Acolytes

By Daniel Fansler

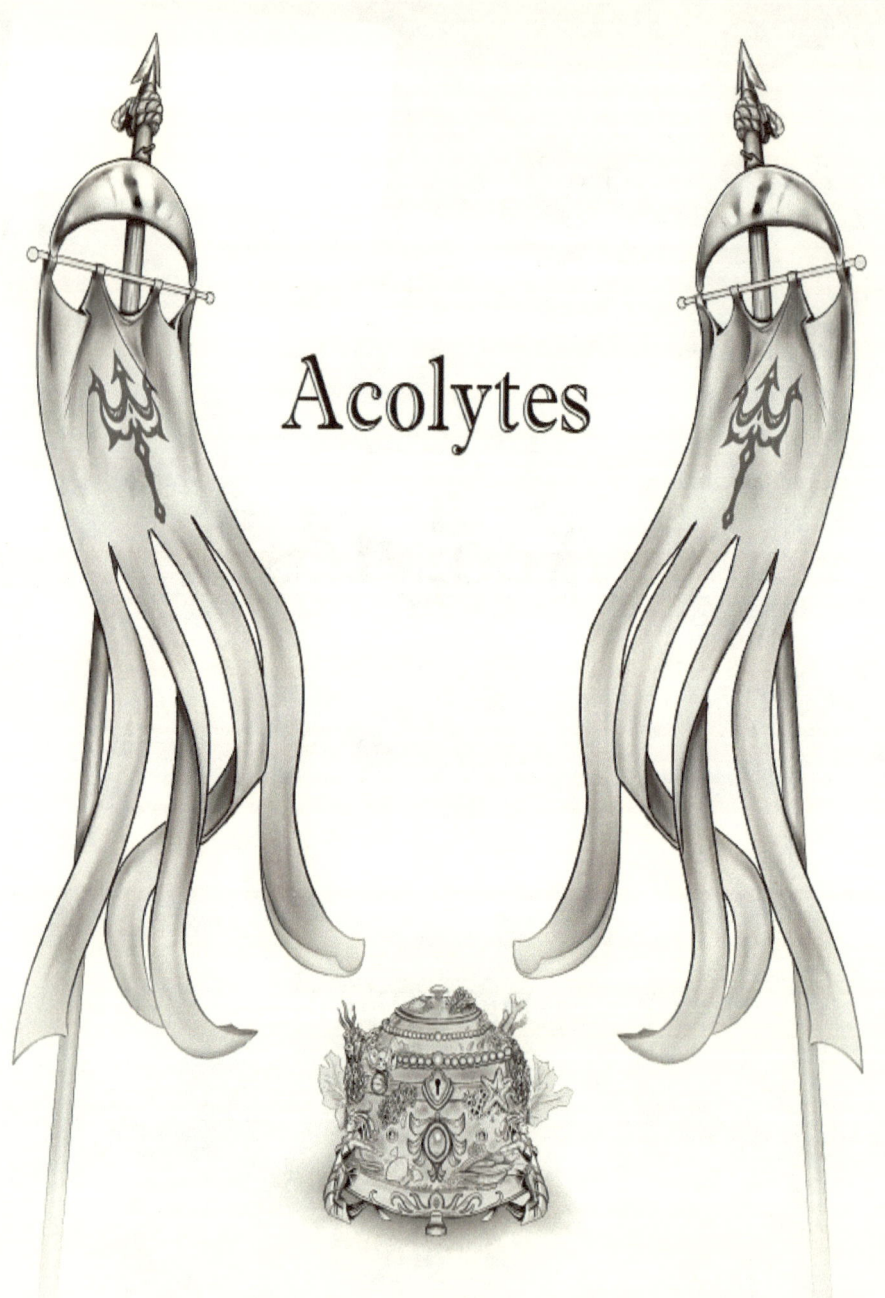

Acolytes

First Paperback Edition, May 2024

ISBN 978-1-7341325-6-4

Map by Daniel Fansler

Title Page illustration by k_olser

Book Design by Bobooks

Visit www.danielfansler.com

Follow me on Instagram and Tiktok
Instagram: @danielfansler.writer
TikTok: @daniel_saurus_rex

For my wife, Ellen, thank you for being who you are

Thank you for buying this book, dear reader! As an indie author, I appreciate each and every one of you for supporting me. The best way to support an indie author, aside from buying and reading their book, is by leaving a review on Amazon and/or Goodreads! If you like this book, I would appreciate it so much if you took the time to do so. Thanks!

TABLE OF CONTENTS

ACKNOWLEDGEMENTS

This time, I must thank my readers first and foremost. In case you haven't noticed, the Chronicles of the First Gods has been in a bit of a standstill. Part of that is due to my life changing completely with the birth of my son, and then years later, my daughter. Things changed so much I simply wasn't able to focus on my writing (even though I completed the first draft of *Acolytes* way back in 2019). I essentially sat on this story for the better part of five years and only resumed working on it and polishing it into what it is now about two years ago. So, for my absence and my unannounced hiatus, I apologize, especially to you readers who were so looking forward to the continuation of the story.

Well, lucky for you, this book ended up being enormous, so I hope that somewhat makes up for the wait. I aim to do better with the remaining three books. Obviously, I don't want a five-year waiting period between each and every one of my publications—from conception to completion.

Like the rest of the installments for this saga, the first outlines for this story were conceived during my late high school years and it was only developed more around the 2017-2018 era. It was around that time that inspiration took hold and the first line of chapter one exploded into my mind, as I was perusing iPads in an Apple store with a friend. Many years later and we finally have this finished project, which I hope you enjoy. Thank you again to all my readers and those who have stuck with me during this journey. Your feedback and encouragement do more for me than you know.

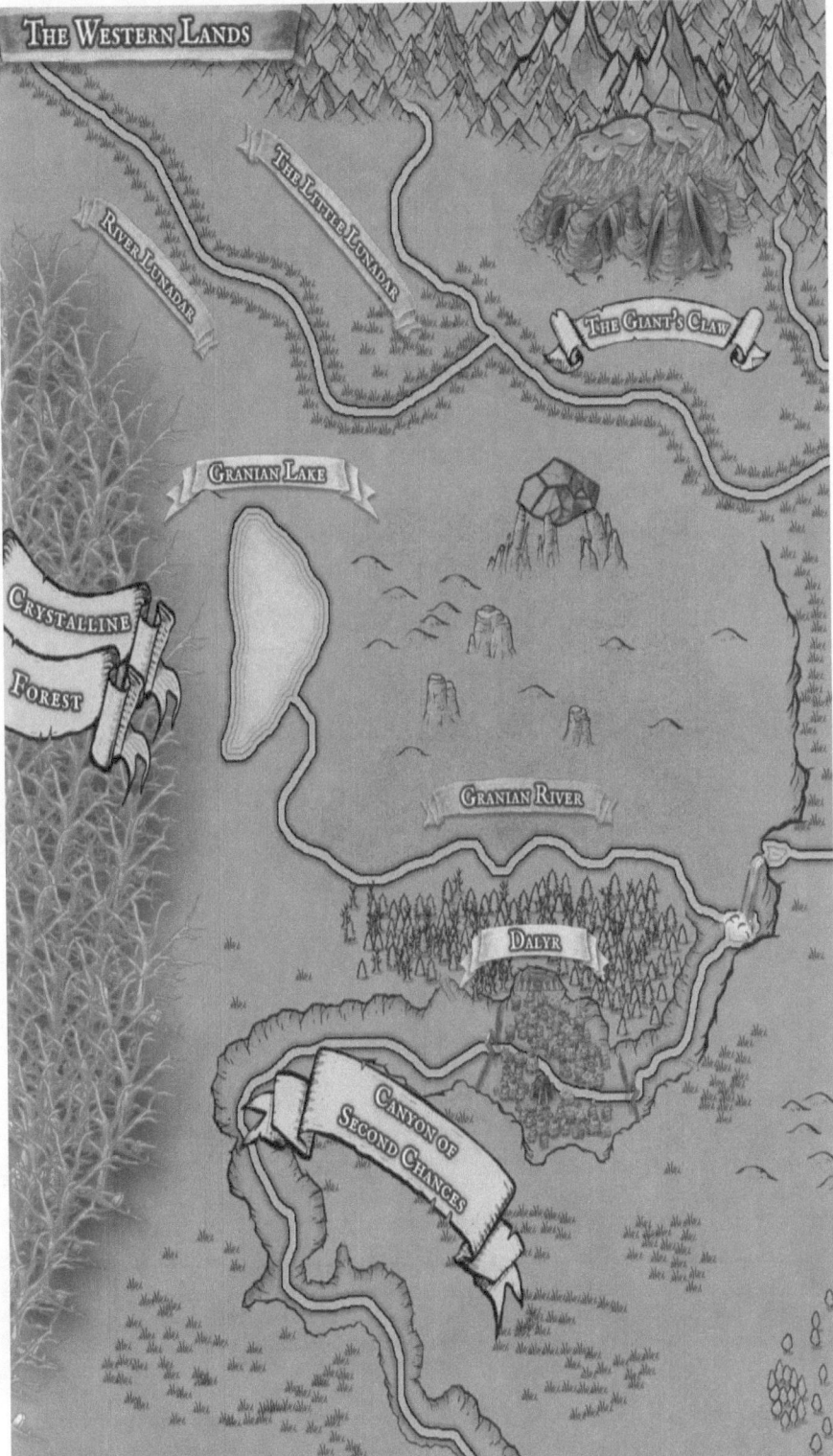

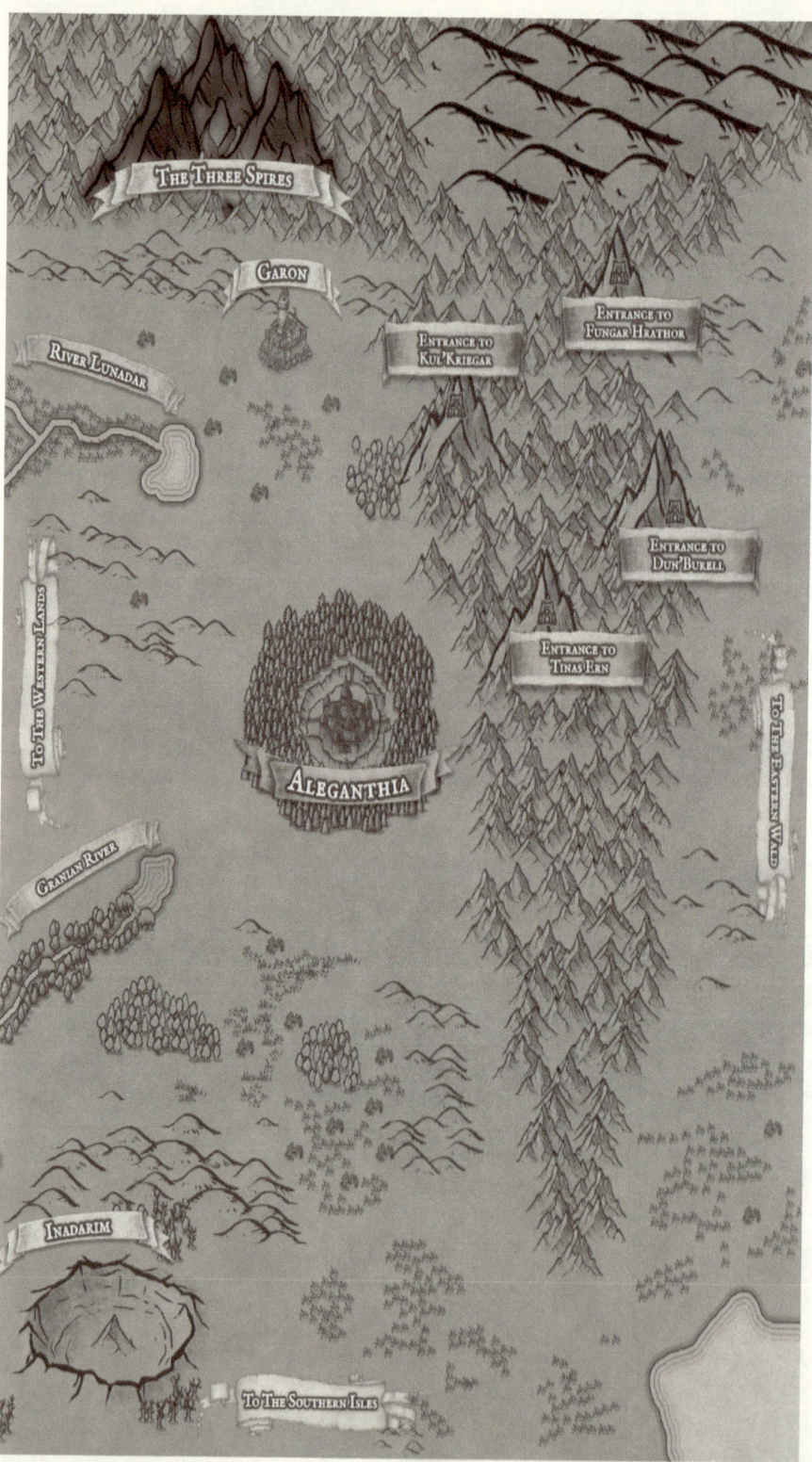

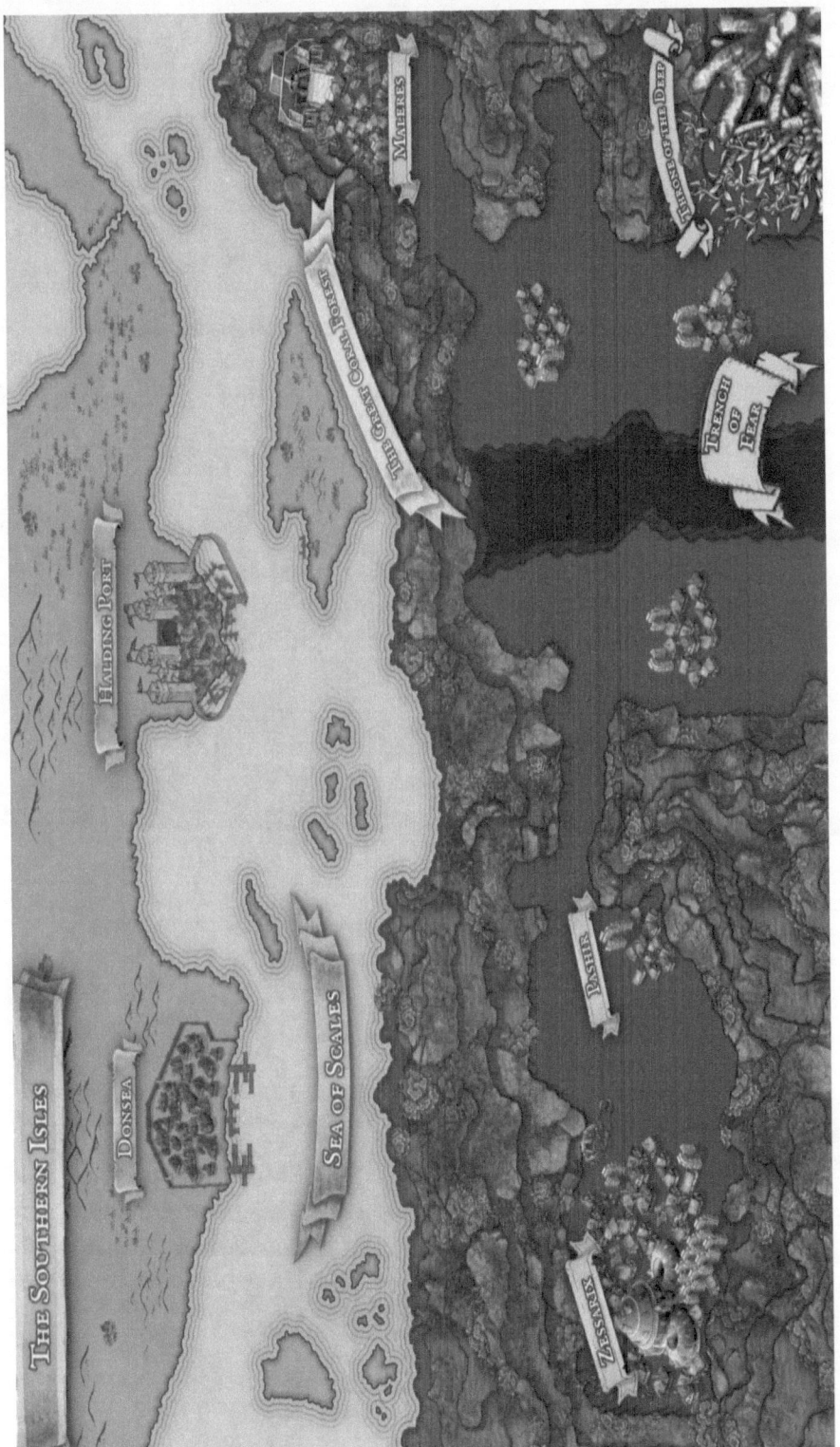

READ WHAT PEOPLE HAVE BEEN SAYING ABOUT *THE LOST KING*

"Daniel Fansler's debut novel is a sprawling adventure in the Tolkien tradition with satisfying new twists to keep the journey fresh. . . readers will want to follow this band of warriors for pages to come."
– John McDermott, Author of *The Idea of God in Tennessee*

"Thuradin's journey to find his king explores the ideas of courage, loyalty, and what it truly means to be a leader."
--Kelley Schorn, Author of *Year 01*

"In *The Lost King*, Fansler takes the trope of the hero's journey and turns it on its head . . . Fans of worldbuilding will delight."
--Lauren Jeter, author of "Lizard Light," *2020 Crab Creek Review Poetry Prize* semifinalist

"This book is extremely captivating. It kept me on the edge of my seat the entire time."
--Amazon customer

AND ABOUT *LIFTING THE SIEGE*

"In this sequel to *The Lost King*, Fansler reminds us of his ability to flawlessly weave together war and wonder. He. . . promis[es] to leave reader again awestruck by the beauty of his world even when all hope seems lost."
--Lauren Jeter, author of "Lizard Light"

"*Lifting the Siege* keeps you guessing—and reading!"

--Kelly Schorn, author of *Year 01*

"Readers of Daniel Fansler's first novel will find even
more to enjoy with the second installment of the
Chronicles of the First Gods . . . a vivid, alluring—and
dangerous—world, one you will want to return to again
and again."
--John McDermott, author of *The Idea of God in Tennessee*

"Reminds me of the fiction books I loved when I was
younger."
--Austin Reichert, Amazon customer

"Never a dull moment."
--Ganonslayer, Amazon customer

AND ABOUT *ACOLYTES*

"It kept me on the edge of my seat and I couldn't put it
down."
--Cindy V, Amazon customer

"This third book in the series is the most intense yet . . .
Fantasy elements are excellent."
--Michael, Amazon customer

OTHER WORKS BY DANIEL FANSLER

THE LOST KING

LIFTING THE SIEGE

A LONGSHIP EULOGY

CHAPTER ONE

"Come, outcast, tell us what you make of this."

A group of about sixty humans stood in tattered clothes on a grassy hilltop, providing them with a commanding view of the surrounding landscape. Plains stretched out for miles to their east and west. To their south was more of the same, though that direction also included memories and a life they had been forced to leave behind. It was no longer in view, but just beyond the horizon, only a few miles west of the Silent Mountains, was their home—at least, what remained of it. Kent, the leader of this small group of survivors, thought he could still see wispy trails of smoke in the distance.

Images of fire and mangled bodies flashed through his mind. He shook his head sadly, thinking of all those they had lost because of the demons' attack.

"Well?" He grunted, turning away and looking toward the north, where a vast forest stood. While this particular forest had always been on the map, few had ever ventured through it. None ever returned.

But something had changed. A significant portion of the giant trees had been felled. Whether by fire or some other destructive force, Kent couldn't tell, but they were gone. And through a newfound gap in the greenery, they could now see a white, walled city hidden within its center. It stood, tall but damaged, on a large mesa separated from the rest of the forest and land by a ravine that ran all the way around.

"I know what city this is," a husky voice sighed. To his left, the wanderer, a man who had been exiled from all towns in the plains for his failure in the Forbidden Lands, cursed to walk the world alone for the rest of his days, now stood. He wore a thin cloak with a large cowl covering most of his face. The only thing visible was a scruffy beard. The man was tall and lanky. Kent had once known him to be a fierce chieftain of the town of Halshire.

"It's talked about in wanderer circles," he continued. "A white city hidden away within the forest, protected by the trees."

"How have we not heard about them before now? The size of this place is comparable to Garon, they could prove a useful ally in our fight against the demons."

The wanderer looked at Kent with hollow, tired eyes. "I don't think you will want their help. This is the home of our most hated enemy; the reason I am where I am today."

Kent stiffened. He knew the wanderer's story just as well as anyone else. Simon, once the chief of Halshire, had had his town attacked by the viatari, fearsome beings with red eyes, silver hair, long, sharp fangs, and a supernatural strength and agility. They often took on the appearance of regular humans to avoid detection.

The viatari's raid had enraged Simon, so he had raised an army to hunt them down. He had chased them into the Forbidden Lands, a large crater south of the plainlands where no one ventured. It was a cursed place with nothing living in it. It was here that Simon's army had first encountered the demons, beasts with the appearance of wolves, bears, hawks, and snakes but far too large, with dull, yellow eyes and a purple aura that seemed to emit from the beasts themselves. They were vicious, bloodthirsty, and they had all but destroyed Simon's army within minutes.

Many had died that day. The hunt had been called off, and the viatari had returned to their home unchallenged. It was a complete failure with no result save the grief of countless widows. And so, Simon had been stripped of his title and privileges, and was sent out into the wilderness to wander for the rest of his days.

For the next several months, no one heard any word from him and many assumed he had died in the wild. However, days ago, after the demons finished destroying his own town of Dün, Kent had run into the former chieftain as he led his people away from their fallen home. He had recognized Simon immediately, even with his disheveled appearance, and captured him, figuring he might be useful as a guide if they were pushed into lands unfamiliar to him.

On their third day of meandering through grasslands they had noticed smoke in the distance to the north, right where the Dark Forest was. Kent had led them toward it, curious to see what might be causing it. He hadn't expected to stumble upon a city, and by the looks of the charred and crumbling buildings within the walls, one that had recently been sacked.

Only the demons would have the numbers and power to take a city of this size. He had wanted to see who might be living here and if they had survived the attack. But after hearing Simon's answer, he wasn't so sure.

"Are you saying—"

"Yes," Simon said briskly. His eyes darkened. "This is Aleganthia, home to the viatari."

* * *

There was not much Thuradin enjoyed more these days than a nice bowl of tobacco. He still preferred a pint of ale— he was a dwarf, after all—and the two put together created a fine evening; but he couldn't drink ale all day without the alcohol eventually affecting his mind. With this pipe, however, and the sweet blend of apple-infused tobacco his friend, Borim, had given him, he could smoke it all day without a care in the world.

He had found many places where he could enjoy his pipe in peace, away from the people in the city. He enjoyed the company of his viatari friends, but sometimes he wanted some time to himself where he could think and reflect on the past several months and the many turns his life had taken. Right now, the spot he had chosen was the southern wall of Aleganthia.

He sat on the ramparts, his feet dangling over the edge in his plate greaves and boots, but only a simple, green tunic to cover his burly chest. A soft wind played lightly with the few thin hairs still on his head, which was nothing compared to the long, gray, tri-braided beard that fell to his knees. Each of his three braids had a thick golden band encircling the top, middle, and bottom sections. He thought back to the last time he had looked at himself in a mirror. His hair had been more white than gray and there were many more lines on his face than he remembered. He supposed the stress of the last few months—discovering the acolytes, fighting darimun, corrupted humans and burrowers, and retaking Aleganthia— were finally getting to him.

His thoughts turned dark as they lingered on the terrible abominations that were the darimun. They were the servants of an acolyte known as the Creature, a being created by the

First Gods to help bring peace and harmony to the world in their absence. Instead, he and his sister, The Turned One, had betrayed their nature, their duty, and as their actions grew more terrible, their essences changed to match. Luckily, they were not the only acolytes the First Gods had created.

Thuradin drew on his pipe and let go of the troublesome thoughts he had brewing in his mind as he blew out a trail of sweet smoke. He glanced over his shoulder to distract himself with the work taking place behind him.

Dwarves bustled through the streets with loads of wooden planks or bricks or cut stone in their sturdy arms, sacks bulging with hammers, axes, trowels, and other tools necessary for the job slung over their backs. Some straddled the higher levels of the wooden scaffolding they had built to reach the taller buildings for repairs and worked deftly as they removed damaged bricks and set down new ones. Even Aleganthia's keep, the tallest building in the city, consisting of many soaring towers connected to a thick, square base that reached as high as twenty stories, had dwarves repairing her gaping holes. They were secured only by ropes as they hung off the walls and towers to paint over the scorch marks and make other repairs.

Thuradin grinned at the sight and then turned back toward the grasslands that stretched out before the city. He felt proud watching his kin work so hard to repair a city that wasn't theirs, it was a sign of how friendly they had become with the viatari ever since their return to the outside world. He only wished he could interact with them, but most dwarves still hated him. Almost ten months had passed since he was exiled from his home in the Dwarven Kingdom, but to him it felt like an eternity. He missed being with his kind, he missed feeling like a dwarf.

Wanting to take his mind off these depressing thoughts, he tried for the tenth time to form a smoke ring but only succeeded in pushing out small orbs. *Well,* he thought, *progress, at least.*

He gazed at the clouds, which spread out as far south as he could see, drifting lazily in an otherwise blue sky, and it somehow made him think of the friends he had made in this strange world, especially Victria. He hoped she was doing well. She had left two weeks ago with Tessa, Natiari, Serania, and Madira for the Southern Isles, an area swarming with human towns and seaports. Her task was to search for the acolyte deep in the Southern Seas to try and convince him to join their war effort but no word had come from her. No report on her progress, no assurance that she was still alive, nothing. The silence worried him—and he wasn't alone—but he knew she was capable. She would be fine.

But she wasn't the only one they hadn't received word from recently. Two months had passed since the last time Thuradin had seen or heard from Borim, right before he had returned home to the mountains with Thuradin's cousin, Garadin. Things were escalating in the Dwarven Kingdom, he knew, because of King Dunkell's ascension to the throne. The fact that there was no word about the situation there was troubling.

He took another puff on his pipe, letting the bittersweetness of the tobacco relax him, and let it gush out of his mouth in a rapid stream of white smoke. In the past two months of inaction, after so much time spent fighting, there had been a lot of downtime for Thuradin to think. And he didn't like it. The thoughts that came to mind were much too heavy and complicated. He was a dwarf of action, but now the only action he could take was to sit and wait. He longed for the days of his youth when things had seemed so simple.

The dwarf reached behind him to pluck more tobacco out of his pouch and into his pipe, but as he turned, he caught a sudden flash of white light coming from the Watcher's Quarter, the highest tower in Aleganthia's keep. One could see the whole city from it, as well as a fair distance past the forest that used to surround the viatari city. Currently, the tower was the holding place for The First One, an acolyte Thuradin and Serania had found in the Crystalline Forest of the Western Lands.

The First One was the only good acolyte they had met so far. He had been the one who told them the history of their world, of the First Gods, of the dwarves' creation by Nythirim, god of earth, and the formation of the viatari by Arokun, goddess of life. It was because of him that they knew where to find the other acolytes and were now seeking them out. Without them, according to The First One, victory against The Turned One and the Creature would be impossible.

Wondering what the sudden burst of light could mean, Thuradin quickly emptied his pipe, gathered up his belongings, hopped off the ramparts and made his way down the wall and into the city streets. He hurried past lines of working dwarves and the few viatari who were still out in the streets window shopping. There were not many viatari who yet lived in Aleganthia while the city was under repairs. Many had gone as temporary refugees to Dalyr, another viatari city in the Western Lands. Those who stayed were mostly the city's defenders, ready to fight at a moment's notice should another attack come upon them, or those who simply couldn't bear to leave their home.

After passing several busy shops and a few buildings that

remained ruined from the siege, Thuradin finally made it to the keep and rushed up the stairs and through the newly-repaired entrance. He had to stop for a minute, not just to catch his breath, but to take in his surroundings. As much work as was being done on the exterior of the keep, there was still much more work to be done for its interior.

Many of the barricades the viatari had hastily crafted when the enemy had entered the city still stood where they had been placed two months ago. Several bronze braziers still lay on their side, their coals scattered on the marble floor, long cold. Some of the railings for the numerous stairways in the building remained splintered. As Thuradin began making his way up these stairs, he saw one group of viatari workers clearing some rubble from a destroyed section of the eastern wall. As they removed the broken stones and carried them away with wheelbarrows, they unearthed a body.

There was a scramble to cover the body, the stench of decay, and the grotesque image of rotting flesh but the dwarf had already seen it. To think, bodies of the fallen still lay where they had been slain all those weeks ago. . . .

Thuradin shuddered, he hoped that was the last one. He didn't think he'd ever get used to seeing corpses. Even though he was a soldier and had seen much death, dwarves didn't decay like the other races, but turned to stone in a process called *entombment.* Statues upon statues of what had once been living dwarves still stood in the Halls of Stone in the Dwarven Kingdom, looking exactly as they had in life. They did not have to deal with something as terrible as decay.

Huffing for breath, Thuradin climbed the last few steps the keep had to offer and opened the simple, wooden door into the Watcher's Quarter. The tower was spacious, with plenty of room to move around and look out the many large, curved windows that provided such a breathtaking view. But this was no time for sightseeing.

In the center of the room stood The First One's artifact, a golden chest with sparkling blue sapphires encrusted into the sides. In the few empty spots where no gems glinted in the day's light were foreign images and symbols engraved into the gold itself. Thuradin had long ago given up trying to decipher what these images and symbols might mean. From the chest, moving erratically like blades of grass caught in a storm, came transparent tendrils of white light, the acolyte's essence.

Standing just to the side of The First One was Felix, leader of Aleganthia, and Salevari, Chancellor of Dalyr, both of whom looked rather alarmed by the acolyte's erratic movements. Thuradin, too, grew concerned. He had never seen The First One move like this, his tendrils had always swayed peacefully, calmly. Now they thrashed.

"What is happening?" Felix asked. "First One, what is it?"

An ancient voice, deep and rumbling like thunder, shook the room as the acolyte cried out in pain. There was another flash of white light and then nothing. The First One's tendrils returned to their usual calm cadence as if nothing had happened. Felix and Salevari glanced at each other.

"What have ye been up ta in here?" Thuradin asked, bewildered by what he had just witnessed.

"We came up here to draw up plans to retrieve the acolyte within the Silent Mountains," Salevari said, her red eyes still glued to the artifact. Though her appearance was young, Thuradin knew she was one of the oldest viatari alive, just like Felix. Both of them had been some of the first Arokun had created.

Salevari shook her head, scratching the buzzed half with

one hand while she tucked the other half of shoulder-length hair behind her ear with the other. She finally looked at Thuradin as if just now noticing that he was there. "And during our discussion we thought we should try to find out what the enemy might be planning. So, The First One tried to see if he could connect to their minds—"

"—and I could not." The First One finished. "Their mental defenses are stronger than most when they are separated, but together they are too formidable a force for me to handle alone. This proves to me beyond a doubt that we will need the aid of my brothers to stand a chance at facing them. I fear my fallen siblings may be growing stronger with each passing month."

"Then obtaining the aid of your brothers will remain our first priority," Felix shrugged, his voice calm and even. "I have yet to hear anything from Victria, but Pulaneus and those who we sent to the Eastern Wald have reported that they are close to entering the first sets of trees. We can only hope they find the Temple before the enemy does."

"Indeed," The First One said. "As for my brother in the Silent Mountains, we must send a party to find him soon. The longer we wait, the higher the chance that my sister will reach him first."

"It would be much easier to find your brother in those mountains if dwarven politics were not falling apart," Salevari muttered.

Felix nodded and addressed Thuradin, "Have you heard anything about the situation there from Borim yet?"

Thuradin shook his head sadly. "No, and that worries me. We all knew Dunkell would nae be liked as King, but the type of tension Borim told me about before he left. . . . Without the dwarven clans maintaining their unity, we will be easily defeated by The Turned One and the Creature's darimun if they shift their focus against us."

"I agree," Felix said, scratching his chin as he continued thinking. "Along with finding The First One's brother we must also do our best to help stabilize our dwarven allies."

"What, do ye intend ta send an army?"

Felix grinned, "Not unless I am invited to."

"I am sure Borim Tomestone will return to us with news that will help decide how we begin our search," The First One said. "In the meantime, however, I sense something approaching us from beyond the walls."

Thuradin glanced outside, scanning the horizon for any sign that a pack of darimun was coming their way, but saw nothing. The viatari looked too.

"I see nothing." Salevari said firmly. Felix sighed in evident relief. The fall of Aleganthia and the subsequent retaking of it had taken more out of the elder viatari than he cared to admit.

"It is not the pawns of my siblings that come to see us," The First One said, a sudden note of interest in his voice, "but humans. They come from the south."

Thuradin, Felix, and Salevari turned their gaze southward. From the Watcher's Quarter they could see the destroyed sections of forest that had once surrounded them and kept the city hidden. Now, just past the newly-built bridge connecting their mesa to the rest of the world, was a small gathering of humans. One of them carried a long stick with a white rag tied at the end. The rag waved limply in the wind.

"Well," Felix said after some time. "That is new."

"What should we do?" Salevari grimaced. "If the humans have discovered Aleganthia, then—"

"Do not fear," The First One interrupted. "I sense that

they only wish to speak with you."

Thuradin frowned, remembering the numerous losses he had suffered at the hands of humans. And his were nothing compared to what the viatari had lost to them.

Felix thought for a moment longer, then spoke with authority. "If they only wish to speak, we will listen. But not without proper precautions."

Salevari nodded. "From behind the wall, then?"

"Yes, sister," Felix turned to leave, "from behind the wall."

The Chancellor glanced once more at the humans before she followed her brother out of the tower and down the keep's stairways. Thuradin continued to stare. The humans stood rigidly where they were, and there were so few of them. He had seen human towns, fought in them. There were always too many humans to count. But with this group he doubted their numbers even reached one hundred. Why would such a small party of these natural enemies of the viatari approach what was clearly a viatari city with a flag of truce?

The dwarf shook his head, there was only one way to find out, and standing here thinking wasn't going to do it. Besides, he was tired of thinking.

CHAPTER TWO

Back on the wall, Thuradin didn't quite know what to make of the humans standing on the other side of the bridge. Most of them were wearing little more than rags. Several were injured, their loose bandages caked with old, dried blood. There were only a few children and elderly, the rest looked like able fighters.

They bore no weapons, though. Whatever they had brought with them now lay on the ground, a sign that they weren't here to fight—or, Thuradin thought, perhaps a trick. He cast the thought aside as soon as he had it. Humans were dangerous and cunning, but if this group of sixty planned on taking Aleganthia by trickery alone, they were neither—only suicidal. Besides, if there was one thing to admire about humans it was that they did not dare do anything that could endanger the lives of their young.

The dwarf glanced at Felix to his right, trying to read the elder viatari's face. Salevari stood next to him and didn't seem to be making any effort to hide her disdain, but Felix was . . . passive. And he was the only one. All along the wall, viatari archers looked ready—no, eager—to kill the small batch of humans before them. Thuradin could hear the tension in their bowstrings, whispering to be let loose so they could unleash vengeful death. But the archers, at least, were disciplined and waited for Felix's order to fire.

Not everyone was so disciplined. Word spread quickly throughout the city about who had approached the walls and a growing sense of panic was consuming the populace. Shops closed. Doors were barred. Those who remained in the streets stood rooted to the spot, staring at the southern wall in dismay as if they expected it to crumble at any minute and a horde of humans to rush through. Seeing them from where he was, however, Thuradin didn't think the humans were a threat, but he still wondered what could have possibly driven them here.

One of the men stepped forward and called out to them in a commanding voice. He stood confidently, his hands on his hips as if he expected the viatari to come down and meet him face to face. His trimmed beard and brown hair all brushed to one side made him look clean and well taken care of. But Thuradin could tell the man was anything but pampered. The long, jagged scar that ran down from his right eye to his neck told him he had seen battle, had bled and continued fighting anyway. The dwarf grunted approvingly. He couldn't help but admire strength, even in a human.

Felix responded in their language. The man took a few more steps forward and began telling his story. Thuradin tried to catch what was being said but his grasp of the human tongue was still rudimentary. He glanced at Felix who listened intently and saw the viatari's eyes soften.

"What is it, Felix?" he asked, unable to bear not knowing anymore.

Felix cleared his throat, thinking for a moment before answering. "These humans have had their home destroyed. They have been on the move for the past several days running from the darimun, taking shelter where they can."

"So, the Creature is attacking the humans too now?" Salevari mused. "Perhaps he's doing us a favor."

"He is doing to them what he tried to do to us," Felix muttered. "I must say, I pity them."

Salevari shot him a look. "What is there to pity? They're monsters. They would kill every single one of us if they got the chance."

"Perhaps," Felix rested his elbows on the wall's parapet, "but perhaps we should listen to what they have to say some more."

There was silence for a moment.

"You can't seriously be considering letting them into the city," Salevari scoffed, a trace of uncertainty in her voice. "Felix, that's just what they want."

"I have ta agree," Thuradin grumbled, keeping his eyes on the humans who continued to do nothing but stare up at them. "We've never had good encounters with them in the past. Nae even my people will speak with them."

"I know, and yet, I feel there is something different this time. An opportunity, if you will."

"What could be different?" Salevari asked, irritation creeping into her voice, "Felix, you are going to endanger everyone's life here because you have a *feeling* that something's different."

"Mm, I misspoke," Felix stood up straight, speaking with authority. "I *know* something is different this time. The Creature is attacking human towns now and they clearly cannot fight against the darimun on their own. How long do you think before more refugees find this place? How long before it is too late for us to try and bring them to our side?"

"Ye want ta make them allies?"

Felix shifted his attention to Thuradin, his eyes stubborn and unrelenting. "I want to hear what they have to say."

Salevari sighed, studied the humans outside the wall and then glanced at the forming crowds of viatari on the other side. Then, she shrugged.

"This is your city."

Felix nodded, "Thank you. If it is any comfort, I do not intend on letting them all in." He called out to the humans again and a handful of them, including their leader, separated from the rest and moved toward the city.

"Archers, keep your bows at the ready, but do not fire on these humans unless I order it, understood?"

Every archer nodded as Felix made his way down the wall's stairs. Thuradin and Salevari followed him. They made their way down the stone steps and moved through the city streets until they reached the southern gate. A group of twenty guards wearing the familiar leather armor of Aleganthia—an X-shaped chestpiece, double-layered spaulders and supple, thick boots that reached the knee—stood at attention behind Felix, who stood just before the gates.

"Open it."

The wooden gates opened slowly, revealing the five humans who would be stepping into the viatari city. Felix inclined his head and spoke a greeting in their language. They responded in kind.

"Make a path for them and surround them once they are through," Felix said, speaking to the guards behind him. "Do not be aggressive, but stay alert for any sudden movements."

The guards split into two groups of ten and stood rigidly, their hands on the hilts of their dirks. Felix explained what was happening to the humans, who looked nervous. But a word from their leader with the scar and they all moved forward, Felix leading the way.

Salevari and Thuradin shared a look.

"My brother."

"Aye, yer brother."

"Let's go," Salevari sighed. "We should see how this plays out."

They caught up to the guards and followed the strange procession to the keep. They passed many of the city's denizens as they made their way. These viatari all stood still, transfixed by the fact that their long-hated enemy now stood only inches away from them, walking through the streets of their city. They whispered, they glared, but luckily none of them tried to attack.

For their part, the humans remained passive. Their leader was an image of calm, his eyes scanning his surroundings but giving no hint of fear as he passed the viatari, every one of whom could kill him in an instant. One of his companions covered himself in a cloak with a thick cowl so his face couldn't be seen, but the other three humans looked to be following their leader's example.

They walked up the marble steps to the keep and passed through its open gates. Felix led them all up a few flights of stairs, down a hallway lined with expensive looking vases and portraits of past viatari. Ahead of them was a small set of wooden doors.

They entered the keep's dining hall, a spacious room with a single, long table and many elegantly carved chairs. Thuradin was brought back to when he had encountered the viatari for the first time. They had taken him and his dwarven companions through the same hall, into this very room, fed them, and asked for their aid. It was where the friendship between their two races had renewed, as well as when the war with the Creature began, as far as he was concerned.

Inside, waiting for them, stood a guard Thuradin only vaguely knew, Zael Windkeeper. He was a serious one, never cracking a smile, with long, soft, silver hair. Had it not been for his crooked nose, broken from past battles, he would have had a perfect face. He faced them as they entered, his steady eyes taking in the situation.

"Humans?"

Felix nodded. "I am glad you are here, Zael. I will need you to translate what they say for Salevari as our discussion continues. I do not have the time to speak with them and my sister simultaneously. Will you do this for me?"

Zael nodded and bowed ever so slightly then made his way to stand next to Salevari, who begrudgingly accepted his presence as a necessity. As Chancellor of Dalyr, she had never had any need to learn the human tongue.

"Everyone take a seat," Felix motioned the humans toward the chairs and, not ten minutes later, large silver plates heaping with smoked meats, grilled vegetables, and seared fish were brought in and placed before them. The humans stared at the food in disbelief.

"What is my brother trying to do, woo them?" Salevari muttered.

Felix forced a grin in her direction, "It is my custom, sister, to feed our guests before any discussions are had."

Thuradin noticed there was no food brought out for the viatari. He thought this was a wise choice. The viatari did not feed on cooked foods like regular creatures, rather they fed on the life-energies of other things. He didn't think the humans would take it well if they watched half a dozen deer walk in only to see their life-energies sucked out by the viatari.

Even the dwarves had been horrified when they first witnessed it.

The humans ate timidly at first, no doubt thinking the food was poisoned. But as time went on, they began eating as if they hadn't eaten in days. Grease from the meat ran down their chins and dripped back onto their plates. Thuradin could hear the crunch of carrots and apples being bitten into and his stomach churned. He hadn't eaten anything since the morning and he suddenly realized he, too, was ravenous.

As Felix conversed casually with the humans, Thuradin grabbed a turkey leg from one of the plates and bit into it. The taste of the sweet, smokey meat burst onto his tastebuds and it took all his willpower to hold in a groan of pleasure. Now if only he had some ale. . . .

"I must admit, I am surprised that you would feed us."

There was silence. The men stopped eating and stared at the human in the cloak. The viatari stared as well. Thuradin stopped mid-bite, unable to believe his ears. Had the human just spoken in Dwarvish?

"You speak Dwarvish." Felix stated.

"I speak Dwarvish." The human replied, still eating as if nothing out of the ordinary had happened.

The human with the scar said something to which the man in the cloak laughed scornfully.

"The man next to me, Kent," he said, licking his fingers, "does not wish for me to speak with you. Says I should hold my tongue."

"How is it ye speak my language?" Thuradin asked.

"For the past six months I have been a wanderer and during my travels I have met other wanderers who taught me the things I now know. I picked up your language quickly enough. There is little difficulty in it."

Thuradin frowned. He felt he had just been insulted. His language was anything but simple. He decided he didn't care for this man in the cloak. But still, he held his tongue as Felix asked him more questions, now in his own language.

"Viatar sha'andi?"

"Viatar sha'andiel."

Felix whistled, clearly impressed. "I've met very few wanderers, even in my long life, but never a human who could speak our language. You are most welcome here, friend."

The man scoffed, drawing looks from his fellows, who didn't seem to approve of his attitude very much.

"I would very much like to punch that arrogant smirk off his face," Salevari growled.

"Ye can't even see his face under that cowl," Thuradin said, his mouth full of meat once more. "How do ye know he's smirking?"

"Trust me, I know."

As the humans finished their meal, the plates were taken away and were replaced with tall glasses of blood-red wine. Here, at least, the viatari joined the humans. Thankfully, a tankard of ale was brought out for Thuradin.

"I know we have fought in the past for many centuries," Felix said, taking a sip from his glass and smacking his lips appreciatively, "hated each other for centuries. And that does not go away with one meal. But you have found our city now. You know where we live. And right now, you are vastly outnumbered. You know and I know that we could destroy what remains of your town within seconds, but we do not want to do that. What we need to know though, is what *your* intentions are."

Kent, the human leader, responded and Zael translated

for Thuradin and Salevari. "He admits feeling hatred for us in the past, but says they come here in peace now, seeking aid against the demons that destroyed their lives."

Felix nodded and glanced at Salevari. "A common enemy can drive hatred away and pave the way to a new friend-ship."

A hoarse laugh came from the man in the cloak as he stood up.

"We are not friends," he said, drawing looks from his companions. Kent tried to sit him back down but the man shrugged him off. He raised his hands to push back his cowl, revealing a face lined with creases, a short tuft of brown hair, and brown eyes that burned with hatred. His face was dirty, malnourished, and Thuradin was sure the rest of him looked the same under that cloak, but something about him told the dwarf that he had once held authority, had once commanded respect.

"We are not friends," he said again.

"Not yet," Felix said smoothly, "but with time—"

"After all you've done, . . ." the man fell into another fit of laughter, which then turned into hacking coughs. "I recognize you, viatari. You were the one who attacked my town of Halshire. You and your band of viatari and dwarves, disguised to look like my people, destroyed my town after cheating your way through a drinking competition."

Felix paled. Thuradin felt his heart skip a beat. Everyone glanced at them with concern, but they couldn't understand. Only Felix and Thuradin, who had been there, could know who this man was. Only they could remember the losses they had suffered because of that one day in Halshire.

"You, . . ." the elder viatari said numbly, "you were the chief of that town."

Kent, sensing the sudden tension in the room, tried again to get the man to sit down, but he was once again shrugged off.

"I was. My name is Simon. You are the reason I was banished from my home, from my kind, made to wander these lands until the day I die. It's because of you and your viatari that I lost an entire host of young men. You *led* us toward those demons."

"Ye led the hunting party. . . ." memories of their journey to Inadarim flashed through Thuradin's mind. He saw the ambush they'd walked through, the viatari they'd lost in the woods to the humans' poisoned blades. The young dwarf who had succumbed to their poison after the battle.

Agrethar.

Rage boiled within Thuradin. Faster than he realized, he saw red in his vision and he was on the table, lifting Simon off his feet, bringing him only inches from his face. He screamed his anger at the man, screamed all the pain he had suffered because of this man's own hatred and if he'd had his axes on him, he would have driven them into his skull without a second thought.

Thuradin felt strong hands pull him away from Simon. Felix's face came into view, calm as ever.

"I know," he said softly.

Thuradin gulped several times and ground his teeth, forcing himself to swallow his rage. He took several deep breathes, trying to clear his mind—to forget. But he couldn't. He saw Agrethar's still, stone body every day and every night he went to sleep.

The dining room erupted into chaos. The humans surrounded Simon, but not to protect him. They yelled angrily at him and looked ready to beat him to death themselves. The viatari guards stepped in to separate them and reestablish order. Zael barked at a few overzealous guards to put their dirks away.

"QUIET!" Salevari bellowed "All of you, QUIET!"

The room froze as the Chancellor of Dalyr pushed her way through the guards and then forcefully separated the humans from Simon, who stood there with an amused expression.

Felix cleared his throat, but before he could say anything else, the doors to the dining room burst open and a messenger rushed in. He saw Felix and made his way to him.

"Felix—"

"We are in the middle of something."

"You will want to hear the news I bring."

Felix sighed, but nodded.

"Borim Tomestone has come with a delegation of dwarves seeking an audience with you."

Thuradin looked at the messenger in shock. "Borim?"

"Yes, he says there's urgent news from the Dwarven Kingdom."

Felix nodded; his mind made up on the spot. "Tell them we will be with them shortly." The messenger nodded and ran back out.

"Come, Thuradin," the elder viatari said. "Let us hear what our dwarven friends have come to say." He turned to the guards, "Take the humans to our guest rooms. Allow those who remain outside the walls to enter our city and find rooms for them as well," he shifted his attention and spoke to Kent and Simon directly now. "Our conversation is not over. We still have much to discuss. However, clearer heads must prevail so, for now, I hope you will take some time to rest. Clean yourselves. Take care of your wounded. My guards will be available for any needs you may have. You are free to explore the keep, but know you will be watched until we have come to a better mutual understanding."

Kent and the other humans—minus Simon—nodded and followed the viatari guards out of the hall with purpose in their steps.

Thuradin stood rooted to the spot, watching them go. A mixture of emotions raged within him. The pain he had felt at losing dwarves under his command burned fresh as did the hatred he felt for the humans who had been the cause of it. And yet, another part of him was distracted by the relief he felt hearing that Borim had returned, though a worm of worry gnawed away at him as he wondered what news came from the Kingdom. He felt a hand on his shoulder and turned to see Salevari looking at him knowingly.

"Come," she said. "There's no use dwelling on it. You need to face these feelings head on."

"Since when did ye become such an expert in that?"

The Chancellor shrugged as she walked out of the dining hall. "I suppose I have my daughter to thank for that."

Thuradin nodded but didn't follow—at least, not right away. He looked around for the tankard he had tossed when he attacked Simon. He found it on the floor a few feet away. Most of the ale had spilled onto the multitude of rugs underfoot, but as he picked it up, he saw there was still enough for a mouthful.

He thought for a moment, then raised it into the air. "This is for ye, Agrethar. I vow, if I ever get the chance ta avenge yer death, I will take it and kill that man."

He downed the rest of his drink, tossed the tankard, and, licking his lips, rushed out of the dining hall.

CHAPTER THREE

Several gruff and powerful voices came from the other side of the doors. Dwarven voices. Thuradin heard them as he made his way down the final flight of stairs and rushed into the keep's reception hall.

Inside this large, stone room, sitting on a half dozen cushioned couches were a contingent of twenty dwarves, all heavily armored with thick plates of steel and armed with heavy axes, swords, and hammers, and sitting right in the middle of them all was Borim. His normally bright eyes drooped from exhaustion and his long, scraggly beard had thinned and grayed since last Thuradin saw him. Clearly, whatever was happening in the Dwarven Kingdom was bringing about many sleepless nights.

Still, once Borim saw Thuradin enter the room, his eyes lit up and a happy smile stretched the deep lines on his face.

"Thuradin, lad, it's good ta see ye!"

"Aye," Thuradin walked up to his friend and they embraced, clapping each other on the back. "Ye're looking old, my friend."

Borim guffawed. "My beard is still darker than yers."

"Only in yer dreams."

Felix coughed behind them and Thuradin remembered

the reason for Borim's presence.

"Ye bring news from home?"

One of the other dwarves scoffed, "It's hardly yer—"

"Shut it," Borim growled. "Thuradin is still a dwarf, so aye, it *is* his home."

The dwarves were silent, which gave Felix the opportunity to interject, "I am sure you have had a long journey from the mountains. We will bring you food and drink and then you can—"

Borim raised a hand to stop him. "No, Felix. As much as I'd like ta accept yer offer, we cannae wait. Time is of the essence and it is heavy news I bring. It weighs on my heart like a mountain of iron."

Felix nodded. "Tell us what has happened, then."

The dwarves shared somber glances, then Borim spoke. "The dwarven throne has been usurped. Dunkell has been ousted, and the Kingdom now lies on the brink of civil war."

Thuradin was speechless, the shock from the news creeping into his mind, turning his thoughts into blurs. The dwarves had always been ruled by an Ironaxe monarch, even during the most turbulent times in Dwarven history. Surely, Dunkell's lack of popularity couldn't be the sole reason for this rebellion.

"Is the King still alive?" he asked.

"Aye," Borim said firmly. "I've made sure of that. Right now, he's ruling those still loyal ta him from Kul'Kriegar. Dranthal, the viceroy of the city, has pledged the support of the Guardian clan as have the Oredwellers in Tinas Ern."

Thuradin's mind turned tactical. Having the Guardian clan on their side meant they had the better warriors— Kul'Kriegarans being renowned for their ferocity in battle— and they would have a steady supply of weaponry, ore, and other supplies from the mining city of Tinas Ern. Both would be vital advantages if war broke out.

"What about Fungar Hrathor?"

Borim shook his head. "The Tiller, Border, and Earth-wrought clans are all on the opposition."

"And Tinas Arsten, Tinas Montig, Kurin?"

"They're with us."

Thuradin frowned. Not having the Tiller clan on their side meant they might suffer from insufficient food supplies, but that could be solved if the dwarven colonies outside the mountains were able to start cultivating crops. He glanced at Borim who looked at him knowingly.

"All the strategizing in the world isn't going ta get us out of this mess."

"Perhaps nae," Thuradin shrugged. "But it's good ta see what options we have."

"This bodes ill," Felix said. "The dwarves are a valuable ally, and with war against The Turned One and the Creature coming, we cannot afford for them to be fractured and leaderless."

Borim laughed, but there was no mirth in it. "We are anything but leaderless. In fact, now we have too many of them. In Tinas Gran, the opposition have set up a Council of five members, one for each clan, ta rule the half of the Kingdom they have stolen." He looked at Thuradin, a sudden uncertainty lining his features as if he was unsure whether he should say more. "Ye should know, Thuradin, that *she* is one of the members on this Council."

"She?"

"Myrna."

A sudden image flashed through Thuradin's head—a memory of a time he thought he had stowed away deep in the darkest depths of his mind. He saw a dwarf with luscious brown hair, rosy cheeks, and a gentle smile that had always made him weak in the knees. Even when he saw it for the last time.

In this memory, he looked down and saw a child. She couldn't have been more than fifty years old, but even so, he knew she would be a strong leader when she grew up. He took in every detail he could: black hair that curled around her face, dimpled cheeks, green eyes glinting with disappointment.

Thuradin gasped and took a step back as the memory vanished. He was still in the keep's reception hall, though now all eyes were on him. He grunted and tried to focus only on Borim.

"Ye're sure of this?"

"Positive."

"Who else is on the Council?"

Borim shrugged. "We don't know. Our spies have only managed to procure the one name so far."

"Who is she, Thuradin?" Felix asked, curiosity heavy with each word.

Thuradin tore his gaze away from Borim. He opened his mouth as if to answer but instead shook his head. "Just someone I used ta know."

Felix nodded, knowing better than to try to dig deeper, though he looked disappointed.

"So, Felix," Borim cleared his throat, bringing the conversation back to their main problem, "now that ye know our plight, I'm sure ye can guess the purpose of our presence."

The elder viatari nodded, though it was not with conviction. "You have come to ask for aid—for us to fight with you. I must say, when I initially offered our alliance to Ronorim and then sealed the pact with Dunkell, I did not have it in mind that we would be called upon by dwarves to fight against other dwarves."

Borim sighed sadly, "True, I can understand yer hesitancy in this matter. But know this, calling for yer aid is nae a decision the King has made lightly. He knows the consequences of yer presence in the coming conflict. He knows dwarves will die by viatari hands, but we must keep in mind that these dwarves have made themselves traitors and there's no guarantee they would be friendly ta the viatari were they ta eradicate all royal support."

"It is a fair point," Felix conceded. "Still, that is not the only issue at stake here. Things have developed here that need tending to as well."

Borim's brows furrowed, "Tell me, Felix, what news comes from Aleganthia that would keep ye from fulfilling yer part of our mutual agreement—an agreement, I would remind ye, that has already called for dwarven blood ta be spilled."

Felix raised his hands placatingly, "Do not misunderstand, my friend, the viatari will send aid; it's just a matter of deciding how much we can send. As I mentioned earlier, our fight with The Turned One and Creature is coming. Not only that, but they have apparently begun to attack the humans in the plains as well."

"Good," Borim grunted, "At least they're good for something."

Felix gave a pained smile as he continued, "Their attacks have brought the humans to our doorstep."

This got the dwarf's attention. "How many?"

"About sixty for now, but more will come as these attacks continue."

Borim stroked his beard, thinking. "I can see how fighting the humans along with the turned acolytes complicates things."

"I do not intend to fight the humans," Felix said, putting weight on each word, "I intend to make them allies."

The old dwarf stared at Felix in bewilderment. "Ye cannae be serious."

"I rarely jest."

"He's let the humans inta the city already," Thuradin said crossing his arms, "including a certain human responsible for chasing us down ta Inadarim, if ye remember."

"How could I forget?" Borim spat. "Why would ye think this is a good idea, Felix? After all they've done."

"It is an opportunity, my friend, for us to bolster our forces against an enemy whose forces, it seems, can replenish effortlessly, no matter how many times we fight them. The viatari and dwarves cannot hope to defeat The Turned One and the Creature alone. I have a feeling this will be a worldly affair, where everyone who lives in Azar will have to choose to fight for it or succumb to the coming chaos. Remember that, Borim, we cannot afford to lose simply because of our desire to hold on to a grudge.

"Which brings us back to the reason you and your dwarves have come here," Felix said, moving swiftly to one of the nearby bookshelves where he pulled out a large, yellowed, rolled-up map of the surrounding area. Then he pulled out a second, this one depicting the Dwarven Kingdom as it was laid out within the mountains and placed it on a table, putting weights on each corner.

"I didn't know ye had a map of our home," Thuradin said in surprise.

Felix nodded, his eyes roving over the detailed drawings of cities and tunnels, "I haven't looked at it in a long time, since before your kind retreated into the mountains."

He took out a plumed pen and marked a few places on the map, separating the cities of Kul'Kriegar and Tinas Ern from the ones controlled by the Council. Borim let out a frustrated sigh, realizing there would be no more talk of humans, and joined Felix at the table.

"As you know Borim, aside from pouring our resources into rebuilding our city, we are sending out our best to retrieve the remaining acolytes, which are scattered across the different regions of the world. I already sent Victria, Serania, Tessa, Natiari, and Madira to the Southern Isles two weeks ago to find the acolyte there. We have also sent a party led by Pulaneus to the Eastern Wald. The only place we have not sent anyone to so far is the Dwarven Kingdom. Now, I am assuming your call for aid is an official request by the King, and not something that is off the record, correct?"

"Aye, he even gave me an official scroll ta hand ta ye with his seal, though I figured it would be unnecessary."

"Looks like you got your invitation to send an army," Salevari mused.

"Our numbers are stretched thin as it is," Felix continued. "We have scouts and spies everywhere as well as a garrison in Garon so we can keep a close watch on any movements from the Northern Mountains." He fell silent and thought for a moment, then began nodding, his eyes hardening with resolve.

"The troubles in the Dwarven Kingdom must be taken care of before our war with the acolytes escalates. I will personally see to it that stability is returned to your realm."

"You?" Salevari turned Felix forcefully so that he would face her. "You can't leave Aleganthia. Who else will run this city, its repairs," she leaned in to whisper, "the humans *you* let inside?"

Felix grinned. "You will."

Salevari took a step back, blinking several times as if she had been struck. Thuradin might have found this amusing had his mind not been so distracted by the plan he was forming for himself.

"Me?" she said. "I . . . I can't lead Aleganthia. I have my own city to take care of."

"Please, sister," Felix's voice was earnest. "Most of your warriors are here anyway, and the danger is here, not in Dalyr—"

"Not *yet*,"

"The Creature is focused on Aleganthia. I cannot leave the city if I do not have someone I know who is capable to take my place. This issue with the dwarves *must* be resolved or we lose our greatest ally in this war. There are few I would trust with this task and all of them are currently on other, equally important missions, so please, sister, lead Aleganthia while I am gone."

"But how will I deal with the humans when I can't even speak with them?" Salevari raised her hands in the air grasping at this last problem, hoping it would be enough to make Felix reconsider and not drop this responsibility on her shoulders.

"You will learn their language with time," he responded quickly, as if he had been expecting this problem to rise up. "In the meantime, Zael will serve as your right-hand man. He will translate for you and do anything you ask him to."

"Drathanar is my right-hand man, why can't I just use him? He has always served me well."

"Drathanar does not speak the human tongue either, so he would be of little use to you in this matter. Besides, I intend on taking him with me to the Dwarven Kingdom."

There was silence for a moment. Salevari looked like she wanted to continue arguing, but instead she clenched her jaw and finally nodded, a determined fire in her eyes.

"And what do you want me to do about the humans while you're gone?"

Felix smiled. "Make an ally out of them. Build trust." He turned back to the map, a calculating look returning to his face. "I will go with thirty viatari to the Dwarven Kingdom. We will be there as peacekeepers to try and keep the dwarves from falling into civil war; but, if need be, we will fight on the side of the King."

He looked into Borim's eyes, "While we are there to give the dwarves our aid, know that our task is two-fold. One of The First One's brothers is somewhere deep in the mountains and we will be searching for him while we are in the mountains so that we can retrieve him for our war against the corrupted acolytes."

Borim nodded. "Dunkell will understand, and I'm sure he'll do what he can ta help ye find this acolyte."

"Then, it is settled," Felix rolled up the maps and put them away. "We'll leave at dawn and with any luck—"

"I'll be going with ye."

All eyes turned to Thuradin, who's tongue felt heavy in his mouth. It had been a struggle to form those words, but now that he had said them, he felt as if a dam had burst.

"I'll be going back ta the Dwarven Kingdom with ye, Felix. I need ta be there ta do what I can ta help bring stability ta my home."

"Thuradin, ye can't," Borim said with sadness. "If ye go back, yer life will be forfeit."

Thuradin looked at his friend, one of the few he had grown up with. "Ye should know better than anyone here that

I would happily give my life for my king and home."

The other dwarves muttered amongst themselves but Thuradin ignored them, waiting for Borim to see, to understand the deeper reason he *had* to risk everything and go back. Soon enough, a new understanding dawned in Borim's eyes. He raised an eyebrow as if to confirm his conclusion and Thuradin nodded.

"Very well then."

The other dwarves looked like they wanted to protest but Borim silenced them with a single sharp glance. "He will be coming back with us," he announced with authority, "in disguise so that no one knows who he is. And if any of ye so much as even think of his name in the hopes that he'll be arrested and executed, I will personally bash yer head in with my hammer. Is that clear?"

The dwarves nodded, though none looked too happy about the decision.

"Are you sure you want to do this?" Felix asked, eyeing Thuradin curiously. "I understand your desire to go back home in these troubled times but the danger—"

"I'm sure, Felix," Thuradin said, his voice light, not wanting to betray the fear he felt creeping through his body as he thought of everything wrong that could happen. "I know the risks and accept them. I need ta help Dunkell in any way I can."

Felix stared into Thuradin's eyes for a moment longer, "Be ready by dawn. Borim, you remember where the guest-rooms are?"

"Aye."

"Make yourselves at home then and get some rest. I will have food and drinks brought to you. For now, I must return to the humans and tend to them."

"We thank ye," Borim slammed his plated fist to his chest in salute.

Without another word Felix and Salevari left the hall, leaving the dwarves alone.

"Right, ye lot go on ta the guest rooms. They'll be on the seventh floor. I'll be with ye shortly."

Thuradin watched the retinue of dwarves file out silently, no doubt saving any discussions they would have about him for when they were out of range of their commander's hearing.

"What took ye so long ta come back?" Thuradin asked once the two dwarves were alone. "It's been months!"

"I know," Borim sighed, the exhaustion clear in his voice. "Sit. There is more ye should know about the situation that I didn't tell Felix."

They sat across from each other and Borim began telling his tale.

"Things have been bad for a while now. As soon as I returned home there was an attempted coup against Dunkell and the generals and officials loyal ta him. The coup failed, luckily, but it encouraged others in the opposition ta try their own methods for ousting Dunkell from the throne."

Thuradin sat still, imagining the events in his mind as Borim told them.

"Soon after the coup, Dunkell called for me and several other dwarves he trusted ta act as his personal bodyguards."

"What about the royal guards?"

Borim shook his head sadly. "They've turned. Therason Kinfriend and the other royal guards are now part of the opposition and guard the Council."

Thuradin couldn't believe it. His royal guards. The dwarves he had led for centuries in service to the King to protect him from all dangers--traitors to the crown.

"Therason . . . if I ever see him again, I'll kill him for what he's done with my royal guards."

"That's nae all," Borim grumbled. "A few weeks ago, there was another assassination attempt on Dunkell's life. There was a skirmish within the royal palace and we were heavily outnumbered. We couldn't push them back so we had ta escape and we only just managed ta do so. We ran through the tunnels under the palace and made it ta the royal stables. We took as many rams as we could and rode hard until we were in Kul'Kriegar where Viceroy Dranthal took us in. We've been holed up in their keep ever since.

"Once we determined that Dunkell was safe I offered ta go ta Aleganthia ta get the viatari's aid, and now, here I am. The Council cannae claim that the King is dead, so they haven't wrested full control of the Kingdom yet. But tensions are growing as the clans take sides and it's only a matter of time before war breaks out between us."

"Does Dunkell have any plans ta stop it from happening?" Thuradin asked. His heart felt heavy with the weight of this dark news and he hoped Borim wasn't here just to get the viatari's military aid in preparation for war. He hoped there was some kind of plan to reunite the dwarves and restore Dunkell to the throne without bloodshed. He needed there to be some hope.

Borim thought for a moment. "Truthfully, I don't know yet. There are too many factors at play. For example, the sounds of digging I mentioned ta ye months ago? That's still happening, and the digging sounds closer now than it did before. People are fearful the burrowers are returning and this all stems from their perspective of what burrowers are—which is why they oppose Dunkell, as well, since he refuses ta go ta war with them."

"Then our only way ta really quell the opposition would be ta convince them that the burrowers are nae blood-thirsty monsters?" Thuradin's shoulders sagged. That was an impossible task. For all that he loved of his people, most dwarves just couldn't get over their hatred and prejudice of the burrowers long enough to see with clear eyes. "There is no hope then."

"Nae necessarily," Borim said, confidence returning to his voice. "We might nae be able to convince everyone, but we don't need to. We only need ta convince the Council. If they're convinced, they'll stand down and the clans can be reunited."

"So, we're going ta talk ta them?" Thuradin said. "We'll just have a nice long chat and convince them that what they're doing is no good for anyone?"

Borim arched an eyebrow. "It's better than just beating their brains in, and it's the only option at this point. While we don't know who they all are, we can hope that they are reasonable dwarves. They're just driven by fear—"

"Which makes them unreasonable—"

"—and if we can quash that fear, we won't have ta resort ta war."

There was silence for a moment.

"Do *ye* believe talking ta them will work?"

Borim looked at Thuradin and suddenly it was as if all his energy were drained from him at once. His eyes drooped, he sat hunched over, and he sighed heavily. "I believe it's all we can do. And Felix can be very persuasive. It's worth trying."

Thuradin chuckled at that, "But," his smile vanishing, "have ye heard anything specific about her? About—"

"Only that she's on the Council," Borim stated grimly. "And I can't imagine what she'll say once she sees ye're back home. It might be best if ye stay hidden while we go talk ta them."

"No, I have ta see her."

"Thuradin—"

"I *have* ta try and fix it."

Borim sighed. "I know ye do, ye fool. I hope for yer sake that she will listen ta ye."

Thuradin nodded and, after a moment, clapped his friend's shoulder. "Come, enough of this talk. Ye need some rest, and I think a pint of ale is in order."

"Aye, I haven't been able ta drink and relax in an age. I would like that very much."

The two dwarves walked out of the reception hall and up to the guest rooms where Borim took off his armor and changed into a more comfortable linen tunic and trousers. They passed a few of the other dwarves on their way down to the cellar where Aleganthia's ale was stored, but the only acknowledgement they received were pointed and disapproving glares aimed at Thuradin.

"I see most of the dwarven world still loathes the fact that I'm still breathing."

"Aye," Borim said regretfully.

"Still, I cannae help but feel excited at the prospect of going back, being in those mountains again. Feeling the crisp chill within the caverns and seeing the rock formations glinting under the light of the braziers. I've missed it all so much."

Borim remained silent as they continued making their way, but once they entered the cellar, picked out a couple of tankards, and began filling them with amber ale, a pained expression spread across his face.

"Ye'll be back in the mountains, Thuradin," he said, shaking his head, "but it won't be the same. Everything has changed, and frankly," he threw back his head and downed his drink, "I wonder if ye'll still be able ta call it home when ye see it."

CHAPTER FOUR

The five riders on horseback would hardly have been mistaken as monsters. Each one wore a long, green cloak with a deep cowl, which was odd in the south because of the heat, but they appeared every bit as human as the farmers, merchants, and travelers they passed on the road.

But they weren't.

The reality was that the figures on horseback were viatari. Their silver hair, red eyes, and sharp fangs were hidden under the illusion of human features, an ability the viatari seldom used. But this was human territory; and all of them, the friendly fisherman who had waved as they passed his hut this morning, the plump woman who had offered to sell them fresh heads of cabbage, the guards who patrolled the roads they were on, would have tried to kill them on the spot if they knew what they were.

And so, they remained hidden under their cloaks.

"How far are we from this place?" Tessa asked. "We've been riding all day."

"It should be close," Madira said, consulting a map of the Southern Isles she had bought from one of the many merchants they had passed on the road. "Just around this bend in the road."

Sure enough, as they neared the bend, they saw in the distance a two-storied inn. It was a cozy establishment named *Admiral's Rest*, made of brick and colored a soft red, like sunset. The garden in front was a collection of multi-colored flowers and well-trimmed hedges, giving patrons something pretty to behold as they made their way to the door. Trees were planted in the back patio, providing shade and a scenic walkthrough for any who wished to take it.

"This doesn't look like any inn I've ever been to," Serania said. "And I've seen a lot of inns."

"And why are we stopping here again?" Natiari asked from the back. "We should be heading straight for Halding Port if we're going to find a ship to take us out to sea."

"We can't do that yet," Victria frowned and turned in her saddle, strands of chestnut brown hair falling out of her cowl. They had been over this already. "We can't go into that port without a guide—it's too dangerous. The person that fisherman contacted for us said they'd meet us here, so we're here."

They rode the rest of the way in silence. A stable boy ran out to meet them as they approached the inn, his freckled face shining with good cheer.

"Good day, madams," he said, bowing low. "Welcome to *Admiral's Rest*. I'd be happy to care for your horses while you go inside and get a hot meal for yourselves."

The viatari dismounted and Victria handed the boy a silver coin in payment. "Will this be enough?"

The boy's eyes widened as he admired the coin. "Thank you, madam," he breathed, nodding rapidly. "Thank you!"

He led the horses away as the viatari walked through the pathway toward the inn's entrance. Victria felt a hand grasp her wrist.

"Be careful flashing around those coins," Serania warned quietly. "We don't want to attract attention to ourselves."

"She's right," Natiari said, drawing close. "I don't want to have to fight off a band of thugs trying to slit our throats in the middle of the night for our money."

"Don't worry," Victria pulled away and made for the inn's entrance. "No one saw us."

"It's a very lovely garden they have here," Madira sighed, oblivious to the hushed whispers happening in front of her as they passed the last of the colorful flowers, "but nothing compared to what I have at home."

"You should take us there to see it sometime," Natiari suggested.

Madira's eyes lit up. "Oh, I'd love to!"

They opened the door and passed through into a large, dimly lit room filled with uproarious laughter, the clattering of plates, and a drunken chorus from a line of men on the stage. As the viatari entered and pulled back their hoods, though, the noise died down instantly as everyone's eyes locked onto the five strangers. Victria noticed that the only women in this inn were the waitresses, all of whom wore dresses showing off their curves. Well, all except for one.

Victria led the others past the congestion of gawking humans, some of whom whistled in their direction, toward a corner table where a lone figure in a dark gray cloak sat.

"Humans," Serania muttered. "How revolting."

Tessa chuckled. "I actually think it's a little flattering. Look, we've mesmerized them. It's as if they've never seen a woman before."

But not all of the men were petrified by the unusual party before them. One daring man tried to stop them by grabbing Natiari's shoulder.

"Ladies, I would love to buy—"

The next sounds to fill the room were yelps of pain as Madira ripped the man's hand off Natiari, breaking his fingers in the process. Victria tensed, worried that the sudden attack might be met with more violence, but instead the men around them laughed; and just like that, the inn came back to life. The man Madira had attacked nursed his fingers as his friends pulled him away, patting him on the back, silly grins on their faces. The drunken songs resumed, and the viatari were ignored. No one else wanted to risk having their fingers broken.

They sat down at the corner table with the lone figure, whose face was hidden behind a cowl. A waitress came to their table to take their order but they turned her away.

"You know, it'll look strange if you sit here without a drink," The stranger said, sipping from her own mug. Victria noted that the voice was light and feminine, but mature.

"She's right," Serania said, flagging back the waitress with a raised hand and ordering them all a glass of wine.

"Wine," the stranger mused. "Interesting choice for a tavern."

"None of us have had good experiences with ale," Victria said, thinking of the time she drank too much of the stuff while negotiating an alliance with the dwarves.

"I see."

Their waitress brought the viatari their wine. They all raised their glasses and took a sip. No sooner had it touched their lips than the stranger began speaking.

"Let's get to business, then," she said. "One of my contacts tells me you need a guide to navigate you through Halding Port."

"That's right," Victria said. "We need to find a ship that

will sail us out past the Great Coral Forest."

"You need to go past the reef?" The stranger repeated. "I know many ship captains and they all owe me favors, but even I don't know if any would be willing to sail in those waters."

"Why not?" Natiari asked.

The stranger studied them for a moment, as if curious. "What are you, foreigners?"

"Yes," Serania said quickly. "We're from the north."

"Hmm, northerners. I don't know how you do it, living in an area without access to the open waters."

"Well, we have plenty of trees at least," Madira said cheerfully. "And open fields."

The stranger paused, "Indeed."

"But you *can* find us a captain who will sail us past the reef, correct?" Victria asked, bringing the conversation back on topic. "I was told you were the only one I could go to with this request."

The stranger thought for a moment, taking another sip from her mug. "It's possible. I might be able to find someone in Halding Port for you—might take a couple days though. But I don't work for free and I don't work for strangers."

"We can pay," Victria pulled out a small pouch and opened it, revealing its contents. The gold and rare gems inside seemed to glow under the inn's dim lighting. "This is just a small sample of what we have to offer. We have connections that can get us more; as much as you need. So, name your price."

The stranger whistled. "Well, I can't say no to a bursting bag of gold and gems. But no matter how rich you are, I still don't work for strangers."

"My name is Victria," Victria pointed to each viatari in turn. "This is Natiari, Madira, Serania, and Tessa is the one sitting next to you."

"A pleasure," the stranger took another swig of her ale.

"Are you going to introduce yourself, so that we know what to call you?"

Victria couldn't see her face very well, but she was sure the stranger was smiling under her cowl.

"You can call me Tera. Now, tell me, how did some fine young ladies like yourselves acquire such a vast quantity of gold and precious gems that you're so confident you can pay whatever price I ask for?"

"We have contacts in the mountains who supply us with what we need," Madira said.

"Ah, so the dwarves are on your side?"

Madira opened her mouth to answer but instead yelped and looked at Serania, who raised her glass of wine innocently to her lips and gave the faintest shake of her head.

Tera laughed. "I'll take that as a yes, then. I've never seen a dwarf myself, but I have heard of them. Being northerners, I suppose you have more dealings with them than we do in the south."

Victria nodded. "We do, and that's why we're able to pay out any price you demand."

"And if I ask for all the gold within their mountains?"

Victria hesitated. "We'd figure something out."

Again, Tera laughed. "I like your determination, Victria. Don't worry, I have no need for so much gold. But I will want, say, three large chests of all the gold and precious gems you can fit."

"Done."

"Excellent!" Tera pulled back her cowl, revealing long, curly blonde hair, piercing green eyes, and an impish smile. Victria thought that she looked to be in her forties. Lines had already begun to form on her face, especially around her eyes as if she smiled and laughed a lot—or used to, perhaps.

"Let's get moving, then. It's a day's ride to Halding Port."

They stood up to leave—Serania taking a moment to down her drink—but before they could move, a man approached them, his friends watching him from the bar.

"'Ello, little lady," he said, looking down at the viatari's guide, who was the shortest one out of all of them. "Why don' you come jo'n me a' the ba'" the man's speech was slurred. Clearly, he'd had one too many drinks. Victria was about to step in and politely push him away but Tera held out a hand to stop her.

"Now, now," she said. "What good would going to the bar with you do?"

"I do-I don' know, have so' fu' I guess."

"What is he saying? I can't understand a word of it," Madira whispered.

Natiari scoffed, "I don't think any of us do."

"You want to have some fun?" Tera flashed a dazzling smile.

"You ha' a pertty nose."

"If you want some fun," she continued, her voice dropping seductively. She traced a finger down the man's chest, "why not meet me in the back room? There'll be no one there except you. And. Me."

The man's eyes widened and he nodded fervently.

"Here," Tera pulled out a vial of dark brown liquid. "Go back there and take this. I'll be with you in just a second." She flashed him another dazzling smile.

"Wha' is it?" the man asked, trying to focus his vision on the vial.

"Let's just call it an enhancer of sorts."

"Wha' would it en—oh . . . oh!" The man flashed a toothy grin and blew a sloppy kiss before stumbling to the backroom. Victria saw his friends at the bar watching him go with some concern.

"Right, ladies," Tera said, her voice back to normal. "Let's go."

They exited the inn and waited in the garden as the stable boy went to fetch their horses.

"That was no enhancer," Serania said, once the boy was out of earshot. "I've seen that potion before, you gave him a laxative."

"Indeed, I did," their guide said happily. "He won't be following us or bothering anyone else anytime soon."

"How did you get him to accept whatever you said like that?" Tessa asked, a bit of awe in her voice. "I've never seen anyone manipulate with such ease before."

Tera smiled, though she did not look too pleased. "I'm sure it's not so different up north. A woman has many ways to get what she wants, but, unfortunately, her most potent tool will always be herself, if you catch my meaning. I don't like to get what I want in such a manner; but, sometimes, it just gets the job done."

Before Tessa could press Tera more about it, their mounts were brought out and Victria paid the stable boy again.

"Thank you, madam!"

They mounted and urged their horses back onto the road.

"Onward to Halding Port," Tera called out. "Follow my pace, ladies, and we will get there within the day."

Halding Port was a large city, the largest the viatari had seen in these southern lands. It seemed to sprawl out for miles from where they were all the way out to the sea. Three giant spires towered over everything, providing enough visibility so the city would have plenty of warning and time to prepare itself if an enemy were to march on them. Of course, looking at the pristine, tall stone walls, it didn't seem likely that there were many enemies willing to waste the resources it would take to lay siege to such a city.

Tera had led them through the city's main gates, where they were stopped by a guard and interrogated. If it weren't for their guide, the viatari might never have entered the city. Her flirtatious ways made it easy to bypass the interrogation and the guard was easily convinced to let them pass.

"I hope to see you soon, miss!" the guard called after them as they passed under the raised iron portcullis.

"In your dreams," Tera muttered. "Come along now, ladies, let's rent a room at an inn first and then we can go about looking for a captain."

They left their horses at the stables and their gear in a room in an adjacent inn, *The Rosy Pirate*, and made their way through the streets toward the docks.

The streets were clogged. Merchants, traders, sailors, and every sort of person bustled through the cobblestone paths, sometimes crowding around a single spot so much it was impossible to move through them.

Victria couldn't help but hold her breath most of the time. She was accustomed to the scent of trees, of the earth. Here, her nose was assaulted with the stench of body odor, sweat, and fish—especially fish. She looked at her companions and could tell they were struggling just as much—except for Serania. Serania caught her gaze and shrugged. "I've visited many places as a wanderer. Most cities in the south smell like this. You get used to it."

After what seemed like an hour of pushing their way through the crowds and declining merchant offers of fresh tuna caught at the edge of the reef, they passed through a second set of stone walls, the other side of which was an array of docks, storage houses, and vessels

The smells were slightly better here. The air was fresh and salty from the sea, invigorating to the senses. There was still the hum of business going about them as sailors disembarked from their ships, hauling wooden crates filled with iced fish onto the docks to be taken into the city.

Masts from the larger warships towered over everything else, their canvas sails furled up tightly. Seagulls glided overhead and converged on the yardarms. The smaller fishing vessels bobbed with the choppy waves, but that didn't seem to faze the fishermen standing in them, who walked about as if on solid ground. Thick, gray clouds were slowly drifting in from the sea. Many of the sailors pointed toward them anxiously as lighting flashed in the distance.

"Looks like a storm is coming," Tera said grimly. "We won't be finding any captains willing to sail out today, but let's see if there are any who will consider taking a voyage after the storm."

They followed Tera as she strode purposefully toward a larger man with long white hair sticking out of a thick woolen cap. He wore nothing but brown trousers and leather boots. Victria noticed the carp tattoo he had on his large belly moved around as if flopping every time he laughed.

"Hey there, Dol," Tera said in a voice as smooth as silk. "It's been a while."

The man looked at Tera and blinked as if waking up from a dream. "Tera? Tera, is tha' really you?" He moved closer and tapped her shoulder. "Flesh and bone," he laughed boisterously, "By the waves! It's good to see ya again!"

Tera chuckled. "Good haul today?"

Dol groaned. "Nothing but bad luck. Had me a beaut'ful marlin on the line, had to be as big as me. Was so close to reelin' 'im in but just when he was 'bout to break through the water, I lost 'im."

"Line broke?" Tera patted Dol on the arm consolingly.

"No," Dol's eyes hardened. "No, I wouldn' be so mad abou' it if it was just tha'. It was those fish people. Stole me marlin righ' from under me. Cut me line and swam 'way 'fore I could throw me harpoon."

"Fish people?" Madira repeated. "As in, half human, half fish?"

Dol's gaze shifted to the viatari behind Tera. His eyes were penetrating and suspicious.

"Brought some lady friends, I see," the captain crossed his arms.

"They're from the north," Tera explained, knowing the question already forming on his lips. "They wouldn't know about the vashi."

"Vashi?"

"Aye, vashi," Dol said grimly. "They look like us in some ways, but that's where the likeness stops. Vicious creatures they are, won' hesitate to kill one o' us when they ge' the chance. Come to think o' it, I guess I was pretty lucky none o' 'em tried to kill me today."

"What were they doing so far in the reef?" Tera asked.

"Ah," Dol suddenly looked bashful. "I may 'ave drifted a fair bit off course t'day and ended up on the edge o' the reef."

Tera smacked Dol hard on the head.

"Dol Holdson, the edge of the reef is vashi waters and

leagues away from your regular fishing grounds, you know that!"

"Ow! I know, I know. But that marlin was so beaut'ful, ya shoulda seen it. Anyway, 'nough 'bout me, what brings ya back to Halding Port? And with friends?"

"That's actually what I came to see you about," Tera said, her voice soft and silky once again. "You see, my friends want to hire a captain to take them out to sea."

Dol's face lit up, "Well I'm yar man, I don' mind showin' these northern beau'ies the wonders o' the sea."

"But they're not looking for just any captain,"

"Oh," Dol's face fell just a bit as Tera continued.

"They're looking for a *brave* captain. One daring enough to take them past the reef. One who knows the ocean like the back of his hand. A captain I know I can rely on to bring them back safely." Tera drew closer to Dol, who had suddenly gone very white. She traced her finger from his neck to the middle of his chest, making him gulp. "Can I count on you, Dol?"

"I-I" Dol took a shaky breath and grabbed Tera's hand with both of his own and took a step back. "I . . . wish I could," he said in a defeated voice, "ya know I would sail to the moon and back for ya if it were possible. But 'yond the reef . . . No, that would be suicide. I may be old, but I still got some livin' left to do."

"Why do you say that?" Victria asked, intrigued. "Because of the vashi?"

Dol nodded somberly. "They don' take too kindly to us humans sailin' in their wa'ers. Their wa'erseers 'ave sunk many a ship in me lifetime. I don' want my own to be the next on their list."

Natiari stepped in next to Tera smiling warmly at the

captain who seemed enraptured by her. She had grown out
her hair, now red in her human disguise, recently and wore
it in a ponytail that touched the middle of her back. She
leaned in close, following Tera's example.

"Don't worry about those vashi, we'll be right there to
protect you."

"I. . . ." Dol shook his head hard and blinked several
times, then he eyed Tera. "Ya're a sneaky one, ya are. Ya
know well I like the ones with the red hair."

Tera grinned and shrugged. "I'd completely forgotten.
You'll do it, then?"

Dol looked longingly at his ship, a small shipping trawler
made of wood and painted green like a forest. A few of his
crew were still onboard, resting from the day's work.

"No," he finally said after some time. "I like ya a lo'
Tera, Trust me, I do. But I like me ship more."

They had no luck finding a captain that day and returned to
the inn sullenly just as the storm they had seen in the distance
earlier unleashed its pent-up fury. Those still outside
scurried indoors as the torrential downpour fell on the city.

Inside *The Rosy Pirate,* patrons ate their dinners of clam
and seaweed soup. The viatari ate too, though they still
hungered afterwards. They left Tera in the dining area to
think over how they should go about looking for a captain as
they made their way to their room. They took turns stepping
out onto the balcony to feed on the life-energies of the
critters they had brought for the journey. They came back in
soaking wet due to the rain, but there were plenty of towels
in the room to dry off with and it was a necessary discomfort. Feeding required them to revert to their viatari
form and they couldn't have Tera walking in on them in the

middle of the process. As it happened, Tera entered the room just as Tessa walked out onto the balcony.

The human raised an eyebrow quizzically, "Is there a reason why our friend has stepped out into the storm?"

"We're using the rain to wash off the stink of the past several days. It has been some time since we've been able to bathe." Victria said matter-of-factly.

"Ah," Tera made her way to the bookshelf and pulled out a thick tome, plopping herself onto an adjacent chair and flipping through the pages until she hit the middle where she began reading. "They have private bathhouses in the city. I should have thought to take you there so you didn't have to use the storm. Next time you feel like you need to bathe, just let me know."

"It's no problem for us," Madira said, wrapping a towel around her damp hair. "We bathe in the rivers up north, so the rain isn't too different."

"Suite yourself, just let me know if you change your minds."

"There's only one bed in here," Serania noted, wanting to change the subject.

"Take it," Tera waved her hand dismissively. "I'm used to sleeping on the floor."

"No, you should have it," Victria said, feeling some sympathy for her. "You helped us so much today."

"Well, you don't have a captain to take you beyond the reef yet, so I haven't done much."

Tessa reentered the room from the balcony and grabbed a towel to dry off. Tera glanced at her briefly before returning to her book.

"I must be getting old. For a moment, I thought your hair was silver instead of black like I've been seeing all day."

Everyone froze. Tessa, who had been scrubbing her hair with the towel, now held it in place, covering her head. Slowly she lowered it and moved on to drying her arms and legs, revealing uneven, shoulder-length, black hair.

Tessa shrugged. "Must have been the moon,"

Tera was silent, staring intently out the window at the sheets of rain falling from thick, dark clouds in the sky. "Right," she finally said, deep in thought, "The moon . . . Still," her tone turned light, nonchalant, "to shower in the rain, it must have been a long ride from—where did you say you were from again?"

"We didn't," Serania stated flatly.

"Well, we're going to be spending some time together, I imagine. Might as well get to know one another. Where in the north are you all from?"

"Just a small city in the north," Victria said dismissively, her heart pounding. "You likely don't know of it."

"There aren't too many cities in the north. I lived up there myself for a time and all I remember is how many small towns and villages there were in the plains. Hardly anything like Halding Port. So, I can assume you're from Garon?"

Madira, who had been dozing in a chair, shuddered at the name.

Tera turned her curious gaze to her. "I'll take that as a no. Such a strong reaction must mean you have some history with that place?"

"Well, we—"

Victria cleared her throat and shook her head ever so slightly, hoping Madira would catch the hint.

"I-it's just not been the best place to be, lately."

"Ah, yes" Tera nodded knowingly, a grin playing on her lips. "I've heard rumors that Garon was sacked recently by an army of viatari. Were you caught up in that?"

"No, we were gone by the time that happened," Natiari said. "If we had been caught in the city we probably wouldn't be here right now since we would have been killed by those . . . *leeches.*"

Victria's gaze kept flicking back and forth between Tera and her viatari companions. They were keeping up with the human's questions and managing to keep their voices steady like they were all having a regular conversation, but she knew everyone's heart was pounding; she could practically hear them. Tera was getting a bit too close to the truth—too many hints had been revealed—she had to find a way to bring this discussion to a close.

Tera nodded. "Those viatari," she repeated, "we hardly ever see them in the south but I imagine you encounter them quite regularly in the north."

"Occasionally," Victria said, yawning. "Anyway, not to cut a conversation short, but I think we should get some sleep. I have a feeling we're going to be at the docks all day tomorrow looking for a captain and the past several days of horseback riding are catching up to me."

"Too true," Tera nodded, closing her book and putting it away while she blew out the candle next to her. "I'll take the floor then, good night."

She grabbed a thin blanket from one of the room's cabinets and laid herself down on the floor next to the door. Not too long after, her breathing turned rhythmic and Victria was convinced she had fallen asleep. She strode to the bed and sat down as if she were preparing to turn in for the night as well. Natiari sat up in bed, watching her. The others drifted closer so they could speak in hushed tones. There was much to talk about. Victria took a breath and turned her eyes on

Tessa.

"'*Must have been the moon?*'" she hissed.

"I didn't know what else to say."

"How could you forget to revert to your human form after eating? The last thing we need is to blow our cover and have Tera run off to tell the whole city there are viatari within the walls."

Tessa frowned. "Maybe I forgot we were in hiding because I've gotten so used to Tera."

"We've only known her for a day!"

"And yet, it already feels like she's one of us."

Victria sighed but forced back her frustration. They didn't need to make a scene and risk waking the human up. "She's still human. We must be more careful around her. That goes for you, too, Madira."

Madira's eyes widened in surprise as she whispered, "Me?"

"You speak too casually. I know you're not used to dealing with humans, being from Dalyr, but you must learn quickly how to answer questions without revealing information that could lead to outing us as viatari."

Madira wrapped her arms around her knees, bringing them to her chin as she nodded glumly. "Sorry, Victria."

"I think we should have a watch," Serania suggested, her eyes glued onto Tera's back.

"What do you mean?"

"I mean, we can't let our guard down around Tera, especially after Tessa's mistake. She could very easily turn on us while we sleep and we'd be defenseless. One of us should keep an eye on her while the others sleep."

"I don't think that's necessary," Victria closed her eyes and rubbed her temples, this whole situation was dangerous but Serania tended to always go for the extreme solution.

"She won't get the rest of her payment if she kills us, and it's unlikely for her to attack us since she would have to be certain beyond a shadow of a doubt about our identities before she acted on it."

"Do you really think she's going to care about some gold when the chance to kill five viatari presents itself? She knows." Serania said with finality.

"She suspects, maybe," Tessa shook her head. "But she can't know for sure."

"Tessa's right," Natiari laid back down on the bed, closing her eyes. "After all, if she knew what we were, how could she fall asleep so easily?"

"Alright," Victria said. "Let's end this discussion. Just remember to be more cautious with how we act from here on out. We don't mention this again until we're away from human ears."

The viatari blew out the remaining candles, gathered what blankets they could, and laid themselves down where there was space. Victria was on the floor next to Tera. She turned to her side so that her back was facing the human. Serania sat upright in one of the chairs across from her, keeping watch.

Victria closed her eyes, half expecting a dagger to suddenly rip through her back, but the other half feeling that they could trust Tera. There was something about her that was unlike anything she had ever encountered in humans before. She wanted to reflect more deeply about the day's events, from their first encounter with Tera to their time in the port, to see if there were any signs of danger she had missed, but she could only dwell on them for a moment before she felt herself drift away into sleep.

CHAPTER FIVE

The sun bore down on Tera and the viatari as they continued their search for a captain the next day. The docks were as alive today as they had been yesterday, though there were less ships present, most still out for their daily fishing expeditions.

Tera closed her eyes and took in a deep breath of ocean air. "Today's a good day for it," she said, opening her eyes and turning to the viatari behind her, all of whom were tired from a restless night. "Not a cloud in sight. At least these people won't be able to use a storm as an excuse this time."

They went around asking the captains of smaller fishing vessels first, hoping the prospect of gold would entice them to make the risky voyage, but all declined with the same look of disappointment and fear. After the tenth sailor declined her offer, Tera moved on to one of the warships moored on the far side of the dock.

"Captain," she called out as she approached the nearest one. A man wearing a long, leather jacket with bronze silk embroidered along the edges turned and looked at her with interest. He had no hair on his head, most of it having grown on his face in the form of a well-groomed handlebar mustache. The two guards stationed at the gangway saluted as he passed them and hopped onto the pier. "What can I do for you, ladies?"

"I have a proposition for you and your crew," Tera said, getting straight to the point. "We need a ship that will take us beyond the reef. We can pay." She tossed the man the sack of gold and gems Victria had given her at the *Admiral's Rest.* "Are you in?"

The man laughed. "So, you're the one who's been scaring off all the honest sailors here. Word is spreading about your rather ridiculous request."

Tera shrugged, "I was hired to find a captain and I intend to do it, no matter the cost."

The captain's gaze shifted to the viatari, who all stood to the side, trying to look natural and carefree. Madira waved shyly. The man grunted and turned his attention back to Tera.

"Why? What business have they to go beyond the reef?"

"I haven't asked. Their business is their own."

"Their business could lead my crew to their deaths," the captain growled. "It may surprise you, but I care for my men, woman, and I'll not be risking any of them for a small bag of gold. Besides, this is a military vessel and my orders are to remain docked at Halding Port."

"There's more of that where it came from," Tera countered, pointing at the bag of gold still in the captain's hands. "Sure, beyond the reef is dangerous, but that's why you have ballistae and harpoon launchers on your ship, isn't it? You'd be able to protect yourselves from any vashi attack."

The man glowered at the bag in his hand and tossed it back. "There's more in the seas to worry about than just the vashi, believe me. And like I said, this is a military ship, not a transport for civilians."

Tera sighed. "Fine, we'll ask someone else, see if they'll be more willing to earn a fine chest of gold for a simple boat ride."

"You may continue asking the local sailors, but if I hear you've been harassing the other military captains for their ships, I will have you arrested and thrown out of this city. I don't care how many mountains of gold you're offering for this expedition; it's suicide." With that, the man stormed off back onto his ship.

Tera turned angrily and made as if to move on to another pier but then stopped, noticing the large number of sailors eyeing them. Clearing her throat, she glared back at each one defiantly. "What are you looking at?"

The sailors snapped out of whatever daze they were in and returned to their work.

Victria was no expert on human affairs but even she could feel the tension in the air as they passed by each individual sailor, all of whom looked their way with a gleam in their eyes, and she didn't like it. "Are we continuing the search?"

"No," Tera said tersely, moving toward the port wall. "We're going back to the inn for the day."

It was a wasted day, they knew, but the abandonment of their search brought no argument from the viatari. They all sensed something had gone wrong with Tera's attempted wooing of the military captain. As they left the dock and re-entered the city proper, they could feel eyes behind them staring daggers into their backs.

They ate a quick lunch of grilled fish with salted potatoes in the inn's main hall. Not a word was said between them as they ate nor as they left the table and retired to their room. Only after Tera had closed the door did the viatari's curiosity manifest itself.

"What was that?" Serania asked breathlessly, "Perhaps we're not accustomed to how things work in the Southern Isles, but if I didn't know any better it seems to me that we have a huge target on our backs now because of today's efforts."

"We do." Tera said calmly.

"So, what's the plan now?" Victria asked. "Do we wait until tomorrow to continue asking around for a ship?"

"No," Tera was deep in thought, her gaze wandering over to the room's large windows, "we'd be stupid to continue our search here after the amount of attention that military captain brought to us."

"What do you mean?" Tessa asked "Those sailors were probably just interested to see if a fight was going to break out between you and the captain."

"Maybe at first. But I'm sure the captain shouting about our mountains of gold convinced them that there were other reasons to be watching us."

There was silence as the viatari let Tera's words sink in.

"They were studying us," Tessa realized grimly. "Looking for weaknesses."

"Exactly, and in their eyes, we have plenty: namely, we're women. They wouldn't hesitate to attack us if it helped their pockets grow."

"I'd like to see them try," Serania said darkly.

Tera grinned. "As would I, but that won't help us with finding a captain here. Though, we likely won't find one in this city at all anymore."

"Why not?"

"Sailors here are big gossips. Word will spread like fire that there are several rich women in the city just begging to be ambushed. It won't be difficult for anyone to find out which inn we're staying at, either."

"Then what's the plan?" Victria asked again. Their goal of finding a means to sail beyond the reef was still her first priority, no matter the danger. The First One had told them one of his brothers was somewhere deep in the ocean. If they couldn't find a captain who would take them there, they wouldn't be able to look for this acolyte. And they needed to find him. Their hope for winning the coming war against The Turned One, for protecting this world, rested on their success. She had known from the beginning that this would be an arduous task, but these constant difficulties were beginning to test her patience.

Tera sighed, then, after a moment, seemed to come to a satisfactory conclusion. "Halding Port is not the only coastal city. There is also Donsea. It's a smaller harbor, but I know one of the captains there personally who I'm sure will be willing to take you beyond the reef—for the right price."

"Then we should go now," Madira said, peering out the window as if expecting a mob of humans to have already formed below them.

"Not yet," Tera grunted as she leaned back into a chair and pulled out the book she had been reading last night. She opened it and leafed through some of the pages, looking for where she had left off. "It will be easier to sneak out at night, when the streets are less crowded. It would be too much of a hassle to move through the crowds on our mounts right now and exposing ourselves out in the open like that would be a nice invitation for an ambush."

Victria agreed. Tera's reasoning was sound. "Then we wait."

"What about the gates?" Madira asked. "They'll be closed

at night, won't they?"

Tera glanced up from her book and chuckled. "You worry a lot, don't you?"

"I just don't want to be trapped in this place," the viatari mumbled, her eyes still glued to the streets below them.

Tera finally nodded. "Fair enough. I'll be sure to head out after dinner to see about that issue. I'm sure one of the guards will keep the gates open tonight if I ask him politely enough."

She smiled and returned to her book. The conversation was over.

The day dragged on for the viatari who could do nothing but sit around and try to catch up on sleep. In the early evening, Tera left them to see about the city's gates. An hour passed before she returned with any news.

"Well," she said. "It pays sometimes to be me. Guard Thomas will leave the gate open for us until midnight. We'll take our leave from this place a couple hours before then. Get some rest, ladies, you'll need it."

They took turns sleeping, all except Madira, who had remained attached to the window ever since they came back from the docks. Night fell and she still sat by the aperture, watching the streets below them.

"Good, it's a new moon," Tera said thoughtfully, joining Madira's vigil for a moment. "We'll have complete darkness on our side. Start packing your things. I'll go pay the innkeeper to stay quiet about our departure and come back to—"

"That man," Madira suddenly said.

"What?"

"There's a man outside who has been standing in the same spot for hours, just looking at us—at our room."

Tera followed where Madira was pointing.

"I see him," she said. "That one, by the café on the other side of the street?"

Madira nodded.

"And you're sure he's been standing there for hours; he hasn't just shown up?"

Again, the viatari nodded.

"That can't be good," Tera muttered. She made her way to the door and tried opening it but the door handle stayed in place. She stood there for a moment, thinking, then shrugged. There was no sugarcoating things. "They've locked our room from the outside," she said bluntly, "which means they've found us. So, we're changing plans. We're leaving town immediately."

"And how are we doing that?" Serania asked testily. "Will we fight our way out? Us against the whole city?"

Tera grinned. "That would be quite the scene. No, there is a better way."

She put the book she had been reading back on the bookshelf by the bed and then pushed the bookshelf to the side. Where the wall should have been was a small, narrow hallway that led to another room. She looked at them triumphantly. "I got this room for a reason; never thought I'd see the day where I had to use this hallway though. Anyway, don't just stand there gawking. Let's make our escape."

After a brief hesitation Victria grabbed her bags and followed Tera through the hallway, encouraging the other viatari to follow suit. Once they were in the other room, Tera immediately went to the door and opened it slowly, just enough to see if anything, or anyone, was outside.

"Whoever locked our door didn't leave a guard to keep watch," she rolled her eyes. "Amateurs. This will be easier than I thought. Follow me and stay silent."

Without waiting for a response, their human guide exited the room, heading for the end of the hallway, where a man-sized window stood. The floor was made of wooden planks yet her steps produced no noise, not so much as a creak. The viatari followed her footsteps, managing to stay just as silent.

"We're jumping out of a window?" Serania asked. "That's your plan?"

Tera smiled and raised her eyebrows curiously. "You have a better one? I'm all ears."

She undid the latch and pushed the glass panel open. A warm gust of sea breeze rushed past them and then nothing. The night was still. Tera leaned out the window and checked the surroundings of the alleyway below.

"I'm not seeing anything to ease our fall, but I don't think we're high enough to break any bones anyway." She hooked one leg over the ledge and climbed out, "Remember, silently now." She let go and landed into the alley below with a soft grunt.

Victria turned to her companions as she climbed out onto the window next, "She knows what she's doing. We have to trust her right now if we want to get out of this city." The others nodded. She let go of the ledge and felt the wind rush past her for a second as gravity took hold. She landed gracefully and immediately sank into the shadows where Tera was.

One by one, the viatari jumped from the inn's second floor into the alleyway. Victria held her breath as each one landed. They were viatari and might be hard to kill, but their bones could still break if they were to land poorly and the pain from that would be enough to make anyone cry out.

Luckily, with Madira landing next to them as gracefully as they all had, that worry vanished and Victria's mind moved on to the next part of their escape: getting to their mounts.

Tera spoke so softly they all had to lean in to hear, "We're moving to the stables which are on the other side of the building we're leaning against right now. Move through the shadows and move *slowly*. The darkness doesn't make you invisible. No sudden movements."

Tera led the way, the five viatari following close behind. Once they were out of the alley and on the main street, there were less places to hide. Some carts still stood parked to the side of the pedestrian path for the night as well as a few stacks of wooden crates and they used these as cover to keep from being seen by the man on the other side of the street, who still had his eyes fixed on their room.

Before they could reach the stables, there existed a gap of open space between the carts for several paces, which posed a problem.

"No place to hide here," Tera said grimly. "We're going to have to leave the shadows to reach the next set of carts. Walk normally, as if you're out for a late-night stroll. We're going to go one at a time. Whatever you do, don't look at the man, don't tense up, don't give him any reason to suspect you. Even if he sees you, chances are he'll think nothing of it. Watch me and do exactly as I do."

As the viatari held their position, Tera stood up straight and began walking calmly through the empty space to the next cart where she then crouched back down and waved them over. Serania took a deep breath and went next. Then Natiari. Then Tessa. Madira followed rather shakily, but made it without raising any alarms either. Tera waved again for Victria to join them.

Victria thought of everything that could go wrong. What if the man looked her way and realized who she was? What if he raised an alarm? They would be surrounded by enemies in seconds. They wouldn't be able to fight off the whole city. They would be overwhelmed. And then . . . what if her companions died because of her, because she froze up?

She closed her eyes and took a breath, trying to think of something, anything that might calm her nerves. Felix's face pushed its way to the forefront. She saw his peppered, short-cropped hair, his ever-calm red eyes as they stood outside Aleganthia's southern gate, the wooden-plank bridge connecting the isolated mesa with the surrounding forest swaying gently with the breeze. White banners with the viatari crest fluttered overheard. The sky was so blue and not a cloud in sight, just perfect rays of sunshine.

"You can do this," she remembered him saying just before she left for her journey to the Southern Isles.

"Why me?" she had asked. "We need these acolytes for the war and if we fail to retrieve even one of them—"

"I know," Felix had taken her hands into his. "This will determine our future, whether we will live to see this world be freed or not," he had smiled at this point, a knowing smile, one she had seen far too many times to count, one that had always comforted her, "and there's no one else I would trust to see this through more than you."

Victria opened her eyes, back in Halding Port, her nerves steady. Not wanting to waste the newfound surge of courage she felt, she stood up and began walking across the open space. It had taken the others around ten steps to reach the other side, so as she walked, she counted in her head.

One . . . Two . . . Three. . . .

She had the sudden urge to look back, to see if the man

was watching her, but she fought the temptation.

Four . . . Five. . . .

Halfway there. It took everything in her not to just sprint these last few steps and be done with them.

Six . . . Seven . . . Eight . . . Nine. . . .

"Hey!"

Victria's blood froze. Her heart pounded in her ears but she kept her breathing steady. *Act natural,* she thought. She turned toward the man who had been watching their room, who was now watching her.

"Where you off to?"

Victria, her mind still on Felix and Aleganthia, said the first thing she thought of.

"Home," she called out, doing her best to keep her voice from trembling. "Home to my . . . husband."

The man nodded and grinned, returning his gaze to the inn. "Lucky man. Not the best night for a walk through this area, ma'am. I'd hurry home if I were you. Wouldn't want to keep your husband waiting."

"Of course," Victria turned away from the man and walked a few more steps, past Tera and the others before her trembling legs finally couldn't take anymore and she sank to the ground.

Tera crawled over to her and put a hand on her back, patting it encouragingly. "You did excellent," she said, "*excellent.* But we need to keep moving."

Victria nodded, taking deep breaths to steady herself as Tera took the lead again. Her heart still pounded relentlessly against her ribcage. She felt the others' eyes on her but ignored them. Tera was right. There was no time to waste on self-pity or comfort.

"In. Quickly." Tera whispered as she pushed the tall

wooden doors to the stables open. They hurried through and heard the doors shut behind them. "Alright," she said, letting out a sharp breath, "get your horses prepped. We need to ride out of this city before the guards close the gate."

The viatari set about putting saddles on their horses as well as tying down their provisions. They didn't talk as they worked, knowing time was not on their side. After a few minutes, they were ready to mount up, but voices could be heard coming from behind the door. There were several of them outside, but two in particular sounded dangerously close.

"Brook said he saw some ladies walk into the stable."

"There's no way it can be them, though, cannit? We been watchin' their room all night."

"Well, that's why they sent all of us here, isn't it? Here, get the other door."

Tera sighed resignedly, "Nothing to do about it, ladies. Get ready to ride through them. Stay close, I don't want any of us getting separated."

The viatari nodded and readied themselves for Tera's signal. Victria felt her body tense as she anticipated the crowds they must surely face once they were out in the open. There was a flicker of flame as the doors cracked open revealing torches.

"Now!"

Tera kicked her horse into a full gallop and the viatari were close behind. Together their mounts rammed the door open and mowed through the twenty or so humans who had assembled in front of it.

"Left!" Tera called out over their screams and alarmed yelps.

They veered their horses away from the mob and galloped

down the street, hooves rapping smartly against the cobble-stone. The humans gave chase, but they were on foot and quickly fell behind. Victria spared a glance over her shoulder and saw them give up as they turned another corner. She should have felt elated, but she had a feeling they weren't the only ones on the lookout for them.

Sure enough, just when the gates came into view, another party of humans, these carrying spears, torches, and rope, burst out of the adjacent houses and formed ranks in front of them.

"Guards, close the gates!" One of them yelled.

"Ride through them!" Tera shouted, pulling out a throwing knife from her left boot. Victria saw a flash of metal as she threw it and one of the guards trying to close the gate crumpled.

The humans of Halding Port were pressed together tightly, but were undisciplined. Many jumped to the side as the mounts came through and the rest were trampled underfoot.

Victria heard a grunt next to her and turned in time to see Serania slide off her horse and onto the street.

"Leave her," Tera shouted, also looking back. "We have to pass through those gates before they close!"

Victria hesitated but found her initial concern was misplaced. Serania pushed herself back up and unleashed a flurry of kicks and shattering blows against the five men who had surrounded her, knocking them all to the floor with broken noses and ribs. She then ran at top speed, catching up to her horse easily, and remounted.

They each passed through the open gates and heard a *thunk!* which told them they had narrowly avoided the closing of the portcullis.

Tera glanced over her shoulder again, sparing a minute

to stare at Serania back on her horse. She said nothing, bringing her eyes back to the road calling out, "We ride to the coast."

They rode at a full gallop for several hours into the night. There was no moon to light their way but the stars were bright and formed many figures in the sky that helped them navigate their way southward and westward toward the ocean. Once they were on the beach, they rode alongside it for some time before Tera finally decided they could stop and make camp.

The viatari dismounted and let their horses roam free. Madira immediately went to Serania's side to check if she was okay, but Serania waved her away.

"I'm fine," she mumbled. "Just got scratched up a bit from the fall."

"No fire tonight," Tera said. "Not that we have time to gather wood, anyway. I don't want to signal any pursuers we may have where our location is."

"I'll take first watch," Victria offered.

Tera nodded. "Kind of you. I'll take second. Wake me up in a couple hours. Serania, are you sure you're alright?"

Serania nodded. "Nothing's broken."

Tera snickered. "Well, that's good to hear. I would be more surprised if you had broken anything and *still* managed to catch up to your horse."

The viatari were silent, avoiding eye contact, even with each other. But Tera was still chuckling, her smile not quite reaching her eyes, as she continued, "Hell, if I were *crazy*, I would say you would have to be a viatari to move that fast. But, like I said, that would be crazy, wouldn't it?"

Serania tried to laugh along with Tera, but her voice sounded hollow as she agreed. "Just crazy."

Tera shook her head and laid down on the sand looking up at the stars. Victria sat on the other side of their little camp, watching and listening to the waves break onto the shore. Within minutes, the human's eyes were closed and she was asleep. Serania came over and sat next to Victria, her face somber.

"She knows."

Victria nodded. "Will you be sleeping tonight?"

"Only if you're watching my back."

"Sweet dreams."

Serania grunted and lay down next to her. A few minutes later, she and the other viatari were also asleep and Victria was alone with her thoughts, watching Tera sleep, thinking of all that had transpired in the short amount of time they had known each other. Could she trust this human? She had seemed different. She had technically saved them just now by leading them out of Halding Port, despite the danger such a task presented for herself.

Looking out toward the ocean and seeing the black waves come in one by one, again and again and again, she came to a decision. Out there, deep within those waters was the acolyte she was charged with bringing back to Aleganthia. And Tera was their best chance at getting to him. Without her, they would be lost.

She would have to be watched closely, but Victria decided they would continue trusting their guide to find them a captain. And if she tried to betray them—well, Victria pursed her lips at the thought, but knew there would be no other choice at that point. She would be sure to kill Tera herself.

CHAPTER SIX

Two days of hard riding brought them to Donsea. It was an uneventful and silent journey. The viatari were mindful of their every word and action, careful not to give away any more hints as to what their true nature was. Thankfully, Tera seemed to have forgotten or lost interest in the subject and hadn't pushed them about it during their trek.

Victria knew they were close to Donsea before they even saw its wooden palisade just by the sheer number of seagulls constantly circling over the same area. Donsea was a city like Halding Port, though much smaller and much cleaner. Victria noticed the denizens here were much more relaxed and ambled leisurely through the gravel streets as they went about their business. Many sat along the porches of their homes or leaned out of their windows, smoking pipe and watching passersby.

"Eyes everywhere," Tessa muttered. "Are you sure this place isn't as dangerous as Halding Port?"

"Don't worry about them," Tera called back as she waved at some of the men watching them. "They're not watching us with any interest. That's just how they pass the time."

They moved through several blocks of the city before

finding a stable to settle their mounts in. The horses nickered and bobbed their heads gratefully as they found a trough filled with water along with a bag full of oats hanging off a wooden post.

"Gather your things and come along now," Tera said, shouldering her own pack and moving on down the road. "We're going to meet an old friend of mine."

"We're not going to the docks?" Victria asked.

"No, not today. This friend is pretty particular about which days he goes out to sail. We're going to his house to ask for his help. He just might be crazy enough to take you all where you want to go. And if he isn't, well," Tera glanced back at them and shrugged. "There won't be anyone else who will be."

They walked the next few blocks in silence. Victria looked around as they passed house after house, trying to guess which one might be a captain's home. When they finally stopped and she saw the structure before them, she wasn't sure if it could even be called a house.

It was a conglomeration of different building materials. Most of the walls were composed of bricks and uncut stones. The roof was mostly wooden with patches of straw here and there. There were three floors to this structure, but they were not stacked directly on top of each other like regular buildings. Instead, they were unevenly stacked as if someone had tried pushing the second floor out from under the third but hadn't managed to complete the task. Two crooked, tin chimneys jutted out of the roof with thin trails of black smoke rising out of them. Victria tried to see through the multitude of windows, but they were all so dirty and full of smudges and rusty stains it was impossible to make out anything within the house.

"How is that building even standing?" Serania gawked at the edifice.

"Thomas built it himself," Tera said with a nostalgic grin. "I said the same thing when I first saw it, but it's a lot homier inside, trust me."

Tera walked up to the door and knocked, then waited a split second before opening it herself and barging in. The viatari stayed behind, uncertain as to whether they should enter.

"You always keep the fire on!" Tera shouted.

"'ey, no need fa shoutin', I be right here."

Coming out of a room adjacent to the entrance was a man with wild hair and wild eyes. He wore trousers that were frayed around the ankles, no shirt, and was well built. His body and face were covered in tattoos of white ink that contrasted well with his dark skin. Most of them looked to be just randomly shaped figures, like the thick white lines that ran from his forehead and over his eyelids to his cheeks, but Victria recognized a few fish that appeared to be swimming around his right bicep.

The man looked at Tera, eyes widening as if he were seeing a ghost. "Tera, be that ya?"

Tera smiled broadly and embraced the man. "It's great to see you again, Thomas. It's been too long."

"Yuh mon, it has. Not to be bringin' up da bad days, but I not seen ya since ya husband was killed."

Tera's smile flickered for a moment, but she shook her head as if ridding it of unhappy memories. She searched for the viatari who were still huddled outside the door and waved to them invitingly, "Come on, come in."

Thomas watched each of them warily as they entered his home. Victria tried to smile so as to appear pleasant but found she couldn't look the fisherman in the eyes. His wide, brown eyes, bordered by white lines of an intricate tattoo design, were disconcerting. It was as if he could see straight through her.

Thomas looked at Tera, crossing his arms. "Ya always be up to someting. What be bringin' ya back to Donsea?"

Tera pointed at the viatari. "These ladies need a favor and I only know one captain crazy enough to do it."

Thomas rubbed the bit of fuzzy facial hair he had on his chin. "Interestin,' interestin.' Come in, come in. 'ave a seat at me table by da fire. I tink we need to be 'avin' a little chat to get to know each other a little bettah."

The viatari followed Thomas through the narrow hallways of his house to a simple wooden table in the dining room. Thomas brought in more chairs from another room and they all sat down, the viatari and the humans on opposite sides.

"So, what ya be needin' from dis 'umble captain?"

Victria took a breath to steady her nerves as she tried once again to look the man in the eyes, but found she still struggled to do so. "We need you to sail us past the reef."

Thomas grinned, revealing several rotting teeth as well as many gaps where others used to be. "Ya be needin' to get past da reef. Dat be no easy task, I tell ya now."

"We've been trying to find a captain in Halding Port with Tera's help, but we ran into some trouble and had to leave," even though Victria wasn't looking directly into Thomas' eyes, she could feel them boring into her, "and now we're here. Tera seems to think you're our last best bet."

"Did'ja now? Run into a little trouble in da big city?"

"One of the captains there proclaimed a little too loudly that we had plenty of gold to pay for the voyage," Tera shook her head in annoyance. "I should have known to come here first."

"Ya should 'ave. Lucky for ya, I not be takin' gold as payment."

"You don't want gold?" Victria asked, slightly worried. She couldn't think of much else they might have that could be valuable to humans. Especially one as unpredictable as Thomas.

"Nah mon, I 'ave no need for it. I make everyting I need. What I be wantin' as payment is da truth."

"The truth?"

"Da truth."

"What truth?"

"First, ya can start by tellin' me *why* ya want to go past da reef."

Victria hesitated. She had been prepared to share most things, but she wasn't sure if it would be wise to share this subject with Thomas, or Tera for that matter. The issue of searching for The First One's brother was strictly a viatari and dwarven problem. The fewer who knew, the better.

"We're from the north," Serania said, coming to Victria's rescue. "We've always wanted to take a trip to the south and see what there is here. We've heard about the Throne of the Deep, and that it lies in the deepest parts of the ocean. Tales of a spiraling structure encrusted with thousands of glimmering pearls that touches the sky reaches even the most northern of towns. We want to see this throne for ourselves so that we can tell our friends back home that we saw a wonder of the world."

Victria was grateful for Serania's intervention and her quick thinking. She was almost willing to believe the rather ridiculous story herself. She shifted her focus to Thomas, hoping to see some sign of understanding or acceptance but all she saw was disappointment.

"Ya be tourists, ya say. Ya just wanna take me boat an' go see da sights of da ocean, ta see da Trone o' da Deep? Ya not be convincin' me wit dat tale and I be close to trowin' ya out of my house fa lyin' to me. But I be a good, gracious man, I know da truth sometimes be hard to come by. So, I be givin' ya one more chance. If ya want my boat, ya need to be givin' me da *truth*."

Victria glanced at Tera, who sat back, relaxed, her eyes locked on them expectantly, and then she realized what was happening. Tera already knew what they were without a doubt. She had dragged them here to Thomas' house to corner them into providing the proof she needed to confirm they were viatari. She wondered what their human guide would do if they dispelled their illusions. Would she attack? Call for help? Or was she above the old human-viatari hatred and only interested in the money she stood to gain for her help?

"We told you already—" Serania began, but Victria raised a hand and shook her head. She closed her eyes and felt herself shimmer as her illusionary disguise faded away.

"Victria, what are you—"

She opened her red eyes and looked straight at Thomas. As she had suspected, Tera and Thomas didn't look the least bit surprised.

"Knew it." Tera said.

"Now tings be gettin' interestin.' So tell me, viatari, why ya be needin' my boat?"

The other viatari sat as still as stone, stunned by what Victria had done.

"It's okay," she said encouragingly. "They won't hurt us.

Besides, they're outnumbered."

One by one, they nodded and removed their own illusion-ary disguises to reveal their true selves. Tera grinned the entire time as did Thomas as if they had won some prize.

"You want the truth about why we're risking our lives being here?" Victria asked, all pretense gone. She was in command now, as far as she was concerned. She would tell the truth, but whether her answer was satisfactory or not, she didn't care. Thomas would sail them past the reef. Even if she had to tie him to the helm. She no longer had time for games.

"Dat's all I be askin' fa."

Victria told him the truth about everything. She told him about the Creature, The Turned One, The First One, and their search for the other acolytes. She told him about the coming war that the dwarves and viatari were preparing to fight to keep the world from falling into chaos. She told him how they had contacted Tera and obtained her aid and how the dwarves were willing to help them pay whatever was needed to get the task done.

"The First One has told us that his brother lies some-where deep in the ocean and we've found that acolytes have only been located within the wonders of the world. That is why we need to go to the Throne of the Deep. We need to get The First One's brother so that we can win this war against the corrupted acolytes."

"You mentioned these . . . darimun," Tera said. "What are they exactly?"

"Servants of the Creature," Victria said. "The Creature corrupts the bodies of animals and turns them into monsters, two times their regular size and many times more powerful. They become bloodthirsty, and can be recognized by their dim, yellow eyes and the purple aura they seem to always emit."

"The demons. . . ." Tera breathed.

Victria nodded, "Yes, I've heard your people call them that," she turned her attention back to Thomas, whose unpleasant grin had only grown more pronounced the more she had shared. "So, now that you know the truth, will you help us?"

Thomas groaned with pleasure, "Da truth be freein', mon," he breathed in deeply as if he could smell it. "Ahh, ya, Thomas be takin' ya deep into da ocean. It be a dangerous voyage though, so I be takin' a few days to prepare and gather supplies. I let ya know when I'm ready to go."

"Really?" Madira said, shocked. "You would be willing to take five viatari onto your boat just like that?"

"Don't push our luck," Natiari muttered.

"I told ya, da truth be me only form of payment and ya just paid in full. Besides, dis be a good chance fa me to catch up on me fishin'." Thomas cackled and rose from his seat. "Ya all are welcome to stay in me 'ome. Ya may as well, Tera, we be 'avin' much to catch up on."

With that the wide-eyed captain left them and went out into the street.

There was a moment of silence as the viatari sat there and waited for Tera to speak. But their human guide simply sat there, eyeing them curiously and without fear.

"We should not have revealed ourselves," Serania hissed in Victria's ear in Viatar so Tera wouldn't understand. "We would have found another captain."

Victria shook her head. "I don't think so. It's clear that Thomas is not like other captains."

"I agree with Victria," Tessa joined in, keeping her eyes locked on Tera, whose smile was growing wider by the minute.

"There was no choice, not if we wanted Thomas' help. And he's *still* willing to help us even as viatari. But what are we going to do with Tera? I don't like the way she's looking at us."

"There's no use speaking in your own tongue," Tera said in perfectly fluent Viatar. "I understand every word you're saying."

Again, the viatari were stunned into silence.

"How?" Victria asked, speaking in the common human tongue again.

Tera shrugged. "I was a wanderer at one point in my life. I met many viatari during my travels who taught me the language, along with a couple of dwarves who taught me Dwarvish—before you say it, yes, I've met with dwarves, yes, what I told you at the inn was a lie; but that was before we knew each other. In fact," she looked pointedly at Serania, "she and I have met several times in the Western Lands and in the human towns of the Grasslands."

Victria looked at Serania, shocked that she was just now hearing this. "You two know each other? Did you recognize her when we first met in *Admiral's Rest?*"

"Oh, she recognized me," Tera chuckled. "She couldn't look me straight in the eye."

"Yes, I knew who she was the second she showed her face," Serania grumbled. "But I didn't think she recognized me in my human form, so I didn't say anything."

"Oh please," Tera rolled her eyes. "There's no one else in the world, not human or viatari or even dwarf, who uses their hair to cover up the entire right side of their face."

Natiari and Madira giggled. "It's a fair point."

Serania slunk into her chair but didn't respond.

"So, what will you do now?"

Tera stood up and beckoned for them all to follow her. "I'm going to take you to your rooms," she said cheerily. "After all, you are paying me to help you, and we're going to need all the rest we can get if we're sailing beyond the reef."

CHAPTER SEVEN

A few days had passed since Felix, Thuradin, Borim, and a band of thirty other viatari, including Aniria and Drathanar, had left for the Dwarven Kingdom. Little was happening in the city, so Salevari used those few days to strategize. She hadn't spoken to anyone and no one had seen her, except those few who brought her food and drink. She knew she needed to be smart about how she proceeded. Felix had left her in charge of Aleganthia but he had also invited humans to come in and stay within the walls. She feared this was a perfect recipe for conflict.

Standing in the main hall of the fourth floor, staring out of one of the large, crystal-glass windows overlooking the city before her had helped bring a new perspective. This was her city now—until Felix returned, anyway—and she would run it as if it were her city.

"Get me Zael," she barked at one of the passing staff. The viatari jumped at the suddenness of her command, bowed, then ran off to carry out the order. Only moments later, Zael came walking calmly down the hall in his captain's uniform. He saluted briskly.

"You called?"

"Walk with me."

They strolled down the hallway in silence at first as Salevari took in the sunlight streaming into the keep. She closed her eyes for a moment and let her mind dwell on the heat on her skin.

"Congratulations on your promotion to captain," she finally said. "Felix told me there are few who he thought would be able to lead the guard so well. You must be very proud."

"It is an honor to serve this great city."

"So solemn," Salevari teased. "Do you know your parents?"

Zael hesitated. Such a question was not uncommon among viatari circles; even now, it was not uncommon for viatari in Aleganthia to not know who their parents were, since most were abandoned as children and left in the wilderness to see if they could survive. This led the subject as being a sore spot for some.

"Yes, I knew them, but they're dead now."

"I'm sorry to hear that," Salevari said truthfully. "But I'm sure they would have been proud of you, too."

Zael nodded. "But this is not the reason you called me to your side, is it? To congratulate me?"

Salevari shook her head, "No, young one, it is not. I want to know your thoughts about the humans being here and what we should do with them."

Zael shrugged, keeping his face neutral. "It is not my place to say. Felix let them into the city and he has led us this far. I trust his decisions."

"But still, you're uneasy about it. I may not know you well yet, Zael, but I can tell."

The viatari captain grimaced, then nodded. "I don't see what use they'll serve in the coming war. They're more likely to attack us from behind than join us."

"I agree," Salevari said, reflecting on the expectations Felix had left her before he had left. "But, as my brother says, he wishes for us to talk with them, try to reason with them, see if there's any common ground that can be reached. And, of course, he leaves the impossible task with his dear sister—me."

Zael chuckled. "I doubt very much we'll find any common ground with them. But if you wish to begin the process, I can summon their leader. As Felix ordered, I will stay by your side to translate."

"Yes, go do that. Oh, and Zael," she called just as the captain was about to run out of sight, "bring me the wanderer, too. The one called Simon."

"Will you need me if he's present? He can speak our language."

"He won't be doing any translating. If he wishes to speak Viatar with me directly, he may, or he can speak to me through you. But I want him at the meeting. Something is telling me that he is as important to convince about a future between our two races as their leader is."

There was no throne room in Aleganthia's keep, something Salevari quickly decided she required. She cleared out the table and the various maps hanging on the walls of what had been the keep's meeting room and brought in an elegant chair from Felix's room. It may have just been a piece of furniture, but it always drew her attention every time she visited her brother.

Once that was done, she looked around. The room was now bare, save her makeshift throne, and she liked it. It wasn't the grand paintings or crystal thrones or gold everywhere that displayed power. True power was displayed by the person sitting on the throne, in how they carried themselves, in how they spoke. And while Aleganthia was under her control, she would be sure to give them a powerful ruler.

There was a knock on the door just as she settled into her chair.

"Enter."

The door opened and Zael marched in, followed closely by Kent and Simon.

"Chancellor," Zael said, bowing deeply.

"Thank you, Zael. Stand by my side while we speak with our human guests."

She turned her attention to the two men and immediately noticed they were looking down at her. She made a mental note to bring in and install a platform to elevate her throne, then stood up.

"How are you finding our city so far?"

Zael translated and the humans scoffed. "They say they would like it better if they weren't being guarded all the time."

Salevari shrugged. "That is for your protection as well as ours. There are many viatari here who would like nothing more than to kill you all, despite my brother's wishes to keep you here, safe behind our walls."

Simon grunted. "That doesn't change the fact that we feel more like prisoners than guests."

Kent said something angrily to Simon, but the human wanderer paid him no mind.

"There seems to be some tension between most of the humans and this Simon," Zael whispered into Salevari's ear. "It seems to me that Kent doesn't want Simon to do any talking."

"Interesting, . . ." Salevari considered asking outright why this tension might exist, but she had a better idea. Felix and Thuradin had both been shocked and outraged when they learned who Simon was, and that could only mean the wanderer knew he had no friends in this city. Such a person, alone with no allies, could prove dangerous if left unattended. They would be unpredictable, a constant worry for betrayal. But if she were to make peace with him. . . .

"Simon, I speak to you directly now," Salevari looked him in the eyes. The human's gaze never wavered. *Hmm,* she thought, *he's not intimidated by us.* "I don't know you and you don't know me—"

"I think I already know where this is going," Simon interrupted, crossing his arms. "So no, I don't know you. But I know you are viatari, and that's all I need to know."

"I understand you suffered great personal loss because of my brother," Salevari pressed on, determined to get her point across. "But I am not him. I, too, was hurt by him. Because of him, I lost many friends as well as my husband. And while I blamed and hated him for centuries, for millennia, I understand now that there are bigger things to preoccupy ourselves with than an old grudge."

Simon frowned, but kept listening. "There is evil in our land now. You experienced it when you chased my brother into Inadarim. Humans everywhere are experiencing it now in the plains. All of their lives are at stake."

"Why do you care? And why should I? They exiled me, sent me off to die."

"But you didn't die," Salevari pointed out. "And they didn't kill you themselves, even though they could have. I know a strong leader when I see one, and I sense that you were strong when you were chief of Halshire. Surely, even now, you still care about your people."

"I . . ." for the first time, Simon looked uncertain. "I grew up with most of the folks in Halshire. I've known them all my life. Of course I care about them—but I failed them. I led their sons and fathers and brothers to their deaths."

Salevari nodded understandingly. "I think if you spoke with Felix, you would discover many similarities. What would you say if I could offer you a chance at redemption?"

Simon's bravado returned. "And what chance of that could you offer me?"

"Those sons and fathers and brothers you led, they must have left wives, daughters, younger sons behind, no?"

Simon's gaze flickered, turned hollow for a moment. "Yes, many."

"They are still alive. And we can keep them that way by saving them from the destruction that will surely meet them if we leave the Creature's darimun to roam the plains unchecked."

"You're saying you would bring them here to save them?"

"That's exactly what I'm saying."

Simon laughed bitterly. "And how do I know you're not just sweet-talking me? What if Halshire has already fallen to those demons?"

The Chancellor of Dalyr turned her gaze to Kent now. "Being chief of his own town, I imagine Kent would have heard if Halshire had fallen. Zael, ask him if he's heard any such news."

Zael did, and Kent shook his head, though he looked confused by the conversation happening without him.

"We can assume your town is still standing for now, then."

Simon thought for several minutes, his eyes narrowed in concentration as he thought of every possible way this could be a trap before he finally nodded. "I agree that the demons controlled by this 'Creature' are currently the bigger threat, and I would stop at nothing to defend my people from the same fate as Kent's, even if they don't see me as their chief anymore and even if it means swallowing my hatred for you—temporarily. So, tell me, what do you have in mind?"

Salevari beckoned the two human leaders closer as she opened a map of the plains for them to look at—during which, Zael translated what was going on for Kent.

"I cannot speak for my brother, and I don't know what he had in mind when he brought your people in, but my plan is to save your kind by bringing as many of them into our city as we can and offering sanctuary."

"And what happens when they begin slaughtering your people, keeping in mind the fact that we humans hate the viatari?" Simon asked.

"Well, when they realize they're too fragmented and exposed out in the plains as they are, and incapable of fighting the Creature's forces on their own—and when viatari forces are the ones saving them from certain death—I have a feeling they'll be more inclined and open-minded about living in a viatari city. They will owe us their lives, and that should safeguard us."

"So, what," Simon brushed his hand across the entire map, "you're just going to fight off the demons wherever they attack and expect the humans to be grateful?"

Salevari grinned. "That's where you come in. You see, having raised an entire army against us, uniting multiple towns in the region against a single enemy, I imagine you will be able to do the same to unite your people against the Creature."

Simon looked up in surprise, the echoes of a laugh in his

words. "You want me to be your spokesperson."

The viatari shrugged. "If that's what you wish to call yourself. I personally prefer to see you as the singular force that united all of humanity. You would be there to ensure the townsfolk don't turn against us as soon as we finish defending them from the darimun and then you would use your words to bring them to our side."

"And if I can't convince them?"

"Then you should at least be able to convince them to let us leave in peace, and the next wave of darimun will come in to destroy what's left. I imagine that won't happen too often, though. You seem cunning enough with your words."

Kent spoke up and Zael translated, though even without the translation, Salevari could hear the doubt in his voice. "He says Simon is a wanderer and an exile. He will be unwelcome in the towns and villages you try to rescue."

"Well," Salevari said, shrugging. "That is exactly why we're doing this. By saving your people from death, Simon can regain the trust he's lost, and together, we can rid this world of the evil that currently roams free. Are you opposed to fighting with us, Kent?"

Kent shook his head, his fierce eyes shining as he spoke in reply. "He says it would be an honor to fight by our side after we so graciously took his people in," Zael translated. "But he cannot speak for the other chieftains."

Salevari dipped her head respectfully. "I understand that. I do not expect for our interactions to bear fruit every time, but this is the best chance we have at saving both your kind and mine from the Creature."

Kent pursed his lips but finally agreed.

"Then what's the endgame?" Simon asked, studying the map intensely. "Say we save all the human towns until we're all crowded cozily behind your walls. What then?"

Salevari cracked a smile. She found she was enjoying Simon's quips. "The goal is to save as many of you as we can while the Creature is still playing with you."

"Playing with us?" Simon scoffed. "You think he's playing with us? He's already destroyed and massacred the residents of several towns!" Kent agreed, nodding indignantly.

"Yes," Salevari replied matter-of-factly. "He has. With small raids."

While the humans stared at her in shock, she continued: "The darimun that have destroyed your towns have not numbered more than a dozen. But the Creature is capable of raising a whole army. Right now, he's playing with you. And while he does that, we will save as many as we can so we can fight him together with numbers when he does finally send his full strength."

She described the many battles she had endured during the first war against the Creature and the high number of casualties they had suffered. By the end, both Kent and Simon were paler than usual.

"So, this really is our only option." The wanderer murmured.

"Yes."

"Fine," Simon's confidence sparked up. "We'll help you with this. Kent and I will send some people out to try and keep track of the demons' movements so we know which towns they're going to attack." Kent glared at Simon for taking charge, but nodded his consent anyway.

"Excellent," Salevari said, relieved at the progress they were making, though she made sure not to make it obvious. "I will be sending out my own scouts to do the same. When we know a town is in danger of being attacked, I will assemble a defense force to fight the darimun off. During the fighting I want you to focus on keeping the townspeople safe. When the battle is over, that's when you will have your chance at redemption, your chance to lead your people away from certain death."

Simon met Salevari's gaze and regarded her for a moment. "You know, this plan requires quite a bit of trust between us. You have to trust that I won't turn the townspeople against you and save myself, and we have to trust that you won't murder us all."

Salevari cocked her head to the side, "I suppose it does."

"Well, I think it may be beneficial to start showing some of that trust now. After all, if you can't trust us, how can we trust you?"

The Chancellor frowned, understanding now what the wanderer was wanting. "You want me to have the guards stop watching you."

Simon nodded. "It would be a start."

Salevari considered it for a moment. The truth was she didn't trust Simon, not really. She had been right in her assumption that he was good with words and that made him dangerous. But if this were the cost to get the humans' help, she might have to pay it. There were other, more subtle ways to keep watch over the humans.

"Very well," she said. "We will remove the guards from your section of the city, and you will be free to roam our keep at will. However, I must insist that you be under guard if any of your people choose to roam through the viatari sections of the city—if only for your own protection."

Simon clapped his hands in triumph. "A decent compromise. Very well, we accept," he turned to Kent, "Don't we, Kent."

Kent continued frowning disapprovingly but nodded and spoke in his own language.

"He says he will keep watch over his own people to ensure peace between us so long as the same is done on our part." Zael translated.

"Tell him it will be done. Now," Salevari sat back down on her makeshift throne, "you two may return to your people and begin preparations for the task ahead."

The two humans bowed respectfully and left the room, leaving Salevari and Zael alone. Zael looked at the Chancellor uncertainly. "Are you sure it's a good idea to leave the humans unattended in our city?"

"No," Salevari said. "We will continue to watch them; we will just have to do it from afar."

"As you wish."

"Tell me, what do you think about what I have proposed to the humans?"

Zael stood at attention, eyes staring straight ahead. "I have no opinion on the matter. You lead us while Felix is away."

Salevari chuckled. "It's quite alright. You can speak freely around me. I have a feeling we're going to be seeing much of each other while I lead Aleganthia."

Zael looked uncertain, but after another encouraging nod from Salevari he spoke his mind, "I think it is risky. It will go one of two ways, and both involve risking viatari lives."

Salevari thought on that. Had she been ruling from Dalyr, she would not have hesitated to lead her people with this chance to create a new ally against the corrupted acolytes. Many of her warriors were here with her in the city, but most of the population was still Aleganthian. Could she command viatari she didn't know, who weren't even truly hers to rule, to their possible deaths?

"What you say is true," she admitted, "but the alternative is to do nothing. And that we cannot do."

Zael did not reply but continued to stand at attention, leaving Salevari to her numerous thoughts. Out of these, only one question kept forcing its way to the front of her mind: what would Felix do?

Knowing she was going in mental circles, there was only one way to find out what her brother would do.

"Zael, get me a quill and ink and some parchment."

Zael bowed and left the room to get her the supplies. Salevari was now alone in her self-proclaimed throne room. She leaned forward and rested her chin on her knuckles, closing her eyes. She could see her brother's face, the ever-present calmness in his eyes, the certainty that was always in his voice.

"Oh, Felix," she murmured. "What would you do?"

CHAPTER EIGHT

Within the week they got their first report of a pack of darimun on the move, as if closing in for the kill. The viatari chosen to defend the humans were already armed and ready to ride out to meet the threat, but it was still uncertain which town would be attacked.

Salevari and Simon walked through the keep's halls going over the plan they had developed and the logistics behind it. This pack of darimun numbered no more than half a dozen, but that was plenty to raze a human town. Those being sent out in defense would be twenty-five strong. For this first attempt at bringing the humans to their side, Salevari would ride out with the defenders to ensure the darimun were defeated. Simon would ride with them and keep the towns-folk from interfering during the battle.

It was strange, but normally having a human next to her would have made Salevari keep her guard up. After all, it would only take one swift dagger strike for Simon to paralyze her with his poisons and then it would be no trouble at all to finish her off. For the moment, though, she felt they were comrades. They would see battle together and they were working toward the same end. She still had no word from Felix about what he thought of her plan, which annoyed her, but she had to go with her instincts. And right now her instincts told her that this was the right thing to do. *Perhaps this is the true beginning of peace between our two races,* she thought.

Just as they were going over which parts of Aleganthia the new influx of human refugees would inhabit, a scout rushed around the other side of the hall, saw them, and made her way to them.

"Which town?" Salevari asked.

"Halshire." The scout said breathlessly.

Simon paled. Salevari clapped his shoulder encouragingly, "It seems your opportunity for redemption has come sooner than even I anticipated."

"Redemption," Simon laughed hollowly, his eyes distant. "More like it's time to see if there is truly such a thing."

They ran down several flights of stairs and out of the keep, going straight to the stables where their forces had been asked to stand ready. They mounted quickly and charged out toward the city's southern gate, their raiding party following close behind.

Halshire was normally a day and a half's ride away at a leisurely pace, but at full-gallop they would arrive within half a day. That would give them plenty of time to assess the situation and to determine where they would be needed most.

As the sun continued its slow journey across the sky, the grasslands eventually turned into a series of hills and small gullies. Salevari kept her eyes peeled ahead, sparing only the briefest of glances at the map she had brought with her to keep her bearings. As they passed another series of inter-lapping hills, she saw smoke in the distance.

She raised her hand and made a circling motion above

her head, signaling for everyone to follow her. Putting pressure on her mount with her left heel, she veered around the next set of hills, only to stop behind the ones after that.

"Dismount," she called out. "We continue on foot."

Now on their feet, they crept their way up the hill, staying low to keep their presence hidden. Once they crested the ridge, Halshire came into view.

It was peaceful. The smoke drifting into the sky came from the town's blacksmiths and a few bonfires that were lit in the central plaza.

"It looks like there is some sort of festival," Salevari observed.

Simon nodded. "Yes, it is the yearly Feast of Gratitude, where we count our blessings and show our gratitude for having lived through another year without famine."

"What do you do during this event?"

Simon shrugged. "It's a feast. We eat and drink and it only ends when everyone has had too much," he chuckled, "everyone always regrets the next day, though, since they all have to clean up whatever mess they made."

Salevari scanned the horizon for any signs of the darimun. The rising landscape made it difficult to spot any attack from a distance, but it looked like they had arrived just in time to see the enemy crest the row of hills opposite them.

One of her warriors pointed them out.

Simon's reminiscent smile vanished and a fiery countenance took hold. "The demons come."

He tried to stand but Salevari held him back by the wrist. "Wait," she said, "we must get into a better position around the town and wait for the darimun to breach the walls first before we intervene."

"What do you mean?" Simon snarled. "If they breach

the gates and enter the town people will die. I thought we were here to protect them."

"We are," Salevari pulled the human back to the ground and came face to face with him. "But for this to work the way we need it to, the darimun must breach the walls first. Your people must believe we are saving them from certain death. What will they think if we intercept this attack and defeat the darimun outside the walls, leaving the humans only as disinterested observers?"

Simon frowned. "Knowing them, they'll think they could have handled the situation alone with their own defenses."

"Exactly, and there would be nothing to prove them wrong because their defenses would never have been tested. But you and I know that they won't hold, no matter your peoples' readiness or determination."

She let him go and he slowly sank back down into the grass. "This is what makes leaders strong. They have to know what is best not just for one person but for all."

Simon nodded, speaking through clenched teeth. "I know, but that doesn't stop me from caring about that one person."

The viatari smiled sadly. "No," she said. "It does not."

The Feast of Gratitude was as successful as most years before it. The town had slaughtered the fattest pigs, cows, chickens, and sheep to provide for the several racks of roasted meats that were consumed each year. Farmers around the area contributed some of their produce: carrots, broccoli, potatoes, asparagus, and a whole variety of fruits so that the town's cooks could create their savory vegetable stews and fruit pies.

It was Garrel's favorite time of year.

There was laughter everywhere he looked, and, he reflected,

plenty of young maidens who had come out in their best dresses. The musicians huddled in the plaza played an upbeat tune and many of these women danced to it, some with each other, and others with men who'd had the courage to ask for their hand.

Garrel's eyes were stuck on one particular girl, Ava. Her pure-blonde hair was well-groomed and ran all the way down her back, perfectly straight. Her bright blue eyes flashed invitingly as they met his own. He grinned, hoping the beer stain on his shoulder wasn't too noticeable as he began making his way to her.

He had seen her every year at the Feast, had even managed to speak with her a few times. It had always been nerve-wracking to do so. But this year he'd had a few more pints of ale than he was used to and felt braver than ever. This would be the year when he finally asked her to dance and, if he could impress her with his light feet—he had been pract-icing—he would ask her to be his.

She smiled stunningly as he approached, but that smile quickly vanished as a thunderous crash sounded near the edge of town. Bells rang but were abruptly cut off as the towers holding them came toppling down. The guards watching over the courtyard drew their swords and axes and rushed toward the western wall, where the crashes had come from. Townsfolk came running from that direction, screaming.

"We're under attack!"

"The demons are here!"

Garrel paled. Demons? Here? He'd heard rumors of their attacks on other towns, towns that had been going through everyday life as they always had only to vanish from the map, nothing but ruins the very next day. He had never believed the attacks would come to his home as well, not

Halshire. He looked for Ava, who was huddled with her friends, scared and unmoving.

"Ava, come to me!"

But Garrel had called too late. A monstrous wolf, three times its normal size, crashed through one of the alleyways into the plaza and leapt onto the group of girls Ava had joined. One tried to run away, but the wolf-demon snatched her in its jaws and tore her apart, its dull, yellow eyes narrow with bloodlust.

It stamped down with its front paws and crushed two others who were under it, leaving Ava alone, lying on her back, her eyes wide as the wolf bared its large, yellow fangs. A thread of bloody drool oozed from the demon's mouth and landed on Ava's face, snapping her out of her petrification. She screamed.

There was nothing Garrel could do but watch as the wolf opened its mouth and lunged. He yelled, reaching out for Ava, wanting more than anything to jump in and push her out of danger. She turned her head to the side and locked eyes with him for what he thought was the last time when the wolf-demon stopped its attack and let out a howl of pain.

Garrel's eyes shifted back to the demon and a figure now perched on its back, a slender dirk in their hands which they used skillfully to penetrate the demon's thick hide. The figure stabbed down several times around the neck and then leapt down, landing below it, bringing their blade with them as they sliced along its belly, eviscerating it.

The demon staggered, its eyes already glazing over. Garrel rushed forward and pulled Ava out from under it just as it crashed to the ground.

"Garrel!"

"Oh, Ava—are you hurt?" He cupped her face in his

hands and turned her this way and that, looking for any serious wounds.

"I'm alright," she said shakily. "But what happened, how did—"

There was a sudden movement in their peripherals that made them both turn their heads. More of the demons surged into the plaza, trying to tear into the townsfolk, demolishing any buildings they ran into, but they couldn't advance much further—and it wasn't the town's guards who were holding them back.

Garrel couldn't quite count them all, but at least twenty viatari were moving about the plaza, jumping from spot to spot nearly faster than he could see, avoiding the demons' attacks while inflicting their own. Before long, the demons were all dead and the viatari were cleaning their blades, leaving the townspeople in awe.

"Are those. . . ?" Ava started to say.

"Yes, I think so," Garrel said, fear creeping back into his voice. "This is just not our day. Where are the guards?"

As more people realized who had saved them from the demons a wave of panic washed over them and the remaining guards who had survived the initial assault formed up between them and the viatari, their weapons raised.

One of the viatari, a female who had half of her hair buzzed and the other half combed over to touch her shoulders, looked almost human, but there was no mistaking those red eyes. She regarded them all curiously, as if she were waiting to see what would happen next.

The guards locked shields and started to advance but they had only taken a few steps when a hooded man stepped out from among the townsfolk, intercepting their advance.

"Guardsmen, hold your advance. Will you attack those

who saved us all from certain death?"

Garrel's insides churned. He recognized that voice, but couldn't believe it. He was supposed to be exiled. He should have been dead by now. He looked at Ava, who drew close to him, clutching at his chest fearfully. The man's words echoed in his ears as he felt Ava's heartbeat against his own. The viatari had indeed defeated the demons, and had they not come, everyone here would have been killed. He would have watched the beautiful woman in his arms be devoured before his very eyes.

He was scared—he was sure Ava could feel him trembling— but he also felt gratitude. And the least he could do to show his gratitude in this moment, even though every nerve in his body and every rational thought told him it was foolish to just stand there, was listen.

Simon took a deep breath. A lot of these people must already have recognized him by his voice. The tension in the air was heavy. But still, he had missed them and was glad to see them alive, though it was bittersweet, as several of them mourned over the bloody remains of the ones they had just lost.

He brought his hands up and removed his hood. He heard several curses float through the air followed by his name.

"I was once your chief," he said, not knowing quite what he was going to say, but knowing he would come up with something just like he always did. "I was your chief and I failed you."

He let his words settle for a moment, then, "I failed you, but I come to you now with a desire to right my wrong, by saving you all from the horrible fate our kind now faces as these demons ravage our lands."

He motioned toward the viatari, who stood motionless and at ease, regarding the crowd before them evenly. "I was exiled from these lands but I know what has been happening. I know of the towns that have been destroyed, and today Halshire nearly joined that growing list."

The crowd was still listening, which was good. It meant they had not yet decided whether they should kill him. "The only thing that saved us from this evil were these twenty-five viatari standing before you. The demons breached the walls of this town in a matter of seconds, ripped through most of the guardsmen with ease and would have devoured you all, except for the fact that they met their match."

He looked at each person he could, trying to read their faces. They were hostile still, but some seemed to consider his words. "So I ask you again, will you attack those who saved you from certain death?"

There was a moment of utter silence. The guardsmen were the first to answer. They lowered their weapons, and turned away from the viatari, passing through the crowd of survivors to try and help those who most needed them. Then a voice came from the crowd.

"So, what do we do now?"

Simon smiled. That was the cue he had been waiting for. "I know we've grown up fearing the viatari, believing they were our natural, life-long enemies. But things have changed. I have wandered through much of the land in the months that I have been exiled. I have interacted peacefully with viatari, dwarves, and other humans. Wanderers of all races do this. And in this current era of evil where demons roam about freely, I think it's necessary for us, the common folk, to do this as well. It is time to join forces—to fight these beasts together—if we want a chance at survival."

"Fight with the viatari?"

"You're mad!"

Simon raised his hands, trying to quiet the crowd as they continued their objections.

"Did the viatari attack this town today?" Simon yelled. "Were they the ones who killed the men and women who lie torn apart on the streets today? Even when I was your chief and led an army into the Forbidden Lands, was it the viatari that destroyed us? No! It was the demons. *They* are the enemy. *They* are the greater threat. If you want to live, you need to trust me when I say our only chance at survival is if we fight together with the viatari."

"Still," one of the men kneeling in the crowd said, a stunningly beautiful woman with blonde hair clutching at his chest, "even if we were to join forces, surely the guardsmen of Halshire and the viatari would not be enough to defeat the demons."

Simon walked over to the man and knelt before him. "You're Garrel, aren't you?"

Garrel nodded and Simon couldn't help but chuckle. "I hardly recognized you with that full beard on your face. I suppose you've become a fine young man in the past year."

He stood up, now among the crowd. "Garrel is right. The forces of Halshire and the viatari will not be enough by themselves to defeat the demons, especially when their master grows tired of his own games and chooses to send his full strength. However, the viatari and I have devised a plan to grow our own strength so that, when this army comes, we'll be ready.

"Just as we came in and saved this town from destruction, more viatari forces are forming up and moving out to protect other towns in the grasslands. With each new town that joins us, our forces will grow until it's not just Halshire that has joined the viatari, but all humankind."

There was a rise of murmuring as a realization of new possibilities took hold. As Simon's words settled, more of the townsfolk looked agreeable to his suggestion.

"What do we do in the meantime?" Garrel asked. "What if we get raided again by the demons and the viatari aren't here to protect us?"

"Ah," Simon stepped away from the crowd and motioned for Salevari to join him. "Allow me to introduce Salevari Mistguide, the current leader of the viatari city of Aleganthia. She has graciously offered portions of her city as sanctuary for those of you who wish to move there while the threat from the demons exists. It will be easier to protect you from their city and you won't be alone; there are already others of our kind living there as we speak."

Salevari nodded her head stiffly as people's eyes moved to her. Simon smiled inwardly. The poor viatari had no idea what was going on, not being familiar with his language. Simon could say whatever he wanted about her and her warriors and they would never know. But he held his tongue. It would serve no purpose to betray the viatari like that—not in the current circumstances.

"Of course," he continued. "I understand it is a big step to leave your home. So for those who wish to stay, you can stay and rebuild Halshire. However, know it will be more difficult for the viatari to protect you, since they do not intend to leave a garrison here."

The crowd began to murmur again and Simon let them. Now was the time for him to be quiet, to let them speak. He had done his part, and with luck, most of the townspeople here would move to Aleganthia as refugees.

"What now?" Salevari asked.

"Now we wait," Simon replied in Viatar. "An idea grows better the longer it festers. We must be patient."

Salevari glanced at her troops, and then at Simon. "And so we will be."

It was night and the moon was only a sliver in the sky, providing little light. Still, that did not stop Anders from strolling down the streets of Aleganthia alone, tossing a pear in his hands, as he whistled an old lullaby his mother used to sing to him when he was a child.

His footsteps were echoed by the viatari guard following him. Anders glanced over his shoulder, seeing the guard's iconic X-shaped chestpiece and layered, leather spaulders clearly even in the dark.

"Nice night, isn't it?" Anders called out.

The viatari grunted.

"I bet you don't even understand what I'm saying, do you?"

Again, the viatari's only reply was a grunt.

Anders sighed and stopped walking, turning to face the viatari and holding out the pear he had in his hands. "Want a bite?"

The viatari glanced at the pear and then at him, his red eyes glowing just slightly under the light of the stars. He shook his head and said something in his own language.

"Ah, come now," Anders smiled warmly. "I insist. It's rude to not accept a gift among my people."

The viatari hesitated, but then shrugged and reached for the pear. Anders placed it in his hands and the viatari took a bite, the fruit's juices trickling down to his chin. Anders' smile stretched across his face as the viatari swallowed and then began to cough.

Looking around to make sure no one was watching, he pushed the guard into a nearby alley and forced him to the ground. The viatari at this point was barely moving, though his eyes stared into Anders', wide with fear as the human slowly unsheathed a dagger.

"Good luck regenerating from this," he said, plunging the cold steel into the viatari's heart. Paralysis having taken complete control of his body, the viatari couldn't even yell as Anders yanked out the dagger and watched his kill bleed out.

The viatari's eyes glazed over shortly after and Anders stood up, cleaning his dagger with a spare rag he looted from his victim. Once his blade was free of blood, he dropped the rag over the viatari's face and spit on him before walking away, back the way he had come.

CHAPTER NINE

Salevari studied the corpse on the table before her, then glanced at the two humans standing on the other side. Simon and Kent looked both shocked and worried by the viatari corpse they were being shown. They were in one of the many cellars in Aleganthia's keep, away from prying eyes, which was exactly what Salevari wanted.

"This guard was slain only blocks away from this keep. His body was found by two other guards lying in a pool of his own blood. They brought him here so I could have him examined. The cause of death was a stab wound to the heart, causing him to bleed out—but viatari don't die so easily. Our alchemists found hints of a new poison in his blood, which seems to have completely paralyzed his body and regenerative abilities. So," she spread her hands outward, and motioned for the two humans to speak, "explain this."

Simon, for once, seemed lost for words. It was Kent who answered, though it took a moment for Simon to come to his senses enough to translate.

"Kent says he's saddened to think one of his own people might have done this. He thought he could trust them."

"Does anyone in particular come to mind when he thinks

of who might have done this?" Salevari asked.

Kent shook his head sadly, but then his face turned resolute as he said his next words, meeting the Chancellor's gaze.

"He says he wishes he could give answers right now," Simon translated. "But he swears to you, on his honor, that he will find out who was responsible for this murder and he will see to it that they are punished."

"The only just punishment in this case will be to hand them over to us."

Kent frowned as Simon spoke for him. "He says he is unwilling to give one of his own to the viatari for them to suck out his life-energies like some beast."

Salevari snarled and slammed the table. "Tell me, Kent," her voice deadly calm, "how would you feel if one of my viatari had murdered one of your people in cold blood? Would you find it acceptable if I told you that I refused to turn them over to you so you could extract justice?"

"He sees your point," Simon said when Kent had finished replying. "But he also asks if you would be willing to give up one of your own to a race that has hated you for centuries for the sake of justice."

Salevari paused. No, she wouldn't, she decided. She would fight the humans if necessary to keep one of her own safe from them. Knowing them, their version of justice would be execution in the most brutal fashion they could think of—the only thing they would think fitting for a viatari.

"Fine," she said finally. "Fine. You will deal with him or her on your own terms. But you will at least present to me who this murderer is when you catch them."

Kent bowed and nodded in agreement.

"Now, the question is," Simon said, looking away from

the corpse. "What will you do about this . . . unfortunate situation in the meantime?"

"Nothing," Salevari said flatly.

"Nothing?"

"That's right." The Chancellor shook her head, disgusted with herself. She didn't like it, but it was the only way to keep the peace in the city. If word got out that humans were killing viatari, how long would it be before the viatari retaliated, before there was bloodshed in the streets? She couldn't allow that to happen. It was not what Felix would have wanted.

"Lucky for you, this guard had no family left. As callous as it is for me to say, no one will notice his disappearance. I've already paid off the guards who brought him in to keep quiet about the matter. I intend to take him out into the forest tonight to bury him in secret. No one will know of this: human or viatari. That should give you plenty of time to find out who's behind this."

The humans nodded and, with a flick of her head, she led them out of the cellar, making sure to lock the door behind her so no one accidentally stumbled upon the corpse. She tossed the keys to the door in her hand before stowing them away in a pouch hanging off her belt. Silently, she escorted the humans back to the keep's gates and watched them exit, heading back to the human parts of the city.

"How much did you hear, Zael?"

Salevari didn't need to turn around to know it was Zael who had been tailing her the entire time, hiding in the shadows where he had thought he could not be seen. It would take a lot more than that to stay undetected by her.

"Every word."

The Chancellor smiled. "Good, then I think you will agree

with me when I say the humans need to be watched closer than even the guards can watch them."

The anger that had been in Zael's voice disappeared. "What do you mean? I thought you told them—"

"I told them what they wanted to hear," Salevari turned and looked into the captain's solemn eyes. "But you should know, as should everyone in this city, that I will always put the protection of our people over the humans."

"So, what are you thinking?"

Salevari looked back at the retreating figures of Simon and Kent, regarding them for a moment. "Those two mean well. I could tell by their reaction that this incident was the last thing they wanted. However, I do not trust them to investigate and discover who the culprit is. I have a feeling they will try to sweep it under the rug and hope it doesn't happen again."

"I agree," Zael said. "So we will carry out this investigation ourselves?"

"Not we," Salevari flashed a smile. "You."

"Me?" Zael walked in front of Salevari, filling her entire vision. "I am a bad choice for this task. I couldn't even avoid detection by you."

"But you avoided detection by the humans," the Chancellor pointed out. "And they're the ones you need to avoid."

She traced her finger across his cheek. "I know we do not know each other very well yet," she said with all seriousness, "but do not think I am playing with you when I say you are the only viatari here who I trust to carry this out. My priority, as much as Felix wants to unite us with the humans against The Turned One, is to safeguard the viatari. Will you do this for me?"

"I am not Drathanar," Zael frowned, taking a step back

from her.

"No," Salevari agreed. "You are not. My general is my right hand, irreplaceable; and yet, you have much potential, much like he did. I trust you, Zael, I am confident that you can find out who was behind this murder, and I trust you will know better than the humans and will bring them to me. So I ask again: will you do this for me?"

There was a moment where Zael was silent and Salevari feared he might reject her request. Finally, he agreed, "Yes, Chancellor, I will do what you ask. I will discover who was responsible for this tragedy."

"Thank you."

With that, Aleganthia's captain turned and marched out, leaving Salevari alone with the dread knowledge of what she must do next.

The Chancellor of Dalyr did not know the city streets of Aleganthia well enough to sneak through them—especially with a corpse slung over her shoulder. And so, realizing there was only one way out, she went to the lyruun stables in the keep's tallest tower, where the Dalyrans kept their flying mounts. It would be much easier to sneak out of the city during the night if she were in the air.

There was no stable master or any beast tender present as she entered the stone room that had been created for the lyruun. The doors, which normally kept them from escaping, were wide open. But the serpentine beasts hadn't escaped today, and instead lay curled up on piles of still-warm coals, their nostrils flaring pleasantly as they dreamed. Salevari snaked her way to one of the blue-and-green mottled ones, larger than the others.

"*As'ven,*" she called out to him in Viatar. "*As'ven, oss*

serath."

The lyruun stirred and one of his green eyes popped open. He saw Salevari and cooed questioningly.

"I know it's late," the Chancellor said soothingly, running her hand across the beast's rough scales. "But I need you to fly me a short distance tonight for an urgent matter—me and another. Could you do that for me?"

As'ven's tongue slithered out and he lifted his neck, unfurling his two sets of wings, flapping them lightly.

"Thank you, As'ven." Salevari grabbed a nearby saddle and strapped it around the mount's snake-like body. She placed the slain guard behind the saddle on the beast itself, tying him and the bag she had brought with her down as best she could, and then mounted.

As'ven cooed again, louder this time. "Shh, easy now. Take me deep into the forest outside the city. Fly swiftly."

The lyruun nodded his head and flapped his larger, scapular wings to gain altitude while his tail wings kept him balanced. Then, without warning, the flying serpent shot out of the stables and into open air.

Below them Salevari saw Aleganthia spread out before her. Torches and braziers burned low, providing enough light for her to see the guards on patrol. Briefly she wondered if she might catch a glimpse of the human who had murdered the guard she was about to bury, but she did not.

It only took a minute for As'ven to clear the city and another before Salevari felt they had flown deep enough into the forest for her to do what she had come to do.

"Down," she called to her mount. "That small clearing to your left will be a good spot to land."

The lyruun veered left and dived, flaring his wings at the last minute to stop their descent before they hit the ground.

Salevari hopped off and patted his head. "Good flying, As'ven."

As'ven purred at the compliment and hovered steadily so she could remove the body she had tied down. Undoing the last knot, she slung the corpse over her shoulder and laid him a few steps away in the middle of the clearing while she went out to grab some wood.

Half an hour later, she returned with enough wood to build a pyre, which she did—laying a row of logs down as a base and stacking the rest of the wood she had gathered strategically before placing the guard's body on top of it. Once her work was finished, she went back to As'ven and pulled out a jar with a few glowing coals inside from her bag.

She had asked a blacksmith in the city to give her a few of them and he had obliged, saying he had plenty. Then she had gone to the city's alchemist, asking them to give her something that could create fire. The alchemist had only been too happy to bring out a vile of what they called "flame sludge."

"What does it do?" she had asked, eyeing the thick, black liquid curiously.

The alchemist cackled. "It can revive any fire no matter how far gone it is. It just needs anything from an ember to a spark to work with. People going outside the walls love this stuff—makes setting up a fire while on the road much easier."

Salevari had bought the flame sludge and took it out now after setting the few coals she had on the pyre. She un-corked the vile with a *pop* and smoke filled her nostrils, making her cough.

Without thinking too much of what she was doing, she poured the black liquid onto the coals and watched as flames burst forth, wherever it touched, spreading quickly. The fire continued growing hotter and more intense until the entire pyre was aflame.

Salevari had to take a few steps back and cover her nose with a clean cloth as the stench of burning flesh reached her. She stayed and kept vigil, though, as the flames consumed the slain guard, turning him to ash. She stayed until the pyre she had built crumbled apart. Only after the fire had died out, as the first rays of dawn were peeking through the foliage, did she remount As'ven and fly back to the city, the desire for justice burning in her heart.

CHAPTER TEN

A cold wind roared past them as the small force of dwarves and viatari trudged their way up another mountain pass. The dwarves, accustomed to these colder temperatures, rode their mountain rams with nothing to cover their skin but their plate armor. The viatari wore several layers of furs to keep out the cold, and still they couldn't keep from shivering as they continued making their way up the path.

One of these dwarves, wearing a long, black cloak with a cowl deep enough to hide his face, caught up with Borim who was leading them. Borim glanced his way.

"How are ye feeling, Thuradin? Ready ta be back home?"

"As ready as I'll ever be."

Borim sniffed. "What, having second thoughts?"

"No," Thuradin said. "I just cannae help but think of how she might react when she hears I've returned."

"Oh, aye?"

"Aye, there's no one else on my mind right now, nae even Dunkell. I never expected her ta . . . I just wonder where it all went wrong."

Borim patted his friend's shoulder sympathetically. "I'm sure she'll come around. Ye were her hero once before, don't forget."

"Aye," Thuradin groaned. "Once."

Felix rode up beside them, his horse nickering a greeting. "How close are we?"

"Eager ta get out of the cold?" Borim chuckled. "Ye know it won't be much better once we're inside the mountains."

"At least there will be no wind," the elder viatari countered.

Borim nodded. "True enough. We should be there soon, just a few more turns up the pass and we'll be riding through the dwarven gates."

"Excellent," Felix glanced behind him and then up at the mountain face as if searching for something. "I have heard of the giant lizards that live on these mountains—the grattles—I am surprised we have not encountered any yet."

The dwarves shared a knowing glance.

"Getting a little bored, Felix?" Thuradin called out.

"Don't mind him," Borim waved away the hooded figure. "Grattles are vicious creatures and a danger ta many on this mountain pass, but nae for us. They may travel in numbers, but they would never try attacking a force this large. We're too difficult a meal."

"Besides," Thuradin added. "They wouldn't be much of a challenge for ye anyway. I've seen Victria decimate a whole pack by herself once."

"Well," Felix said, keeping his eyes on the mountain's face above them. "That is comforting."

They rode on, Thuradin falling behind and eventually riding with the contingent of viatari. There were thirty in total, including two he was well familiar with. Aniria Windryder sat on her horse numbly, her thick hood pushed away and her shoulder-length, silver hair flying back with the wind. She was pretty to look at, though the blank, emotionless countenance she always wore now was rather disconcerting, especially when Thuradin had known how happy and care-free she had once been.

Drathanar Sungard rode beside her, the only thing pro-truding from his thick hood being his pointy chin and strands of wild hair. The dwarf was sure that, under the hood, the Dalyran general's eyes were moving everywhere, scanning for possible threats and analyzing every potential obstacle in their path.

"Aren't ye cold, lassie?" Thuradin asked Aniria, who continued to stare blankly ahead.

"I feel nothing," she said in a hard voice.

Thuradin didn't quite know how to respond to this, so he thought he might try changing the subject. "We should be arriving within the first set of tunnels ta the Dwarven Kingdom soon. Everything ye've always wondered about my kind and how we live ye'll get ta see first-hand now and—"

Aniria glared at him and Thuradin felt more ice in her eyes than in the wind blowing around them. "Let's not fool ourselves," she scowled, her lips barely moving. "We are not going to your home to sightsee. It's hardly your home any-more, anyway. Your people are on the brink of civil war, so if you think this will be a time to reminisce and show me all the wonders of your kind, think again. This is going to be a hard time for all of us, especially you, I imagine, and the only way we're going to get through it with any success is by looking at the situation with some realism."

Thuradin felt his spirits dampen, but he brushed the feeling off. After all she had been through, he couldn't blame Aniria for how she had changed. Months may have passed, but it took more than that to heal from the terrible wounds war had inflicted upon her.

They rode in silence for a moment before Thuradin

thought he would try to coax some feeling out of her one last time.

"I haven't seen ye around lately—which, I know ye've been busy with yer own preparations and everything, as we all have—but I just want ta make sure ye're alright, lass. How have Balinarus' parents been? I hear they've—"

In an instant Aniria's face contorted in rage. She moved to slap him, and, had Thuradin not been living with the viatari for months and adapted to fighting at their level, the blow would have knocked him clear off the mountain before he even knew what hit him. As it was, he raised his plated arm just in time to deflect the strike inches from his face.

Aniria looked shocked for a moment, but then her anger returned and she bared her fangs. "Don't you *ever* mention that name again." Turning away, she urged her horse forward at a faster pace. Thuradin watched her go.

"Not your fault," Drathanar said in a thick accent. Not many Dalyrans spoke Dwarvish, and those who did didn't speak it very well—though Salevari had picked it up rather quickly after living in Aleganthia for a while.

"And how are ye today, Drathanar?" Thuradin said with a sigh, rubbing his bruised arm. "I wish I knew how ta help her. I know what it is ta lose those closest ta ye, but I've also come back from it."

Drathanar nodded. "I as well. But for her, she has not. Will take more than just time to heal."

Thuradin nodded. "Perhaps ye're right," he glanced at the Dalyran general, a note of humor in his voice. "Ye're getting better at speaking my language."

The viatari grunted. "Still need practice."

"Well," Thuradin looked ahead at the two massive pillars

of stone that stood flanking a large gaping hole in the side of
the mountain. "Ye'll get plenty of practice where we're going."

Next to the pillars were two gigantic statues of dwarven
warriors in full plate armor, thrusting their large war-
hammers into the air. The gate was wide open, two thick
slabs of stone that took twenty dwarves each to push open.
At the top of the tunnel hung another slab of stone with an
inscription in Ancient Dwarvish etched into it that read:
*Welcome friend, beware foe, ye are now entering the
Dwarven Kingdom.*

"We're here lads and lassies!" Borim called out from the
front. "Form up in pairs of two as ye enter and mind those
on the sides."

Thuradin urged his ram forward so he could ride next to
Borim again. "What do ye mean by 'those on the sides?'"

Borim grimaced and motioned for Thuradin to look
ahead. Before them, a thin line of dwarves, lightly clad and
bearing bulging bags of their own belongings trudged from
the entrance tunnel to the mountain pass leading to the
Dwarven town of Kurin. Their eyes remained downcast as
the retinue of dwarven warriors and viatari passed them.
Darkness enveloped them as they entered the tunnel. For
several minutes nothing could be seen but then the first line
of torches came into view.

Around them, marching solemnly along the sides toward
the tunnel exit were more haggard-looking dwarves. Many
were families, a few guards, but all of them looked exhausted, ragged, and without hope.

"What is this?" Thuradin asked, his voice barely above a
whisper.

"This is the result of the Council taking Tinas Gran. Those
still loyal ta the crown were ousted from their homes or

escaped on their own. All of them were forced upward through the tunnels into Kul'Kriegar."

"But Kul'Kriegar wasn't built ta take in this many refugees." Thuradin stated.

"No, it was nae," Borim agreed. "And so they're on the move again, this time ta the outer colonies. There's sure ta be space in those new towns—they seem ta be expanding every day. But still, it won't be their home. For many of them, this will be the first time they step foot in the outside world."

Thuradin frowned, watching a young dwarven boy lift what looked like his grandmother and carry her along. The elder dwarf leaned her head against the boy's strong shoulders and closed her eyes.

"This is wrong," he finally said. "These dwarves shouldn't be forced ta leave their homes just because their loyalties still lie with the rightful ruler of our Kingdom. We should nae be doing this ta each other."

Borim looked at him grimly, "Tell that to the Council."

Kul'Kriegar was a rather simple city compared to Aleganthia, but it was dwarven—exactly what Thuradin had been missing.

He had missed the hanging stalactites and the towering stalagmites of the dwarven caverns, had missed the thick smell of frying ram meat from the markets, the constant sound of hammering from the blacksmiths. Boisterous laughter came from the city's many taverns, adding to the din. He had missed the feeling of being a dwarf again and was glad to be back, but now, so close to his kin, he couldn't help but feel small stones of doubt form in his stomach as they moved toward the city's gates.

He was under a thick cloak, it was true, and the cowl did well to hide his face; but still, what if someone recognized him?

He was sure, had his face not been covered, he would have looked as gray as the walls around them from the sudden trepidation he felt. As it was, the guards let them all pass without a second glance. Thuradin looked behind him, making sure they weren't being followed and let out the breath he only now realized he had been holding.

Borim snorted. "Were ye nervous?"

"A little."

"I didn't force ye ta come."

"I'm nae complaining."

"Good," Borim turned in his saddle to face the rest of their group. "Let's drop off our mounts at the stables and head straight for the citadel."

Everyone nodded and split up into smaller groups so the stables could more easily accommodate them. The stablemasters who took their mounts raised a few eyebrows among the viatari as they noticed they were wearing full plate armor as if ready to go to battle at a moment's notice. In fact, looking around, Thuradin noticed that every dwarf he could see was wearing full armor and carried one or two weapons hooked onto their belts.

"If I didn't know any better, I would have thought we were in Dun'Burell," Thuradin muttered.

Borim shrugged. "Times have changed. There's the looming threat of war now. Ye know how this city is. It was built for war, it breeds warriors. I don't think it should be so surprising ta see them like this."

"Nae surprising," Thuradin said, doing his best to keep his cowl up as he dismounted. "Just saddening, I suppose."

Borim clapped Thuradin's shoulder and turned him back to the streets. "Aye, my friend, that it is."

Kul'Kriegar's citadel was not the most aesthetically pleasing thing to look at. It was a giant, cylindrical structure, acting like a support pillar for the cavern. It was made of the mountain's hard stone and had taken years to conform to the dwarves' will. It was surrounded by several smaller towers and a series of connecting walls, all with their own garrisons.

They passed through these walls without a problem, Borim's new status as the King's protector granting him and any he wished instant access. As they neared the citadel itself, Thuradin took a moment to appreciate its formidable design. He had seen it many times, but never this close. There was only one entrance—an iron-wrought door that had a guard of five dwarves heavily-clad in plate armor on each side. Windows weren't part of the cylindrical design until twenty stories up, allowing nothing but bare rock and steel for the citadel's base.

They entered through the single door and marched straight for the stairs across the hall, a pair of the citadel's guards escorting them. Before long they were all huffing— even the viatari—as they climbed the steep, spiral stairwell. It took at least half an hour before they even reached the first set of windows, where Thuradin could at last appreciate the city below them.

"How much—longer—will we—have to climb?" Felix asked, his face dripping with sweat.

Borim looked down, breathing hard but grinning. "Bet ye wish ye'd left those furs back with the horses, aye? Don't worry, he's in one of the central floors of the citadel. It would be too obvious, I think, for assassins ta guess where he was if we had put him at the very top."

They climbed up several more levels before they finally veered right into another hallway. Thuradin took a moment to catch his breath, as did most of their group, which gave him a chance to gather his surroundings.

This hall was much dimmer than the one on the first floor. The torches here barely burned, creating long shadows. The walls looked bare, but on the floor were several iron barricades that made it difficult to maneuver. Thuradin snagged his cloak on the iron spikes sticking out of these barricades twice before they stopped in front of a plain, wooden door.

Borim knocked loudly three times, the sound of his knuckles rapping the wood echoing in the stone hall.

The door did not open. Instead, a booming voice spoke from the other side, "Declare yerself."

"I am Borim Tomestone, defender and loyal servant of the King, former captain of the wall guard, and friend ta Dunkell and the name of Ironaxe."

"State yer business."

"I've returned from my expedition ta the outside world and have brought with me those who can aid us in our coming conflict with the Council."

The door creaked open and Borim marched through, followed closely by his retinue of dwarves and viatari.

The room they entered was no throne room, but it was large, and sitting on an elevated, stone chair at the other end of it was Dunkell Ironaxe, King of the dwarves. There was no mistaking the mess of dark hair or the two braids hanging from his short beard. He looked almost the same as he had when last Thuradin saw him, but there was also something different.

Despite being ousted from his throne, he had more of a

regal air about him. He held himself in a manner that de-manded respect, his armor was a thick and glossy set of plate, gilded along the edges with patterns made of encrusted emeralds in the center. His eyes had also changed. Gone was the idealistic optimism from a year ago. Now they were tired. Thick bags of skin hung under them. The light that had once lit a fire in those eyes was no longer there.

"Borim, ye've returned," the King said, lifting himself from his seat with a groan and walking over to embrace him.

"I have, yer majesty, and I've brought the aid I promised."

Felix stepped forward, "On behalf of the viatari I offer my condolences for the loss of your throne and promise to not leave your Kingdom until we have helped you regain it."

Dunkell smiled, but it was weak. "I thank ye, Felix Draka, for yer kind's aid. And while I understand one of ye could battle all the dwarves in this room inta submission, I must wonder at yer numbers."

The elder viatari nodded. "I understand your concern. If I am being honest, I hope there is no need for us—that we can avoid war entirely. However, if there is a need, I will call for reinforcements. I would rather not do this, however, as our forces are stretched thin at the moment."

"Stretched thin," Dunkell repeated. "I understand yer city was sacked a couple months ago and ye must have lost many a lad and lass in the fighting to save yer city. But how is it that ye're still stretched thin?"

"I can explain that," without thinking, Thuradin spoke, and then realized that his voice would be recognized. Dunkell's attention snapped to him as did most of the guards in the room.

"Don't tell me that the dwarf behind that cloak—"

"Sorry ta disappoint," Thuradin said, pulling back his

cowl, annoyed that he had blown his cover mere hours after having returned home. There was no turning back now.

"Seize him!" one of the guards shouted. A few pulled Dunkell behind them as if to protect him while others reached for their axes or hammers and advanced on Thuradin.

"Hold on—Agh—Get off me, Farell. I said, HOLD!" The King's voice was like cannon fire and rang in their ears for several seconds.

"Ye will nae do anything ta this dwarf without my say so," Dunkell said, stepping between Thuradin and the advancing guards.

"But, yer majesty—"

"And ye will obey my orders without question," Dunkell barked.

The guards saluted smartly, and went back to their station, eyes looking anywhere but their King. Dunkell turned back to Thuradin and embraced him.

"It has been too long."

"Aye," Thuradin mumbled, unsure whether he should return the embrace or simply stand there. "Aye, it has."

"Listen here," Dunkell's attention was back on his guards. "No one will dare harm Thuradin while he is in this city. He is now under my protection. He has come ta help us retake my throne and in return I will revoke his exile so that he may live amongst us once again."

"Dunkell," Thuradin whispered, nearly yanking on the King's shoulder to get his attention before he remembered his place. "What are ye doing?"

Dunkell turned to him, smiling. "Giving ye yer freedom, of course," a sudden thought crossed his mind, "ye have come ta help me take back my throne, haven't ye?"

"Aye, I have, but hopefully nae through war."

Dunkell looked at Thuradin, then at Felix, then back again and nodded before returning to his throne seat. "I understand yer hesitation ta fight against yer fellow dwarves. We all feel it, none of us wants this ta happen. But believe me when I say there is no other way for me ta regain my rightful place."

"We can talk to them," Felix said.

"We *have* talked ta them—or tried ta, anyway. They won't listen ta reason, so we must get them ta listen with our axes."

There was a murmur of assent from the guards, though none looked too happy about it.

"They won't listen to you," Felix agreed. "But maybe they'll listen to me—" the elder viatari spoke for several minutes, explaining the existence of the acolytes and the war between them. He explained everything that they had learned, everything The First One had told them and about the war that was coming that would determine the fate of their world.

"This is much bigger than just politics," he said when he had finished explaining. "This is a time when all races: viatari, dwarves—even humans—must band together to defeat the evil that threatens our world."

"So, ye've nae come ta help us in our time of need, but ta look for this artifact that ye believe lies within our mountains," Dunkell said with disappointment.

Felix shook his head. "Do not misunderstand. Even if we did not have this pressing matter of finding The First One's brothers and bringing them over to our side, we viatari would still have come to your aid to honor our alliance, just as you did for us not so long ago. It just so happens that we have the opportunity to accomplish two important tasks at the same time."

"If I had my throne back, I would be able ta help ye by putting all the resources of the Dwarven Kingdom inta finding that acolyte," Dunkell said after a moment's thought. "So I don't understand why ye want ta talk with them so badly instead of just forcing them out—which would be quicker."

"It *could* be," the elder viatari pointed out. "But there's no guarantee that it will be. Tell me, Dunkell, how will we be able to find The First One's brother if the Dwarven Kingdom is thrown into a chaotic civil war? What if the fighting does not end as quickly or as easily as you hope? What if it lasts for months?"

"So, what if it does?"

"We do not have months to wait for your Kingdom's stability," Felix said calmly, though his fingers twitched. "We need to try to accomplish both tasks in a timely manner, and for that the best option will be to keep trying to talk with the Council in hopes of a peaceful solution. That way we can begin our search right away."

There was silence as Dunkell considered his words.

"Ye said these acolytes only show up in areas that could be labeled as 'wonders of the world' but as grand as my Kingdom is, I cannae think of where an acolyte would have remained hidden. Surely, we would have found it by now."

Felix lips stretched, a gleam in his eyes. "As vast as your Kingdom is, you do not own the entire mountain range."

The King's eyes widened with understanding. "Of course! I can send a courier ta ask them if there's such a place deeper in the mountains."

"And while you do that," the elder viatari motioned toward those standing behind him. "I will leave you half of my forces for your protection and take the other half to go to Tinas Gran."

"Aye," Dunkell nodded enthusiastically. "I'm starting ta like this plan, Felix, and the possibilities that come from it—I give ye my blessing ta go. And if ye're somehow able ta convince the Council ta surrender and return my throne, all the better for us all."

"It is settled, then."

Thuradin looked between the two leaders, unsure of what sudden understanding had passed between them—but for the moment, he didn't care. There was something more pressing on his mind right now.

"I'm going, too."

Dunkell's excitement turned to puzzlement as his gaze shifted to Thuradin. "Ta Tinas Gran?"

"Aye."

The King leapt off his throne and approached him, his voice low as he spoke his warning, "I don't think that's a good idea, Thuradin. I cannae protect ye there like I did here. The Council *will* kill ye if they catch ye."

"I have ta talk ta her. If she's one of their leaders, I have ta get her out of it."

Dunkell sighed heavily and glared at Borim, who looked at the floor with interest.

"Ye've heard, then."

"Of course I have," Thuradin said gruffly. "Ta think, Myrna, my own daughter, usurping the throne."

The King gripped his shoulder sympathetically. "I understand. Go, then. I will nae stop ye—though I cannae promise that she will be too happy ta see ye, knowing her."

Thuradin grinned weakly. "Aye, I don't think she will be."

"I'll go with him," a feminine voice said from their right. They both turned to see one of the guards approaching.

"Forgive me, yer majesty, I couldn't help but overhear—being so close—but I would be happy to accompany Thuradin and the viatari for this task."

"Why would ye want ta join me?" Thuradin asked. The voice that had spoken sounded familiar, though he felt like he hadn't heard it for a long time. He looked the guard up and down, trying to think of who she might be, but he couldn't think of a name.

"Do ye nae recognize me, Thuradin?"

"I'm trying," he said, not wanting to insult her. "Forgive me, maybe it's just because of the armor, but I cannae place who ye are."

The guard laughed, a soft, playful sound, and took off her helmet, revealing a tight bun of blonde hair secured by a mithril pin. Had her locks been let loose, they would have fallen brightly over plump cheeks and soft blue eyes—eyes Thuradin had last seen downcast, her shoulders trembling when he had called her name to join him in his task to find King Ronorim almost a year and a half ago.

"Lyrie?" he breathed, a sudden burst of euphoria flooding into him that was quickly stemmed by his last memory of her. He couldn't understand why she would now want to go with him to Tinas Gran. "Lyrie Swordmeist?"

Lyrie smiled at him warmly. "Hello, Thuradin, it's been too long."

Minutes passed and all he could do was gawk at her. At a loss for words, Dunkell took care of asking the question he was wanting to ask.

"Do ye mind telling us why ye want ta go with him, lass?"

"Aye, yer majesty," Lyrie said, all business again. "Two reasons. First, having more dwarves in these talks will give the impression that we are sending the viatari nae as a threat, but as an outside party able ta sit in on our dialogue neutrally, ta see which of our claims has greater legitimacy.

"Second," she said, putting her helmet back on. "I have a feeling Thuradin talking alone with Myrna will nae end well. I intend ta watch his back."

Dunkell nodded approvingly and grinned at Thuradin, who was still too bewildered to say anything.

"I don't have anything against the idea," the King said, returning to his seat greatly amused. "And I look forward ta hearing the results of these talks. Ye may join them, Lyrie. Take a day ta rest here, and leave tomorrow, Felix. I'll make sure that ye are well-provisioned for the journey."

"Thank you, your majesty," Felix bowed. The viatari turned and left the room—Borim nudging Thuradin in the ribs to get him moving.

"Well," Felix said with mirth. "I do not believe I have ever seen you so flustered, my dwarven friend."

Thuradin didn't respond, his mind still reeling. Seeing Lyrie again had opened a whole avalanche of mixed feelings and thoughts in the moment, but now the only thing he could focus on were her calm, blue eyes. And he wasn't sure how he felt about that.

CHAPTER ELEVEN

Thuradin quickly found that he had missed Lyrie. Before leaving for the outside world, they had been close friends; so close, it was often joked about with her husband, Hork Anvilgar, that he should keep a closer eye on his wife. Hork never had appreciated this joke and neither had Thuradin, the dishonor that joke implied insulted him. But now he found himself laughing about it with Lyrie as they reminisced on the second day of their journey to Tinas Gran.

They rode in the middle of the fifteen viatari accompanying them. The viatari kept quiet on their horses, which allowed the murmuring between the two dwarves to echo loudly in the dimly lit tunnels.

They had just finished laughing about their time in Dun'Burell, where Lyrie had once mistaken a drunk and haggard Borim for a burrower and had nearly run her sword through him, when her face grew serious. "It's hard ta believe that was so long ago."

"Aye," Thuradin said thoughtfully, already wishing they could go back to laughing—he had missed feeling so carefree.

"Is it true what I've heard about ye?" Lyrie asked, her blue eyes studying him deeply. "I do nae judge ye Thuradin,

I'm sure ye had yer reasons for whatever ye did."

"That's just it," Thuradin said grimly. "There's been so much exaggeration about what happened that by now I'm sure the story is that I murdered an entire clan, skinned Ronorim alive, and drank his blood in a dirty stein—none of which is true, by the way."

Lyrie snorted and for a moment Thuradin hoped they might go back to lighter topics, but it looked like she was determined to get her answer. "Obviously I don't believe that load of ram's dung. I swear, the lies people come up with . . . but now I want ta know the truth. Will ye tell it ta me?"

"I will if ye do the same for me."

Lyrie cocked her head to the side, "What do ye mean?"

"Why did ye reject my call ta go ta the outside world ta find Ronorim?"

Lyrie blinked rapidly, a slight shade of terror coloring the edges of her eyes. "I—oh, Thuradin, ye don't know how much I wanted ta accept yer call—"

"—and I had been so sure ye would—"

"—but I couldn't," she looked away, her eyes downcast. "Hork would . . . never have forgiven me had I left with ye for what everyone thought ta be a suicidal quest."

"What could Hork have said? It was for our King that we took such a risk."

"He wouldn't have liked it—" Thuradin saw Lyrie open her mouth as if she wanted to say more, but instead she bit her lip.

There's more ta this, he thought, fingering the end of his beard.

"Anyway," she continued, swallowing whatever she had been about to add. "I was so proud of ye for taking a stand like that when Dunkell usurped the throne initially—I mean, back when we all thought he was up ta no good. If ye want ta know something embarrassing, I mourned when ye left because I thought I'd never see ye again. I was sure ye were a goner."

"Thanks," Thuradin grinned. "Glad I could prove ye wrong."

"Me too," she turned to him. "Now spill it. I want ta know what really happened."

And so Thuradin told her. He left no detail out as he described the Creature, his curse, the burrowers, and the plan he thought of and executed to save the dwarves from committing genocide. By the end of it, Lyrie was about as pale as he had expected her to be.

"Well," she said, clearly struggling to express just what she felt. "At least ye didn't drink his blood."

Thuradin was so struck by this comment he couldn't help but burst into laughter. Lyrie joined in, and soon the two were once again reminiscing about the old times—the more recent, darker stories out of the way. Thuradin was so absorbed with their conversations that he didn't even notice they were out of the tunnel until they were entering the streets of Tinas Gran. He hurriedly pulled out the black cloak he had been given to wear to hide his identity and put it on, pulling the cowl over his face.

He looked around, taking in all the sights he could of the city he had once called home. He marveled at the many pillar-like buildings that stretched all the way to the top of the cavern floor and the gargantuan braziers that hung from thick chains above the city, lighting the whole area. But the joy he felt for being back in the dwarven capital was short-lived.

This was not the same cavern he had left all those months ago. Like Kul'Kriegar, the dwarves here were ready for war, most wearing their armor. The populace here was clearly hostile, glaring at them as they rode past or spitting on the path ahead of them. Some of the guards looked ready to come out and harass them, but a quick, threatening look from Felix was enough to convince them to continue with their patrols.

Around them, yellow flags with gray rams' heads were draped over most buildings, replacing the regular red and black flags that had always been there. Most of the former banners had been ripped apart and cast to the side, the royal insignia of a double-bladed iron axe unrecognizable now.

"What's that smell?" Thuradin asked, doing what he could to cover his nose as a putrid stench filled his nostrils. He saw many of the viatari do the same. Lyrie rode normally, her eyes fixed on the palace ahead.

"Garbage," she said. "Sewage. Before Dunkell left the city he made sure its water supply was cut off. They've been living in their own filth for weeks now."

Thuradin tried breathing from his mouth but the stench started to acquire a taste and he decided he would rather breathe in the rot than eat it. "No wonder the dwarves here look so haggard and . . . well, angry."

Felix raised his fist for them to halt as a band of one hundred dwarves, all with their weapons drawn stood before them. A dwarf with a short, red beard stepped forward, his eyes hard. "State yer business, outsiders."

"We have come to speak with your Council," Felix announced in a loud, clear voice. "We mean you and them no harm."

The dwarf with the red beard spoke with another, who

then went off running toward the palace.

"We'll see if they wish ta speak with ye. If nae. . . ." The dwarf fingered the blade of his axe and grinned with a glint in his eyes.

Moments later the runner came back, out of breath, but nodding his head. The red-haired dwarf's face fell in disappointment.

"Alright, lads, let 'em through."

The band of dwarves split in half, giving the viatari a narrow walkway for them to pass through. Thuradin couldn't help but notice that their eyes never left them once as they rode past.

Their mounts were taken to the stables and they continued on foot, walking under the shadows of the various large statues of dwarves holding hammers or axes into the air. They entered through a series of ornate archways, bordered by massive columns and soon were making their way through the royal halls of the palace.

Royal guards lined the walls and stood rigidly in front of many of the doors they passed, blocking their way most of the time. Thuradin was ashamed to see them. Most of them would be the same dwarves he had fought beside before his exile.

So lost in thought by their betrayal, he didn't notice which room they were approaching until the large metal doors sealing it off creaked open. They passed through into what had once been the throne room.

Much of it still looked the same. It was a circular area filled with large, thick columns spread out evenly along the walls. In the center of the room stood two of the largest, thickest stone pillars in the Kingdom. So often had these columns acted as a symbolic barrier between the royal authority of the King and the people he served. No longer.

The biggest difference in the room were the extra thrones. Normally, only the crystal throne of the King would have been there as they entered the room. Now, however, Thuradin counted four others, made of marble, set up alongside it. On these thrones sat the members of the Council, whose faces were hidden in shadow.

Thuradin studied them, trying to make out any identifiable features. One of them was Myrna, his daughter. He felt Lyrie grab his hand and give it a little squeeze.

"Keep calm, Thuradin, we will speak with her soon."

He nodded and fought to control the nervous swelling he felt in the pit of his stomach as Felix began speaking, "Grand Council, I am Felix Draka and have come to speak with you on behalf of your King, Dunkell Ironaxe."

"Hah! He's no King of ours." A shrill voice Thuradin recognized but couldn't quite place called out from a throne to his right.

"Aye, no King of ours—no King at all."

Now *that* voice was familiar. He felt his veins turn to ice as he remembered the famous tracker he had called upon to join him on his task to find Ronorim. One of the most respected and renowned dwarves of the realm at the time, she had survived the dangerous expedition with him and Borim and had fought in the final battle against the burrowers. He looked to his left, where the voice had come from and could just make out a spear with an iron crescent head that was the iconic weapon of choice for Ayrie Hearthkeeper.

"She's supposed ta be imprisoned," he whispered.

"Who is that?" Lyrie breathed into his ear. Sound echoed in these halls and she did not want to be heard.

"Ayrie Hearthkeeper. I'm sure of it. I heard that after she

discovered what I had done, and that Dunkell had ascended ta the throne, she went mad. She killed several royal guards before she was subdued."

"Quiet now," another familiar voice said directly in front of them. The dwarf sitting in the crystal throne stood and walked forward a few paces so that his face was revealed by the surrounding light. Thuradin groaned inwardly as he recognized his cousin, Garadin Stoutshield, now a leader of the Council. "It is good ta see ye again, Felix Draka. Forgive my colleagues for their hostile tones, but passions spike when there is any mention of a king ruling over us."

"Garadin," for a moment, Felix, looked lost for words, but he recovered quickly. "I must admit I am shocked to see you here."

Garadin nodded knowingly as he moved closer to them. "I expect ye would be, after I helped defend yer city under the King's orders. But though not much time has passed, they were still different times."

"Surely, things are not so bad that an attempted coup and assassination are justified."

The dwarf gave a short burst of laughter. "I see ye're up ta date on what's been happening, then. Aye, we orchestrated that but nae out of nefarious desire. We were left with little choice."

"And how is that?" Lyrie asked. "King Dunkell wasn't doing anything ta threaten yer little group of dissenters."

Garadin smiled kindly. "That's just it, lass—he wasn't doing anything at all! Meanwhile, we have burrowers digging closer ta our caverns each day. It's only a matter of time before they reach us. And if that happens while we're unprepared, many will die."

"Who says it is burrowers that you hear digging toward

your caverns?" Felix asked.

"Who else could it be?" Garadin shrugged. "We have no enemies aside from them."

Felix leaned in close so that hardly anyone could hear his next words, "I think you know, as I do, that the dwarves have more enemies now than just burrowers."

Garadin's face darkened. "Aye, I know what ye're implying. It would be no surprise ta me if we have ta face the evil we faced in the outside world again soon. In fact," his eyes lit up as if seeing the world around him for the first time. "I would bet my own brewing recipes that those corrupted acolytes are the ones behind this coming invasion."

Felix arched an eyebrow. "I hope you realize though, Garadin Stoutshield, that there are two different kinds of burrowers. There are the ones you faced in the outside world which are indeed under the control of The Turned One, and then there are the ones that live in the caverns below your cities who have not been heard from since Thuradin forced shut the tunnels connecting your people to them."

Garadin glanced sharply at the viatari and then at Lyrie and Thuradin. Even though his face was hidden under a cloak, he knew right away that Garadin recognized him.

"Please," he said, his voice low and hot with resentment. "Do nae tell me that ye brought him with ye. That the dwarf I'm looking at next ta the lass isn't who I think it is."

"And what if it is?"

"Then his life would be forfeit for foolishly returning from exile."

"Ah," Felix grinned. "But that was a sentence carried out by a judge appointed under the authority of King Dunkell, a king you have renounced and a king who has already granted

Thuradin a pardon. So, if you were thinking of taking his life under those pretenses, you would not have the right to do so, and it would be unwise for you to attack a member of our party when we have come under a banner of peace."

Garadin looked between Felix and Thuradin sourly, muttering curses under his breath.

"Och, Garadin, what's all the banter for?" A light, but commanding voice called out from one of the thrones to the left. "Are ye gunna let them talk ta us or are ye gunna run them out of the palace?"

Thuradin recognized this voice instantly, and he wished that the dwarf it belonged to was anyone but his daughter. Myrna Stonebeard hopped off her throne and walked into the light next to Garadin. It had been at least two centuries since he had last seen her, yet it seemed to Thuradin that she had hardly aged at all—her thick black hair was kept in a tight bun and her green eyes were still alive with the fire of youth.

She spared a glance his way and he felt as if a bolt of lightning had suddenly struck him. Even with the frown she wore, and her guarded expression, she still reminded him so much of her mother, Agata. But as quickly as the sensation had come, it left

"What's the plan?"

"Easy now," Garadin glanced between Thuradin and her, a sudden dawning in his eyes. "They're only here ta talk," he called out to the others, "Ayrie, Lunthir, Andarthol, come on down."

The other leaders of the Council came out into the light as well and Thuradin saw each of their faces. None were malicious—though Ayrie's seemed a little harsh. In fact, except for the three dwarves he knew, the other members of the Council looked more frightened than anything.

Garadin turned to them. "Now ye know who we are, ye know our names and what we look like. So ye can tell Dunkell ta call off his spy in the palace who's been trying so hard ta see who we are and ye can tell him yerself."

Felix bowed graciously. "For those who do not know me, I am Felix Draka, leader of the viatari in Aleganthia. Ayrie, it is good to see you again."

"Bet ye wish I said the same," Ayrie muttered, fingering her spear's iron tip.

"I will get straight to the point," the elder viatari said, ignoring the jibe. "I have personally come here because of our alliance with your people. We know of the tensions in this Kingdom and that they are nearing to the point of civil war. We want to prevent that."

"Why do ye care?" the dwarf named Andarthol asked. He was a shorter dwarf with a short red beard that was trimmed into a perfect point. "Ye made yer alliance with Dunkell, nae with us."

"Indeed," Felix replied. "However, that does not mean I want these tensions to escalate. Instability in the Dwarven Kingdom would be a disaster."

"For yer kind?" Ayrie spat, her eyes narrowing angrily. "And why should we care about the viatari after what ye monsters did ta our last true king?"

"For the world," Felix said calmly. "What is happening in this Kingdom will affect more than these mountains. With the dwarves divided, there will be nothing standing in the way of The Turned One and the Creature from moving against my people and wiping us out before they move on to yours."

Ayrie opened her mouth to retort but Garadin beat her

to it. "Easy, lass, he has a point. Believe me, I've seen the evil that they are preparing ta face," he thought for a moment, "Believe it or nae, Felix, but we do nae want war either. Those dwarves on the other side, as wrong as they are ta follow an imposter, are still our brother and sister clans. I would want nothing more than ta reunite with them, but nae if it means surrender. So," he spread out his hands as if waiting for the viatari to strike him, "what do ye propose as a solution?"

"That is the problem," Felix said, "This movement to form a Council seems to be based on the idea that Dunkell is an imposter to the throne, but he is not. He is an Ironaxe, whether you like it or not. His father was Thelm Ironaxe, his grandfather was Ranth Ironaxe, his great-grandfather was Geothur Ironaxe, who I dealt with personally. The dwarves have always been led by an Ironaxe; it is a lineage that has persevered throughout the millennia. I implore you to see reason, Garadin. You have no right to oust Dunkell simply because of a disagreement in policy—he is your rightful king. Give him back the throne peacefully, and we can address together what to do about the imminent invasion you believe is coming to your caverns."

"That's nae a solution," the dwarf named Lunthir muttered. "That's a surrender, and Dunkell will have all of our hides the minute we give his throne back."

"I assure you he will pardon you, but only if you return the throne to him peaceably. He is your rightful ruler; you must see this. The dwarves cannot be led and united by those who would be called usurpers. If you continue down this path you will have centuries of unrest. And in the mean-time, the evil that threatens all of us will consume our world."

Garadin sighed. "If that is yer so-called solution, Felix, at least now we know which side yer on. Dunkell was doing nothing about the invasion when he had the power. He would continue ta do nothing if we gave it back ta him."

"I am not on either side," Felix's voice was still calm and soothing. "I am on the world's side, and right now all of Azar needs the dwarves to stay united."

"Ta Nythirim's foot with the world," Ayrie shouted. "What happens outside our mountains is nae important right now— but this *is* important because it will determine how we live as a people from now on. And how we're going ta live is by putting our own kind above all else."

"Ayrie, if you would listen—"

"We're through listening ta the likes of ye!" Ayrie continued to shout. "And ye can quit pretending ta stand there, calm and such, and just attack us like—"

"OY!" Lyrie stepped in between the two parties, looking from one to the other. "No offense Felix, ye were doing a wonderful job, but I think they're done listening ta a viatari telling them what they should do," she turned to the Council members, "but we should still talk, dwarf ta dwarf."

"Then speak," Garadin said. "But only if ye have something ta add ta this conversation that Felix has nae already said. We will nae surrender the throne ta Dunkell any time soon."

"Aye, ye've made that clear," Lyrie glanced at Thuradin. "For these talks though, I think it best if they were done in a separate room with fewer hot heads. I request that my companion and I speak with Ayrie and Myrna."

Garadin's eyebrows raised. Lunthir and Andarthol looked at each other with amusement.

"And why should it just be ye four?"

Lyrie shrugged. "If the lads cannae reach an accord why

nae try having a discussion with just us lasses?"

Garadin chuckled at this, "A talk between just lasses, hmm?" He shook his head and began walking back to the crystal throne as he called back, "Very well, ye and yer *companion* may take Ayrie and Myrna ta the side room if they're willing ta listen ta ye. Felix, ye and yer viatari may wait in the outer halls for yer companions ta return. It is clear we have nothing more ta discuss and I doubt any of our minds will be changed by further talk."

"I am saddened to hear you say that," Felix said, "I had hoped for more reason to come from you, Garadin." He motioned for the viatari to follow him as he strode out of the throne room.

"And why should we go with ye ta the side room?" Ayrie asked suspiciously. "Why nae just say what ye have ta say? We're lasses regardless of what room we're in, if that's the angle ye wish ta take."

"Ye'll want ta hear what I have ta say," Lyrie said simply as she began leading them to the door that opened into the throne's side room.

Myrna watched her leave, then turned to Ayrie. "I don't know, Ayrie, it cannae hurt ta hear what they have ta say."

Ayrie thought for a moment and scoffed. "It can hurt in more ways that ye know, young one. But I suppose we'll just have ta follow her and see." She took a few steps forward then turned a suspicious eye to Thuradin.

"I have my eyes on ye, stranger. No funny business. I've noted ye've nae said a word yet."

Myrna, too, looked at him and the same shock he had felt earlier passed through his body again as her eyes met his hidden ones. He took a step forward, following them to the side door, wondering what exactly Lyrie had had in mind when she presented this idea to Garadin. Moreover, he was shocked that Garadin had allowed it.

Once they were all inside and the door closed behind them, Ayrie rounded on Lyrie, her spear in her hands, the iron tip right under Lyrie's chin.

"Alright, start talking. What's in yer mind that ye wish ta talk with Myrna and me so badly but cannae do it in front of the other Council members?"

"Ayrie," Myrna sighed. "She cannae speak with a spear ta her throat. Let her explain herself before ye get physical," she turned to Lyrie, "And don't think we won't get physical if we don't like what ye have ta say."

Lyrie nodded as Ayrie withdrew her spear. "It's nae so much what I have ta say." She looked at Thuradin and he suddenly realized why she had asked for a private audience. Garadin already knew who he was under the cloak, but hadn't done anything about it. Now, it was time for Ayrie and Myrna to find out. Though what good it would do, he would have to ask Lyrie later—he already knew how they would react.

"I ask only that ye give me a chance ta explain myself before going for the attack," Thuradin said, lifting his hands to pull back the cowl of his cloak.

Ayrie's and Myrna's eyes widened.

"I know that voice," Myrna whispered.

"Aye," Ayrie growled. "Aye, lass, I do, too."

Thuradin's hood fell completely back, revealing his thick gray beard and weathered face. He watched Ayrie's features twist into absolute rage, saw the grip on her spear tighten so that her knuckles turned white. He looked at Myrna and felt a chill run through him as those once comforting green eyes now looked at him with an intense coldness. Her frown deepened and she took a step back, her hand reflexively on the hilt of her sword as if she were about to draw it.

"Hello, Ayrie," Thuradin said gruffly, knowing how precarious the situation now was. He had his axes on him and Lyrie had her sword, but if Ayrie and Myrna attacked, he wasn't sure he would have the will to fight either of them. "Hello Myrna," he looked at his daughter again, hoping she could see the regret that he felt and his intense desire to gain her forgiveness.

"I'm home."

CHAPTER TWELVE

Myrna drew her sword. Her features, which were controlled a moment ago, now as fierce and hostile as Ayrie's. Her voice thundered as she spoke.

"How dare ye speak ta me with such familiarity? After all these years. How dare ye?"

Ayrie moved to thrust her spear into Lyrie, but Lyrie must have anticipated this. Sword already out of its sheath, she parried the attack easily and stepped forward, swinging the pummel of her sword down hard on Ayrie's cheek, stunning her.

"Enough," she said. "Myrna, Ayrie, *listen* ta what he has ta say before ye attack him."

"And why should I do that?" Myrna rounded on Lyrie, pointing her sword at her.

"Because he's yer father," Lyrie's eyes were fierce, refusing to back down.

"Oh, he's my father, is he?" Myrna looked at Thuradin again, the disgust plain on her face. "What father abandons his own child just so he can go and play war for decades on end with his friends? He renounced his place as my father centuries ago."

"I never abandoned ye," Thuradin said so quietly he

almost didn't hear himself.

Myrna looked incredulously around the room. "Never abandoned me? Ye abandoned me and mum! Ye're the reason she isn't here with us now. Ye broke her heart with yer absence!"

"DO NAE TAKE THAT TONE WITH ME, LASSIE." Thuradin's voice blasted through the room. Myrna stared at him, for a brief moment in a state of shock and awe. Thuradin looked between Ayrie, who had remained silent, glowering at him the whole time, and Myrna.

"Myrna, I swear, I didn't abandon ye. I know I wasn't present, but it was nae out of a lack of desire ta be with you and yer mother—I wanted nothing more than ta be with ye. But my duty ta our King and Kingdom bid me ta fight in Dun'Burell, ta keep fighting there until the burrower threat was eradicated. In that way, I did my best ta keep ye and yer mother safe—so ye two would never have ta see the brutality of war as I have."

Ayrie sneered at this. "Funny ye should speak of duty ta our Kingdom when ye're the reason our last true king was killed. Ye're the reason we have this imposter on the throne. If the dwarven clans fall inta civil war it's because of yer actions."

Thuradin shook his head. "Ayrie, where's yer reason? Ye know Dunkell is no imposter. He has Ironaxe blood in his veins and succeeded the throne properly after Ronorim died. Ye are wrong to oppose him like this, and I would have thought a dwarf who values duty and loyalty as much as ye do would realize that herself."

Ayrie's eyes narrowed. "Tell me this, Thuradin, did Ronorim die of natural causes or did Dunkell kill him—or is what I've heard about ye having a hand in his death the truth? Because the memory of Dunkell trying ta usurp the throne himself is still fresh in my mind, and I can never align myself with a dwarven prince who would stoop so low."

"What Thuradin did, he had ta—" Lyrie began to say, but Ayrie swung her spear at her again, forcing her to step to the side to avoid its iron tip.

"Ye be quiet," she seethed. "I want ta hear this directly from Thuradin," she looked back at him, "I considered us friends after our time in the outside world, so I at least owe ye enough time ta explain yerself. But if ye ever respected me, ye know ye owe me the truth."

Thuradin nodded. "Ye're right—" and he told Ayrie and Myrna the truth of what happened and the reasons behind it. He told them of the curse, of what he saw during the last battle they had with the burrowers, his sudden realization, and finally, the details of Ronorim's death at his hands as he lit the fuse that caved in the tunnel they had been in. By the end of it, everyone in the room looked ashen, but Ayrie's and Myrna's anger had not quite faded away.

"I do nae doubt that the Creature did something ta ye," Ayrie said, shuddering slightly. "I remember well how evil that thing felt. But that doesn't excuse yer actions. Ye should have trusted yer King."

"And sacrificed my honor? Nae just mine, but that of our entire race? No, Ayrie. That was never an option for me. Without honor, we are no better than what we imagined the burrowers ta be."

"What they *are*," Ayrie growled.

Thuradin turned to Myrna to see what she might say, but he couldn't read her face. She kept it guarded too well, much like he used to do.

"What say ye, my child?" he asked, hoping her silence

meant something had gotten through to her. "I raised ye well enough, I think, ta instill what it means ta know honor and true loyalty and duty."

"I think," Myrna said slowly, her eyes hardening with each passing second. "I think ye should leave."

Ayrie laughed. "Ye're too kind, Myrna, lass. They cannae leave now—at least, *he* can't," she rounded her spear on Thuradin so that it was only inches away from his chest, "ye, Thuradin, are going ta stay and pay for the crimes ye committed against our Kingdom. Once I reveal ye ta Garadin, I'm sure he'll—"

Her eyes rolled back and she collapsed to the ground hard, her spear clattering away, as Lyrie struck her temple with the flat side of her sword. Myrna swung her own blade, but Lyrie was quicker and had her under sword point within seconds.

"Don't try it, girl."

"What are ye doing?" Thuradin sputtered, gawking at Ayrie's crumpled form and then at Lyrie.

"I've decided this talking is getting us nowhere," Lyrie said. "It isn't going how I had hoped so I'm doing what I must ta end it."

"Ye've just signed yer own death warrants by attacking us," Myrna seethed, her chest heaving with every angry breath. "Once Garadin—"

"Oh, please," Lyrie rolled her eyes back to Myrna and pushed her away, sheathing her sword in the same movement. "Ayrie was threatening us first. Besides, do ye think Garadin doesn't know yer father is here already? He recognized him almost immediately but didn't do anything about it."

"He knew . . . and still he allowed Ayrie and me ta be

alone with ye?

"Aye," Thuradin said. "I must admit I was surprised, too."

"He had ta have known the futility behind it."

"Perhaps he did, lass," Lyrie moved for the door. "But I suppose he also thought the opportunity for a different conclusion was worth the risk. Anyway—" she opened the door and beckoned for Thuradin to follow her, "—we must go now. I have no doubt that the minute Ayrie wakes up, she'll set the guards upon us."

"But—" Thuradin looked back at Myrna, into her fierce, green eyes. The talk hadn't gone as he had hoped at all, but for a moment, it seemed to him he had swayed his daughter—at least, a little bit—to think differently of him. She was right to be angry with him, he knew, and he was sure she would be angry for a long time. But that didn't dash his hope that she might give him a chance to make things right between them.

"We have ta *go*, Thuradin," Lyrie insisted. "We must get back ta Dunkell."

"Aye, ye should go."

Thuradin's heart clenched sharply as he heard the bitterness in his daughter's voice.

"Myrna. . . ."

"Go," she said. "Go back ta yer pretender. Follow yer sense of duty, as ye call it, and serve that imposter king—while ye still can."

Thuradin frowned, alarm bells ringing in his head. "What do ye mean by that?"

Myrna shrugged, but her lips curved into a vicious grin. "Let's just say we at the Council do nae see him remaining King for much longer."

For a moment, Thuradin stared at his daughter, hoping

he wasn't reading too much into her words, but his instincts told him with certainty that her meaning was clear. The King was in danger.

"Ye're right, Lyrie," he said, his voice hardening. "We must go."

He stepped toward the door and said, without looking back, "Farewell, daughter."

"Goodbye, *father.*"

He heard the door close behind them and, without giving anyone else from the Council a chance to stop them with questions, he and Lyrie rushed out of the throne room and into the outer halls where the viatari were waiting.

"Well?" Felix asked when he saw them.

"We'll tell ye on the way," Thuradin said, walking at a fast pace. "Right now, we need ta head back to Kul'Kriegar and get ta Dunkell as quickly as possible."

Within a few minutes they were back in the stables, getting their mounts ready to ride out. Thuradin pulled his ram out of the stalls and had just hefted his thick, leather saddle onto the beast when he noticed a pair of soft, blue eyes watching him.

"Do ye need some assistance, Lyrie?"

"No," she said, a trace of regret in her voice. "But now that the adrenaline from the moment has passed, I wanted ta apologize for putting ye in a position like that without warning or asking ye. I just assumed back in Kul'Kriegar that that was the reason you came down here."

"It was," Thuradin replied gruffly, tightening the saddle straps onto his ram a little too tightly, bringing out a bleat of protest. "Sorry, girl—it is what I wanted, and I expected it ta end the way it did, but I cannae lie and say that I feel fulfilled, or that I don't feel saddened by what was said."

Lyrie nodded, mounting her ram and bringing it close to his, reaching out a hand. Thuradin took it and allowed her to swing him onto his saddle, his face suddenly close to hers. He could feel her breath on him as she sighed, could have counted her individual eyelashes if he'd wanted to.

"Well," she said, lingering for just a moment before pulling away and urging her mount toward the exit. "If ye ever want ta try again, I'll be there ta keep ye company in case ye ever need support."

For a moment, Thuradin felt his breath leave him, but he shook his head, bringing himself back to the present. He wondered what had come over him.

"Aye," he said. "I'll keep that in mind."

They rode out of Tinas Gran at full speed, and wound their way up the steep steps leading into the tunnel to Kul'Kriegar. As they continued riding, Felix came up next to Thuradin, his eyes fixed on the path ahead of them, but his mind clearly elsewhere.

"Tell me what happened," he shouted so he could be heard over the hoofbeats.

Thuradin grimaced. "Nothing good. Ayrie tried ta attack us when I revealed who I was and my daughter continues ta despise me."

"You have a daughter." Felix looked taken aback.

"Aye, Myrna. She's on the Council."

"So, that is why you were so determined to come back to the Dwarven Kingdom even when to do so would risk your life."

Thuradin nodded. "I have ta save her from this, Felix. But she wants nothing of me and I have no clue how ta reach her."

"You have my sympathy." Felix let a moment of silence

pass between them out of respect before continuing, "I am sure that one day you will make amends with her. But if that is all that happened, why are we riding to Kul'Kriegar with such haste?"

"Because before we left, my daughter said something that makes me fear for Dunkell's life."

"And what was that?"

"She told me ta serve the King while I still could. She, nor the Council, seem ta think that Dunkell will nae be around for much longer."

Felix frowned. "I am confident the viatari I left behind will be enough to keep him from danger."

"Maybe," Thuradin put more pressure into his ram's sides, urging her to go faster. "But I don't want ta risk it. We're going ta ride all night so that we can arrive ta Kul'Kriegar within the day, so ye might want ta spread the word."

Felix said nothing more and fell back to relay Thuradin's intent to his people, leaving the dwarf alone with nothing but the sound of hoofbeats to accompany him.

They were all exhausted by the time they arrived to Kul'Kriegar, especially the mounts. Their legs shuddered and their chests heaved with each breath as they finally reached the stables. They looked ready to collapse as their riders dismounted.

"Take good care of them," Thuradin told the guard gathering their harnesses. "They've earned it."

The guard nodded and Thuradin took off toward the citadel, followed closely by Lyrie, Felix, and the rest of the viatari. They made surprisingly good time up the many flights of stairs they had to climb, and, before long, were barging through the inconspicuous wooden door into the room where Dunkell had established his headquarters.

The sudden entrance grabbed everyone's attention. Dunkell sat straight on his throne, his eyes widened for a moment in surprise but then relaxed when he realized who had entered. The guards as well as the viceroy of Kul'Kriegar, who had been about to surround their King to shield him, also relaxed. Only the viatari seemed unperturbed by Thuradin's dramatic entrance.

Thuradin took in his surroundings. The room looked much the same, though the torches and braziers burned a little low, allowing long shadows to cover the room. Dunkell looked unharmed and in no immediate danger. Guards—both viatari and dwarven—stood in place all throughout the space. He sighed in relief. The King was safe. Perhaps he truly had read too deeply into Myrna's words.

"So," Dunkell said, scratching his short beard as he looked at the tired group before him. "How did the talks go?"

It was right after he said this that Thuradin saw the shadows moving and realized what was about to happen.

"TA THE KING!"

Within seconds, half a dozen dwarven guards lay face down on the floor, stiff and oozing blood. A few viatari also bled from multiple stab wounds but their regenerative abilities were keeping them in the fight.

The remaining guards looked around wildly, their shields raised as the shadows around them seemed to melt from the wall, revealing a dozen dark-clad dwarves, each one dual-wielding curved daggers or sabers. One of them advanced on Dunkell, who easily dodged the assassin's attack and came crashing down with his massive double-bladed axe, cleaving the dwarf in two.

The other dwarven guards let loose war cries and clustered together into tight formations, protecting the few Enurg'en with them as well as their King while they engaged the assassins. Thuradin drew his twin axes and rushed in, ramming one assassin into the wall while cutting into another's arm. The dwarf yelped in pain as Thuradin kicked him to the side, finishing him off with a quick strike to the neck.

The viatari joined the fight. The room was small, so their maneuverability was extremely limited, but still, they managed to move quickly enough to avoid most attacks, and before long, more than half of the assassins lay dead, the viatari's blades moving too quickly for them to block.

Thuradin looked to his left and saw Borim fighting two of the remaining assassins with several of his guards. The next moment he felt a sharp pain tear into his kidney and rip up his spine. He felt himself fall and tasted blood. There was a furious cry and he saw through his peripherals another assassin slam into the wall to his right, Lyrie standing over him, her sword ready for the final blow.

"Stop!" he heard Dunkell shout. "Keep that one alive."

The next minute, Thuradin felt a gentle warmth rush through his back, and his pain slowly disappeared. He spit out the last bits of bitter blood from his mouth and found that he could move again. A dull ache remained, but he pushed himself onto his back and saw an Enurg'en standing over him, his hands touching the ground as he healed him with the earthen powers Nythirim had blessed the dwarf with.

"I give ye my thanks," Thuradin said, standing and reaching behind him. He felt a jagged hole in his armor where he had been struck.

The Enurg'en nodded, though Thuradin still detected hints

of distaste in the healer's face.

Lyrie and Felix approached him, their weapons bloodied and their faces full of worry.

"What happened?"

"One of the assassins snuck up behind you and stabbed you in your lower back, slicing upward until their dagger hit your shoulder. That wound should have killed you," Felix said.

"Ye were bleeding everywhere," Lyrie said, a tremor in her voice.

"I'm fine now," Thuradin assured them. "I'm just glad we had some Enurg'en with us." He looked around the room. Several guards were dead, none of the viatari, and all the assassins, save the one Dunkell was currently securing into a chair with thick coils of rope. The torches burned much brighter now.

"How did they get inta this room?"

"That is a good question," Felix's gaze roved over the viatari until he found the two he was looking for. "Aniria, Drathanar!"

The two viatari walked over, their faces stern. They already knew what was about to be asked of them.

"I left you two in charge while I was gone so you could protect the dwarven King," Felix began, "so tell me how so many assassins managed to sneak into this room and stay hidden for who knows how long?"

Drathanar shook his head in shame. "I have no excuse."

Aniria glanced sharply at him, then at Felix, her eyebrows furrowing as she crossed her arms. "Well, obviously, we didn't see them come in."

"And why not?"

"Because," Aniria shrugged. "They didn't just waltz through

the door and plaster themselves onto the wall while we were looking. They must have been watching this room for days—hidden, I might add—and found a perfect time to infiltrate without detection. They were probably waiting for the right time to strike, too, until you barged in."

"Lucky we came when we did, then." Felix said, clearly not pleased with her answer.

Aniria scowled. "We could have handled them fine just by ourselves, Felix."

Before Felix could respond, she was already walking away to the other side of the room where the captured assassin was now coming out of his daze.

"*Ith sula, Aniria o'alor.*" Drathanar said in Viatar.

"*Ith shala,*" Felix replied.

The Dalyran general bowed his head then walked over to Aniria, placing a comforting hand on her shoulder which she shrugged off.

"She's still healing," Thuradin noted.

"Yes," Felix frowned. "That is essentially what Drathanar just told me. We must leave that for another time, though. Let us go see what we can find out from this assassin."

They walked over together, Lyrie lending her body to support Thuradin with her weight as if he were still injured. He was about to remind her that he was already healed when Dunkell's angry voice captured his attention.

"Now we shall see the mastermind behind this attack."

The King pulled off the assassin's black mask, which had been hiding most of his face, and revealed two large, hairy ears, a shock of jet-black hair, a pudgy nose, and a face that was unnaturally darker than the rest of the dwarf's skin. The question left Thuradin's lips before he could stop himself.

"Why is yer face so dark?"

The assassin shifted his cunning eyes to him and gasped. "Bloody hell, is tha' Thuradin Stonebeard I almost killed? What a trophy tha' would 'ave been, shame the Enurg'en go' ta ya in time," He struggled for a moment, trying to loosen the knots tying him down. "As ta yer question, I shade me face with charcoal so I can match the res' of me wardrobe, which is black, in case ye didn' notice." He let out a quick bark of laughter before returning to his bindings.

"Wait a minute, . . ." Dunkell's eyes widened in shock. "Morteth Shadowmeld, is that ye?"

The assassin froze. "Ah, yer majesty," he said, clearly uncomfortable at the notion of being recognized. "Nice ta see ye again. Looks like yer doin' well! Glad ye survived tha' little attack."

"*Ye* tried ta kill me?"

"Oh," Morteth laughed, but it was a hollow sound. "'Twas nae personal. If ye must know, I quite enjoyed carryin' out tha' job for ye last year and would gladly work for ye again. But this . . . ah, 'tis just about the money I need. Nothin' personal—yer majesty."

"I don't think I even need ta ask who hired ye," Dunkell grumbled. "It was the Council, wasn't it?"

Morteth's eyes shifted between everyone looking at him. "Ye know, if I could move better, I would shrug."

"Wait," Thuradin said, a sudden thought coming to him. "Ye said ye've worked for Dunkell before?"

"Oh, aye, 'twas a challenging job! 'Twas when I had ta—"

"Now let's nae get distracted," Dunkell said firmly, though he refused to meet anyone's eyes.

"If the Council ordered this assassination, they came close to achieving their goal of ridding this Kingdom of their King," Felix said. "And the fact that there was even an attack today means that they know where the King is, what room he is in, and how to get past the guards," he looked pointedly at Aniria who glared back defiantly.

"What's yer point?" Dunkell asked.

"My point is that you cannot stay here if you wish to live. They will know this assassination failed when they do not hear back from the dwarves they hired. And once they learn that, I believe they will try again."

Morteth cackled. "Perhaps, but there's no way they'll find anyone better than me ta do it and even I couldn' do it, even with me best team! If I cannae do it, no one can do it. No, ye're quite safe, yer majesty."

The elder viatari regarded the assassin for a moment. "I still suggest you move somewhere safer. Somewhere the Council would never suspect you to be."

Dunkell thought for a moment. "Ye don't mean—"

"I do. It would also give you a perfect opportunity to ask about the acolyte we seek as well if you have not already sent an emissary."

The dwarven King stumbled back into his seat. "And what of my Kingdom? Who will run it while I'm away? Who will keep the dwarves here in check so that we do nae fall inta conflict?"

"If that is the only thing stopping you, then rest assured," Felix stepped over the dead bodies around them and stood before Dunkell, bowing low. "I will ensure your Kingdom does not fall into disarray while you are gone. I will keep the dwarves from falling into civil war."

Dunkell laughed incredulously. "Leave a viatari in charge?"

"I cannot go to them," Felix shrugged. "They would not listen to me; they do not even know me."

The dwarven King sat back in his chair and thought for a

moment.

"Who are ye talking about?" Thuradin finally asked, frustrated by the coded conversation the two leaders were having.

"The burrowers," Dunkell said, deep in thought. "Felix wants me ta go inta their caverns and speak with them ta see if they know anything about this acolyte yer trying ta find."

"It would also be the safer place for you to be, since the Council would never guess that you went into hiding in burrower territory," Felix added.

"Burrowers?" Thuradin asked, his mind reeling at the thought. "But how would ye get ta them? I destroyed the only tunnel connecting us ta their territories. Besides, Dun'Burell is controlled by the Council."

Dunkell grinned knowingly. "The main tunnel, aye. But I still have my own ways of getting there," he thought for a moment longer, then nodded, "Alright, Felix, I will do as ye say. It will give me a good chance ta see if we can create a stronger bond with the burrowers anyway, and we might learn more about what's behind the digging we've been hearing lately."

"Ye'll need a guard, of course," Borim stepped in. Thuradin could tell by the somber tone in his friend's voice that he wasn't too agreeable to Felix's plan. "Ye cannae go alone."

"I'll be fine," Dunkell said. "The burrowers have never been hostile toward me."

"Even so," Borim grimaced. "I must insist that I accompany ye."

"I'll go with ye," Thuradin said. He couldn't have drawn more attention to himself if he tried. Several of the guards shouted their protest, their distaste for him plainer than ever. The King raised a hand and at once the room fell silent.

"I am fine with Thuradin accompanying me," he said pointedly, staring each of his guards down. "He has my trust and he's a skilled warrior. He will be able ta protect me."

"I'll go, too," Lyrie raised her hand, her eyes on Thuradin.

"I wouldn't expect anything less," Dunkell chuckled. "However, I will need at least one trusted dwarf ta remain and ensure the safety of our home so I can feel a little more confident about my absence."

The King looked around the room but couldn't seem to find the dwarf he was looking for, "Where is Dranthal?"

"Here," one of the guards said heavily, looking down at the eviscerated body of the viceroy of Kul'Kriegar. "He has fallen."

"I see . . . I will mourn his death," Dunkell said, his face falling for a moment. "But he died as a warrior—better yet, protecting his king—and for that I honor him."

"We will have to mourn his loss and the loss of all those who fell with him another time," Felix said not unkindly, turning and focusing his attention now on the assassin who had been listening intently to their whole conversation. Morteth looked away, feigning disinterest and tried half-heartedly to undo his bonds. "But for now, there is another matter we must attend to: what to do with this assassin."

The elder viatari took a step forward, his sharp fangs bared menacingly. "He cannot leave this room."

Morteth's eyes widened and he put more energy into trying to undo his bonds. He didn't speak, but his eyes flicked from Felix to Dunkell to Thuradin, then to other parts of the room as he tried to figure out how to escape the red-eyed creature coming toward him, hand in hand with his doom.

CHAPTER THIRTEEN

Victria awoke to the sound of Thomas singing. Having lived in his home for the past week, she had grown accustomed to being woken up for random reasons. Today it was because of Thomas. She lay in bed for a few more minutes, listening to his deep voice as he sung a ballad about the seas.

Getting up, she dressed herself in an airy, white shirt and tight trousers, a common set of clothes seen among the denizens here. On top of that she put on her leather armor and then finally wrapped a thick, green cloak around her body to cover it all.

Yawning sleepily, she made her way downstairs and into the dining room where she found everyone seated. Serania and Madira grinned excitedly as she approached.

"What's going on?"

"We're leaving," Serania said.

"Leaving?"

"Yuh, mon," Thomas said, coming out of the kitchen with a large plate piled high with grilled fish. "Aftah we eat we be goin' ta me boat an' castin' off."

Victria looked at the plate of food with a mixture of longing and disappointment. The fish smelled delicious and she was sure the taste was equally as pleasant. However, it would not fill her in the slightest if she were to eat it as it was. The viatari had run out of their supply of live animals for feeding and had been forced to hunt for rats during the night in the city streets, often with little result. Donsea was a rather clean city.

Thomas must have sensed her thoughts because he flashed her his toothy, knowing smile. "Don'chu be worryin', mon. I be havin' more where dis came from dat I tink ya be appreciatin' more."

He went back into the kitchen and returned with a bulging sack of live, wriggling fish. "Today's catch."

Tera coughed and looked away for a moment as the fishy aroma reached her. "I'll never get used to that stench."

The viatari, too, wrinkled their noses. "Why can't live fish smell as good as the cooked ones?" Natiari muttered.

They all ate, the viatari even indulging in some of the grilled fish after they had their fill of the live ones. After eating, they took their plates back to the kitchen and set about washing them with water and sand, as well as finishing up any other chores that needed to be done for the care of the house.

"I've run by the stables," Tera said as they gathered in the front hall with their things. "They'll continue to watch our horses while we're gone."

Victria nodded and looked at Thomas, who was sitting in one of his many stuffed chairs, the white tattoos on his face twitching every time he blinked. In one movement the ship captain stood up, stretched, and turned to join them, a toothy grin stretching his face.

"Ya be ready?"

The viatari nodded. Victria's heart pounded with excitement. They were finally going out to sea. One step closer to their goal.

They walked out of the house and down to the docks without a word. The viatari did what they could to remain unproblematic but no one really seemed to mind them as the citizens of Donsea went about their morning work. Victria wondered if they would have been noticed even without their human disguises.

They reached the docks within minutes, the strong salty air hitting Victria hard so that she had to rub her nose a few times to get used to it.

"So, which one is yours?" Natiari asked, looking around at the numerous small to medium-sized sail boats that were docked.

"It be dat one," Thomas pointed to the far end of the docks. Victria's eyes widened. There was no way this was the ship—if one could call it that—they would be sailing in. A quick glance around told her that her companions thought the same thing.

Thomas' ship was as much a conglomeration of materials as his house. Most of the hull was made of wood, though the types of planks used seemed to vary in both age and type as well as size. The deck wasn't overly wide, but it was rather long, with the stern of the ship rising into a secondary plat-form where the helm was. There was only one sail and Victria wondered if it would even be able to catch any wind. The canvas was grayed out from age and patched all over the place. The bow of the ship ended with an iron shaft that narrowed and sharpened at the end like a spear.

"Uh. . . ." Natiari scratched her head absently as she studied the vessel. "Does it work?"

Thomas glared at her, and for a moment Victria feared they might have insulted their one hope of setting out to sea.

But the next second, Thomas was moving on, cackling.

They boarded without issue. Victria learned that Thomas had named the ship *Lady of the Sea*. She dared not voice her opinion on how poorly the name matched the appearance of the boat. The viatari went below deck to store their belongings while Tera and Thomas set to work casting off. By the time Victria returned above deck, they were already underway, the docks receding in the distance.

"Mmm," Thomas closed his eyes as he rocked with the ship's movement. "Good winds today, we be makin' good distance."

There were a variety of swiveling chairs bolted onto the deck that the viatari made use of. With little else to do, they spent the hours watching the waves lap against the hull. Victria caught Tera staring at them.

"You know you don't have to remain in your human forms anymore," she said. "We've left the human world behind us, as far as you need be concerned."

The viatari shared cautious glances. Tera had a point and Victria had to admit she longed to return to her viatari form, to be rid of the human illusion she had been wearing for weeks.

Shimmering under the sunlight, she closed her eyes and felt her hair return to its natural silver color. Her eyes reverted to their blood-red and her fangs grew sharp. The other viatari followed suite, Tessa and Madira sighing with relief.

Tera continued appraising them. "You know, now that I see you up close as you really are, I'm reminded that you're not as bad as other humans have made you out to be. What do you think, Thomas?"

Thomas was still at the helm, steering with his eyes closed

as he enjoyed the sea breeze. "Ya, mon, dey be charmers alright."

Victria had to admit, she was impressed by these humans. They were different than any she had ever met. She felt that Tera had grown more trustworthy with each passing day, and though she wasn't quite sure if they were there yet, she hoped that one day they might be friends.

The hours passed by slowly. The viatari were fascinated by the surrounding waters and enjoyed watching the land behind them disappear under the horizon. And while Madira and Serania seemed to be struggling to contain their breakfasts, Victria found the rocking of the ship mixed with the salty sea air and the brilliant heat from the sun incredibly relaxing. She felt she could sit out on the deck as she was forever. The only thing that was missing, she thought, was company. *Like Felix*, her mind added automatically.

She chided herself. Lately thoughts of Felix had been barraging her at every free moment. She understood why—had understood for many months now—but now was not the time to think of such luxuries. Now was not the time for distractions.

Still, she thought, maybe once this conflict was over they could come back here to the south and speak to Thomas about sailing away. She laughed at herself. Maybe it had to do with being out at sea but she felt her imagination was running wilder than usual.

Victria heard retching sounds come from the other side of the deck. She turned to see Madira lean over the railing, her chest heaving as more of her breakfast left her stomach. Natiari stumbled over to her and put a hand on her back, took one look over the railing and then leaned over as well to add to the sickening chorus.

Tera laughed as she strode over to Victria's side. "Sea-sickness. Not everyone is made for the waves."

Serania checked on them to make sure they were okay but promptly returned to her seat next to Tessa, for fear of catching the urge to join them. Victria turned away from the spectacle and closed her eyes, letting in all the natural sounds, smells, and feelings around her. She sighed contently. It was a good time to rest.

Even after a couple of days of sailing, Victria still had not grown tired of the beauty of the ocean, though Tessa, Natiari, and Madira had. There was a different sort of beauty here. The sun was brighter, the clouds fuller. The ocean, so blue it seemed to swallow them up as she looked into its depths.

They had passed only a few islands so far, which Thomas had claimed were of no import. No humans lived on them as there was nowhere suitable to farm or build or do any-thing to sustain civilization.

"Though," he said with a mischievous smile, "I like ta go dere meself sometimes. Get away from all da othah humans. Even in Donsea dey be too much for 'umble ol' me."

"What do you do on those islands by yourself?" Tessa asked. "Surely the isolation would drive anyone insane after a while."

"Ah, but missy, I like bein' left alone. It be da best way ta be. Besides, I don' be sittin' dere doin' notin'. I fish—all day, all night. Da perfect life. In fact—Tera, take da helm if ya would."

Tera did, and Thomas went below deck, returning with a long, metal fishing pole.

"Dis be some good fishin' time."

"Thomas, I wouldn't if I were you," Tera warned. "You

know how the vashi get with that type of stuff."

Thomas waved her away lazily as he took a seat in one of the swiveling chairs and cast a line out. Victria watched the lure sail quite a distance before plopping in the middle of the waves, where it swam back to them as Thomas reeled it in.

"We still be in da reef. Besides, I done made a deal wit' dem."

Victria climbed the short set of wooden planks leading up to the captain's roost, as Thomas liked to call it, to join Tera at the helm.

"What is it with you humans and your fear of the vashi? Everyone we talked to in Halding Port was terrified of them but you never told us why."

Tera shrugged. "They should be no issue for you since you're a powerful viatari, but the vashi and humans of the south have had a long history of conflict. It's a long story."

"Well, I think we have plenty of time."

Tera glanced at her and shrugged again. "Very well. Once upon a time, all this water you see around you—all of it, up to the shore—belonged to the vashi. Humans came roaming to the south from the northern plainlands and built settlements along the shore, the first port cities. The two races soon went to war with each other when the humans refused to stop fishing in vashi waters. The humans needed to fish for food, but the vashi saw this as an invasion.

"The humans won the war, as I'm sure you can guess, since the vashi no longer control the Sea of Scales in its entirety. Their waters now begin when the simple reef we fish in turns into the Great Coral Forest. The vashi were a brutal enemy, and even now we hear stories all the time of fishermen who sailed off-course into the Great Coral Forest and were dragged to the bottom of the sea by the vashi."

"Do the humans fear another war against them?"

Tera raised her hands as if in surrender, "I know as much as you on that one. I don't pay too much attention to the politics of the south. But I'm sure they do, that's why the port towns—Halding Port, especially—are so well-entrenched with walls and battleships and the like."

"And you don't think the vashi will have a problem with us crossing into their waters to get to where we need to go?"

Tera smiled knowingly. "Oh, they'll stop us, and soon. We're about to cross into their waters right now, it just so happens. I doubt they'll drag us to the bottom of the ocean, though, seeing as you're not humans. They might be more interested in learning about you."

"But you're human."

"I can take care of myself, sweetie."

Lady of the Sea rocked dangerously, nearly tilting all the way portside into the waters. The viatari latched onto the railings, the chairs, wherever they could to keep from falling over.

"What was that?" Victria asked, shocked. It was as if they had hit something.

Tera grimaced. "They're here."

Victria looked over the railing and saw that the water had begun to churn. Bubbles frothed to the surface as if the ocean was boiling. Then, ever so slowly, a head popped out, followed by another, and another, until a total of twelve heads were bobbing with the waves. They surrounded Thomas' ship and began to climb up the hull, their webbed hands and feet sticking to the planks.

"Stay calm," Tera called out. "And Thomas, get your damned hook out of the water!"

Thomas rolled his eyes and uncrossed his legs as he finished reeling in his line and put away his fishing pole. "Why ya gotta be suckin' out all da fun?"

The first vashi climbed aboard and Victria got a good sense of the type of people these were. They were humanoid in figure, but that was where the similarities to humans ended. Their skin was shiny and looked like it was covered in a thin layer of mucus. There were three cuts on either side of their necks which reminded Victria of the gills on a fish. Their arms and legs were covered in scales, and as they climbed aboard, the viatari witnessed their feet—which had been more like flippers before—transform into something more human.

Each vashi had long locks of thick hair and had bodies built for fighting. Their torsos rippled with muscles underneath their pale-blue skin. They wore enough armor—made of what, Victria couldn't tell—to cover the essentials. Victria studied their lower halves and saw that each vashi had a different color to them. Some were red, others green, still others were black or other hues. After she had finished observing this new race—something, she realized, they were doing with her and her companions as well—she then noticed that each vashi carried a weapon, from tridents to spears to rusty sabers, as if ready for a fight.

The vashi began hissing, their tongues sharp at the end. Victria guessed this was what their language was comprised of. If so, they were in more trouble than she had realized because she could not begin to understand anything they were saying. She wondered if Serania, who had been a wanderer, perhaps understood it. She could tell, though, by the viatari's bewildered expression that she did not.

The vashi glared, waiting for a response, then realizing

none was coming, looked at the humans and spoke in their tongue, obviously disgruntled that they had to do so.

"Why have you come into our watersss, humansss?" The vashi who Victria presumed was the leader asked. He wore a spiked helm that seemed to rise and end in a half-oval. "You know it isss not permitted."

"We not be comin' ta do any major fishin', mon," Thomas said, walking casually toward the vashi and extending one of his tattooed hands, which the vashi took. "We be bringin' dese ladies who wanted passage past da reef."

The vashi studied the five viatari curiously. "What are thessse?" he asked. "We have not ssseen them before or heard of their kind."

"We are the viatari," Victria stepped forward so that she was face to face with the vashi leader. She fought the urge to wrinkle her nose. The vashi smelled heavily of fish. "And we have come with specific purpose."

She took her time explaining their situation, detailing the brewing war with The Turned One and the Creature, what the acolytes were, that they were searching for one of them here, and how necessary it was for them to find him if they wanted any chance of winning the coming war.

"It isss quite a tale," the vashi leader said. He bowed. "Pleassse, allow me to introduccce myself. I am called Esseld, I am commander of the border forcesss, we who patrol the watersss between the Great Coral Forest and the reef to ensure the humansss don't wander into our watersss. If what you sssay isss true, then I fear we may sssoon have more than humansss to worry about."

Victria bowed back. "My name is Victria Bloodletter. Will you let us pass, then? We were told by The First One, the acolyte who advises us, that his brother resides in a place

CHRONICLES OF THE FIRST GODS BOOK THREE   173

called the Throne of the Deep."

Esseld's eyes bulged. "None but the high priestsss are permitted to enter that holy area. If that isss where you must go, then you must first come with usss."

"Where will you take us?"

"To our Sssupreme Overseer, he leadsss usss all. He will decide whether you and your kind may be permitted to travel to the Throne."

"But how are you to take us when we cannot breathe underwater?" Serania asked, stepping forward herself. "I assume your home is deep under the waters, is it not?"

"It isss," Esseld said with a glint in his eyes. His gills flared happily. "Worry not, viatari, our waterseer will be able to aid you with that particular problem."

One of the vashi with a green lower half stepped forward. He carried a staff made of coral and thick hair also covered his chin.

"Greetingsss, viatari," he said, inclining his head slightly. "My name is Cotovas. I am the waterseer for thisss company. I have the ability to transform you temporarily ssso that you are able to breathe underwater and ssswim asss fast asss we ssswim."

"Transform?" Natiari repeated. "What kind of transformation?"

Cotovas chuckled. "It isss nothing major. We will just give you gillsss and webbed feet. However," the jovialness in his face evaporated and was replaced with a deadly seriousness. "Thisss particular transformation requiresss a sssacrifice for it to take hold. You must each sssacrifice sssomething you hold dear."

The viatari looked at each other with the same question in their eyes. What would they sacrifice? They huddled together, away from the vashi, to discuss in relative privacy.

"We didn't bring anything for a sacrifice," Serania said.

"What if they don't require a physical object for the sacrifice," Madira wondered. "What if we sacrifice one of our abilities as a viatari?"

"Why would they care about us sacrificing that?" Natiari asked.

"Because it holds value to us," Victria answered, looking at Madira with approval. The Dalyran was most likely correct in her thinking. Now the question would be what should they give up. They only had so many options and she didn't relish the idea of parting ways with any of them. They were what made them viatari, and she treasured each of her abilities equally.

"It should be our speed and strength," Tessa suggested.

There was silence as they waited for an explanation.

"Well," she shrugged. "It's what we use the most. We would feel their loss the greatest, so it would be a worthy sacrifice."

"I agree," Serania said.

"Me too."

"Yes."

"Alright," Victria turned back to the vashi. "We have our sacrifice."

Cotovas revealed a line of sharp teeth in a shark's smile. "Good. Join usss in the water and we will begin the ritual."

"I'm going too," Tera said, joining the viatari by the railing.

Victria considered her for a moment. It would be great if Tera were with them, if only to add to their numbers; however, they had only hired her to find them someone who would sail them this far and she had accomplished her task.

"You don't have to come," she said. "You've done every-thing we've asked you to. You'll get your reward when we return, I can assure you of that."

Tera scoffed, putting her hands on her hips. "I'm not offering to go because I have to. I'm going because I want to. I want to make sure you all stay out of trouble."

"We can take care of ourselves," Natiari said.

Tera drew close. "Are you sure about that? Even with you sacrificing your extraordinary speed and strength? You'll be little more than humans at that point when it comes to fighting, and if there's one thing humans know when it comes to a fight is strength in numbers."

Victria nodded, conceding the point. "Very well," she turned to the vashi. "She is our guide. If it is possible, we would like her to join us as well."

The vashi hissed with distaste, but did not refuse and beckoned for them to enter the water. They did so and Victria felt like needles had stuck into her skin as the cold water shocked her. She tried opening her eyes but immediately regretted it as the salt burned them.

She breached the surface and floated there as the vashi encircled them. For a moment she thought this might be a trap, but that thought vanished once Cotovas began chanting. He raised his staff and a large bubble enveloped the space where they floated.

"Name your sssacrificesss," the waterseer hissed softly.

The viatari looked at each other and nodded. "We sac-rifice those traits that make us viatari. We offer our powers of speed and strength."

The vashi nodded approvingly. "And you, human?"

Tera reached into her shirt and pulled out a golden locket. She opened it, stroked whatever was inside, and then closed it again.

"I offer this locket, within which are strands of my late husband's hair, the only thing left I have of him."

The golden locket floated to the top of the bubble and the viatari gasped as they felt their power leave them, as if they were having their energy drained. There was a blinding flash and suddenly Victria felt a warm surge rush through her body. There was a burning sensation around her neck and her feet felt cramped. The rush reached her head and she was suddenly light headed, trying to comprehend what was happening.

She reached for her neck where the burning had stopped and felt slits. She felt her feet and saw that her toes had been joined together with a thin webbing.

"You have been granted thisss temporary transformation as a sssign of goodwill by our patron, Ocaeusss, who gave usss the powersss of the watersss. Come now, viatari and human, we will take you to our Sssupreme Overseer."

The viatari looked at each other with uncertainty and a little trepidation as they realized the scope of their trans-formation. Tera was the only one who seemed to still have all her wits about her.

"Well come on, then," she said. "We don't have all day. Thomas, what will you do?"

He grinned down at them, his white tattoos stretching across his face. "I be headin' over ta da nearest island, have some time ta meself and do some fishin'. When ya be done wit' what ya need ta do, just come over and let me know and I take ya back. Tera, ya know what island I be talkin' 'bout. We made some good memories dere, if ya remembah."

Tera chuckled. "Understood. Take care of yourself."

Thomas' smile melted, his face turning unusually serious.

"Ya as well, Tera. Watch ya back."

And with that he disappeared over the railing.

"Come on, girls," Tera said encouragingly. "We've got a Supreme Overseer to meet."

CHAPTER FOURTEEN

Victria submerged her head contemplating if she would ever see the surface world again. The blueness of the ocean was, at first, overwhelming. It stretched on forever. She could not see the ocean floor. While sunlight was visible from the surface, it didn't do much more than provide blurs of white light when she looked up. She twirled to see if there might be a landmark—anything that might orient her, but there was nothing. It was all just so . . . blue. Not even a school of fish swimming around them could break the monochromatic world they had just entered.

The viatari and Tera swam using their newfound webbed feet and found that their swim speed had increased significantly. It did not take much to travel a great distance and, after some effort, they caught up to the vashi. Victria tried to push herself to surpass them, as she would normally do when traveling with humans or dwarves, but without her usual speed all she could do was struggle to keep up. She bared her fangs in frustration. She did not like feeling so powerless.

They swam down until the ocean floor came into view, which was a relief to Victria. While the reef the humans fished in wasn't much, it was at least something new to look at. Small clusters of coral, like tiny jewels of color, were scattered throughout the otherwise blue-gray floor. There were some ocean creatures moving across the sands as well—many of which Victria had never seen or heard of before, but others, like the sea turtle, she recognized and admired as she watched it cruise gracefully below her.

Once they reached the floor they sped off, moving away from human waters. Despite the peaceful scenery, Victria kept alert and focused. Water rushed against her face as they swam with speed. Clusters of coral below passed her by quickly and soon turned into large kelp forests. These large, thick stalks of green, yellow, and brown algae reached up from the ocean floor to great heights, so much so, Victria thought they must reach the surface. They reminded Victria of the forests surrounding Aleganthia in a way. They swayed back and forth with the currents even as the vashi and viatari swam through them, slimy arms brushing against their darting figures.

Some time passed and Serania let out an aquatic gasp—a stream of air bubbles escaping her mouth and floating all the way to the surface—as she looked ahead. Ahead of them was another reef, but unlike the humans,' everything about this place was colossal and vibrant in color. Giant coral arms stretched out every which way like intertwining tree trunks—many of them differing in color. Sea anemone populated much of the empty spaces in between, their long pink, purple, and blue tentacles flowing back and forth with the current.

The vashi hissed to get the viatari's attention and signaled that they should continue swimming, which they did. A new sense of wonder enveloped Victria as she marveled at the giant reef. There were corals of all types here, some that looked like gigantic mushrooms, inside of which vast colonies of fish and other small sea creatures made their home, others that looked like towers.

The wildlife, too, was vastly different from what lived in the human waters. Here the fish were larger and more colorful. They came in every shade and pigment, from pearly white, to yellow with green stripes, to ruby red. There were more sea turtles here, swimming in packs, as well as other wildlife like sting rays, small sharks, barracudas, and others Victria couldn't name.

She was so distracted by the sheer number of new sights and living things and even scents that her gills could pick up through the water, that she did not register they had dived well below the reef, delving deeper into the sea until they reached a lower floor. She looked up and saw that the giant arms of coral worked together, reaching outward, providing a roof-like structure for them.

Here, too, in this lower level of the ocean floor everything was different. There should not have been any light to see, being so deep underwater and away from the sun, yet light permeated everywhere through bioluminescent, giant jellyfish, which floated in place in large bubbles. The vashi set foot upon the ocean floor and began to walk. The sand was soft underfoot as the viatari followed suite. Victria was careful where she stepped so as not to disturb the large, green crabs, sea cucumbers, and other smaller critters scavenging through the pure, white sand for food.

"Come, we go to the town of Pashir, where our Sssupreme Overseer residesss." Esseld said, pointing with his harpoon to a cluster of stones that Victria had initially mistaken as ruins. The stones that the vashi structures were made of were ancient and cracked, moss and seaweed having grown across most of them. Some of the buildings appeared to be shaped out of coral as well.

The houses, towers, and even a sort of wall that looked more like an aqueduct, had clearly been built in a planned grid. And as they drew closer, Victria noticed more vashi, swimming between buildings, floating above the wall, and going about daily life.

They entered Pashir through an archway and continued down the main road. As they passed houses and a handful of elegantly carved statues of sea life, some of the town's residents approached cautiously to investigate the new arrivals. They stopped short when they noticed the silver hair and the blood-red eyes of the viatari. Murmurs broke out in the vashi's own bubbling tongue.

They neared one of the larger edifices in the center of town. It was an assembly of white coral and marble slabs. The stone doors were already opened and so the vashi entered without so much as a knock. The viatari followed and were stunned to find themselves instantly dry the second they stepped inside. In fact, they found that there was no water within the building at all—it rippled just outside the doorway as if held back by an invisible wall.

"Our powersss," Cotovas explained, "are used for many thingsss to assist our way of life. The ocean obeysss our commandsss ssso long asss we respect it, which isss why it restrainsss itself from entering our dwellingsss."

"I will call for the Overseer," Esseld said, walking up the marble stairway to the second floor and out of sight.

The vashi indicated that they should all take a seat on the various couches and chairs that stood along the edges of the foyer. Victria took the opportunity to look around. From the outside, the building had appeared aged, but inside everything was shiny and new. The floors glistened from a recent polish.

The coral walls were smooth and vibrant. She saw large pots of green fire hanging from the ceiling, which kept the room lit. There didn't appear to be any wood burning in it and she wondered how the flames stayed lit.

"Everlasting fire," a deep but friendly voice said from the stairway on her left. She whirled around and met a vashi who she could only assume was the Supreme Overseer. His long, thick hair was braided and wrapped around his shoulders. He wore an elegant, light-yellow robe that seemed to float with every step he took and covered the golden scales of his lower half. A chain of pearls rested across his neck.

The Supreme Overseer's green eyes flicked to Tera and he raised his eyebrows in interest. "A human, Esseld, how surprising."

"They insisted we bring her, my lord."

"I see," the leader of the vashi took a moment to study the viatari, taking in their features, making note of their subtle mannerisms. He bowed respectfully, "I am Araxie, Supreme Overseer of the vashi. Might I ask who you are and what you are doing in our waters?"

Victria noticed Araxie didn't speak with the hiss at the beginning or end of his sentences like the rest of his kind. She could only assume his grasp of the human language was better than theirs, enough to be rid of any speech impediments.

"I am Victria Bloodletter. My companions are Tessa Shadowweaver, Natiari Lunglow, Madira Starglow, and Serania Mistguide. This human's name is Tera, she was our guide as we crossed the humans' lands and helped us find our way here. We have come because of recent events in the surface world. . . ."

Again, Victria went into detail in explaining the events of the past year as well as explaining her task to find the acolyte in the Throne of the Deep. By the end of the long tale, Araxie had taken a seat, his chin resting in his hands as he looked thoughtfully at a statue of a manta ray to his right.

"Esseld was right to bring you to me. These events on the surface may prove consequential to us if these corrupted acolytes get their way. However, as I'm sure my commander has already told you, no one but the high priests and waterseers may enter the Throne of the Deep. Indeed, few have entered that place in the last few centuries."

"Why is that?" Serania asked. "Clearly the Throne holds some religious meaning for your people."

Araxie nodded. "It does. However, let's just say that there are a few . . . obstacles keeping us from entering the Throne."

"Are you not able to help us, then?" Victria asked. She was beginning to fear they had come here only to be told there was no way forward.

The Supreme Overseer thought for a moment. "I believe this issue must be taken before the Assembly, which is our body of government. They are a cluster of representatives from different regions of our waters who bicker to no end; nevertheless, we must see if they think it is wise or not before any decisions can be made. Then, if they agree to it, we would need to ask the high priestess in Maleres for permission to enter the Throne."

"But if you're the Supreme Overseer surely you don't need their say in the matter," Natiari said.

Araxie laughed, an echoing boom in his marble halls. "Do not mistake my title for one of power. I may be Supreme Overseer, but I do not have absolute power, nor would I want it. All issues that concern the vashi must be brought before the Assembly to be debated. I get final say on what's done, but I cannot do it by myself without consulting the representatives."

"Then what will we do while you do that?" Victria asked, the sinking feeling in her stomach growing by the second. "We cannot simply stand by and wait while events unfold outside of these waters."

"Well—"

A sudden movement to their left caught everyone's attention. Victria caught only a glimpse of whatever had approached them before it ducked behind the door.

"Come in, my son," Araxie called.

There was a slight hesitation, but finally the door swung open and Victria witnessed a younger version of Araxie pass through. She had no idea how the vashi aged, but this boy appeared to be in his later stages of adolescence. His thick hair was long and curly and he had the same green eyes of his father. He wore a similar silk robe that nonetheless revealed much of his muscular chest. The scales of his lower half were silver, like moonlight.

"My guests, if I may introduce my son and heir to the Overseership, Avmoshir."

Avmoshir eyed them all warily, but nodded his head respect--fully. Then he turned to his father. "Mother wants to know what you desire for supper."

Araxie glanced at the viatari and grinned. "Tell her she need not slave away tonight. We will go out to eat with our guests and show them the wonderful fare that Pashir has to offer."

Avmoshir shrugged and, the next moment, was gone be-hind the door again.

"Lovely boy," Madira noted.

"He's a tad shy," Araxie chuckled. "Still growing. I have much to teach him so that he may lead our people well when I'm gone. But back to our discussion—I find truth in your story, which is why I am inclined to help you with your struggle against this Turned One and Creature. Tomorrow, I will send word to our capital city of Zessarix and call for the Assembly to gather. Then, we will do what we can to convince them of your cause."

While it wasn't much, Victria was at least grateful they hadn't simply been turned away. With the vashi's aid, they could set about their task with renewed strength. Perhaps even gain a valuable ally.

"I offer no promises, though," Araxie warned, reading the newfound hope in her eyes. "Convincing the Assembly will be no easy task."

"Why not?" Tera asked. "Surely the representatives of your people are as reasonable and intelligent as you are."

The Supreme Overseer laughed again, revealing his sharp teeth, of which there were many.

"Flattery is not something I encourage in our world, human," he said, not unkindly. "But you shall soon see why I warn you. Even we vashi have our flaws. Like everywhere in the world, I'm sure, power has a tendency to corrupt. Many in the Assembly have held on to their power for far too long and have created factions in the process, which has led to more infighting and not as much productivity."

"Why not change how your government works since you have the final say?" Tessa suggested.

Araxie's face turned stony for a moment, but then relaxed. "I don't know how the politics of the surface world work, but I am no dictator. I have no desire to seize more power for myself even if it were to make things more expedient in the political realm. My people already waged war on each other once—long before I was ever a thought—over the style of government they wanted. That war led to the creation of the Assembly, but it also caused much bloodshed, tragic loss, and dark days. I'd rather not risk recreating those times."

Tessa shrugged, conceding the point.

"Enough politics, it is a heavy subject," Araxie stood up. "Esseld, you and your company are dismissed. You may resume your patrol of the border waters."

"Yesss, my lord." Esseld bowed, as did his troops and they quickly exited the room.

"As for you, my guests," the Supreme Overseer beckoned for the viatari and Tera to follow him, "I will take you to your accommodations. We will stay here a few days while I give the Assembly time to gather, and then we will journey to Zessarix. Rest a while. I will call for you when we are ready to head out to eat. Have any of you ever eaten eel?"

They all shook their heads,

"I thought not. It is an exquisite delicacy. Prepared properly it can leave your mouth watering even as you finish your meal. . . ."

Araxie continued with his descriptions of vashi cuisine as he led them down the spacious halls of his residence. Victria was only partially listening, though. As she passed a window, she found herself taking in her new image. Her skin had gone paler than usual. She reached up to feel the three slits on her neck that allowed her to breathe underwater and shivered. Her hair and eyes were still their usual color, but she could hardly recognize herself. Tearing her gaze from the ghostly image, she was left with a slight sense of unease.

CHAPTER FIFTEEN

They spent two days in Pashir, during which Victria learned much of what vashi life was like. Every morning the men would set out into the open waters to hunt with seaweed nets. The women remained in town, fixing armor or weapons, weaving silken cloths out of the kelp, sea silk, and other finer materials they managed to procure from the ocean, and generally helping with the upkeep of the town.

Around midday, the men would return with large hauls of fish in tow. Some would also return with baskets full of a fatty substance that remained a mystery to Victria, but which the vashi used for everything; from keeping the fires lit, to gluing things together, they even used it in some of their foods.

The food had proven delicious, as Araxie had promised; though, it did nothing to sate their hunger. When they had first told the Supreme Overseer of their method for obtaining sustenance, he had thought they were joking but had humored them anyway and ordered a full net of fish and other living creatures to be brought in.

He had stood there, speechless, when the viatari began draining their life essences. By the time Victria and her companions had finished eating, the fish were no more than flattened, brittle versions of themselves.

"It appears there is much my people must learn about yours," Araxie had said after he recovered from his shock.

During their stay, Victria had also made an effort to learn more about Tera. Often, she found herself sitting in on Serania and Tera as the two shared stories from their time as wanderers—from scaling the Silent Mountains and traversing its peaks for weeks to surviving the brutal heat of the deserts of the Western Lands while on the run from a pack of carnivorous anta.

The day they were to leave Pashir for Zessarix was a hectic one. Araxie was shut in his office, writing last minute letters, and so his son, Avmoshir, had taken the responsibility of directing the servants as he made sure the preparations were complete. Servants rushed in and out of Araxie's residence carrying scrolls, foodstuffs, bulging packs, and a variety of other items.

Victria couldn't help but notice the light of excitement in the young vashi's eyes. He glanced her way, caught her staring, and shrugged. "It's always a treat to go to the capital."

"Do you go often?"

"Every now and then,"

Victria was surprised. Avmoshir had been consistently silent around them the past two days, no doubt wary of their strangeness. Now, though, he spoke freely, as if they had known each other for years.

"My dad goes there a lot on business, but never stays and only takes me when there's something important he wants me to learn."

"I imagine there's much to learn in your people's capital. Why would he not just let you live there? I would think it would help you prepare for a role in leadership."

A servant approached Avmoshir with a bundle of food and, after inspecting it, the young vashi directed him to take it out to the front.

"You would think so," he said, turning back to her with his green eyes. "But dad says it's dangerous for us to live there. Too many enemies. Plus, he thinks city life might corrupt me."

Victria thought of Aleganthia. When it came to her own home, it was not her experience that it was particularly dangerous or corrupt. Granted, she had been there for the founding of it and with a leader like Felix, corruption had never really had a chance to take root. Perhaps the vashi were more like the humans in this.

"Tell me about Zessarix."

But Avmoshir was already shaking his head, though he flashed her a shy grin. "You have to see it for yourself. There's no describing it. Even for me, who has seen it dozens of times, it still takes my breath away. Dad would say the same."

Minutes later, Araxie emerged from his office and led them all outside where a small caravan of servants and tuna floated, waiting for them. Victria glanced at the tuna. She knew the vashi ate them because they had been served it several times during their stay. *These must be the lucky ones*, she thought. They were destined to bear the weight of the vashi's supplies like pack mules instead of being eaten.

"Are we all here?" Araxie asked, counting heads.

Victria looked around and noticed Tessa was not with them.

"Where is Tessa?"

Natiari turned to Madira, confused, "I thought she was with you."

Madira rolled her eyes. "She was. But then, while we were

walking down the street, she caught the eyes of a few vashi guards and told me to go on ahead."

"And you just left her there?" Victria asked bewildered.

"She can take care of herself," Madira shrugged. "Those vashi are no match."

"Madira," Serania stepped in close, her one visible eye bulging in disbelief. "We gave up our strength to be here, remember?"

Madira instantly paled.

"Where did you leave her?"

"By the fountains," she said, pointing a shaky finger toward the town center. "I left her by the fountains. How could I have forgotten?"

"We've been too relaxed here," Victria muttered more to herself than to Madira. "Come, we'll get her together."

"If there's a problem, I can send some of my guards as well," Araxie offered.

But before anyone could say anything else, Natiari pointed at a handful of approaching figures. "Is that—?"

"It is."

Walking toward them was Tessa in the middle of a small band of vashi, all of whom appeared to be struggling to keep their balance. They all wore massive grins on their faces and laughed loudly at every little thing that passed them by. Victria had a sneaking suspicion as to what had happened.

The vashi stopped a few yards away as Tessa stumbled the rest of the way toward her friends.

"Why, 'ello," she said as a fit of giggles overtook her. Victria had never seen her like this. Tessa was almost never open to strangers; always serious, even during lighthearted occasions. The only one she had ever really opened up to, as far as she knew, was herself and Natiari—and they had known each other for most of their lives.

"What happened?" she demanded

"Oh, nothing," Tessa cleared her throat. Victria could tell it was taking a lot of effort to make the words come out without a slur, but still they sounded heavy as they left her lips. "Those vashi gentlemen just offered to buy me some drinks so I decided to accept their offer. Figured we had some time to spare. Simple as that!"

"Was it an orange drink?" Avmoshir asked. "A little fizzy?"

Tessa pointed at him, eyes wide. "Yes! And it tasted like how flowers smell!"

Avmoshir grimaced. "Potent stuff."

"And you know this, how?" Araxie asked from behind, his arms crossed. Avmoshir paled.

"Well, I—"

"Since when do you accept drinks from strangers?" Natiari shook her head. "That's just reckless."

"Just thought I'd try something new, my apologies," Tessa muttered, not looking the least bit sorry.

"Regardless," Araxie said, drawing everyone's attention. "Now that we are all here, we must move out if we wish to reach Zessarix before nightfall."

The caravan set out on foot, passing the tall stone arches of Pashir. Once they were a few hundred meters away, they jumped lightly off the ground and began to swim to a higher depth. Victria couldn't help but let her eyes rove over the countless vibrantly colored coral that seemed to surround them wherever they went.

Before long, they came upon a large cave carved into a cliff that extended for miles in either direction. There was a small party of vashi sitting on the edge of the cave's mouth, playing a game with marked cubes made of bone. They stopped what they were doing and stood at attention as the caravan approached.

"We will need mounts for everyone in my retinue," Araxie said. He was not commanding but his voice held a natural air of authority over those who heard it.

"Right away, lord."

All but one of the mount wranglers broke away and swam into the cave. Moments later, they came out holding harnesses made of seaweed attached to a creature that both surprised and unnerved Victria. There, hovering peacefully behind the wrangler, was a giant manta ray. There were at least a dozen of them, one for each of them to ride, including the servants.

The manta rays were at least triple Victria's size and yet they did not appear aggressive. In fact, as she looked into the nearest one's eyes, it seemed to be studying her curiously. Its triangular pectoral fins flapped slowly, lazily, as it settled down around the members of the caravan.

"How do we ride these?" Tera asked, for once sounding uncertain.

"Do not fear," Araxie crawled onto the back of the closest manta ray and gripped the harness. "They're harmless. Just mount them like so—"

The other vashi mounted just as easily. Victria shrugged and tried climbing across the back of hers. It was as easy as Araxie had made it look. The manta kept still for her, keeping its fins straight across so it did not accidentally throw her off. Once she had gripped the harness and found a comfortable riding position, the manta began to flap its fins like wings, maintaining its depth.

Tessa had the hardest time mounting her ray, but with Serania's and Natiari's help she finally managed to find her way to the harness.

"Use your body to direct your mount," Araxie instructed. "Leaning left or right on your elbows will tell the manta which way to turn. Leaning forward will direct it to dive, leaning up, to rise."

"How do you make it stop?" Serania asked.

"Three swift pats on the head will tell the manta it's time to stop." With that, Araxie leaned up and to the right, leading their party to Zessarix. The mantas flapped their fins, twisting their bodies away from the cave. Once they were back in open water, they began picking up speed.

Victria would have never guessed such large creatures could move so quickly with so little movement, but the giant manta rays did. Her surroundings passed by almost in a blur and she couldn't help but grin to herself once she realized she was enjoying the ride. It was like what she imagined flying to be—but underwater.

The vashi servants formed a loose circle around them as they traveled. Victria thought this was rather defensive and wondered what could be considered a threat by the vashi. Even here, in a place as beautiful as this, she concluded, it would serve her well to remain vigilant. She could not afford to let herself relax and grow complacent.

They rode for hours and, unlike with horses, were no worse for wear. Before too long, Victria could make out shadowy clusters forming ahead. The water became clearer as they drew close and she could see that these clusters were buildings—of which there were many.

Zessarix stretched out for as far as the eye could see. Victria stared, her mouth as wide as her eyes as the blue and white city passed by underneath. Large, thick stalks of seaweed shot up high over the city like pillars, swaying back and forth

with the movement of the water. The mantas easily maneuvered around these stalks and descended toward an open
sand field in the city center.

Before the surrounding buildings could block her view
completely, Victria noticed a huge blue dome rise high above
the rest of the city. She had a feeling this was where they
were ultimately heading. It seemed an appropriate place to
house a government.

The mantas landed smoothly, just barely skimming the
sandy floor as they halted their momentum. The vashi
hopped off and attended to the tuna, which had followed
them faithfully the whole time. The viatari dismounted less
gracefully, Natiari and Madira tumbling off the side of their
mounts while Tera slowly crawled off hers.

A wrangler, keeping a guarded eye on the viatari, took
the harnesses of each manta, leading them to a nearby cave
where the other mounts were kept.

"Come," Araxie said, wasting no time on rest, "my servants
will take our belongings to my residence in the city. Avmoshir,
go with them and your mother and make sure everything
gets settled."

"But dad, I want to go to the Assembly!"

"No arguments, my son. I will take you another day. Right
now, I will have enough to handle with introducing our
guests."

Avmoshir looked crestfallen but did as he was told and
went with the servants. Araxie faced the viatari, his face
serious.

"The Assembly should be gathered by now. We will head
straight there, though I cannot promise you we will get much
done today aside from introductions."

They all nodded and followed him as he led them through

the city. There was little said, a cloud of tension having fallen around their small party. Araxie had made it sound as if the Assembly was an unreasonable or perhaps unpredictable entity. Victria wasn't the most skilled when it came to politics, Felix being the one who did the brunt of the work in that arena, but she had witnessed enough between the dwarves, the humans, and her own people to know what civil politics could look like. She had the impression this was not going to be the case with the Assembly.

The streets of Zessarix were made of marble and wound their way in many confusing directions between buildings. They would have easily lost their way had Araxie not been leading them.

As they exited yet another street crowded on both sides with residential buildings made of coral and marble, the water finally opened up around them and they saw the largest building they had yet encountered in this underwater world. It was the dome Victria had seen as they descended into the city. It was a colossal edifice, made entirely of marble. A wide, long ramp led up to the entrance, statues of several—Victria assumed—important vashi figures lining the flanks. The dome was held up by a series of fluted pillars and, as they passed under these pillars, the viatari couldn't help but gawk at the intricate detail and the amount of work that must have been put into building this. She wondered what Thuradin or any of the other dwarves might have thought of the craftsmanship, had they been here to see it.

They entered the Assembly Dome, as it was called, through a moss-covered archway, their bodies once again drying instantly once they passed over the threshold. Araxie continued to silently lead them. They passed paintings made of seaweed with vivid colors that Victria couldn't identify. There were also many representatives, or so she assumed, dressed in fine robes who openly gawked at them, whispering to each other as they passed. At one point they passed a statue of a massive beast which made Victria stop in her tracks.

It was serpentine in nature. The statue's mouth was open, revealing rows upon rows of dagger-like teeth as long as Victria's legs. A thin crest rose up from the beast's head and ran all the way down its spine to the very end of its tail. It also boasted a multitude of limbs that seemed to sprout from the side every foot or so, perfect for crawling on the ocean floor or swimming. Victria counted at least fifty sets of limbs.

"That is a saran," Araxie said after noticing Victria had lagged behind. "It is a legendary beast of mass terror. Not much is known about them as they're very rare. There have only been two confirmed sightings of a saran, though whether it was the same one we're not sure. They're extremely dangerous beasts. Not many who see them live to tell the tale. It is a monster of the ocean, said to even be able to devour the giant blue whale."

"A serpentine monster," Serania breathed, her one eye staring intently at the statue of the saran. "Makes me wonder if there's a connection between this thing and the stories of the monsters in Granian Lake."

Araxie gave them another moment to admire the fearsome creature but eventually had to urge them to move on with him. They did, and a few minutes later they stopped between two marble doors, with more ocean imagery etched into them. Two guards stood on either side at attention as Araxie approached.

The leader of the vashi turned to them, "Do not speak in the Assembly unless requested to. Only the vashi have the right to speak here at will." It looked like he wanted to say more but seemed to decide that was enough and motioned for the guards to let them in.

The heavy doors swung open, revealing a tiered arena with pairs or trios of finely dressed vashi sitting in giant clams that circled the room and went up as high as the ceiling. Victria was surprised to find that, while the halls leading up to this place and their subsequent rooms had been devoid of water, this room was filled with it. A massive upheaval of surprised hisses vibrated through the waters as the vashi representatives discussed amongst themselves the meaning of their arrival.

Araxie led them toward the back of the room, where there were a few coral benches that Victria perceived were for guests. The vashi leader indicated that they should sit in them and then made his way to a clam shell in the center of the room with a healthy plating of gold lining the edges. From a stand placed next to him, he drew a long, golden harpoon and struck the butt of the shaft against the floor three times, bringing the Assembly into silence.

"The Assembly will take their seatsss," a female vashi, with flowing yellow hair floated next to Araxie's seat and held a list before her as her voice rang out. "The Assembly callsss on Koranam, the representative from Kesmur, to resume hisss opening of debate from our last gathering."

From the middle tier of shells, swam a hulking vashi with waves of green hair. Unlike most vashi Victria had seen so far, this one was all one color: black. He looked powerful, his bulky limbs surging him forward to the assembly floor within a matter of seconds. He looked around the Assembly for a moment with vivid orange eyes before beginning.

"I thank the herald for calling on me to begin. But before

I do, I must ask the reason we are opening this Assembly in the disgusting tongue of the humans?"

There were loud hisses of approval from most of the vashi gathered. Araxie once again stood and hit the butt of his harpoon's shaft against the floor to regain control.

"As I'm sure you've noticed, Koranam, we have guests with us today," and now he spoke to the rest of the Assembly, "they are a race from the far north called the viatari and they have come to speak with us about a matter of great importance. They do not speak our language and we do not know theirs, yet we must understand each other. For this reason, we speak in the human tongue."

Koranam grunted but didn't press the matter, instead bringing his focus back to whatever debate had been started in the last Assembly.

"As the Supreme Overseer sees fit," he bowed. "My fellow vashi, I once again bring up the topic for debate of returning to a state of war with the humans—"

"Not this again!" Someone shouted from one of the higher tiers. There was an uproar as vashi factions took sides and began to argue with one another.

"Silence!" Araxie demanded, his voice booming through all the noise. "We will have order in this Assembly!"

The vashi representatives quieted down, looking sheepishly at their leader. Araxie turned to Koranam.

"Tell me, why do you return to this subject as a topic for debate?"

"I do apologize for the repetitiveness," the representative said without sounding apologetic at all. "But my reasons remain as clear and obvious as they've always been. The humans continue to fish in our waters, they encroach on our territories. They pollute our waters with their trash and waste. In addition, we have no business abandoning half the Sea of Scales and leaving it and the wildlife who live within its waters to the mercies of the humans. We are the protectors of this realm. Look what they have done with the half we ceded to them. It has disintegrated little by little and continues to do so. It pales in comparison to our beautiful reef when once it used to be just as beautiful. We must put an end to this travesty."

Another representative stood to speak. The herald, quick on her webbed feet, read from her scroll. "The Assembly recognizes the representative from Maleres, Varaxir, to speak."

"Thank you, madam herald," Varaxir said. "Koranam, you speak the same drivel but you forget, there is no winning against the humans. We tried in the past and look what happened, we lost the war and *were forced* to cede the upper part of the Sea of Scales. There can be no positive outcome from going to war with the humans. I am, however, interested in hearing what our Supreme Overseer has to say about these guests he has brought from the surface."

There were murmurs of approval from several of the other representatives. Araxie stood up to address them. "Koranam still has the floor, but I will tell you there is a grave threat, worse than humans I daresay," he looked pointedly at Koranam, "that could bring disaster to our world as we know it if we do not lend our aid."

There was a hushed silence as the Assembly took in the Supreme Overseer's words. "The viatari have told me of an ancient evil from the far north whose sole desire is to throw our world into chaos, a state which would include enslavement of our people, violence, destruction, death. It must not come to pass."

Koranam looked skeptically at the viatari. "And how is it

that you are taking them at their word. They are strangers to us."

"Strangers, yes," Araxie agreed. "But not deceivers. Had they come to deceive us, the waterseer's ceremony for transformation would have killed them rather than transform them, as you can see it has done."

Koranam took another look at the guests and his orange eyes widened with rage.

"Perhapsss my eyesss deceive me," he said, so full of rage that he could not properly control his speech as he had been doing. "But it appearsss to me that a human isss among them."

There were exclamations and shouts of rage as all attention shifted to Tera. Victria glanced at her and was unsurprised to see she was as calm as ever, she even let loose the briefest of waves before she crossed her arms and legs.

Araxie sighed. "Yes, one of their members is a human who guided them to us. She is no threat."

Koranam whirled around. "With respect, Sssupreme Overseer, *all* humans are a threat," he turned back to Tera and loomed over her, his sharp tongue sliding out of his mouth and licking his lips. "I want a world without them. Without your kind, human."

Tera did not rise to the challenge but instead remained seated, staring into Koranam's eyes as if to say "bring it on."

Koranam seemed to sense the same thing and put his face even closer until they were almost touching noses. "With my will I will ssset fire to your citiesss, drag your shipsss and men down to the depthsss of the Trench of Fear, drown your women and children until there are none of you vermin left. I vow to wipe your race from the face of thisss world and reclaim what is rightfully oursss."

Tera smiled openly, her eyes glinting dangerously. "What's stopping you, sweetie?"

CHAPTER SIXTEEN

Salevari was thankful there had been no new murders in the weeks that had gone by. It seemed to her that word of the slain guard had not spread either. As she looked out over the city from the Watcher's Quarter, though, she couldn't help but dwell on a feeling of bitter disappointment. So far, there had been no progress in the humans' investigation of the murder.

She thought back to a few days ago when Kent had suggested that perhaps the guard's death had been an accident, to which Salevari had wondered out loud if it would be considered an accident were she to stab him through the heart. The human chief had quickly dropped the idea, but such a claim had shown to Salevari how little effort the humans were putting into their "investigation," especially if they could not come up with a single lead in all this time.

"Am I taking the right course of action, First One, letting all these humans roam our city?"

Behind her, the translucent, white tendrils of The First One filled the room, shimmering as they flowed out.

"Difficult to say," his ancient voice echoed within the stone room. "Even I am not adept at predicting the future."

"But can you not sense any malice or evil intent in

them?"

The First One paused for a moment. "I sense nothing specific. There are strong feelings here and there, but none that would prove treacherous to you. Whoever it is you're worried about is hiding their feelings toward your people—and doing it well."

Salevari shook her head. Sometimes she wondered what use the acolyte served. The First One seemed to sense her thoughts.

"Were the human alone, or were there a multitude with the same feelings, I would be able to sense them and tell you who and where they were. As it is, there is such a sea of souls out there that to find any individual person with a specific hatred hidden in their heart proves difficult."

"I apologize," the Chancellor said, turning to the acolyte and dipping her head. "I did not mean to offend. I just cannot help but worry that I'm leading Felix's city into peril by bringing in what once was our most hated enemy. The time will come when they will outnumber us within the walls. What if they plan to fight us once they have gathered enough strength?"

"I would sense such a nefarious plot, were it true. You may rest assured, that there are no such feelings from a majority of these humans. Whoever is trying to sow discord, is doing it on their own or away from the prying eyes of the public."

"Should I continue as we are, then?" Salevari asked. "If you have some wisdom, I ask you to share it. Felix has not responded to my letter and I fear he may never do so if things in the Dwarven Kingdom are as bad as Borim suggested. I remain unsure of what to do."

The First One thought for a moment. "You have been

successful in your campaign to defend the human towns, have you not?"

"Yes. We've saved many towns and villages and most of the time the humans agree to come live in Aleganthia. Those who don't at least let us leave in peace. Though, we haven't been able to save every town as we used to ever since the Creature increased the size and frequency of his raids."

"The time will come when my brother will cease playing games and will attack the humans in full force with the intent to wipe them out. He sees them as a particular threat, especially were they to join our cause. If he believes the humans are valuable, I will believe it as well. My advice is to continue as you are. Bring them to our side. This world is theirs to defend as well. They have every right to fight alongside us, should they choose to do so."

Salevari nodded. The door to the Watcher's Quarter opened and one of the younger staff entered, her gaze downcast as she approached Salevari.

She gave a small curtsey before speaking, "The human, Simon, wishes to speak with you, madam. He waits for you outside on the stairs."

"Thank you," Salevari nodded encouragingly with an easy smile. The girl visibly relaxed and curtsied again before leaving.

The Chancellor moved to leave. "You will warn me if there is imminent danger, won't you?"

The Turned One's tendrils twitched as if shrugging. "I will do what I can, but remember I am spending most of my energy and focus these days on the mental probes I send out against my corrupted siblings. You may not be able to depend on my abilities for your sole use at this time."

"I understand." Salevari exited the room and almost

immediately came face to face with Simon. She tried her hand at the human tongue, which she had been practicing for the past few weeks.

"How you?"

Simon cracked a grim smile. "It's 'how *are* you.' Good try, though."

The Chancellor felt her face flush. She was no expert at Dwarvish either, but the human tongue was proving difficult for her to master. She switched back to Viatar.

"Why did you wish to see me?"

Simon glanced at the door behind her. "What lies behind this door? Your little messenger girl was quite adamant that I do not enter."

"Something I will introduce you to when the time is right. Come, walk with me."

Simon didn't seem too pleased with the deflection but he followed nonetheless. "My scouts have reported three attacks heading for the towns of Tur, Marlow, and Brewton at the same time."

The viatari pictured a map of the plainlands to their south. The three towns Simon had named were several miles away from each other and if they were attacked at the same time, the viatari wouldn't be able to focus on each one individually before moving to the next. No, they would need to raise the number of viatari defenders sent out.

"It seems the Creature has increased pressure again. No matter. We have plenty of viatari to fend off these attacks. Have they already been sent out?"

"Yes," Simon said, but there was something in his voice that hinted that he had more to say.

Salevari raised an eyebrow and looked at him. "Is there something wrong?"

"I just worry," the human said, meeting her eyes with his typical haughty expression. "Will your viatari be able to continue to match the Creature's forces? My scouts tell me the demons' numbers grow with each raid."

"We cannot guarantee victory in every battle," Salevari shrugged. "But so long as they remain raiding parties and not a full army, my warriors will pull through. However, if these raids grow too difficult, I will send out lyruun riders to help, which should bring the tide of battle back in our favor."

Simon nodded. "Very well. I will trust you—for now."

"And I, you."

Simon was tricky, manipulative, too clever for his own good. Still, Salevari could not help but respect his natural leadership abilities and his crafty tongue. Perhaps, if trust truly grew between them, a real bond could be made, bringing their two races together and ending the centuries of fighting they had endured.

They reached the ground floor of the keep. At the bottom of the stairs watching her was Zael. The meaning in his eyes was clear. He needed to speak with her. Alone.

"Now, Simon," Salevari said, trying to dismiss the human as smoothly as she could without having him raise any questions. "I have a prior engagement I must attend to. Keep me updated on your scouts' movements and I will do the same for you."

Simon glanced between Zael and her. With some suspicion in his eyes, he bowed.

"As you wish."

He continued down the stairs, passing Zael who he eyed before walking on and out of the keep. Salevari made her way to the captain, who did not say a word until she was right next to him.

"I want to show you something." He turned without another word and walked out into Aleganthia's streets. Salevari followed close behind. They said nothing as they walked toward the human quarter of the city and no one they passed paid them any mind. Salevari was about to question where Zael was taking her when they turned left into one of the few inns Aleganthia had to offer, *Nomad's Hut.*

It was dark inside, but that didn't keep her from quickly registering that there were both viatari and human patrons within the *Hut.* Viatari guards were here as well, most likely keeping watch over the humans as per her orders—since they were outside of the human quarter. She had to admit, she was surprised the humans would come to a viatari inn for their drinks and meals rather than establish their own.

The two viatari walked straight to the bar where the innkeeper was busy opening a fresh bottle of wine.

"Busy day, Valar?" Zael asked.

The innkeeper grunted. "Had to hire new help with the influx of humans—have to try to cook to their tastes now. Luckily, most of them like their meats on the rare side. What can I do for you two?"

"Just a plate of rabbits, please."

Valar rapped the bar with his knuckles and relayed the order back to the kitchen. "It'll be out in a few minutes. Sit wherever you like and let me know if you need anything else."

They chose a table nestled in the corner of the inn and sat down.

"Is this what you brought me to see?" Salevari asked, keeping her eyes on the humans. "Humans mixing in with viatari?"

"Yes, for two reasons," Zael said quietly. "It is a good sign, first of all, because it tells me that there are at least some humans who are not afraid of us and who are willing to live and work with us."

"And the bad?"

"It's a security risk. Any human with ill-will toward us could easily make his way through our city at his leisure and strike whenever and wherever he pleased. I don't know which humans we can really trust."

Salevari understood his point. Even now, after weeks of working with Kent and Simon, she wasn't entirely sure if she completely trusted them, though she claimed otherwise. And she was sure the feeling was mutual.

One of the barmaids, a tall viatari with curly, silver hair came up to their table and placed a platter of live rabbits between them as well as a bottle of wine and two glasses.

"Enjoy!"

Salevari grabbed one of the rabbits, which squealed in fear as she bared her fangs. She bit into it, sucking out its life-energies. She felt a rush through her body as they mixed in and added to her own. By the time the rabbit was a dry husk, there was an earthy aftertaste within her which she let sit for a while before washing it down with some wine.

She glanced at Zael as he finished his own rabbit. He caught her gaze and seemed to read her thoughts.

"You wish to ask about the investigation."

"Yes, but that can wait. This isn't the place."

"On the contrary," Zael said, reaching for a second rabbit. "This is the perfect place. With all the drinking and eating, no one will notice us. And the humans have yet to learn our language. So, as long as we only speak in Viatar we have nothing to worry about from them."

"How can you be sure of that? They've been here for weeks now. I would think at least some of them should have learned Viatar by now."

Zael shook his head and laughed scornfully. "Humans. Because we speak their language so well, they don't see the need to learn ours, so they don't. That is something I've learned recently."

Salevari frowned, but if anyone knew the humans at this point it was Zael. She would trust his judgement.

"Very well, then. Have you discovered anything?"

Zael shook his head. "Nothing concrete. There are whispers. Rumors. The murder of one of our guards hasn't been proclaimed throughout the streets of the human quarter—probably due to Simon and Kent publicly running their own investigation. But there are some who have heard something about a planned attack. There's supposed to be a meeting tomorrow to address these rumors. I intend on going."

"Good. You should bring a guard with you—in human disguise, of course—just in case there's trouble. Better there are two of you than just one."

"I will be fine on my own," Zael licked his lips and threw away another emaciated rabbit. "Besides, a sudden stranger among them would bring some suspicion. It's taken me some time to gain the trust of the humans I've been talking to."

Salevari frowned. She didn't like the idea of Zael going alone. But he knew best in this case. Again, she would have to trust that the young captain knew what he was doing.

"Very well, just be cautious. Don't do anything that might give you away."

She finished the last rabbit and they stood to leave, leaving behind a few silver coins for the food and service.

They made their way back to the keep, Zael parting ways with her after a few blocks to return to his living quarters. The next time they met, he promised, he should have some more information to give her.

Salevari watched him go, hoping he was right. There was one thing she was certain of, and that was that she would not be able to hide the fact that a viatari was murdered within Aleganthia's walls forever. Someone would find out eventually, and she had to have the culprit in custody by the time that happened.

She resumed walking toward the keep but had only taken a few steps when she heard someone calling for her.

"Salevari Mistguide?"

She turned around, hand on her sword, ready to defend herself, but saw it was only one of the city guards. She relaxed.

"Yes, can I help you?"

"I think so," the guard said. "My name is Aleir. I am currently stationed on Aleganthia's southern wall."

"You do important work keeping watch for us all," Salevari said. "Are there extra supplies you're needing?"

"Well, no, madam, we're well-provisioned," Aleir said. Salevari sensed he was rather nervous to be around her. "What I wanted to know was if you have access to guard records—where all of us are stationed and all that—being in charge of the city as you are."

"I do," the Chancellor replied, a feeling of dread reaching into her heart and making it beat faster. "Is there someone you need to know about?"

"Yes!" Aleir jumped at the question. "I need to know where Loran Nusol is stationed. He was stationed as city patrol, but I haven't seen him in weeks. I was wondering if perhaps he had been reassigned somewhere else."

Salevari's blood froze. It felt as if ice were slowly creeping up from the bottom of her feet to her head. Loran Nusol was the name of the guard the humans had murdered. The one she had burned in the forest, leaving nothing but charred bones buried deep with his ashes to make it seem like he had never existed.

Several seconds passed in which the guard looked expectantly at her. Finally, she found her voice. "And why are you asking for Loran, exactly?"

"Oh," Aleir shrugged. "We've been friends for a long time, since childhood, in fact. I just found it strange that he would have been reassigned without giving me word first, so it had me wondering. . . ."

The guard's voice faded as he noticed the look on Salevari's face.

"Is something wrong, Chancellor?"

"I'm sorry," was all she could say before turning and quickly making her way back to the keep.

"You're sorry?" The guard ran to catch up with her. "Why are you sorry? Has something happened to him?"

Salevari would not meet his eyes. She felt sympathy for him, felt terrible for keeping the fate of his friend from him, but she couldn't reveal what had happened. Not now. She had to maintain the secret or she risked losing control of the situation.

"I cannot tell you where he is right now. I suggest you go back to your station, Aleir. When I can tell you something I will summon you."

The guard stopped in his tracks and she pushed on, reaching the steps leading into the keep before he called to her one last time.

"What has happened to Loran, Chancellor?"

She did not answer, did not stop walking, did not turn around, but went straight through the keep's doors and up the stairs to her makeshift throne room. Once inside, she slumped into her chair, her head drooping into her hands. She closed her eyes, trying to think, but no clever ideas came to mind.

This proved beyond a doubt that she would not be able to hide the death of one of her own forever. In fact, it looked like the incident would be discovered sooner rather than later if Aleir continued digging for the truth. Her only hope was to catch the murderer in time, so she had something to show the people when Loran's terrible fate was discovered. Her only hope rested with Zael.

She sat up straight, regaining her composure, her eyes landing on a portrait of her brother hanging on the wall across from her. In it, Felix had his calm, calculating expression. He looked capable, confident. Well, so was she. She was as much of a leader as Felix and then some. She had led Dalyr through some of its most trying times and had come out of it triumphant. She would lead Aleganthia just the same, no matter the cost.

CHAPTER SEVENTEEN

Zael Windkeeper woke with a start. The dim light of dawn crept into his room through open windows. But it wasn't the light that had woken him. Nor was it from any noise outside. As far as he could tell, the only thing he could hear from the streets below were the shuffling steps of a few passersby. The day had not yet begun for much of the city.

No, he felt it was a dream that had woken him. What that dream was, though, eluded him. However, he couldn't shake the feeling that it had something to do with his past—with the Rauans. He shook his head. Now *that* was a topic he did not want to think about. Too many bad memories. Too much bad blood . . . the sole reason he had been left orphaned in this world. The Rauans had once been family friends of his parents. They had known each other for centuries, had suffered through much together before and during the war with the Creature. And yet, when his family had needed them most, the cowards had saved their own skin, abandoning Zael and his family, leaving them to die. Zael had survived, but only through the sacrifice his parents had made for him.

He shook his head. He didn't want to dwell on those times. He didn't want to waste any time thinking of the traitorous Rauans. It was not often that he did. He tried to keep his eyes forward at all times, in the present—as well as his mind.

He pushed himself out of bed, fighting the urge to keep sleeping. He had work to do today, and people—particularly Salevari—depending on him to pull through. He grabbed one of the many meandering chickens in his room and bit into it, a rush of new energy flowing through his body as he consumed the chicken's life-energies. He tossed the animal's remains into the chute built into the side wall of his room where it would be sent into the collective compost heap used to help the few viatari farmers working outside the walls.

He grabbed a sword rather than the dirk he usually wore on his belt. He would be going into the human quarter today disguised as one of them. It would do no good if he blew his cover right away by wearing a viatari's weapon.

Not needing anything else, he left his room, exited the communal building he lived in, and made his way to the human quarter. He lived a few blocks from that part of the city, which would give him plenty of time to plan as he walked.

With any luck, this would be the last day he would have to pretend to be human. What he had heard about this coming meeting had been promising. It had been sold to him as a chance for change in the city. He had a suspicion on what that change could be, especially if the one enacting such change was their murderer. If they revealed themselves at this meeting, he would have everything he needed to go back to Salevari so that she could have them arrested. Then, there would be justice.

But he couldn't get ahead of himself. First, he had to attend this assembly without rousing suspicion.

Over the past few weeks he had done well in making himself known to the humans. He was known to them as "Kurt," and his sudden presence had not been questioned as an almost daily influx of new refugees meant there were now many strangers living here. He had made some quick friendships—at least, in human terms—particularly with a man named Garrel. It was he who had mentioned the meeting to Zael. They were to meet by the western wall and then head to the place where the meeting was to be held.

Approaching the human quarter of the city, Zael nonchalantly took cover in one of the city's many alleys and changed into his human form. When he emerged from the alley, his long hair was now blonde, he had flat teeth like the humans, and his eyes were gray. He saw his reflection in a store window and shook his head in disgust.

So far, Salevari's plan for him to spy on the humans like this had proven to be sound. She was a good, natural leader—one he had come to respect. He was still wary of becoming her pet, as Drathanar was, but even he had to admit that he liked her leadership and enjoyed serving under her. He trusted she would lead them through these troubling times well. Still, he could not help but hate the fact that this mission forced him to don his human illusion too often and for such long periods of time.

As he made his way through the streets, the sun had risen high enough to wake the rest of the city. More people were out now, especially humans, and some called out to him as he passed.

"'Ello Kurt!"

"We missed you last night, Kurt!"

"Blimey, you look tired, Kurt, have you been out all night?"

Zael responded to these calls as well as he knew how, often resorting to a simple shrug or nod. He was well-known among the humans as a serious, non-talkative type so he figured such a response shouldn't turn too many heads.

Garrel waved as Zael approached, his bushy red hair helping him stand out against the white stones he leaned against.

"Morning, Kurt. Rough night?"

Zael shrugged. "Why do you ask?"

"You just look like you could use some sleep."

"Bad dreams, I guess. So, when does this meeting take place?"

Garrel laughed. "Ah, always down to business. It should be starting soon. Let's go. The house that's hosting it is nearby."

They walked in silence the entire way. Zael wasn't sure how he felt about Garrel. The young human seemed nice enough, but it was also him who had tipped Zael off about this meeting. Though, Zael knew, it was always possible he had read too much into the human's meaning for "change." Garrel hadn't mentioned any specifics about what this meeting was about and, Zael thought, it was likely because he didn't know the details himself.

They stopped outside of an unassuming house at the very edge of the city. Zael had to admit, if the subject matter of this meeting was what he suspected, the humans leading it were quite brave to hold it in a place so close to the wall where viatari guards regularly patrolled.

Garrel knocked, and a voice bellowed from inside.

"Name?"

"Garrel and Kurt."

"The sun rises,"

"And winter is on the horizon," Garrel responded without hesitation.

The door opened and they were quickly ushered in. Zael blinked, helping his eyes adjust to the dark room. All the windows were covered and the only sources of light were a few candles. He saw several faces he recognized from the streets as well as many he did not. It was quiet here, only a few mutterings and whispers reaching the viatari's ears.

Several tables and chairs had been set up as well as a stage in the back of the room. Garrel led him to a center table where they took a seat.

"I'm suddenly nervous," Garrel muttered.

"Why is that?"

"I don't know. What if the viatari catch us?"

Zael raised an eyebrow. "Are we doing something that the viatari should be worried about? I thought the purpose of this meeting was to make changes in the city."

"That's what I was told." Garrel shivered. "Still, I feel like they're always watching, waiting for the chance to pounce on us. Just nerves, I guess."

Zael nodded, trying to refrain from smiling. Oh yes, the viatari were watching. And he was their eyes and ears.

The low buzz of conversation ended abruptly as a seemingly normal couple entered from an adjacent room and took the stage. The man was grizzled, with a scraggly beard and bushy brown hair. His eyes were hardened, but he looked out at the group of gathered humans with an air of satisfaction and gratitude. The woman had short, jet-black hair that barely reached her shoulders. It was tied back tightly into a bun that stretched her already tight face even further. She was cunning, that much Zael could tell from her eyes, and more than physically fit to partake in battle. Lithe, too. Good traits for an assassin.

The woman was the one to begin the meeting.

"Good morning, everyone. My name is Lyna and this is my husband, Anders. First of all, we'd like to welcome you all to our home and to thank you for coming even if it's just to hear what we have to say. We know you're busy with your own lives trying to survive in this new world so it really means a lot to us that you, too, want to make some changes for the betterment of our lives here."

Zael frowned. So far, Lyna sounded amiable, and he feared that this meeting might be a waste of his time after all. If the humans wanted to make some changes in their part of the city to make themselves more comfortable, that was not really his business. It certainly wasn't nefarious.

Now Anders was the one speaking, "We also know that many of us come from different towns, and so it might seem strange at first to work together, but we're all human first— let's remember that. And that should unify us in working to free ourselves from the viatari."

Low murmurs came from the crowd at the mention of the viatari. Zael's doubts vanished and now he listened with rapt attention.

"We believe, my wife and I," Anders continued. "That our leaders have grown soft with recent events, that this softness has led them to seek the aid of our most hated enemy, an enemy we can never and should never forgive. It's become clear to us that petitioning them to take us out of this pact we have been forced into with the viatari would be pointless. We must put in the work ourselves if we wish to be free again."

"What makes you think we're not free?" A voice from the crowd asked.

"There are guards everywhere," Lyna spat out the words as if they were venom. "Always watching us, always patrolling near our part of the city, no doubt ready to take action against us. I wouldn't be surprised if they had some agents hiding among our homes to keep an even closer eye on our activities. This is a prison, not a haven."

How quickly they forget that this is our city first, Zael mused. He was glad he had come. It was clear now that these two humans were trying to create some sort of uprising—to what end, he did not know yet, only that it was to rebel against the viatari. But that did not necessarily make them the assassins he was looking for.

"Why not ask the viatari to give us more freedoms?" Garrel asked, bringing Zael's attention back to the present. "It worked last time when Simon did it."

"Can you really trust the viatari to keep their word? Do you truly believe they've stopped watching us as Simon promised?" Anders asked. "I don't. Not for a second. None of you should. We have, all of us, felt their evil in our lives at one point or another. They've killed our sons, our brothers, our families. We should all, for at least one reason or another, harbor some ill-will toward these monsters."

"Which is why we called you here," Lyna placed a hand on her husband's chest, as if to calm him down. The faintest smile traced his lips and he let her have the stage. Clearly, as Zael had suspected, she was the clever one, the mastermind behind whatever was being presented.

"Some of you might be comfortable as you are, and that's fine. When this meeting is over you are free to leave and carry on as you were. We only ask that you not speak a word of what happened within these walls. We cannot risk the viatari discovering what we have planned. It would endanger the lives of everyone living in the city if they did. But those of you who feel as we do, we wish you to join us as we work to destroy the viatari from within."

There was a series of chuckles from one table. A beefy man with very little hair stood up. "How do ya plan on doin' that, then?"

Lyna beamed confidently. "It might not seem possible because of their strength and agility, but our leaders have unwittingly given us the perfect opportunity to destroy the viatari once and for all by bringing us into their city. We will weaken them and demoralize them with assassinations, sabotage, whatever we can do to cause damage. With a continuous influx of refugees, our numbers will continue to grow. And once we have enough brave souls fighting for the cause, we can take out their leader—this Salevari Mistguide—who keeps us imprisoned within her city with one swift stroke."

There was a heavy silence as the gravity of what was being conspired sunk in. But it did not seem to put off most of the people here. In fact, a lot of them were nodding their heads in agreement. Zael glanced at Garrel to see where he might stand. The young man's eyes were wide. He looked conflicted, but clearly not enough to have him turn away from the meeting. A few people did though, and Zael watched them leave, making a note of their faces so he could remember which humans were the good ones.

"Why should we risk our lives with this foolishness?" One woman asked. "Even if we could carry them out—which I don't believe we can—what will a couple of assassinations do, except anger them. Anyone who has fought the viatari like I have knows how much stronger and faster they are than us. Plus, with their regenerative abilities . . . what chance do we have?"

A crazed smile spread across Lyna's face as she replied, this time with more venom in her words. "The assassinations we carry out will not just be on random targets—though that is where we will begin. We have a list of important viatari within the city who we aim to take out, with our most important target being Salevari herself. We will need training and practice before we can carry something like this out, true, but it can be done."

Zael's skin crawled. Anger built up inside him as he realized where this conversation was leading to.

"How do you know it can be done?"

Anders and Lyna looked at each other triumphantly.

"Because we've already done it!"

There was another series of murmurs, this time more excited. Anders stepped forward, a dagger in his hand which he thrust outward to present to the crowd.

"A few weeks ago, we created a new paralytic poison that not only paralyzes the viatari, but also disables their regenerative abilities, making them as easy to kill as you or me. We tested the poison out ourselves on two viatari guards, who we killed. One in the city, and one by the edge of the forest surrounding us. That's two fewer guards we have to worry about."

Zael wished he could unleash his rage and kill everyone then and there, but he bit back his anger, allowing a bitter sense of satisfaction to come over him that this had not been a wasted trip. He had found the assassin—worse, assassins—and their sinister plot to topple the viatari. He would also have to tell Salevari that there had been another murder that so far remained undiscovered.

"The best part is," Lyna said, her voice high-pitched with

excitement and elation. "The viatari don't even know. If they had discovered what we'd done, we're positive there would have been some word of it already, some alarm raised or a heavier watch put against us. But nothing has happened since we killed those two guards. Our goals are attainable, friends, we just need more help—"

"—so we can regain our freedom!" Anders voice boomed through the house and the crowd cheered. They were all in. They were ready to join, ready to kill the viatari, to end their reign of terror, to win their freedom.

Again, Zael had to bite back his anger and keep his face passive. He had to relay all of this information to Salevari without tipping the humans off that he was not with them. He relaxed his face, flashing a grin at Garrel who was clapping along with the crowd, though still uncertainly.

"Just one question," Zael said it rather quietly, yet it pierced through the din, silencing everyone as they turned to listen to "Kurt," who so rarely spoke.

"This is obviously a dangerous ordeal, and there are bound to be some failures along the way. So what happens when one of us gets caught in the act and taken by the viatari? How can we be sure that the viatari won't discover this plan?"

"An excellent question," Lyna nodded approvingly. "And something that we will now address. You all must understand how serious and important our task is, and the most vital factor in it will be secrecy. No one outside this house can know of what we're doing. Understand that if anyone is caught by the viatari, we cannot save you. You must die with dignity."

"Yes," Anders agreed gruffly. "As my beautiful wife says, it will be the greatest honor to die in this, our quest for freedom. The stakes are just as high for us as they will be for you. But if fate chooses that you must die for this cause, die knowing that the rest of us will carry on. We will continue the fight and avenge your death with our inevitable victory!"

"Thank you for your question, Kurt," Lyna said, dazzling him with a bright smile.

He grinned back, wishing he could give up his human illusion and bring forth his fangs just to tear through her throat.

"That's all I needed to know."

CHAPTER EIGHTEEN

"Does your incompetency know no bounds?"

Salevari leered down at the two humans before her as she sat in her now-elevated makeshift throne. Simon and Kent glanced at each other, unsure as to why they were being greeted with this question.

"What is the meaning behind this question?" Simon asked.

"It has become apparent to me," Salevari seethed. "That whatever investigation you say you are conducting to unveil the murderers in this city either has very little to no effort being put into it, or is being led so incompetently that no results shall ever come from it. I choose to believe the latter rather than the former, as I'm sure you would not dare tell me you are investigating these murders and then simply choose not to do it."

Kent spoke, and Simon translated. "He says our investigation has been underway for many weeks now. Just because we have no results yet doesn't mean any fault on our part. He says it is unfair for you to accuse us like this without waiting for the investigation to end."

"Your 'investigation' need not continue," Salevari said with a note of finality. "I have discovered what you could not in the same amount of time."

Simon's eyes bulged. "You've continued spying on us?"

"Yes," Salevari didn't hesitate to admit it. She would not be rebuked for her actions when the results had proven invaluable. "And it's a good thing I did, or we would all still be in the dark and in danger. Tell me, Kent, what are your impressions of the humans named Lyna and Anders?"

Kent thought for a moment, then shrugged.

"They're hard-working people," Simon translated. "Always kept their heads down around him. But they're not murderers. They never quarreled with any of their neighbors."

"Maybe they're not murderers when it comes to humans," Salevari closed her eyes briefly, wondering how much information she should divulge. She still wasn't sure she could completely trust Simon or Kent, but if she wanted to obtain what she needed to counter the attack Zael had warned her about, she would need their help.

"My agent discovered that a meeting was to be held at their house and attended it. During this meeting, he has told me, it was admitted by Lyna and Anders themselves that they had murdered not one but two viatari guards with a new poison that paralyzes both our bodies and regenerative abilities. They intend to conduct more assassinations, with me as their main target. They are currently recruiting those of you who might feel opposed to the fact that they live peacefully among the viatari to join them so that they can—as my agent said they put it—destroy us from the inside."

"If what you say is true, we can look into it," Simon said, though he still looked displeased. "We will take Lyna and Anders into our custody and question them ourselves and put a stop to this little uprising."

Kent added to that, and Simon nodded in agreement.

"Kent says he hopes you understand that Lyna and Anders do not represent us as a people and they will be punished."

Salevari shook her head. "You will do no such thing."

Simon's eyes narrowed. Kent looked between them, confused and concerned.

"What do you mean?"

"If you barge into their house and arrest them and question them about this rebellion, which is supposed to be a secret, even from you two, then not only will you fail to destroy the movement—as I'm sure it would be continued by others—but you also risk exposing my agent. It is the same reason why I do not just send my guards into their home to kill everyone who was involved in that meeting. We would only make them martyrs."

Simon relayed everything to Kent, who grunted and shook his head, clearly troubled.

"What are we to do then? And who is this agent of yours?"

"That is none of your concern," Salevari waved her hand dismissively. "Needless to say, I had him and a discreet group of viatari go out to collect the body of the second guard who we discovered had been slain. As for what to do," she sat back in her chair and crossed her legs, a wicked smile playing on her lips. "We let these meetings continue. Let Anders and Lyna recruit. My agent will remain embedded within their organization and he will keep us updated on any attacks that are planned out. If we know what's coming against us, we can avoid or counter it."

"But that won't stop them," Simon said, his eyes still uncertain, trying to understand what the viatari was thinking. "You risk your people falling to their blades if you let these dissenters grow and operate."

"They will not operate forever," Salevari held up a finger. "We cannot wipe them out right now because it would make them martyrs, as I said. The only other option, then, is to wait for them to attack us first—that way it looks like self-defense when we destroy them."

Simon blinked several times as the words sunk in. "So, you intend to kill them all."

Salevari's eyes flashed dangerously. "Very good, you are coming to understand my plan. We cannot allow these humans to continue living in our city if they hate us so much. It will cause problems between the viatari and humans who *do* want to live and work together against the greater evil. Do you not agree?"

"Yes, but—"

"Would you rather I imprison them? Exile them? Don't think my first option was to kill them. But if I choose to imprison or exile them, they would still have the ability to incite hatred against my people. They would still have the chance of being seen as martyrs. They must be cut down to the last man, but only in self-defense."

Simon hesitated, then translated all that had been said for Kent. The human leader took a breath and paused for a moment but eventually nodded, though it visibly pained him to do so.

"He agrees with you," Simon said, distaste in his voice. "He says if this is our only option for us to continue having a working relationship with your people, he will allow it to happen. Personally, I still think there must be another way—though, he doesn't care what I think."

"When it comes to this particular matter," Salevari said. "Neither do I."

The two humans bowed and began walking away but

Salevari called out to them once more.

"Simon, there is one more thing I must ask of you."

Simon turned around with a skeptical look, sarcasm dripping with his every word. "How can I be of service?"

"I agree with you that allowing these operations to continue does put the lives of my people, and the relationship between our two races, at some risk. While we have the advantage of foresight with my agent in place, the poison they are using has proven quite potent. I know, as do all viatari, that humans are masters when it comes to creating poisons as well as antidotes."

"You want to know if there is an antidote for this particular strain." Simon finished the Chancellor's thoughts.

Salevari nodded. "Would you be willing to provide us with one?"

Simon hesitated. "I don't know that I can give you such a thing."

The Chancellor frowned. "Is it because you don't know what the antidote is or do you simply refuse to share human secrets with the viatari? Is your fear, perhaps, that if you give us this antidote, it will make us impossible for you humans to kill?"

"I just don't think—" Simon began to say, but he never finished his thought. Instead, he regarded Salevari with a small frown, and she knew she was correct in her assumption.

"Ah, Simon, if you humans work and fight with us in this war against The Turned One and the Creature, do you really think we will go back to how we were before? Do you really believe that nothing will change, that your people as well as mine will not come to realize that we work well together? Is there still no trust?"

Simon was clever, Salevari knew. Perhaps in the beginning,

he had thought there might be a way to take advantage of the viatari's hospitality just as Anders and Lyna were now doing, but she didn't think he was that kind of adversary anymore. If anything, ever since Halshire had been saved, and he was once again accepted by his people, he had become much more willing to help the viatari with their needs.

The human closed his eyes, conflicted, but nodded. "You are correct, Chancellor, in all you say. I, however, remain unsure whether granting your people this antidote is the best move for all of us. Still, you must believe me when I say that Kent and I intend on helping you oust those among us who still wish to destroy your people. I just . . . I need some time to think on your request."

Salevari shrugged. It was better than nothing, she supposed. "Very well, just make sure not to think too long. I wouldn't want—"

Just then, the doors burst open and a viatari scout ran in, breathless, a wild look in his eyes. Those eyes landed on Salevari, and he ran to her, brushing past the humans without noticing them.

"Chancellor," the viatari bowed low.

"What is it, has something happened?" Salevari asked, though she could tell by the scout's face that such a question was unnecessary. Her heart began to race.

"Reports from the three defense parties we sent out recently have come in," the scout said, his voice trembling. "The darimun attacks on all three towns were successfully repelled. The citizens of Brewton and Marlow have agreed to come under our protection, but Tur—"

The scout's voice broke and he seemed to be at a loss for words. Salevari's patience was already thin. Now she stood up, her face livid as she feared the worse.

"What is it? Speak!" she snapped. "What has happened in Tur?"

"We—after repelling the darimun, the humans turned on our forces and—and killed them. They killed them all."

Simon paled to such an extreme that he could have been mistaken for a ghost. He relayed what had just happened in the human language. Kent closed his eyes, running his hands through his hair anxiously.

"They killed them all," Salevari repeated, her voice hollow. "What of the human speaker sent with them? What happened to him? He was supposed to ensure their safety."

"He still lives," The scout spat out the words in disgust. "Though, he was wounded in the battle that ensued. He says the humans attacked before he could stop them. Our forces defended themselves, but there were too few to fight off the whole town. The speaker fled after receiving his wound. It is from him that I heard this news. There are also reports from other scouts in the area that say a second pack of darimun is moving to attack Tur again."

A deadly calm came over Salevari's mind and she knew what had to be done. She had feared this would happen eventually. Now it was time for humans—all humans—to learn who the greater enemy was, the viatari or the darimun, and to decide which side they wanted to be on. She would send them a message they would not forget.

"How many darimun?"

"At least thirty."

"Good. Gather our warriors. I want one hundred of our best fighters ready to move out within the hour. We march for Tur."

"Yes, my lady!" The scout ran off to do her bidding. Once he was gone, Simon and Kent approached Salevari, shaken by the news.

Kent asked something softly. Salevari did not need to speak the human tongue well to know that he was giving his condolences. She nodded her head in thanks. She didn't blame Kent for this betrayal, nor humans in general. But that wouldn't stop her from carrying out her plan of action to ensure this never happened again.

"Do you intend on attacking the town in revenge?" Simon asked.

Salevari chuckled, though there was no humor in it. "I am not so simple. I have a better idea in mind."

Kent muttered something. Salevari's grasp of the human language was enough now for her to understand that he, too, was asking for her to spare the town.

"I assure you, I will do nothing to Tur," she said again. "But I cannot allow this betrayal to go unpunished. The remaining towns and villages in the plains must learn what will happen if they attack us after having defended them from the darimun. I expect both of you to ride out with me."

"Of course," Simon said, still worried. He shared a glance with Kent but the two said nothing more and left the room to prepare for the journey.

Salevari sank back into her seat, letting out the breath she had been holding in. With it she let the mask fall and threw her face into her hands, her mind blank except for the faces of those viatari she had sent to their deaths.

Tur was relatively close to Aleganthia. It took only a day for them to catch sight of it. As they marched, Salevari saw a few small hills to their left. They would provide a good vantage point for her to overlook the area surrounding Tur. It would also give the townspeople the opportunity to see her with her forces.

She led her warriors up the hill, where they stood glaring down at the town. The humans had not yet noticed them. They were still going about their own business, making repairs on the sections of wooden palisade and buildings that had been destroyed by the recent darimun attack.

A series of disgusted murmurings rippled between the viatari ranks. Some of them pointed at the town's gates, where fifteen stakes rose up out of the ground. Nailed to these stakes were the bloody, dismembered remains of those who had originally been sent to protect the town from the Creature's attack.

Salevari clenched her jaw. The anger she had been holding in rose to a boiling point once more. Simon and Kent sat on their mounts and peered her way nervously.

The Chancellor tore her gaze away from the stakes and scanned the surrounding flatlands, which made up much of the region here. In the distance, south of Tur, she saw a cloud of dust. She had no doubt what might be causing it.

"The darimun are coming. Let us see how long it takes for the humans to notice."

It did not take long. Within a minute, alarm bells were ringing throughout Tur and there was a swarm of activity within the streets as guards formed up and manned the walls. Screams of terror could be heard as civilians ran for the town center, seeking protection.

At this point, several of the townspeople noticed the small host of viatari warriors standing on the northern hills, still as statues. They pointed, catching the attention of some of the guards. The guards hesitated, then beckoned desperately for the viatari to enter their town.

"I think they're calling for us to help them," Simon noted.

Salevari glanced at him. "Indeed."

As some of the humans continued waving for the viatari to come help them, the first line of darimun crashed into the town's palisade, easily knocking down the recently repaired sections of the wall. Men went flying as the second wave crashed into them, only to fall directly into the maws of the Creature's servants.

The screams within the town took on a new fear as the darimun, unchecked, ravaged through the small garrison as if they were nothing. They smashed into buildings and toppled over braziers, setting fire to others. Some civilians who hadn't made it to the town center tried to run away but the darimun quickly caught them and tore them apart.

The remaining guards now cried out desperately, opening their northern gate for the viatari to enter. Some fell onto their knees like beggars. Still, Salevari did not give the order to attack.

Simon and Kent, white as snow, looked on in horror as the town of Tur was utterly devastated. The town center soon fell, its bell tower toppling over to the side as the roof caved in. Some of the darimun rummaged through the rubble, digging out the humans within only to devour them.

Those few guards who had been asking the viatari for aid finally abandoned their hope and turned to meet their fate. They didn't even bother to defend themselves as the darimun pounced on them.

Salevari looked on with cold eyes as the last of their pitiful screams died out. The darimun continued their rampage, destroying building after building until there was nothing but ash and debris. They smelled the viatari, and a few moved forward as if to attack, but sensing their opponent

was too large a force for them, they regrouped and moved
eastward toward the Silent Mountains.

A chilled wind swept through the viatari ranks, all of
them looking on with the same pitiless expression that the
Chancellor had. Kent leaned over to the side of his horse
and vomited. Simon stared in disbelief. Crows circled overhead.

Without a word, Salevari veered her horse around and
made her way down the hill, her warriors following her.
They were returning home. For several minutes, only Simon
and Kent stayed behind, paralyzed by the terribleness of
what they had just witnessed. Finally, they too turned their
mounts around and followed the viatari, their faces stricken
with grief. Smoke from the ruins of Tur rose high into the
bright, blue sky, mixing in with wisps of white cloud, and
eventually blown out of existence by a strong gust of wind.

CHAPTER NINETEEN

Dunkell, Borim, Lyrie, and Thuradin were surrounded by darkness. They descended carefully, step by step, down a stone stairway they couldn't see deeper into the mountains. Dunkell had brought a torch with him, but its flickering flame penetrated only enough to light their faces.

The tunnel they stumbled through was one of the secret ones Dunkell had created when he had temporarily claimed the throne from his brother. It was narrow. Thuradin could touch both side walls as well as the ceiling just by stretching out his hands. Still, it was so dark he couldn't see them. The only senses he could rely on here were touch and his hearing, but all he could hear were the occasional drips of water into underground pools that Dunkell said were further down the tunnel.

They were silent as they pushed on, and this silence gave Thuradin plenty of time to reflect on recent events. He thought of yesterday. He had nearly died. A small part of him wished that he had, but he quickly pushed those feelings out. He didn't want death, he decided. Not now. Not yet. There were still plenty of things he had to see through, the first of which was getting his daughter out of the claws of the Council.

Once the Council was defeated—and they would be, he was certain—he knew those in charge would be tried for treason against the Kingdom. If they were not lucky enough to be exiled, they would be executed. He had to get his daughter out of the grave she was digging for herself before it was too late. The only question was how.

He had thought much on this issue but, so far, a solution eluded him. He shook his head, frustrated, but glad no one else could see the conflict he was sure was plain on his face and tried turning his mind to something else.

He thought of Morteth Shadowmeld, the young assassin who had almost killed him. Morteth himself had nearly seen the jaws of death, and would have by Felix's hands, had Dunkell not stopped him.

"Stop," the King had said back in the throne room, causing Felix to turn, puzzled.

"We cannot let him leave this room," the elder viatari had repeated. "He knows too much."

Dunkell had left his throne and walked up to the assassin until they were face to face. "If I let ye go, will ye try taking my life again?"

Morteth chuckled uneasily, then, realizing it was a serious question, responded quickly, "No, no, course nae. I've be'er things ta do than risk me own life again an' all that."

"I do not believe him." Felix frowned.

"Nor I," Dunkell agreed, but with an amused grin. "Tell me, Morteth, how would ye like ta make more money than what the Council is promising ta pay ye?"

Morteth's eyes lit up at the mention of money, but a moment later his face became guarded. "They're payin' me a handsome sum. Ye sure ye can top it?"

"Oh, I'm sure they can pay ye in mounds of gold—as could

I—but I have something that might be more precious ta ye. Whatever weight in gold they're offering for ye ta kill me, I can offer the same weight but in ernen diamonds."

The assassin's eyes bulged. "Ye couldn't," he whispered. "They're so rare."

Dunkell laughed. "Ye forget, Morteth, I'm the King. And Tinas Ern remains under my control—*and* I've received a report recently that a new vein has been found which I can have miners harvest as soon as I see fit."

Morteth sat there, stunned for a moment as he imagined his very rich future.

"Ye've go' a deal. Bu' wha' do ye wan' me ta do?"

Dunkell's grin widened as he patted the assassin's shoulders and turned away. "Come see me before I leave for the burrower caverns and I will tell ye. But for now, I must decide on a new viceroy ta appoint for Kul'Kriegar," he motioned to the guards as he returned to his throne. "Release him."

Now, Thuradin's mind back to the present, he remembered Morteth had said something about working for Dunkell in the past, and he had a sneaking suspicion what the job had been, but he wanted to hear it from the King's own mouth before he gave the thought any credence. It was a terrible thing to believe, if true.

"So, Dunkell," he tried to keep his voice light and conversational, but everything sounded muffled in this narrow tunnel. "I've been thinking about yesterday. Now that we're nae in any immediate danger, would ye tell me what ye hired Morteth ta do for ye?"

Dunkell snorted. "Oh, I'm just having him sabotage any plans the Council might have for attacking us in the near future. He's ta do anything he can ta put off the coming conflict between the dwarven clans. Mind ye, I told him specifically nae ta assassinate the Council members—so, rest assured—yer daughter's safe."

"Aye," Thuradin said, he had never considered his daughter to be in any immediate danger, but he appreciated the gesture. "I appreciate that, I'm only sorry she's on the other side right now. I thought I raised her better than that."

"In yer defense," Lyrie said from behind. "She doesn't seem ta think ye raised her at all."

"Ah, thanks."

"It sounded better in my head."

Thuradin could hear Borim laughing silently in front of him. He slapped him over the head, forgetting he was wearing a plated gauntlet.

"Agh! Oy, Thuradin, are ye trying ta kill me?"

Thuradin patted the spot he had struck. "Sorry, wasn't thinking."

"Skies of *hell*, Thuradin," he could feel Borim duck out of the way and move behind him. "Stop patting my head with yer gauntlet on. I think ye've bruised my skull."

"I never knew ye were so fragile," Thuradin said, this time unable to hold in his own laughter.

"It's the old age."

Their laughter died down and they continued on in silence for several more minutes before Thuradin realized that Dunkell hadn't really answered his question; at least, not the right one.

"Dunkell,"

"Hmm?"

"When I asked ye what ye hired that assassin ta do, I meant what was the job ye gave him in the past."

There was a long pause.

"What do ye mean, Thuradin?"

Were he better friends with Dunkell, and had Dunkell not been his King, he would have struck him over the head much like he had Borim for playing dumb.

"I think, ye know what I'm asking. Morteth mentioned yesterday that he had worked for ye before. What did ye hire him ta do?"

Another pause, and Thuradin feared that his suspicions were correct.

"Did ye hire him ta assassinate yer father, Thelm?"

He could hear Lyrie gasp. Borim kept his silence, listening. Dunkell sighed.

"Nae just him, but Ronorim as well. He only managed ta get one of them, though, as ye well know."

Thuradin was speechless. He had always harbored mixed feelings about Dunkell, especially when Ronorim had been King. Their ideas of who the burrowers were were so vastly different that it had been thought—and proven true—that Dunkell had been trying to take the throne from his brother in order to protect them. However, Thelm had always been in the middle of the two extremes.

As the commander of the royal guard at the time, Thuradin had always suspected Thelm's death was the result of him swinging in favor of campaigning against the burrowers, but he had never suspected the King's death would have been orchestrated by one of his own sons.

"Yer own father, Dunkell."

"Thuradin, before ye judge me, remember the reasons why ye killed my brother. With that in mind, would ye do it again?"

Thuradin thought for a moment, remembered the burrower city he had seen, the burrower families cowering as the dwarves fought just outside their doorstep. He remembered the moment he realized that his people were committing genocide. Yes, he decided, he would do it all again if he had to.

"Aye, I would."

"Ye had ta make a terrible decision for the good of many," Dunkell said. "I understand that better than most because I've had ta make similar decisions. Above all, even above kin, there must be honor, or there is little for us in life. As a prince of the dwarven people, I saw it as my duty—as I do now as King—ta safeguard our honor. And so, I did."

Thuradin let this all sink in and found that he could agree with Dunkell's words. Still, would he have done what he had to do had his family been involved?

Thoughts flashed through his mind of his father, his brothers, all of whom were killed in Dun'Burell over the centuries. He thought of Agata and her lying figure at rest in the Halls of Stone. He thought of Myrna, his only living family, and put her in Ronorim's place. Could he do it? And, stunned by his own realization, he knew that he could not. Whether that was a good or bad sign, he couldn't determine.

There was a splash ahead as a pebble was knocked into a pool of water ahead of them, snapping Thuradin out of a daze. He noticed with a start that the temperature around them was rising. Instead of the constant chill that permeated the dwarven caverns and kept them all cool, he felt a sweltering heat as if he were lying out in the sun with nothing to protect him from its rays. He wiped the sweat from his brow and took a deep breath of the musty air.

"How much farther until we reach the end of this tunnel?"

"Feeling a little claustrophobic?" Borim called out, though

by his own short breathing Thuradin could tell he, too, was having issues with the heat.

"Hardly," Thuradin grunted. "I was just worried about ye and yer old age."

"We're the same—"

"Children!" Lyrie shouted over them. "Just ask what's really on yer mind. Why is it getting so hot down here suddenly?"

"It's because we're closer ta the center of the world," Dunkell responded with nonchalance, continuing to hold his dim torch out in front of him.

"I don't remember it being so hot when Ronorim led us inta burrower territory," Thuradin muttered, now using his beard to wipe off the beads of sweat pouring down his face.

"That's because it wasn't. It's always been warmer, but the burrowers having a large tunnel connecting them ta us gave them access ta our airways which helped cool everything down. Now, though, without it, the heat has nowhere ta escape."

"Why haven't they tried digging a tunnel ta the outside world ta make some vents?"

"They have," Dunkell said. "Or, at least, they're in the process of setting those vents up. Ye have ta remember, Thuradin, they're much deeper in the mountains than we are."

"That still doesn't answer the question," Borim huffed. "Of how much longer we have until this blasted tunnel ends."

No sooner had he said this, though, than they stepped out into a large familiar cavern. Giant stalactites hung from the ceiling and seemed to threaten them like spearheads as they walked to the edge of the ledge they were on. Ahead of them was a cluster of twinkling lights. *Bonfires,* Thuradin thought.

"Right," Dunkell took a moment to extinguish his torch and left it leaning against the tunnel entrance which was just a narrow cut in the rock wall. "Let's climb down."

Being dwarves, the climb down was as simple as walking. Within minutes they were on the cavern floor and making their way toward the burrower city.

"Dunkell," Thuradin said, a sudden thought occurring to him. "Do they know we're coming?"

"Eh," Dunkell chuckled rather nervously. "Nae exactly, but they'll recognize me—most of them know me—and if they don't, their High Chieftain certainly will."

"They have a High Chieftain?" Lyrie asked with some interest.

"Aye," A twinkle came into Dunkell's eyes as he talked about the burrowers. "Ancient fellow. Amiable, too. We've come ta know one another quite well over the past year. He goes by the name of Gruk-Gruk."

"Gruk-Gruk?"

"The burrowers are going ta have different names than us, obviously. It's nae as if they speak Dwarvish."

"If they don't speak Dwarvish, yer majesty," Borim said. "How are we going ta speak with them?"

The King winked at the old dwarf reassuringly. "Because I've learned how ta speak Bru-Noot, their language—and I've taught Dwarvish here ta some of the burrowers I've met. I'm sure they can hold a conversation by now."

Lyrie leaned in close to Thuradin and muttered, "I don't know about that."

"I guess we'll find out, won't we," Thuradin shrugged.

As they drew closer to the burrower city, guards began appearing on several of the rocky outcrops surrounding the outer edge of huts. The burrowers glared at them as they passed. A small party came down from one of the outcrops and approached them, hunched over, and just as ugly as

Thuradin remembered.

Their blue-gray skin was like leather and had a thick coat of dust and dirt. Their faces were egg-shaped, with very little hair but an abundance of creases, making them look like ancient pieces of parchment. They wore individual pieces of armor such as a single spaulder or boots, but other than that the only thing they had on was a loincloth.

They spoke in their guttural language. Their primitive spears came down threateningly, iron points only inches from the dwarves' bellies. Clearly, these burrowers were ready for a fight.

"Easy," Dunkell said calmly to the dwarves behind him. "Let me do the talking."

Borim scoffed. "Ye're the only one who can."

The King responded in the same guttural language with perfect pronunciation as far as Thuradin was concerned. This seemed to throw the burrowers off, though a few still looked wary. Thuradin heard the name Gruk-Gruk mentioned several times by both parties and when the guards surrounded them and started escorting them into the burrower city, he assumed they were being taken to the burrower High Chieftain.

Their city was nothing compared to the dwarven ones. There were no soaring towers touching the cavern ceiling, no buildings made of steel or iron with golden mosaics etched into them, no statues of any sort except one small, crude one made of stone depicting a vaguely familiar humanoid figure.

What Thuradin saw plenty of, though, were huts, but these were no primitive huts. They were hewn from the rock—in many cases leading down into the cavern floor. As they walked through the bare stone streets, he took in his surroundings. He saw many blacksmiths, their fires glowing purple and their hammers singing as they struck the metal they worked on with consistent, measured strength.

That was one thing that the burrowers surpassed the dwarves in, he knew. It was deceiving because their weapons appeared primitive—such as the basic spears the guards carried. Most wielded clubs or long daggers wrapped in a layer of metal that even the dwarves were unfamiliar with. Many dwarves believed the burrowers just used iron, but no iron could be so strong as to slice through dwarven mithril, as had happened in many a battle.

They passed a few small arena circles, where two burrowers would wrestle in the mud in front of a crowd of spectators. Several of the city's residents watched them pass with a mixture of fear, hatred, and curiosity. These were the burrowers Thuradin had sacrificed everything for. He took it all in, wanting to feel some sense of satisfaction, but he felt nothing.

After walking for almost thirty minutes, they arrived to the town's center, where a series of larger huts stood, connected by earthen hallways to form one large building.

"This is the High Chieftain's dwelling, similar ta our royal palace," Dunkell explained as they walked in.

"I wouldn't exactly call it similar," Borim muttered.

"Nor I," Thuradin agreed.

Lyrie leered at them. "Hush."

"Mind yer manners," Dunkell warned. "We're guests here, and don't forget, while only a few speak Dwarvish many more can understand it. We don't want ta offend."

The burrower guards led them through several wooden doors into a spacious hall with a large red-moss mat in the center. There were more burrower guards in this room— slightly more equipped with armor and better weapons—and a much shorter, much more stooped one sitting in the middle of the mat. Thuradin noticed that this shorter burrower sat in the center of four colorful orbs that looked to be made of glass or perhaps crystal and were placed in a square around him.

He had white wisps of singular hairs on his oval head and resting over it was a simple headpiece made of bleached bone and layered with rat fur, which draped down the sides of the burrower's head.

The burrower made no move to turn in their direction but seemed to already know they were there without the guards having to announce them. His voice was deep and raspy as he spoke in his own language.

Dunkell responded in kind, which seemed to give the strange burrower pause. He stood up and flexed his back, which looked deceivingly bony and brittle, but in reality was packed with muscles; another feature Thuradin had learned from his many battles. The High Chieftain turned to face them.

He had a hard face, weathered, as if carved from stone. He was clearly old, with most of his teeth missing, and while one of his eyes was dark and focused, the other was milky white and blind. He carried a medium-sized brass scepter with a glowing red orb at the head and as he moved several burrowers popped out from around the room to aid him. He waved them off and looked each dwarf in the face for several minutes before speaking again

"King Dunkell," he said in perfect Dwarvish. "It is good to see you again. We welcome you to our city of Trek-ti."

Dunkell bowed graciously and was about to return the greeting when Gruk-Gruk held up a hand.

"Now, tell me why I shouldn't kill you all."

CHAPTER TWENTY

For a moment, Thuradin thought he'd heard wrong, or that maybe the burrower High Chieftain's grasp of the dwarven language wasn't as good as Dunkell had claimed, but the guards moving in around them with their weapons ready seemed to imply that what Gruk-Gruk had asked was indeed a real question.

He widened his stance, hands on his axes, ready to draw them at a moment's notice. Lyrie and Borim readied themselves as well. Thuradin felt a war cry itching to escape his throat.

Dunkell raised a hand. "Don't do anything, ye fools. Stand down," he smirked at the High Chieftain. "Gruk-Gruk, nice ta know ye still have yer sense of humor."

There was a moment where everything was still, then Gruk-Gruk's face broke out in a toothy grin and he bent over in a fit of cackling laughter. The guards joined in. Thuradin took in the scene with some confusion, unsure if he should relax or not.

"Ah, Dunkell," Gruk-Gruk said, raising his arms invitingly. "I could never harm you, as you know. You, who have helped my people so much, saving us from your own kind even at the risk of losing your throne. Come, embrace me."

Dunkell stepped up and the two leaders embraced, the High Chieftain looking like a frail child compared to the King's bulkiness.

"Now," Gruk-Gruk turned his gaze to Thuradin, his smile vanishing. "Tell me why I shouldn't kill your friends."

The guards moved in once again with their weapons ready. Thuradin hesitated. Was this another joke? He had no idea how to read the situation, but by the cautious look on Dunkell's face, he thought it likely that he, Lyrie, and Borim might be in some potential danger.

"Surely, ye wouldn't—" Borim began to say but one of the guards swung the butt of his spear and rapped him on the head, silencing him.

"I speak only to the one in the middle," Gruk-Gruk pointed with a wrinkly finger. "Even among us you are famous, Thuradin Stonebeard, commander of the royal guard. How many of my people have you slain?"

"I am commander no longer," Thuradin said, "And for the burrowers I have slain, I do nae apologize. Just as I do nae expect yer apology for the dwarves killed by yer people."

"Thuradin—" Dunkell warned.

Gruk-Gruk cackled. "We killed in self-defense. There is a difference."

"That's nae how we saw it."

"Oh no," Gruk-Gruk took a few steps forward until he was face to face with Thuradin. Thuradin stared into the High Chieftain's eyes, refusing to break eye-contact. He would not be intimidated. "No, you simply thought we were pests, parasites, rats to be squashed under your steel boots."

"We," Thuradin spread out his arms, motioning to Borim and Lyrie behind him, "do nae think that anymore. We have learned from our mistakes."

Gruk-Gruk's good eye studied him, looking for any hint of deceit while his blind one sat still, staring blankly ahead. Finally, he snorted and stepped back into the center of the mat.

"Still," he said, gripping his scepter tightly and swinging it like a club. "A change of heart does not convince me to let you leave my city alive."

"Then, perhaps this will," Thuradin told his tale about the Creature, The Turned One, and the coming war between acolytes and the created races of the First Gods—of which, he mentioned, the burrowers were one.

"—Nythirim created our two races for a purpose and that purpose can be none other than ta help bring peace and balance ta our world. The viatari are doing their part—more than their part, if I'm being honest—and we've now started working with the humans. It's a start. But more importantly, we need ta find the other acolytes, and if ye kill us now, then the one that lies within these mountains will remain here, isolated from a war that, without his aid, we cannae hope ta win."

The burrowers shared uneasy glances while Gruk-Gruk stared at the ceiling, deep in thought. He turned to Dunkell, who nodded, affirming the authenticity of Thuradin's tale.

"What you tell me of these acolytes, especially the corrupted ones, disturbs me."

For a moment Thuradin felt hopeful that he had gotten through to the High Chieftain, had explained everything well enough to convince him to help them with their task. But that hope faded as quickly as it had flared with his next question.

"But why should my people care?" Gruk-Gruk asked, twirling his scepter in bored fashion. "We live in the mountains, not the outside world. We live deeper in the mountains than even your people—so if these acolytes decide to attack us, they will have to get through your people first and we are more than happy to let the dwarves weaken the enemy before we must face them."

Thuradin grit his teeth, anger bubbling in his stomach. "My people cannae fight off the Creature's darimun or The Turned One's corrupted warriors. And ye *should* care," he heard his voice growing louder with each word as the sudden surge of fury he felt rushed into his head, "because without yer aid, without all the acolytes together, we *will* lose this war. And once the corrupted ones have subjected my people, they'll enslave yers, just as they did ta the burrowers who live outside the mountains."

Gruk-Gruk suddenly stopped twirling his scepter, his face frozen in shock. "What burrowers?"

Borim put a hand on Thuradin's shoulder, pulling him back before he could yell anymore. "Chieftain, a few months ago, our allies, the viatari, were attacked by a large force under the command of The Turned One. A large part of those forces were burrowers she had enslaved with her corrupting influence ta fight for her. These burrowers had no will of their own, and fought with a savageness that even ye would have trouble matching. We believe they were once their own civilization, much like yers, but in the outside world, living peacefully with their neighbors until they fell under the corrupted acolyte's control."

The High Chieftain's blue-gray face turned grayer. "Is this true, Dunkell?"

"Aye," Dunkell said grimly. "One of my commanders—before he betrayed me—mentioned they had fought burrowers in the outside world. I knew right away from his description of them that they had ta be a different tribe or something of the sort, since yer people have no access ta those parts."

"Yes," Gruk-Gruk breathed. Thuradin could see the gears running in the old burrower's head as his thoughts went into overdrive. "And perhaps it is good that we have no access to such a world. Still, corrupted or not, those burrowers are our brethren. If they are inflicting pain to the world, spreading evil, then my people will do what we must to put them down so that we may save our honor as a race. Our kind's name will not be sullied by these acolytes."

"Ye'll help us then?" Thuradin asked, snapping out of the mad haze he had been in.

"I will allow you to help yourselves, yes." Gruk-Gruk said, though he didn't sound too happy about it. "Dwarves have never roamed our caverns freely before, however, and I do not wish for this to become a regular occurrence."

He turned away from them and walked to the back of the room, which was hidden in shadow. He returned, moments later, carrying a medium-sized pillar with a statue of a black chest on top. Encircling the pillar were many pictographs which, Thuradin imagined, told the story behind the statue. He only spared these a glance though. He was more interested in the chest on top.

It was a small, rectangular crate, black like the night but with similar precious jewels around the sides that the other acolytes had.

"Is that. . . ."

"No," Gruk-Gruk said, placing the pillar down on the center of the mat. "This is just a statue of what you seek."

"Why do ye have a statue of it?" Lyrie asked, moving closer to get a better look. "Does this mean ye know where it is?"

The burrower nodded. "I do, we all do. For as long as

anyone can remember, we have had this chest in our presence, protecting us, empowering us, aiding us when we needed it. I never knew its origin, but I knew it was a being of immense power."

"So, is he a god ta yer people?" Borim asked, rubbing his fingernail across the statue and inspecting the bits of rock he had scraped off. Gruk-Gruk lightly tapped the dwarf's hand away with his scepter, the red orb at the end flaring brightly.

"I would ask you to please not touch our statue or damage it as you dwarves are prone to do with everything. And no, he is not our god. The only god we acknowledge is our maker, Nythirim, just as the dwarves do."

"What's the story behind this acolyte being here then?" Thuradin asked. "And where is he so we can find him ourselves?"

"I will tell you, but first," Gruk-Gruk turned a wary eye to the dwarven King, "Dunkell, am I to trust these dwarves you have brought into my home?"

Dunkell nodded without hesitation. "I trust them with my life."

Gruk-Gruk nodded, though he still did not look too happy, and gazed again at the statue, his one good eye passing over the lines of pictographs encircling the pillar.

"The black chest has always been with us. Our first High Chieftain, Gul, my ancestor, was the one who discovered it. Gul had been foraging for food for this city, which had just been founded at the time. He traveled down to the larger caverns below us until he stumbled into one filled with an ocean of molten rock. There, he fashioned a boat out of two thick slabs of stone, and set off in that dangerous sea with the hopes of finding food on the other side.

"During his journey, he met many dangers from fire giants

to fire spiders, and of course all the magma around him, which, had he touched it, would have destroyed his flesh. But no challenge was so fierce as the mighty Ta'Ka, the fire bird.

"Gul fought bravely, and was elusive when necessary to avoid these dangers. Finally, when he reached the center of Magmasea, as we have come to call it, he discovered the black chest. He spoke with the mysterious being living within, and the being, having taken a liking to the daring Gul, promised him and his descendants protection against hardship and taught him how to summon and control the living element of fire to enchant metals and rocks, a skill that has been passed down to this day."

Gruk-Gruk closed his eyes, mumbling a few words in his own guttural language, as if in prayer.

"That is the story of Gul and the chest," he finished.

"So, the acolyte is in the center of an ocean of magma," Thuradin said, finding much of what he had heard difficult to believe. But he would say nothing of his doubts. "How are we supposed ta get ta it?"

"Weren't ye listening?" Lyrie said, wonder in her voice. "Gul crossed Magmasea by crafting a boat from two slabs of stone. I imagine the burrowers today can do the same thing."

Gruk-Gruk nodded, his one eye twinkling as he looked approvingly at Lyrie. "The female is correct. We have stone boats already built, docked on the shore of Magmasea."

"And how will we get there?" Borim asked, his brows furrowed. "We'll need guides."

"And you will have them." The High Chieftain clapped his hands and called out in his own guttural language. Immediately one of the guards ran out of the room. Several minutes passed before he returned with four more burrowers in tow. Gruk-Gruk spoke to them for a few moments, leading to all four of them making the disappointment they felt plain on their faces.

"They do nae look too happy about their task," Lyrie muttered.

"Aye," Thuradin agreed, his fingers twitching ever so slightly toward his axes.

Gruk-Gruk turned back to them. "These four burrowers are named Brap, Krunt, Thrak'mig, and Hrack. They will be your guides for your journey to Magmasea. Only Brap speaks Dwarvish with any decency, though the others can understand it."

Dunkell stepped forward before any of the other dwarves could say anything and bowed gracefully. "On behalf of my people and the world, I thank ye, High Chieftain, for the aid ye're providing us."

"This aid is not without cost."

Dunkell hesitated before rising from his bow, caution printed on his features. "How can we pay you?"

"You can pay me, Dunkell," Gruk-Gruk said, a smile creeping along his lips, "with your company. You are to remain here with me in my halls while your friends are guided through the magma caverns to do what they must."

"And why must our King stay with ye?" Thuradin demanded.

"Because I don't really trust you," Gruk-Gruk stood up to his full height, his hunch completely gone, and towered over all the dwarves. "I do not trust you, Thuradin Stonebeard, or any dwarves. And you must earn my trust if my people are to assist you any further. Your King will stay here with me—well-protected, I should add—to ensure your good behavior in my caverns."

"Go ahead, Thuradin," Dunkell said, moving next to the

burrower High Chieftain, "I'll be fine. I trust the burrowers and I trust ye nae ta make a mess of things. I will remain here and see what I can do ta convince Gruk-Gruk ta aid us even more with our war effort."

Gruk-Gruk chuckled. "You have an agenda, I see. Trying to rope me in with the world's affairs."

Dunkell nodded with a mischievous grin. "It's time the world knew the full might of the burrowers." He looked back at the dwarves, who remained where they were, uncertainty plain on their faces. "Go. That is an order from yer King."

With smart salutes, the dwarves marched out of the burrower High Chieftain's hall, their new burrower guides leading the way. One of them, rather thin but with several lines of tattoos darkening his creased face, walked next to Thuradin.

"I am Brap," he said in a thick accent. "I help you with task, though I no like."

"Ye're nae alone in that sentiment." Thuradin muttered. Despite having saved these burrowers from certain annihilation at the hands of his own people, he still found it difficult to interact with them. Centuries of prejudice and hatred and a history of fighting didn't just disappear with a single day, or even a year.

Brap eyed them all as they walked through the city streets.

"Follow," he said. "We see blacksmith."

"Why?" Thuradin asked. "We already have armor and weapons. We don't have time ta waste."

Brap and the other burrowers spoke in their own language and snickered. "Armor and weapons, yes," Brap croaked, his eyes glinting with distaste. "But they melt when we fight fire giants, or cross Magmasea. Armor and weapons need enchantment to protect against fire. You no have any, you die."

"Let's get it over with," Borim said, shrugging off Thuradin's bewildered look. "What harm will it do? Ye and I both know that the burrowers possess a skill with metallurgy that we don't have and if we need these enchantments, as Brap says, ta withstand the creatures we'll be facing, then we need them."

"Come along, Thuradin," Lyrie shoved him forward. "It won't hurt."

"We'll be out of our armor while the blacksmith is working," Thuradin warned as they followed Brap toward the thin trails of black smoke rising in the distance. "We'll be vulnerable."

Lyrie placed a hand on his shoulder. "We need ta trust them—Dunkell does. So why can't ye?"

"I don't know," Thuradin said, though it wasn't true. He glanced into Lyrie's calm eyes, and shook his head, a sense of surety now with him. She was always so convincing and he had no idea why. "Fine, we'll do it, but stay alert."

"Aye, commander," Borim said with a mock salute.

They walked through several blocks of Trek-ti with no significant change in the city's appearance. Not until they were in the metalworking district. Here, dozens of blacksmith forges stood lined up along the street, each one sending up clouds of smoke from the constant fires raging within various furnaces.

"Come," Brap said, shuffling along. "We ask my friend for help. He only one who will help us."

"Why's that?" Borim asked.

Brap glanced at him and sneered. "Because he *my* friend."

They were led to one of the smaller forges in the center of the district.

"Lurt!" Brap called out, waving.

"Brap!"

The two burrowers ran at each other and smashed heads, laughing as they both collapsed onto the ground, dazed.

"At least now we know why their heads are shaped like that," Lyrie whispered into Thuradin's ear. Thuradin snorted, managing to pass it off as a sneeze.

The other burrowers bumped heads with Lurt and they all began grunting rapidly in their own language. Brap pointed at the dwarves several times and then at the forge. Lurt didn't look too happy, but by the end of the exchange the two agreed on something and bumped heads happily.

"They're like a bunch of rams," Borim remarked.

"Perhaps," Thuradin agreed, keeping his voice low as Brap approached them. "But I wouldn't dare ride any of them inta battle."

Borim chortled, drawing a look from the burrowers.

"Lurt take armor now," he said. "Enchant it, make it strong. That way you no die by fire."

Thuradin glanced at Lyrie, then Borim, who both nodded.

"Very well, lad—and lass—let's get this over with."

As he moved to undo the straps of his armor, Lurt let out a beastly yell, pounding his fists onto his chest and then went to work on the bellows as he continued yelling the same word over and over. The flames in the furnace turned from red to blue with green sparks shooting out. Tongues of purple flame mixed in with the blue like veins, and Thuradin stood, transfixed for a moment, as the flames in the furnace grew a pair of arms, legs, eyes, and then a mouth.

A distorted voice came from the living flame.

Lurt beat his chest and swung a fluorescent hammer made of green iron onto his anvil, creating a burst of slow-moving sparks. Before they could hit the ground, he gathered them up and threw them into the flaming beast that had been born from the furnace. The elemental roared in agony, its arms reaching skyward as solid chackles, formed by Lurt's sparks, encircled its wrists.

Ignoring the wailing from the elemental, Lurt hurriedly took hold of the dwarven armor Brap passed to him and chucked it into the living flames. After a few minutes, he would take out the plate, hammering away while muttering guttural incantations over each piece. Multi-colored sparks erupted with each blow of the hammer, dazing Thuradin as he stood there in awe, listening to the elemental's desperate cries and the constant ringing of hammer on metal.

CHAPTER TWENTY-ONE

The rooms Felix and his viatari were given in the Kul'Kriegaran citadel were small, with only the bare necessities provided. There were three beds, a torch casting a soft glow for light, a small brazier for warmth, a simple, wooden table, and—Felix felt lucky to have this—one of the few thin windows that allowed them a narrow view of the city. After Dunkell had left, announcing Edana Hartshield as the new viceroy of Kul'Kriegar, the viatari had been given these accommodations so that they might have a chance to rest.

But Felix couldn't rest, he could hardly do anything but pace their small, stone room as he reflected on their current situation. He thought of how he might go about stopping a dwarven civil war, he thought of the letter he had received only hours ago from Salevari, reporting on the precarious situation in Aleganthia, he thought about Thuradin and the dwarven King, hoping they would be successful in finding the acolyte they needed for the coming war. He seemed to be drowning in thoughts.

"Felix," Drathanar said soothingly in Viatar. "You must rest. You're no good with a tired mind."

"I cannot rest," Felix responded. "Unless you have already thought of a way to stop this coming dwarven conflict *and* ensure the dwarves continue to aid us afterwards for our own war against The Turned One."

"Should we even try to stop this war?"

Aniria lay on one of the beds, her eyes fixed on the ceiling. She seemed to be lost in her own thoughts, or memories, though what those might be these days Felix couldn't guess.

"Of course we should stop it," he said, still pacing. "We cannot have the dwarves fall into chaos because of—what? An impossible fear that the burrowers might be returning to attack them."

"Maybe they are though."

Felix shook his head, frustration beginning to take root as his mind came to a standstill. "Please, Aniria. The burrowers are not the dwarves' enemies."

"Perhaps not the burrowers that Thuradin and the King have gone to see," Aniria yawned. "But you and I both know there are others out there."

Felix stopped pacing. "While you are correct that any potentially imminent invasion the dwarves may be facing will be at the hands of The Turned One's forces, that does not change the main problem. The dwarves cannot, whether by choice or by sheer ignorance, differentiate between the burrowers The Turned One has enslaved and empowered with her essence and the ones that live deeper in the Silent Mountains."

"Plus," Drathanar said, his gaze fixed on Aniria. "If it is The Turned One digging into the dwarven caverns, that should be even more reason to keep the dwarves from fighting each other."

Aniria glared at him and Drathanar quickly dropped his gaze, now more interested in the sharpness of his curved sabers, which he had just pulled out.

"If we can get the dwarves to unite against a common enemy, they would forget their grievances against each other. This civil war would be banished from their thoughts as they protect their home. We just have to let The Turned One make her move."

But Felix was already shaking his head. "We cannot do that."

Aniria sat up suddenly, her brows furrowed. "Why not? If you're afraid of the dwarves being unable to fight off The Turned One's forces by themselves—well, that's why we're here, isn't it? They will be no match for our combined strength."

"She's right," Drathanar said softly, his eyes still on his swords. "It's essentially what happened between our two peoples when Dalyr came to your aid. Fighting together united us even though our two cities hated each other not too long ago. It could work."

Felix took a deep breath. *They are like children,* he thought, *they cannot see the bigger picture.*

"I am not denying that the idea itself could work, but it would work for the wrong reasons. We accomplish nothing if we get the dwarves to unite under the pretense of hating the burrowers. It would not unite them under their King—who does not hate the burrowers—and they would still not understand the difference between The Turned One's corrupted burrowers and the ones Thuradin has gone to deal with."

"Why should we care about that?" Aniria groaned, laying back down.

"Because it is not a permanent solution." Felix's voice rose as his frustration boiled over. "It is like putting a single square of cloth over a severed limb. We need a long-term fix, because there is no telling how long this war against the corrupted burrowers will last and we *need* the dwarves to help us or we are lost."

Aniria shot out of bed again with a vengeance. "Well, do you have any better ideas, then? Because right now we're just sitting around in these tiny rooms when we should be outside of these mountains fighting and killing the enemy!"

"Aniria," Drathanar tried to pull her away but she shoved him off.

"Stay out of it, Drathanar. I don't need your help."

"That will not stop me from trying," the Dalyran general murmured as he once again tried to pull her back. This time, she let him, and he sat her back down on the bed, his arm still around her both for protection and comfort.

"Believe me, Aniria," Felix sighed, regretting now that he had raised his voice. If he was being honest with himself, after having seen Aleganthia sacked, it was becoming increasingly difficult to maintain his composure as he had once always done. "We will be out there killing darimun and corrupted burrowers and men soon enough, but if that's all we do, we gain nothing but our own inevitable deaths. Their numbers can always be replenished, ours cannot—not as easily, anyway."

"So, the only solution we have is to make all the dwarves accept Dunkell as their King," Drathanar stated, his voice low and calm as he continued holding Aniria, who had calmed down and now looked dazed and tired. "Do you have a plan?"

Felix grimaced. That was the question, wasn't it?

"Not yet," he admitted. "But I am thinking. What is certain, though, is that we will need the new viceroy's help in keeping those loyal to the King in check so that no rash decisions are made that could spark something major. That should buy us some time."

"Go talk to the new viceroy, then," Drathanar said. "We will stay here a moment."

Felix nodded and left them, the sound of Aniria's stifled sobs just managing to reach his ears as the door clicked shut. Again, a great swelling of regret moved through him as he reflected on his own behavior during their heated exchange, but it quickly passed as his mind moved on to the matter at hand.

He walked through the ever-circling halls of the citadel, his steps echoing, until he finally found himself in front of the viceroy's work chambers. Two guards stood stationed in front of the iron door, much of their face covered by their thick armor.

"I seek an audience with her."

One of the guards grunted and entered the chambers. A moment later, he returned.

"She'll see ye," the guard said. "But she's very pressed at the moment, so she urges ye ta make it quick."

The guards stepped aside and Felix pushed through the iron door into a spacious room filled with maps, tables, armor stands, and all kinds of weaponry leaning against the wall. There were also several stone bookshelves lining much of the walls with huge tomes and dusty scrolls sitting in them. In the middle of all this, speaking quickly with one of her aides, was the new viceroy of Kul'Kriegar, Edana Hartshield.

She had short, orange hair and a bright smile, but in her eyes Felix could tell she was a warrior through and through. She had seen battle and did not fear death. The aide bowed low to her before running out of the room to carry out whatever orders he had just been given. Edana shifted her attention to her new visitor.

"If it isn't one of our powerful viatari friends," she said with a beaming smile. "What can I do for ye today?"

"I have come to speak with you for a moment on the matter of keeping your people from falling into civil war and I need your help."

"I see," for a moment Edana's smile faltered, as if she didn't want this conversation to continue, but in the end she shrugged, saying, "go on."

"I am in the process of finding a way to keep your people from warring against each other by uniting under King Dunkell, but I need more time. To get this time, I need your help in keeping those loyal to the King in check, to make sure they do not go out seeking a fight."

Edana sighed and examined the maps and charts on the table before her. A line marked her forehead as she considered his words, though he didn't think there should be much to consider.

"I'm sorry, Felix," the viceroy finally said. "Truly, I am. If ye'd already had a plan in place I would have been all for it, but I cannae gamble with time. Right now, I need ta spend what little time we have for preparations."

Felix felt like he had just been punched in the stomach. "You intend to pursue war with the Council."

"Aye. They're rebels, traitors ta the crown, and I'll have none of it. We will march swiftly upon them, crush them before they can organize inta a proper fighting force. Once we've done that, we'll execute the traitors who led this rebellion. Then, and only then, will we be able to reestablish peace in our realm."

"But . . . but you are dwarves! You cannot just go killing each other because of a difference of opinion."

Edana frowned with a mixture of pity and some annoyance. "Were it so simple. Look, I admire the viatari because yer people are strong. So, I expect ye ta understand this. If we do nae strike now because we're waiting for ye ta come up with some plan ta save us all, there are only two outcomes."

She raised her hand, holding one finger, then two, up. "One: ye find some way ta keep us all from going ta war and Dunkell returns ta a united Kingdom, and we all celebrate because we didn't have ta shed dwarven blood. Or, two: Ye cannae think of something in time and the Council raises an army and attacks us while we're waiting for ye. We either go ta war or we don't."

"I understand that, but—"

"I'm nae finished!" Edana wagged her two fingers in Felix's face, which he would have found ridiculous because of her size had the situation not been so serious. "If we go ta war, there are—again—two outcomes. One: we get lucky and the war ends in ten years because of our superior warriors and supplies. Or, two: we are unlucky, and this war lasts one hundred years or more, which means countless dwarven lives will be lost. Now—"

The viceroy took a deep breath, calming herself, "—as the newly appointed viceroy of Kul'Kriegar, and general of the King's forces, I'm nae willing ta gamble all of those dwarven lives on the *hope* that ye'll think of something in time. So aye, I intend ta wage war with them—soon—so we can end this threat ta the realm as swiftly as possible. There is a time for talk, but now is nae that time."

Felix was so stunned he didn't know how to respond. Moreover, he was surprised to find that he couldn't think of anything reasonable to counter the points Edana had made. From her perspective, while her actions would provoke a full-blown war between the dwarven clans, she was sure an early strike would mean less casualties and an early end, and Felix didn't necessarily disagree. However, that didn't make him satisfied with the end result.

"Does Dunkell know you are doing this?"

Edana pursed her lips, and that told Felix all he needed to know.

"He doesn't," she admitted. "I am doing this by my own judgement. While I am loyal ta the crown, I know he can be a little too hopeful at times—and in this case, that can be dangerous. I'm sure that once the rebels are subdued and he returns ta find a Kingdom united, he will appreciate what I have done and understand the necessity of it."

"He will return to nothing but a Kingdom in ruins, with streets soaked in the blood of his own people," Felix muttered as he turned to leave, determined now more than ever to find a way to resolve this conflict. He was only disappointed that he and those he had brought with him were on their own in this endeavor.

"I trust the dwarves can still rely on yer peoples' aid?" Edana called out as he reached for the door.

Felix stopped for a moment and turned back, regarding the dwarf sadly. "If you must, but know I will strive to find a peaceful solution until the end."

The viceroy nodded. "I wouldn't trust ye as allies if ye didn't. Thank ye, viatari."

Felix exited the chambers and shuffled back to his own room where he found Aniria asleep and Drathanar sitting at the edge of her bed, his eyes fixed on her peaceful features, studying them, memorizing them. The Dalyran general jumped off the bed when Felix spoke, clearly unaware that he had entered, and returned to his own bed.

"The viceroy will not help us."

Drathanar frowned. "That is not good."

"No," Felix agreed. "It is not. We are on our own. But I think I have another plan that can buy us some more time."

For being the Dwarven Kingdom's most renowned assassin, Morteth Shadowmeld was not difficult to find. A quick trip to the first tavern he saw, and Felix immediately identified the charcoaled skin and the large, hairy ears of the stout dwarf.

The tavern was loud and Felix, accompanied by both Aniria and Drathanar, stood out like large diamonds in a mound of gravel. The tavern's occupants glanced their way as they entered, stared as they briefly wondered what a few viatari would be doing here, then shrugged away their curiosity as they returned to their drinks.

Morteth, too, was drinking. He sat at the bar, cradling a mug of the brown liquid dwarves so loved. He seemed distracted, though, because he wasn't drinking any of it, instead staring into the mug like it was telling him a story.

"I'm surprised you haven't left the city yet," Felix said, cheerfully sitting down next to the dwarf. Drathanar sat on the other side of the bar while Aniria stood behind the assassin, arms crossed.

Morteth didn't jump, but a few quick glances and he knew he was surrounded. He laughed dryly, "Hör, how 'bout a drink for me new red-eyed friends."

Hör, the bartender, glowered at the assassin and the viatari surrounding him as he took our three more mugs. "I do nae want any trouble in me tavern, ye hear?"

Felix nodded and raised his hand in a peaceful gesture. "There will be none, you have my word."

The bartender slid the three mugs of frothy ale to the

viatari and returned to cleaning the bar, though Felix knew his attention was still on them.

"Well, drink up," Morteth chuckled, taking a sip himself. "The best part's the froth!"

"That is actually why we have come to speak with you," Felix said, taking his own mug and leaving the remaining two where they were. "I have a proposition for you."

"Interestin'," the assassin squinted at Felix as if he were having difficulty seeing, or as if he were already intoxicated. "I'm a fan of these propositions, 'tis true, long as they come 'long with some nice, shiny gold."

"You will get your payment from the King," Felix replied easily, taking a sip from his own mug and very much wishing he could spit it out. He was not particularly fond of ale. "But we want to change the task the King gave you."

"O-ho!" Morteth chortled as ale dripped down his short beard. "Defyin' the King, are ye?"

"Not defying," Felix shrugged. "Just switching things up for a better result."

"Wha' would ye wan' me ta do?"

"We know the King wants you to infiltrate the Council and sabotage whatever plans they might have for an attack on the King's remaining strongholds, correct?"

"Aye."

"Well, we want you to do the same thing, but against the new viceroy of Kul'Kriegar," now Felix lowered his voice to ensure they weren't overheard. "We want you to spy on the viceroy for us. Keep us informed on what she's doing. Sabotage, incapacitate, do whatever you need to do to keep her from going to war with the Council."

"I see, I see," Morteth hurriedly finished his mug and ordered another, his face shining with curiosity. "Now, o'course, I'm nae on anyone's side, mind ye, I just wan' me payment, but why would the King pay me if I go against his own interests?"

"Because we," Felix indicated himself and his companions, "will be going down to the Council's caverns in your stead to ensure that war doesn't break out. What we need to acc-omplish this is time, which is what you will be providing for us."

Morteth belched loudly as he drained another mug. "Tha' is pret'y gutsy of ye, and I won' deny tha' the task intrigues me. Bu' I'm a sure-money kind of dwarf, ye see. Seems ta me tha' only one of these tasks has a be'er chance of me ge'ing paid."

"Then let us make this interesting."

"Oh?"

Felix finished his own mug off and pulled in the other two the bartender had brought for the viatari toward him. "Let us have a drinking contest to decide which task you will do."

Like most dwarves, Morteth's eyebrows shot up and his eyes bulged at the prospect of a drinking contest. "Tha' would be fun . . . bu', och—" he frowned. "I've already 'ad several pints; it'd be no fair for me ta start as we are."

"I have already finished one," Felix countered, "and I am no dwarf. We viatari are not exactly known for our drinking stamina."

Morteth's face scrunched up as he tried to think. "Then why would ye challenge me when ye know ye're goin' ta lose?"

"Did I say I would lose?" the elder viatari asked bringing the mug close to his lips, waiting.

Minutes passed, then the assassin's face broke out into a

large grin. "Ye're on!"

Hör worked hard to keep their mugs full as they drank pint after pint. After three rounds, Felix called for a bucket.

"Al-oof-already callin' it quitsh?" Morteth taunted, swaying in his stool.

Felix gagged, but held down what he had just consumed. "Just a precaution."

The contest continued and Morteth downed mug after mug, his words slurring more with each round. It came to the point where the dwarf couldn't keep his balance on the stool and he collapsed, but continued drinking on the tavern floor.

Unknown to the now severely intoxicated assassin, after their third drink, Felix would take each mug he was given and pour its contents into the bucket and then show the empty mug to Morteth as proof he had finished it.

"That's cheating, you know," Drathanar said in Viatar, as Hör walked away after bringing another pint, grumbling about wasted ale.

Felix shrugged, swaying a little himself. "I will do what I must, and he will not remember a thing." He bent down from his stool to show the dwarf another empty mug.

"Uh, Felix," Aniria said tentatively. "I think he's unconscious."

Felix tried to focus on the dwarven assassin's face but found it difficult, though he could hear Morteth snoring, and registered a thick pool of drool already spreading under him. The elder viatari sat back up, and slammed the mug down on the counter.

"I win."

"Ye'll be paying for all that wasted ale, I hope ye know."

Hör growled.

For a moment a silence hung between them, during which the bartender's face turned red.

"Ye *have* the coin ta pay for all that ale, do ye nae?"

"I—"

A bag of coins landed with a *chink* on the bar and Felix turned to see Aniria had been the one who threw it there.

"Where?—"

"Off him."

He looked again at the drunken dwarf asleep on the tavern floor and nodded. "Right, let us get him into a room in the citadel, we will continue this tomorrow to discuss details."

Aniria picked Morteth up like a child and walked out of the tavern without waiting while Drathanar took his time to help a stumbling Felix leave the dark building. Behind them, Hör counted the money he had been given, his face relaxing more and more with each coin he took out.

CHAPTER TWENTY-TWO

Silence settled in the Assembly Hall as the vashi realized Tera had talked back to them. Victria thought that if a bubble had burst in the center of the room, everyone would have been able to hear it.

Then an eruption of noise filled the water as vashi on all tiers of the hall shouted their protests or defenses and began bickering with one another. Some reverted back to their native tongue while others continued in the human language. Several of the representatives from opposite sides of the hall swam out of their tiered shells to confront one another, yelling in each other's faces.

Koranam looked like he was ready to strike Tera, blades that curved all the way around his arm to his elbow suddenly appearing in his hands, and he might have, had Victria and the other viatari not suddenly stood and placed themselves around their human companion like a wall. The vashi representative glared at them distastefully, but did not attack.

Araxie struck the butt of his golden harpoon against the marble floor hard, the sound bouncing off the marble and coral walls, catching everyone's attention instantly as if the very water around them were vibrating. The Supreme Overseer stared disappointedly at each member as he spoke.

"There will be order in this Assembly. The guards will escort the wayward representatives back to their seats."

The guards, who had intervened to keep some of the representatives from fighting each other with more than words, herded them up and did as the Supreme Overseer ordered. Almost all of them returned to their respective shells without fuss, though Koranam initially brushed his guards off as he tried to approach Tera once again. But he, too, was eventually brought back to his seat.

Araxie looked around for a minute more before addressing the room, "What just occurred here was a shameful display—one that happens too often, I regret to say. It is clear we are not, and most likely will not, come to a consensus on war with the humans today. But I ask you this for all to ponder before I dismiss the Assembly for the day: should we go to war with the humans, and this course of action winds up aiding the evil these viatari have told us about, what then? We will have aided in the world's own destruction rather than helped save it."

"I object to that," Koranam rose from his seat, his fist raised high over his head. He looked much calmer now, though Victria could see him eyeing them every now and then, disgust still in his eyes. "These viatari have brought no evidence to prove that this evil even exists, they've only told a story as far as I'm concerned."

Araxie frowned. "What reason would they have to lie?"

"Furthermore," Koranam ignored the question. "There is no evidence that this 'evil,' if it truly exists, would even prove a threat to us."

"The purpose of this evil being the viatari have called 'The Turned One' is to throw the world into chaos. The world, Representative Koranam, includes us vashi. Even if this thing were not to attack us directly, she would surely wish to enslave us."

"The vashi will never be slaves," Koranam declared. There was scattered applause throughout the hall.

"Indeed," Araxie settled back into his own seat. "But to ensure that never happens we must act. I urge you all to reflect on this until next we meet. This Assembly will now end. We reconvene in a week's time."

The vashi representatives left their seats and swam to the hall floor, a low buzz filling the room as they discussed amongst themselves. Araxie waded over to the viatari and sighed heavily, the displeasure clear on his weathered face.

"Was that . . . normal?" Serania asked.

"Unfortunately so," Araxie said. "Very little truly ever gets done in the Assembly anymore. I told you before it would be difficult to convince them to help, but I am still hopeful that we may get the result you're looking for in the end."

"But the Assembly doesn't meet again for a week," Victria said, suddenly anxious as she began to wonder how long they might have to stay here in Zessarix. "And there's no guarantee that they'll have a decision ready by that time. What do we do until then?"

Araxie shrugged. "For now, we will make our way to my residence in the city, have a meal, relax. Tomorrow, I will go meet with some of the more moderate representatives privately so that I may tell them the full extent of the danger we could soon be facing. I will probably be in such meetings all week. As for you, well, Zessarix has many attractions for newcomers to explore," the Supreme Overseer cracked a smile, "I'm sure my son, Avmoshir, will not object to acting as your guide for the next few days."

With that they left the Assembly Hall and returned to the

city streets. There was much to think about, so much that Victria almost couldn't focus. She wanted to think of a plan, a next step to get them closer to their goal, but right now they were stuck in a waiting game, and they couldn't move on until the allotted time had passed.

Araxie's house in Zessarix was not as large as the one in Pashir, but it was just as elegant, both inside and out. Avmoshir had done much with the servants to prepare the house for Araxie's arrival. The marble floors sparkled from a recent waxing. Vases stood on counters and miniature pillars all over with fresh ocean flora. Everything looked neat and clean as if every aspect of the edifice was looked after each day of the year.

Despite this pleasantness, Victria was eager to leave the next day. She did not want to be cooped up in this house—in this city—for a week, but she knew there was little she could do.

"It'll be fine," Serania reassured her when Victria brought up what was consuming her. "We have time to spare. It's not like any of us were expecting success overnight."

"I know, but still, I feel so useless."

Their plan the next day was to explore the city. Avmoshir had reluctantly agreed to his father's request to be the viatari's guide and had created an itinerary for them. They would leave early, see the morning markets, go to a couple museums, visit a city park, have lunch, dinner, it was all just so . . . un-eventful. Victria could appreciate the opportunity to learn about the vashi—they were an intriguing people—but to do it right now felt counterproductive.

They made their way down the stairs and ran into Madira, who had been hunched over one of the many vases in the house examining the flora.

"Morning, Victria, Serania!"

"What are you looking at?"

"Just these plants," Madira brought her eyes close to the vases. There were some that looked like miniature seaweed, some sea anemone, and other plants or creatures that Victria could never hope to recognize. "They're fascinating. A little small for my taste, but still. I never imagined there could be such diversity of flora under the sea."

Victria didn't quite know how to respond. Luckily, she didn't have to as Avmoshir rounded the corner and saw them.

"There you are," he jerked his head back toward the lobby, indicating that they should follow him. "We're ready to leave. Tessa, Natiari, and Tera are already out the door."

The three viatari followed him outside where they greeted their companions. They walked a short distance before stopping by a sign with a coral "x" on top. There, they waited.

"What are we waiting for?" Tessa asked.

"Transportation." Avmoshir yawned. "Watch."

Only a minute later, something large loomed in the distance. Victria couldn't make out the shape, but as it drew nearer, she realized it was a giant sea turtle, one with strange seat contraptions strapped onto its shell. A rider sat at the head and pulled back on the reins, bringing the turtle to a stop right by the sign. Here, a few vashi jumped off the turtle and swam on to wherever they were going. Avmoshir hopped on, indicating that the viatari should follow. Once they were all onboard and seated, the turtle lurched forward and began surging through the water.

"What is this?" Tera asked, bewildered.

"Public transportation. We have giant sea turtles carry us from the outskirts of the city to the center. It's faster than swimming," he shrugged and added as an afterthought, "the turtles are well taken care of."

The buildings around them flew by and became more clustered. Within minutes they had stopped again. Avmoshir stood and hopped off the turtle, Victria and the others right behind him. They looked around. Here there were many more vashi, all walking along the streets on their own business. A few cast them some curious glances, but none lingered.

"We'll hit the markets first," Avmoshir pointed toward a number of multi-storied buildings, each with a fancy sign posted out front in a strange script that Victria couldn't read. Several well-dressed vashi stood in front of each store, hissing at the crowds in their own language, trying to entice customers with bargains.

Victria glanced at a few shops but wasn't entirely interested in buying anything—plus, none of them had any vashi money. She felt like these people might take gold, but she couldn't be sure. While gold was very valuable on the surface world it might not be here.

They spent very little time in the marketplace. Once Avmoshir realized they had already grown bored of it, he heaved a sigh of relief and said they should move on to the terrarium.

"What's a terrarium?" Serania asked.

"You'll see," Avmoshir grinned. Victria had the sense he liked the feeling of being in charge and more knowledgeable than them. "It's actually pretty fascinating. It's one of the places I enjoy going to the most."

They arrived to a long, rectangular building that seemed

to be made of several different materials, including one section that was composed entirely of seaweed. Once inside, it did not take long for them to realize what a terrarium was all about.

Smaller, bioluminescent jellyfish hovered in hanging globes of water around them, lighting the many enclosures that housed animals and beasts from the surface. Walls of thick marble separated them from each other, but as they walked through the building Victria saw horses running through small fields of artificial grass, a bear trying to save her cub who had climbed too high on a coral tree, even small creatures like rabbits and squirrels had their own enclosures—which seemed to attract the vashi children more than anything.

"How—" Tera, for a moment, was lost for words. "How is this possible?"

"We vashi have the ability to command the waters to transport us," Avmoshir explained. "We can appear any-where on the surface world as long as there is a body of water for us to emerge from. Some of our hunters do this and bring back beasts from your world so that we can study them and see what otherwise we would never be able to see."

"These poor beasts will never see the sun again—" Natiari muttered.

"Or feel the wind—" Serania added.

"Or brush against soft beds of grassy meadows," Madira stifled a cry.

Avmoshir frowned, sensing their displeasure. "I apologize if this upset you, I did not think it would. I thought you might enjoy seeing parts of your world for a change."

Victria shook her head and flashed the young vashi a forced smile. "No, we appreciate the gesture, Avmoshir. We just . . . would rather see more of your city."

Avmoshir shrugged and they left the terrarium, opting to walk through the city streets and wander around instead. As they walked, they passed the rear end of the Assembly Dome, where they had been only yesterday. On this side of the city was the military quarter. Several troops of vashi were out on spacious fields practicing maneuvers or dueling each other.

The vashi were silent as they fought, reminding Victria slightly of her own kind. They were opposite the dwarves, who liked to yell fearsome war cries during battle.

"Victria," Serania muttered. Something in her voice caught Victria's attention, making her head snap around. Serania stared stiffly ahead. She noticed Tera had moved closer to the viatari as if for protection. Her eyes followed their gaze until she saw what had caused such a reaction.

Stalking toward them, his curved blades out, was a hulking figure with long green hair and vivid orange eyes. Koranam, a subtle look of triumph on his face, smiled, revealing several rows of sharp teeth. Avmoshir saw him coming, too, and called out to him.

"What are you doing here, Koranam? I rarely see you with the troops," the young vashi didn't seem to share the viatari's unease about this particular representative.

Koranam glared at the viatari, lingering for a moment longer on Tera and licked his lips. "Avmoshir, it has been too long. I'm here to practice. It is always good to stay sharp when it comes to one's fighting ability. But what are you doing out in the city? I had thought you would be cooped up all day with your father."

Avmoshir sighed. "Father wanted me to give the new-comers a tour of our city."

"I see," something in Koranam's voice made Victria's stomach tighten. It was like he was a snake preparing to strike.

"What a shame the young prince has been put on guide duty rather than sticking by his father's side to learn his . . . masterful ways of leading our people."

The young vashi chuckled, oblivious to the tension that stained the water around them.

"I'm no prince."

"Perhaps not in title, but with your father's death you might come to lead our people."

Avmoshir frowned, taken aback with where the topic of the conversation had suddenly swung to. "Well then, it is good that my father is not dead yet."

"No," Koranam agreed with a grim smile. "Not yet."

Once again, the representative eyed the viatari. Victria knew he must be studying them to see what kind of threat they presented. He most likely saw their slender dirks as non-threatening compared to the heavy weapons the vashi carried. Normally, she would welcome such an under-estimation, as the viatari's supernatural strength made up for their light weaponry. But they didn't have that advantage anymore.

"You should return home, young prince," Koranam finally said.

"I'm not—"

"Tend to your father. Send him my regardsss."

With that, the representative from Kesmur turned and waded away, returning to the training grounds.

"Perhaps we should go back to your father," Tera suggested. "Something about the way he said that doesn't sit right with me."

Avmoshir only seemed to hear the first part. "Yeah, okay," he muttered, his thoughts elsewhere. "We've seen the better parts of the city anyway."

As they walked back, not much was said. Avmoshir, at one point mentioned how Koranam had changed, how they used to be the best of friends before falling silent once more, as if he had been talking more to himself than the viatari.

It took thirty minutes for them to reach the giant sea turtle transport and another ten to arrive at the stop near Araxie's house. They leapt off the turtle and walked for only a few minutes before they were stopped in their tracks. Victria's eyes widened.

"No," Avmoshir whispered.

Tera bent down and pulled out two daggers from her boots.

"Let's go," she said, and charged in, prompting the others to follow.

Ahead of them, Araxie's house lay in shambles. The windows had been shattered as if someone had broken through. The same was true for the door. Nothing but cracked marble and shattered coral remained.

Once inside, they saw the extent of what had happened. All the servants who had come with them from Pashir, lay on the marble floor in unnatural poses, their blood staining the white stone. A few other vashi bodies, clothed in black garments and wielding silver harpoons, also lay scattered across the floor.

Victria scanned the bodies and saw that none of them were Araxie. Avmoshir seemed to notice the same thing and he exhaled in relief.

"Dad! Mom!" he called out.

"Quiet down!" Serania put a hand to his mouth to keep him from yelling anything else, her curved saber held out in front of her. "We don't know if whoever attacked this place is still here."

Victria drew her blade as did the other viatari and they carefully crept up the stairs to the second floor, careful not to make any sound that might give them away. They rounded the corner into a connecting hallway and saw more bodies, this time some guards mixed in with the servants and assassins. Again, Araxie was not among them.

"Araxie!" Victria hissed, "Where are you?"

Silence, then coughing coming from the room at the end of the hall. The viatari rushed through, Natiari and Tessa keeping to the flanks and making sure the rooms they passed were clear as they ran. They burst through the door into the room, weapons at the ready, but no one was there to greet them, save more bodies on the floor.

Here were the most vashi in black that Victria had yet seen. Many had died here. It was clear this was where the fiercest of the fighting had taken place. She saw movement out of the corner of her eye and turned quickly, her dirk at the ready, but what she saw next nearly made her drop her weapon as her heart lurched into her throat.

Near the window, leaning against the wall, his pale-blue chest ragged with wounds and drenched in his own blood, was Araxie, leader of the vashi. In his arms was Avmoshir's mother, eyes staring up at him yet unseeing. Streaks of red painted her midsection. Avmoshir stared in disbelief for a minute before rushing to his father.

"Dad! Mom!" he whimpered. "What happened?"

Araxie opened his mouth to speak but coughed up blood instead.

The viatari glanced at each other, a knowing look passing between them. Araxie was dying. And Victria thought she knew who was responsible for the attack. The signs were too clear and the motive—painfully obvious. They were not safe here.

Serania seemed to come to the same conclusion. "You all stay here. I'm going to check the rest of the house, make sure we're really in the clear."

"I'll go with you," Tera said, sparing one last look at the vashi leader before running out.

"They . . . will come again," Araxie gasped.

"Who's they, dad? What do I do?" Avmoshir's voice broke.

"You do nothing . . . My son—I am dying."

"No, you can't. You can't!"

Araxie grinned feebly. "Apparently, I can. There is still so much you must learn, but—"

Araxie coughed again, struggling to take in another breath. "No time," he looked at his son for a long moment. Victria briefly thought he had died, but then he let out another rattling breath. "No matter, you will know what to do . . . It is—natural—in our family."

His eyes glazed over briefly, but then he caught sight of Victria. A new energy seemed to surge through him, sharpening his mind.

"You . . . you must promise me something."

His voice was faint. Victria knelt next to Avmoshir, who held his father's hand, tears streaming freely down his face.

Araxie continued, "You must promise me . . . Protect my son, at all costs. Keep him alive."

Victria didn't know what to say. Of course, her natural instinct was to keep Avmoshir alive, to put those evil forces who had orchestrated this attack down. But how could she promise any of that? She was without her viatari abilities, she was weak. In the forefront of her mind was the idea that she would fail, and she couldn't shake the feeling.

"Promissse me. . . ." Araxie's voice was now barely a whisper. Victria saw his eyes close. The grip on his son's hand slackened.

"Promissse. . . ."

"I promise." Victria said, knowing there was nothing more to be said.

Araxie, leader of the vashi, gave the faintest of smiles and then he was still.

CHAPTER TWENTY-THREE

"Come away now, Avmoshir," Victria said as gently as she could. Her mind was in overdrive as she thought of what they should do now that their one ally in this alien place had been killed, but at the same time a numbness was settling in, keeping any coherent thoughts from forming. All she knew at the moment was that they had to escape. "Come, we must go."

Avmoshir, who had been staring at the still faces of his parents in disbelief, turned to look at her. There was a moment where he seemed to not recognize her, but as his wits returned, his face contorted in anger. He hissed.

"I'm not going anywhere. You go, you have no reason to be here anymore."

"Avmoshir—"

Before Victria could continue, however, Serania and Tera burst back into the room.

"The house is clear," Serania reported. "Everyone in here, aside from us, is dead. But whoever did this is already on their way back. Tera and I saw them coming from the ridge south of us."

"At least a dozen of them," Tera added.

"Who could have done this?" Madira asked as she inspected the killing blows one of Araxie's guards had suffered.

"Koranam," Victria said, voicing her suspicions for everyone to hear.

She remembered only hours before when they had encountered the representative from Kesmur. She had felt that something was off about him at the time. He had seemed shocked and fairly disappointed to see Avmoshir out and about. His ominous words echoed in her head.

Tend to your father. Send him my regardsss. . . .

"It was Koranam, I have no doubt. He sent us back here, and then told what remained of his assassins to return and finish the job."

Natiari nodded as she peered out one of the windows. "That would explain why we are under attack so suddenly after returning."

"I think he meant to take out both Araxie and Avmoshir in one fell swoop. That's why he was surprised when he saw us in the military quarter, and why he urged us to go back home."

Avmoshir, who still knelt by his parents, laughed incredulously. "Please. You invent wild stories. Koranam disagreed with my father on many things, but he would never do something as terrible as this."

"No?" Tessa pursed her lips. "Tell me, young one, if both you and your father were to die, who would become Supreme Overseer?"

Avmoshir stuttered for a moment. "K-koranam, most likely, but that's beside the—"

"Well, if that doesn't convince you, maybe this will," Madira pointed at an insignia tattooed into the arm of an assassin she had been inspecting. Victria thought it looked like three fish sprouting out of an endless hole.

"That's—" for a moment the young vashi seemed lost for words as he drifted from his father's side to where Madira was so he could get a better look, "—that's the seal of Kesmur . . . Koranam's province. . . ."

"Well, now that we've got that settled," Tera waved her hands to get everyone's attention. "I would like to remind us all that we will soon be under attack by a force that outnumbers us."

"She's right," Serania said. "There's no time to waste on further investigation. What should we do?"

They all looked at Victria.

Victria blinked. "You want me to decide?"

Serania shrugged. "You've led us this far."

She thought for a moment. If Tera was right about the numbers of the enemy, they wouldn't be able to fight them off, especially in their weakened state. Their only option, then, was to run, though how they would outrun vashi in their own territory she had no idea. Suddenly an image of the manta rays entered her mind and she clapped her hands.

"Mounts! Madira, Tera, go out the back door of the house and swim as quickly as you can to the stables. Get enough mounts for us all and an extra one to carry supplies."

Madira and Tera nodded and were out the door without another word.

"Tessa, Natiari, go to the kitchens and gather as much food as you can."

"Food? But we can just hunt—"

"Not for us," Victria pointed to the young vashi who had returned to his father's side. "He's coming with us and if we're going to keep him alive we need to keep him fed. Get all the food you can carry."

The two nodded and left as well, leaving only Serania.

"Serania, watch my back. I don't know how the assassins plan to attack—they could come through the front door or through any of the windows. Hopefully we're gone before they do, but if we're not. . . ."

"Got it. I'll keep an eye out."

Now Victria returned her attention to Avmoshir, who had been ignoring the proceedings, his attention available only for the corpses of his parents.

"We need to bury them," he mumbled.

"There's no time," Victria said sadly. As much as it hurt her to not give the young vashi what he needed to grieve properly, the dire circumstances they were in demanded she get the boy up and moving now.

"Avmoshir, we need to go now if we are to survive this. We cannot fight our way out."

Avmoshir scoffed. "More like you don't want to fight." He eyed the golden harpoon still in his father's limp hands and took it. "I'm not afraid to fight. I will avenge my father and mother. Curse those scavengers of Kesmur!"

"There will be a time for fighting in the future," Victria said firmly, gripping the vashi's shoulder. "But now is not that time. You need an army of your own if we're to take back the city."

Here Avmoshir shook his head, confused. "Take back the city? Zessarix is mine. The armies here are mine."

"They were your father's and should be yours," Victria agreed. "But Koranam has had plenty of time to plan things out beforehand. I have no doubt he has swayed the military, the Assembly, even the citizenry to his side so that he can assume immediate control. He does not expect you to live for much longer."

Avmoshir's defiant mood reared up again. "I'll take my

chances. I may not look it, but I am a skilled fighter. I will kill any assassin who dares attack me and then I will appear before the Assembly and challenge Koranam for the throne."

Victria pictured the bulking figure of Koranam looming over the smaller frame of Avmoshir. While the younger vashi might be a skilled fighter, as he claimed, experience would be the deciding factor in such a battle. But she did not want to hurt his pride any more than she had to.

"Don't be foolish," she warned. "I saw how many were on Koranam's side when I was in the Assembly with your father. You would not just be facing him. You'll need help if you're going to claim power."

"Are you not going to help me?" He asked accusingly.

"I will—I am—but even my help and that of my companions will not be enough. We need more aid."

Avmoshir looked once more at his father.

"Araxie told me to protect you at all costs and I promised him I would do so. But to do that right now we need to leave the city."

The young vashi sat there for a moment longer and finally nodded, turning away from his father. Victria could see it was taking everything in him to keep his emotions in check. But there was no time for comfort, they needed to act.

"Now, what's the best way out of this house so that we can put distance between us and those assassins without being seen?"

Avmoshir thought for a moment, then nodded as he came to a conclusion. "We can't do this all the time, but we will for this one instance. Call your companions back in here. You will all need to hold on to me for this to work."

Victria did so, and moments later everyone was back in the room, Natiari and Tessa with three filled sacks full of whatever they were able to find.

"They're nearly upon us," Serania said. "They could rush through the doors within the next minute."

"Hold onto some part of me and do not let go until I say so," Avmoshir instructed.

They did so. Victria wondered what Avmoshir had in mind when suddenly she felt like jelly. The feeling was gone as soon as it had appeared and now she found herself outside of the house and on one of the several ledges that surrounded the back end of it, providing a fair view of their surroundings. The other viatari gasped as they, too, felt the same strange sensation. Only Avmoshir remained unaffected.

"You may let go now."

They did so and collapsed onto the ground, their legs shaking.

"What—happened?" Victria breathed hard. One moment they had been in the house, the next, within the blink of an eye, they were on top of this ledge.

"As I told you before, we vashi have the ability to command the waters to transport us anywhere in the world, so long as there is water to do so and we know the location of our destination's water source. It is called *liquefaction*. It is an instant method of travel. It cannot be done all the time, though."

"Won't the assassins be able to just 'liquefact' to us, then?" Serania asked, using her sword to push herself back onto her feet, albeit shakily.

The young vashi shook his head. "They could only follow us if they had seen us liquefact—there's a small glimmer left behind when we do this that can be used as a trace for someone else to follow—but it only lasts for seconds. It should be gone already."

From the ledge they could see every inch of the house as well as every assassin that surrounded it. There was a shout from one of them—more like a loud hiss—and then they all barged into the building from multiple points.

"They're in," Serania noted. "They'll see we aren't there and will likely comb through the surrounding area to see if we've made a run for it."

"So, we're still in danger," Natiari grimaced.

"Yes."

"I just hope Tera and Madira don't bring the mounts straight back to the house," Victria said. The thought had just now occurred to her that those two wouldn't know they had escaped by non-conventional means.

"If your two companions have any brains," Avmoshir said, looking up. "They will come riding in from high above so as not to be seen by our assailants. They should find us easily from such a vantage point." He smiled, the tragedy of the past few hours temporarily forgotten, "Lucky for us, it appears they do have brains."

He pointed to their right and slightly upwards where eight black dots were quickly growing larger and taking shape. The cluster of mantas circled high above for a single rotation before diving down with great speed. The creatures flapped their fins heavily, swinging themselves upward just before they hit the ground.

They mounted quickly, tying the bags of food and their other supplies onto the last manta, and then they were off. No words were spoken. It was not the time for idle chatter. They leaned back on their harnesses, urging their mounts forward and upward. The mantas swam with haste and the city of Zessarix passed by quickly underneath. Before too long, they were nearing the large, stone arches that marked the city's entrance.

Victria looked over the side of her mount and saw a small party of vashi standing just before the gates, all dressed in black.

"I think we have some company waiting for us."

"I see them, too," Serania said.

"Think we can outrun them?" Tera asked

Serania shook her head. "No, they've already spotted us. We'll have to fight them."

"Finally!" Avmoshir cried and raised his harpoon high above him, the jagged tip pointed toward his enemies below. "I will destroy my father's killers."

And with that he urged his mount into a steep dive straight at the group of black-clad vashi. Victria counted at least nine—one of them looked to be a waterseer based on his ornate headdress.

"Let's go," she said. "But be careful. Serania, focus on that waterseer. If they're anything like the dwarven Enurg'en I don't want them to turn the battle against us."

They all leaned forward, the mantas responding instantly to their body weight, and dove. The vashi hissed in anticipation, their tridents and nets ready for the first strike.

Avmoshir's manta barreled through them, slapping them with its large fins and scattering their tight formation. The young vashi drew first blood, impaling one of Koranam's henchmen straight through the heart and dragging him along for a distance before ripping out his harpoon and leaving the body to float in a growing mist of blood.

Fighting on a manta ray was unlike anything Victria had ever experienced. Thankfully, the mount gave her an advantage in speed and maneuverability that she would not otherwise have had against the likes of the vashi. One tried to jab

at her mount with his spear, but she batted the tip away with
her dirk. The attempt angered her manta, though, and the
beast turned suddenly, swiping at the vashi with one of its
fins, sending the enemy spinning in the water. Victria jumped
off her mount quickly, speeding toward the spinning vashi
before he could regain his balance and finished him with a
quick slash across the throat. The vashi's eyes bulged and
then slowly closed and he grew still. The manta glided under
Victria and she took hold of the seaweed harness, once
more speeding through the waters.

The other viatari seemed to be managing well. Serania
had slain the waterseer easily with her saber, lopping his
head clean off. The water around them was saturated with
blood as if they were swimming in a cloud of it as the battle
continued. Victria observed that there were only three more
vashi to deal with. Avmoshir dove from above again, picking
one off the same way he had before while Tessa, Natiari,
and Madira worked together to fight off another. Tera
handled the last one by herself, swimming swiftly to avoid
the vashi's attacks while she came in close and jabbed her
daggers into her opponent's belly, slashing outward and
eviscerating him.

Within minutes, the battle was over and the viatari were
remounted, speeding away from the city. Victria glanced back
and saw the thick plumes of blood had spread with the
currents. It would not take long for someone within the city
to notice and investigate. She was sure Koranam would realize they had escaped once he saw the bodies. He would
send more assassins after them.

"Where do we go from here?" She asked. She didn't
know these waters. As far as planning went, the next step
was up to Avmoshir to find a safe haven.

The young vashi thought for a moment. "If Koranam was as devious as you suggested and planned this out, it is likely he has brought the nearby towns, including Pashir, to his side. We will have to avoid them and make for Maleres, which is on the other side of the Sea of Scales, past the Trench of Fear. A three days' ride."

"You don't think he would have brought the people of Maleres to his side as well?" Madira asked. "Why stop with the small towns?"

"No. He's not one for tradition, despite what he says and how he looks. He could care less for the temple-city of Maleres and its inhabitants. They are mostly waterseers and high priests. Few warriors. He wouldn't see them as a potential threat, so he would never bother to try and sway them. He probably assumes they'll do whatever he demands anyway."

"Will they?"

Avmoshir glared at Victria, who had asked the question. There wasn't anything necessarily hostile in his gaze, but she could tell he did not appreciate the question. If he was wrong about Maleres, then they had nowhere to go. Still, he eventually answered.

"They will not. The waterseers and high priests of Maleres were always extremely loyal to my father. They will be our safe haven and a place from which we can plan how to re-take my city."

And with that, they rode in silence. Several things went through Victria's mind during this time, first and foremost the knowledge of how silence can allow one to delve too deep into their own thoughts, their own feelings, especially once the adrenaline of battle had passed. She looked at Avmoshir and saw his shoulders trembling ever so slightly. She looked away, wishing she had something comforting to say. But words failed her.

CHAPTER TWENTY-FOUR

It was strange, Victria thought, how everything in the ocean remained beautiful despite recent events. Life still abounded, even as they rode out into the open ocean. Shoals of different kinds of fish swam gracefully above them, hovering just below the surface. Sword fish darted past them, disappearing into the blue depths as fast as they appeared. At one point, a pod of dolphins swam with them for the better part of an hour, whistling and trilling as they went.

With all this seemingly undisturbed life around them, Victria couldn't help but feel at peace as their journey continued, so much so that at times she would almost forget why they were out in the open ocean in the first place.

Their first day of travel passed by without incident. They saw the murky silhouettes of a few towns in the distance but steered well clear of them. As Avmoshir had mentioned before, it was likely these towns were already under Koranam's control. They would find no refuge there. And so they had continued riding, eventually making camp in a small cave they found tucked away within a series of small ridges.

They set a watch that night, with Victria and Natiari taking the first shift. There was no campfire, though they had brought a few vials of everlasting fire, and so the two sat in the dark by the mouth of the cave.

The ocean was much more menacing at night. Here, where there was no civilization, and thus no captured bioluminescent jellyfish to light the waters, there was nothing to see but blackness. And yet, Victria could still sense creatures skittering about in the dark. She heard the faint shuffling of crabs hunting for prey. Every now and then a sudden vibration in the water reached her, prickling her skin and telling her that something had moved suddenly, as if to strike.

"I'm finding it hard to see what the use of a watch is if we can't see a thing," Natiari commented, as if reading Victria's mind.

Though she had a point, Victria could only shrug. "It feels safer than not having one, I suppose."

As the night wore on, Natiari began to hum. Victria recognized the tune as an old traveling song the viatari used to sing during their days as nomads, back in a time when they had been hunted by the Creature's darimun. It was a solemn song.

The humming stopped. "What do you think about the boy's intention of retaking Zessarix?"

"I don't see how it can be done," Victria said truthfully. "I only encouraged him to get him to escape with us. If Koranam has really taken as much control of the seas as we believe. . . ."

"Why are we here, then?"

Victria glanced questioningly in her direction, then remembered that Natiari couldn't see her face. "What do you mean?"

"I don't mean to sound unsympathetic, or unkind," Natiari started. "But we have our own task here: to find and obtain the assistance of this acolyte residing in the Throne of the

Deep. Aren't we wasting time by sticking with Avmoshir and meddling in political disputes of a people who clearly don't want anything to do with us?"

Victria had to admit, the thought had occurred to her as well many times throughout the day. But she knew she could never truly entertain the idea of leaving Avmoshir on his own. There was something about the young vashi that made her want to protect him. He was just a boy.

"Our paths are still the same for now. Araxie told us that only the high priests of Maleres can enter the Throne of the Deep. Since Avmoshir has a mind to go there, I don't see why we should part ways. And besides, coming here has presented a new opportunity for us, I think. One that Felix did not foresee."

"What would that be?"

"Seeking an alliance with the vashi."

Natiari laughed. "You can't be serious. Koranam only cares for his people. He would never even discuss the idea with us. Any chance of the vashi joining our fight against the Creature and The Turned One died with Araxie."

"Yes, but perhaps it can live on with his son."

"You think Avmoshir would be willing to join us? He seems to hate us. Or, at least, he's uninterested in our troubles."

"He's grieving—" Suddenly she turned around, looking back into the cave, though she couldn't see anything. She thought she'd heard something from within—a movement. But they had checked this cave thoroughly before making camp inside it, there should be no danger.

"He's grieving," she repeated. "But I don't think that puts him against us. If we help him and manage to take back Zessarix, he might be inclined to help us in return."

There was a moment of silence, then Natiari chuckled. "So, it's a trade of services we're performing?"

Victria frowned. "I don't see it as such, but I suppose you could say so—though, it's not the only reason I think we should stick this out until the end."

"Ah, you promised his father you'd protect him." Natiari stated.

"Yes," Victria said softly. It was a promise made in the moment, and one she did not like to make. She thought of all those in the past she had tried to protect, but failed. She should not have made such a promise. Perhaps it was not too late to renege it? She shook her head, fresh determination coursing through her. No, she thought, this would not be like those times. "I never break my promises."

With the second day of travel came the Trench of Fear. Victria had seen it coming from a distance, an endless chasm that ran all the way down from north to south as far as she could see. It was blacker than night within and as they began to cross over, she couldn't help but feel a sense of doom that she would fall in and become lost to the world forever.

"What is this place?" Madira asked in a hushed tone.

"The Trench of Fear," Avmoshir answered stiffly. He might be from these waters, but Victria had a feeling even he felt uneasy about crossing over this area. "No one knows how deep it goes or what lies within. It's too deep, even for us vashi, to swim into without suffering permanent brain or lung damage or even death from the water pressure. We often send convicted criminals to their deaths by tying an anchor or stone to their ankles and pushing them in."

There was silence for a while, until the ocean floor behind them disappeared from sight and all they could see below them was the black void.

"I feel like I'm about to fall in," Tessa noted. Victria tightened her own grip on the harness of her manta.

Avmoshir chuckled. "You won't fall in, believe me, unless—" A shadow fell over them, cutting off Avmoshir's words as they all looked up and froze. Victria wasn't quite sure what they were seeing. All she knew was that it was a beast of massive proportions; the biggest she had ever seen.

"Keep the mantas moving at a steady pace," Avmoshir whispered urgently, his eyes glued to the monster above. "No sudden movements."

"What is it?" Serania asked.

The beast swam slowly, gracefully, and moved its body similar to a snake, despite having many limbs that moved back and forth, propelling it forward. Victria thought of the statue they had seen back in Zessarix. Araxie had told them what it was.

"It's a saran," Avmoshir whispered, now in awe as it became clear that the saran had not seen them and was continuing on its way. "They're incredibly rare, even though they constantly travel across all parts of the ocean. Super dangerous, too. My dad says pretty much no one survives an encounter with them."

"How do you know people have encountered them if no one survives to tell the tale?" Tera asked.

The young vashi shrugged. "We find their remains in saran droppings, which sink to the ocean floor. They're pretty easy to find."

Their mounts continued gliding through the water and, within minutes, the saran's enormous form faded into the endless blue that surrounded them. Though the danger of the saran had been brief and was now past them, it still took almost half an hour before they saw the ocean floor, dispelling any fears of falling into the Trench below.

"We'll continue past the trench for a couple of hours to put some distance between us and this place and then we'll set up camp for the night." Avmoshir said, urging his mount to a greater speed.

They made camp out in the open. It felt risky, Victria thought, but they hadn't seen any caves or seaweed forests where they could conceal their position so there had been little choice. She sighed. It looked like there wouldn't be a fire tonight either.

After letting the mantas loose to roam freely, Tessa and Madira set out to hunt for some fish. Avmoshir and Tera went through the provisions and pulled out several uncooked filets of eel and snapper. Avmoshir seemed to have no issue with the raw fish as his sharp teeth sliced through the meaty flesh. Tera grimaced, but forced herself to eat until she was satisfied.

"New experiences," she said with a pained grin as Victria glanced her way.

"I'm sure we'll reach Maleres soon where you can get a hot meal."

"I hope so. We should be arriving tomorrow, right Avmoshir?"

The young vashi looked up from his food and glared at Victria and Tera. He turned away and shuffled off without saying a word.

Tera watched him go. "I wonder what's got him in a mood."

Victria shrugged. "He is young, and he's just lost his parents."

Tera eyed her last piece of eel and tossed it over her shoulder. She laid down and stretched out, eyes already closed.

"Well, we've all lost, haven't we? It's what we do after that defines who we really are."

Victria tried to think of something to reply with, but found she couldn't deny what had been said. It made her think. And for the rest of the night as she took first watch again, now with Serania, memories of her past and everyone she had lost during her lifetime returned to the forefront of her mind.

As they woke up the next day and resumed their journey for Maleres, Victria began to wonder why they hadn't seen any signs of pursuers yet. Surely Koranam would have known they had escaped the city. To secure his power over the assembly and the Sea of Scales, he would have to kill Avmoshir, the only one who could challenge his legitimacy, and he would need proof of his demise. And yet, their journey had been surprisingly smooth for the past two days.

She mentioned this to Serania as they gathered the mantas and strapped on their harnesses.

"Maybe we're lucky," the wanderer suggested. "We didn't stop at any of the towns so it's not like we left a trail of witnesses for them to ask about our whereabouts."

"It is strange, though," Tera said, walking up to them, having heard their conversation. "I haven't even seen much ocean life since we passed the Trench of Fear aside from the fish Tessa and Madira managed to bring back yesterday."

"That's because you're not looking," Avmoshir yawned as he picked up his sack of belongings. He pointed upward and to his left. "Look, there's a gam of sharks over there in the distance. It looks like six to eight of them. Where there are sharks, there's food, which means there's other life around us."

They mounted up and headed out, the mantas picking up speed with each flap of their fins. Victria thought about the young vashi's words and kept her eyes on the sharks to their left. She couldn't help but question if they might be the food that attracted them to this part of the ocean.

"We should arrive at Maleres within the hour," Avmoshir called over his shoulder after a few hours had passed. "Look, you can already see the grand temple rising in the distance."

Ahead of them, still only a dark blur in the water, rose a structure that looked to be made up of countless columns. To be seen from this distance, Victria was sure it had to be at least as large as the Assembly Dome back in Zessarix.

"Keep an eye out," Serania called. "If there was ever a time for Koranam to attempt some sort of attack, it would be now."

Victria agreed and looked over her shoulder once more to see if the sharks were still keeping pace with them. She was glad to see they weren't. That brief breath of relief was pushed out, however, when Tessa pointed above them and cried out.

"Sharks!"

She looked up. Eight sharks were charging in on their position, their maws open, revealing rows upon rows of jagged teeth. Avmoshir's eyes widened.

"Scatter!"

Victria leaned hard to her right, causing her manta to balk, and just narrowly avoided two sharks that had targeted her. She drew her weapon quickly and slashed to her left, only managing to graze the tail of one of them.

The two predators circled her, their large black eyes staring through her as they positioned themselves for another charge. She wouldn't give them the chance. Leaning forward suddenly, she urged her manta to go full speed toward the two beasts. One of them jerked suddenly, trying to catch her as she sped by, but missed. She held her dirk high as she passed under the other shark, opening its belly and creating a thick mist of blood.

She felt a small sense of victory, but that quickly vanished once she saw that the blood in the water had only caused the remaining shark to fall into a frenzy. It charged her with incredible speed. She tried to dodge the attack, but without her regular speed, she wasn't quick enough.

Teeth sank into her left arm like butter. It was like several daggers had been shoved into her at the same time along with two huge weights as the pressure of the bite crushed her bones. The shark thrashed, pulling her off her mount and nearly ripping her arm out of its socket. The pain was incredible. She felt her limb go numb and, not knowing what else to do, swung her other arm wildly so that her blade went straight through the shark's eye and out the other. The beast instantly went limp, and Victria was able to force its mouth open and remove her ragged arm from its jagged teeth.

She held it close to her, thankful that they at least had not given up their regenerative abilities. As she waited for her arm to heal, she watched her companions finish off the remaining predators. It seemed she wasn't the only one to have struggled during the fight.

Tera had been nipped on the foot, but it didn't look too bad. Serania had been bitten on her sword arm and was now nursing it just as Victria was. Luckily, all of their mounts, except for one, had survived as well. The unlucky manta looked like it had been attacked by several sharks at once, its body torn up in several places with large chunks of flesh missing.

As the last shark was impaled through and through by Avmoshir's golden harpoon, he turned to them. Seeing that they were all still alive, he nodded and pointed toward the city. "Quickly, we must reach Maleres before more sharks try to attack us."

"Is it normal for them to attack like that?" Tera asked, wincing slightly as she poked at the shallow wound in her foot.

"No," the young vashi replied grimly. "Not even when they're hungry. Not against the vashi—and with you being around the same size as us, they wouldn't do that to your kind either. No, those sharks were being controlled."

"Koranam," Tessa stated.

Avmoshir nodded. "He must have some waterseers in Zessarix who captured the sharks and bent their will to theirs. Sharks are much better hunters than we vashi are, so it would make their search for us easier even with us avoiding the towns."

"Do you think there are more, then?" Victria asked, slightly concerned. Battling sharks had been unlike anything she had ever done. They were fast, smart, and without her natural fighting prowess as a viatari, very dangerous. And if they had to fight more. . . .

"I would be surprised if there weren't," the young vashi scoffed. He pointed once more to the city before them. "Which is why we should hurry. The sharks will not dare attack within the city limits, even under the control of a waterseer."

Without another word, he urged his manta onward and the viatari and Tera quickly followed. Before long, the city's archway towered over them. Victria turned back to see where they had been attacked. There was still a great cloud of blood in the water from the slain sharks, and though they were now quite a distance from the spot, she was sure she could see the outlines of more hunters moving in to inspect the carnage.

306 ACOLYTES

CHAPTER TWENTY-FIVE

Flames illuminated the darkness, bathing the white walls of the city with their red and orange tongues. Salevari watched from where she stood, rooted to the spot in the middle of Aleganthia's plaza as the city burned.

The humans rampaged around her. They threw bricks at windows, dragged out the viatari from inside and slew them on the spot. They set more fires to those few buildings which had yet been untouched. They passed her without seeing her, a frenzy in their eyes. And she could do nothing to stop them. She turned her gaze to the flames eating away at the city walls. They grew brighter and brighter until finally she was forced to close her eyes.

When she opened them again, she was in her room. Sunlight streamed through the windows, blinding her.

A dream, she thought. But certainly a very troubling dream. She pushed the sheets off her bed and forced herself onto her feet, stretching as she did so. Why would such a dream come to her?

And then she froze as an idea came to her. She remembered how the Creature had often sent images to Thuradin when the twisted acolyte had been in the dwarf's mind. These visions often proved to show near-future events of disaster, much like her dream. She wondered if perhaps, somehow, the Creature had entered her mind. She splashed her face with cold water from a large bowl on her dresser. There was only one way to be sure.

She strapped on her leather boots, hooked her sword to her belt, wrapped a cloak around her shoulders and headed for the door. Leaving her room, she made her way upstairs. There were low murmurs of greeting from the staff as they passed her by, busy with their own work. She looked outside as she passed some of the keep's tall staircase windows. The city was bustling with activity just like any other day. In the distance the white walls of Aleganthia stood, not a single disturbance in sight.

This calmed Salevari significantly. Even though she knew her dream had been just that, she had still half-expected to see something wrong, some sign that could mean troubling times ahead.

"Salevari."

The Chancellor turned as Simon and Kent approached her from behind. They were both out of breath, having run up the stairs to catch up to her. Both of them also looked exhausted. Dark bags hung under their eyes and their hair—at least, Simon's hair—looked unwashed as if the two had been consistently busy for several nights.

"Can I help you gentlemen?"

"Hopefully," Simon grimaced. "We must discuss what happened at Tur. The news has spread among our people and—"

"If your people are worried about the same thing happening to them you may assure them that they need not fear it. The warning was only for those who kill my people."

Kent grunted.

Simon began to translate, "He says—"

But Salevari's mind was elsewhere. She raised a hand for silence. "We can discuss this another time. I have something I must check on first. You may wait in my throne room. I will send Zael along shortly to keep you company."

Simon looked like he wanted to say more, to hold her there, but she was already shaking her head before he could speak. "I promise you, we will speak on these matters. I will come by later so we can do so, but I must deal with this first."

Begrudgingly, Simon finally nodded, and he and Kent turned to make their way down the stairs and out of sight.

With a sigh, Salevari continued her climb until she was outside of the Watcher's Quarter. She hesitated for just a moment, and then went inside, being sure to close the door behind her.

The First One stood in the middle of the room, white, transparent tendrils swaying peacefully as always. A sense of calm overcame her as she approached the acolyte. For a moment she just stared at the golden artifact, and then she turned her gaze to the city below her and the surrounding forest.

"You have been busy," The First One noted.

"To lead well requires it," Salevari muttered. She focused again on the acolyte. "Have you discovered anything about your brother and sister and what their intentions might be?"

"No," Salevari could hear dissatisfaction in the acolyte's voice, which was rare. "Whatever blocks or wards they have set up to prevent me from reaching them are working well. They are obscured from my sight, which can only bode ill. I have sensed my other siblings, however, and they all appear to be awake—though it does not look like any of them are aware of our situation yet."

"So none of our forces have managed to reach them yet."

"It would appear not. But I sense this topic is not the only reason you have come to visit me today."

Salevari nodded. "I had a dream last night, a terrible one. The city burned because of the humans. They slaughtered us and I could do nothing to prevent it."

"Mmm," the acolyte's tendrils curled as if in thought. "An appropriate dream for the times, I would say."

"Is there a chance of it coming true?" Salevari asked, a trickle of fear entering her voice despite her best efforts to contain it. "Could this be a vision of the future like the ones the Creature used to show Thuradin?"

There was a pause. Then a couple of The First One's tendrils approached the Chancellor, planting themselves on each side of her head. She closed her eyes and felt the acolyte's presence take command of her mind.

"I do not sense my brother in you," The First One finally said, withdrawing his tendrils. "I do not believe this dream you had is his doing."

"So, it was just a dream."

"Yes, though one that appears to bear a great potential of coming to pass, nonetheless."

This caught Salevari's attention. "Do you mean to say you sense danger from the humans we have allowed into Aleganthia?"

"The humans are not dangerous in themselves, I believe," The First One seemed to hesitate, as if he wanted to choose his words carefully. "But they can be made so if they are not respected and are instead influenced by fear."

"They have no reason to fear us."

"Do they not?"

Salevari looked away. She knew what the acolyte was referring to. It was the same thing Simon and Kent had wanted to talk to her about.

"I did what I had to. They killed my people. A lesson had to be taught."

"I believe you did what you thought you had to do," The First One said, his voice soft. "But all actions have consequences. One such consequence from the events at Tur is this new and growing resentment the humans have toward the viatari."

"Even though we saved them?"

"The act of saving someone means nothing if the reason behind it is to use them for your own personal reasons."

"But it's not for my own personal reasons!" Salevari shouted. She felt the need to defend herself, to justify herself. It was the humans who were in the wrong, not her. Her first responsibility was to her own people, not them. "Didn't you say we needed them for the war?"

"Yes, I did," The First One replied, his voice still calm. "But not as pawns. We must have them help us through a relationship built on trust, or we risk losing them to my brother and sister."

The First One's aura seemed to double down on Salevari, but she blocked it out. She would not be forced to feel any kind of calm when she was being accused like this. As if *she* were the villain.

"What happened at Tur was a tragedy," the acolyte continued. "But your response, I fear, was not proper for our goal of uniting the humans and having them work with the viatari. It has only sown fear and division, which leads to resentment."

Salevari would hear no more. She turned on her heels

and stormed out of the Watcher's Quarter without another word. Anger burned through her body as she walked down the steps all the way to the keep's main hall. And with that anger, she felt hunger. She stormed out of the keep and into the city streets, making her way to the inn Zael had taken her to before. She would have a meal. She would spend some time alone, outside of the sphere of leadership. And then, once she regained her composure, she would go back to leading Aleganthia.

She burst into the *Nomad's Hut*, ignoring the stares she received as she entered and went straight to Valar, who looked rather distressed.

"Who is it now? Ah, Salevari, how may I help you?"

"Get me a pig. A large one."

Valar cracked a smile. "Hungry, are we? Pick out a seat and I'll get it right out to you."

Salevari sat in the same corner table she and Zael had taken last time. She kept her gaze down, not wanting anyone to think about coming over to talk with her. A moment later, the same barmaid as last time with the same silver, curly hair placed a large platter in front of her, a well-sized pig standing on it with bits of green garnish tucked behind the ears.

The pig snorted softly as Salevari stroked the back of its neck. With a quick motion, she wrapped her hand around the animal's snout and bit into its neck, consuming the animal's life-energies as it struggled and squealed in a panic. With such a decent-sized pig, it took her several attempts to consume all of the animal's life-energies. Each time, the pig struggled less and less until it moved no more.

Salevari licked her lips. Now that she was satisfied, she felt some of her anger dissipate—not all, but enough for her to start paying attention to her surroundings. There was a loud clatter only a few feet away and then the shuffling of chairs and footsteps. She glanced up and saw a human patron facing off against a viatari.

"Get out of my face!"

"I don't take orders from humans."

"You won't take orders from anyone if you don't back off."

The viatari chuckled. "An empty threat. If you don't like what my friends and I are discussing, perhaps you shouldn't listen."

"I don't give a damn what you and your friends think, but when you bring up what happened at Tur in such a disrespectful manner—"

Salevari had heard enough. She stood up and stormed over to where the two customers were. Valar remained behind his bar, eyeing them warily, as did most others in the inn. The tension was palpable. Any more escalation and she knew the bystanders still sitting at their tables would jump into action. Bloodshed would be inevitable. She would not permit it.

"Sit down, both of you," she growled. "This will not be tolerated in Aleganthia." She moved in between them and pushed them away from each other. She pointed at the viatari. "You should know better."

The viatari shrugged and went to rejoin his companions, his distasteful gaze still on the human. The human, too, returned to his seat, his eyes just as dark.

Salevari remained there for a moment longer. Seeing that there was no longer an immediate threat from either of them, she knew it was time to leave. She moved for the door.

"Continue with your meals," she ordered, her voice

carrying in the silent inn. "In peace."

She walked quickly back to the keep. It was time for her to speak with Simon and Kent. She had been so hungry and angry after talking with The First One, she had completely forgotten that she had told them she would come speak with them afterwards. Now, though, after seeing what had almost happened in the *Nomad's Hut*, she knew there could be no more delay. Things were escalating between the humans and viatari. They had to find a way to stop it while they still could.

The keep was eerily empty as she entered. She climbed the stairs, making her way to the throne room and thinking all the way. The streets had been rather empty as well. Perhaps it was her imagination, but it felt like a stone was sitting heavily in her stomach as a fear that something had already happened permeated through her mind.

She entered the throne room and found it full of staff members as well as Simon and Kent. The buzz of conversation died abruptly as they noticed her presence. Zael looked her way and shook his head grimly. That was all she needed to see to confirm her gut feeling. Something had indeed happened.

"What is it?" she asked.

A guard answered her, "There has been a murder within the walls."

Salevari's heart sank. Another one. And worse, the public knew about it this time.

"Who was it?"

"One of ours," the guard replied. "Esko Flurwind. He was off-duty, so it's possible the perpetrator didn't know he was a guard, but still. A viatari has been slain."

"I understand," Salevari said, her mind working in overdrive. "Do we know anything about the murderer?"

The guard frowned. "No. No one saw it happen, but based on the wounds, it looks like a single dagger strike was what slew Esko. I would bet there is poison involved as well."

Salevari thought that was a safe bet.

"I ordered the guards in the area to form a perimeter around the body to keep civilians from approaching. It's waiting for your inspection."

"Good, I—"

"Chancellor, there's something else."

Salevari recognized one of the scouts who typically brought her reports of imminent darimun attacks was present. "Is there another attack?"

The scout shook his head. "No, worse. The humans have formed a mob and are marching for the keep. They carry torches but nothing else as far as I could tell."

For a second, bitter anger returned. The humans would *dare* march so openly against the viatari in their own city? Salevari was tempted to send out every viatari warrior to wipe them out. The viatari would handle the corrupted acolytes by themselves if they had to. But she pushed the temptation aside and took a deep breath. Her gaze shifted to Simon and Kent, who both wrung their hands nervously.

"Go," she said. "Go to your people and stop them. Calm them down. I will go to the body and see what I can do there, but we need to move quickly to keep this situation from spiraling out of control. With any luck, we will have peace in Aleganthia again by nightfall."

The two humans nodded and stood abruptly, quickly leaving the room.

"Zael, you're with me."

The viatari captain saluted and joined her by the door. Salevari looked at the guard who had provided the report and took another deep breath. She had no idea what she was going to do, what she could do, to stop the viatari if they decided to take matters into their own hands and retaliate against the humans. They had every right to, this was their city.

The First One's words pulsed through her mind, *all actions have consequences.* She knew what the consequences would be if such action was taken. She had dreamed about it only last night.

"Alright," she said, steeling herself. "Take us to the body."

CHAPTER TWENTY-SIX

The viatari rushed out of the keep, heading for the northern parts of the city, their leather boots producing a light pattering against the cobblestone paths. With such a beautiful blue sky above them and a fair breeze at their backs, one would have never guessed that the city was on the verge of an explosion of violence. And yet, Salevari thought, here they were. She let the guard run ahead of them, just enough so that he was out of earshot.

"What happened?" She turned to Zael. "We were supposed to get some sort of warning before the humans attempted something like this so we could prevent it."

Zael pursed his lips. "There has been no word about taking action like this yet. Whoever did this did it of their own accord."

"I need you to find out who was responsible. We need to keep a closer eye on them in case they plan on going rogue again."

Ahead of them a crowd of viatari came into view. Many of them were crying, some tried to push past the guards, who formed a perimeter blocking off one of the city's many intersections. Salevari followed the guard's every step as he maneuvered his way through the crowd. The circle split just long enough for them to get through. As soon as the Chancellor was on the other side, she saw the body and sighed.

The slain viatari, Esko Flurwind, was none other than the one who had almost gotten into a fight with a human at the *Nomad's Hut*. She grimaced. If this was who was slain, she thought she could guess which human might be responsible for the murder. She tried to remember his face, but couldn't think of any specific features. He had been so bland, so typically human—they all looked alike in her mind.

"What should we do?" the guard next to her asked.

She looked at him, at the guards around them, and at the crowd of civilians who now stood silently, watching her. She looked at the body again and thought of what The First One had told her. *This* was the cost of her vengeance at Tur. This life, and a city on the brink of chaos. Felix would not have allowed things to get this far. He would not have gone to Tur at all—that way the viatari could not have been blamed for the town's inevitable destruction. Life would have gone on. This was her fault. But now she knew what she had to do to fix it.

"Take the body and bury it," she said. "I must go to where the humans are gathering and help Simon and Kent calm them down."

"But what about the humans?" the guard asked. "What if they do this again? What are we going to do to protect ourselves?"

"I'm still working on that. For now, do what I have told you and spread the word among the patrols to stay alert from now on. Do not consume or take anything that may have been made or handled by humans."

"The humans did this!" someone from the crowd shouted. "They must pay!"

"She let them in, this is her fault, too," another yelled.

"We must take the fight to them!"

Salevari gazed at the crowd, found where the voices had come from, and walked over to them. The few viatari who had made the calls glanced at each other nervously but held their ground. She took her time studying each one. They were average. They didn't look like fighters, probably had never partaken in a battle.

"Is that what you want?" she asked softly, and then raising her voice so everyone could hear, "do you want more violence?" She looked around waiting for a response but none came.

"I may be new to this city, but even I remember the streets of Aleganthia streaming with our people's blood not too long ago. Do you really think we should have that happen again? I may have continued letting the humans in, but Felix was the one who started the process—with the hope of helping us get over our hatred for the humans and the humans letting go of their hatred for us. You trust Felix. Now I ask you to trust me when I say I have Aleganthia's best interests at heart."

Her gaze returned to the three viatari who had called for retaliation, waiting to see if they would say anything else. When they did not, she took it as a sign that they were willing to stand down—at least for now.

"I go now to the humans to give them the same message. We must work together if we are to fight against the great evil we face today. And you may all be rest assured that the person responsible for this murder will be caught and brought to justice. Zael—"

She looked around, but the captain was nowhere to be seen. She could have sworn he was right behind her the entire time. Evidently, he had slipped away unnoticed before they had even reached the body. She sighed. She would have to face the humans alone, then. Her ability to speak the human tongue was still limited, but she thought she might know enough to convey her message to them. She could only hope it would be enough to calm them down as it had her own people.

She turned her attention to the guard who had led her here and motioned at the still body of Esko. "Bury him. The two of you," she pointed at two other guards who were part of the perimeter, "with me."

She made her way through the crowd again, the guards in tow, and ran back toward the keep. With any luck, Simon and Kent would have managed to slow the mob down enough for her to join them before they reached the keep.

As she ran, the sun sank below the horizon and covered the city in darkness. In the distance, Salevari could see the glow of many fires a few blocks from the main plaza. She pointed toward it and motioned at the guards following her.

"We'll get there faster on the roofs."

With a single motion, she jumped onto the top of the nearest building and started running along it, the guards following right behind her. As one section of roofing came to an end, they jumped over the alley gap onto the next one, again and again, each time drawing closer to the ominous glow ahead. The ribbons of smoke drifting into the sky began to thicken.

"Fires have taken hold," Salevari muttered. If the fire was still in the early stages, it could be contained easily enough. She just hoped the humans didn't cause any more damage before she had the chance to speak with them.

They made it to the end of their grid of rooftops again

and stopped in their tracks. Directly below them was a sea of humans, torches in hand and rage in their voices as they chanted something in their own language.

Salevari looked to her left and saw that a small barricade of carts, crates, and barrels had been hastily assembled to keep the mob from moving any farther. Behind this barricade was a small force of viatari guards, Dalyrans by the looks of their armor and large shields, who were facing off against the humans.

"Quickly!" Salevari called to the two guards behind her. "We must get to the barricade and head this mob off."

The viatari jumped across a few more roofs and before long had joined the guards by the barricade. Now that she was closer, she also saw Simon and Kent were there, doing what they could to appease the crowd, but it looked like the humans were having none of it. Simon stood there, his arms raised, trying to quiet the mob so he could be heard but they would not be silenced. Their voices penetrated the night and seemed to mix in with the heat from the fires they had set.

They weren't the only ones who were angry. Salevari could see the desire for violence in her guards' faces as they watched their homes burn. She had no doubt they would have no issue rushing forward and cutting down every last man and woman before them. She, too, felt a similar urge, but she swallowed it. Giving in to that desire would bring Aleganthia nowhere except destruction. She had to diffuse this situation and reestablish peace. But first, she needed their attention.

She yelled. All the anger and frustration she held within her, she let out with one penetrating howl. Her guards, Simon and Kent, and all the humans before her fell silent as her

voice caught their attention. All eyes turned to her, stunned that such ferocity could come out of someone so small.

Salevari took a deep breath, trying to recall as much of the human language as she could, and hoping it would be enough to convey a coherent message.

"Humans, I speak to you now," her mouth felt awkward, heavy. She knew her accent must be thick, foreign to human ears. She only hoped it was not so thick that it could not be understood. "I speak to you from heart. I know why you chant, why you march through Aleganthia. Anger and fear. It is what I felt when I heard news of my people's deaths in Tur."

The humans were ominously silent. The only sound in the night came from the crackling of fires.

"I forget the greater enemy. We face evil stronger than humans and viatari alone. We must face together, or evil will spread. More human towns fall. Aleganthia fall. Humans and viatari are stronger together. Only together, we have victory. Begins with trust. You must trust us and we must trust you— or we all lose."

"She's right!" Simon stood on one of the tipped over carts to project his voice. "If we allow ourselves to fall to our most basic fears and prejudices, we will have nothing but violence amongst ourselves, and those who are left after will be nothing but game for the demons to finish off. The viatari have shown their good faith by saving us from the demons' attacks and letting us live in their city, rather than leaving us to perish. We must return the favor."

People in the mob looked at each other, their feelings conflicted. Finally, a few in the middle ranks lowered their torches, followed by more and more. Buckets of water were brought out by the viatari so the humans could extinguish them, which they did. Then, with nothing left to do, many of them walked back the way they had come—slowly, as if they had much weighing on their minds. Some stayed behind and helped clean up the mess they had made.

The fires were put out, the extinguished torches picked up, the barricade removed, and the night was peaceful once again.

"Thank you," Salevari said to Simon as the last of the humans and viatari guards left. "I don't think I would have been able to convince them without your help."

Simon cracked a smile. "You did fine. I think hearing that sentiment from a viatari—in their own language, no less—was what made the difference. Kent and I were barely able to keep them from pushing past us before you came. If this city is saved it's because of you."

Salevari nodded, letting out a sigh of relief. "I think it is time for me to get some sleep. Will you meet me tomorrow? Since we had such a heartwarming discussion over the topic of trust between your people and mine, I think it is time we go over those antidotes."

Simon hesitated, but inclined his head, "We shall discuss it tomorrow, then."

The Chancellor left them and made her way back to the keep, a satisfied grin on her face. She looked up at the stars and thought of her brother, what he might say had he seen how she had just handled the situation.

She couldn't help but laugh at how she used to think of him not so long ago. The thought of pleasing Felix would have sickened her, but she no longer felt that way. He had given her a huge responsibility and shown that he trusted her more than anyone by giving her his city. She did not want to disappoint him.

And perhaps now she wouldn't, she thought, as she passed through the keep's large doors. They had come close to disaster tonight, but had managed to avoid it in the end. Perhaps now things were starting to look up.

CHAPTER TWENTY-SEVEN

Zael could hear the chanting of the mob from where he stood. He glanced over his shoulder. Only a few blocks away he could see the glow from their torches reach over the roofing of the residential buildings. He bared his fangs and faced forward, stomping toward the human quarter of the city.

He was furious. It had only taken a single glimpse for him to recognize that the dead viatari was murdered by a human. The single puncture wound was the same as the other two victims. The humans had struck again within the viatari's own city and it didn't look like there was anything Salevari could do about it.

That was another thing that angered him, though he tried his best to concentrate all his anger on the humans and not on Salevari. He couldn't believe the Chancellor had chosen to do nothing about Anders and Lyna after he had told her their plot to start an uprising. And now another viatari was dead because of her inaction.

Zael shook his head, still snarling, as he ducked into a narrow, dark alleyway. He began to shimmer and fade away, returning seconds later in his human form. Though he looked different now, his eyes burned with the same fury.

He walked with purpose through the human quarter. If Salevari was too cautious to do anything about these people, he would take care of them himself.

His plan was simple. He would stride into the resistance group's headquarters and he would kill every last human he found inside. He would have to be careful to not make it obvious that the humans died by viatari hands, though, so his people did not pay the price. His blood might be hot, but he was not foolish enough to think there would be no repercussions if he didn't at least try to make it look like the humans had killed each other.

The chanting from the mob teetered off into silence. The night grew still and Zael briefly wondered what could have caused the mob to stop. Whatever it was, it would not save them from his wrath. They had gone too far this time, marching toward the keep as if to burn it down. If the humans were to continue living in Aleganthia, they had to learn their place—and he would show them where that was.

Zael was only a few minutes away from his destination when he noticed two crouched figures just barely visible poking out of the shadows of a nearby alleyway. He stopped in his tracks, wondering if he should ignore them or investigate. Almost the entire human population within the city seemed to have taken part in the march. He wondered what could have kept these two from participating.

He crept forward, careful with his steps so he didn't kick any loose pebbles and give himself away. The two humans were just within the alley. Zael pushed himself against the wall adjacent to them and stood still, controlling his breath so he could hear every word they said, despite their whispers.

"—sure you killed him?" asked one of the voices. He

sounded afraid.

"I'm sure," Zael knew he'd heard this voice before but he couldn't quite put a face to it. "I saw the wretch stop quivering. You should have seen it, Dave. He just kept twitching and whimpering like a helpless critter. The poison Anders gave us really works!"

Zael's blood boiled. All thoughts of attacking Anders and Lyna's headquarters evaporated. The only thing registering in his mind now was that he had found him; the human who had murdered one of the viatari. He thought of what he should do, and only one course of action came to mind. This man would meet justice. *His* justice. There would be no taking him prisoner, no parading him through the streets. And he would make sure the human knew *who* had killed him.

"That's wonderful news, Barty!" the first man said again. Zael prepared himself for what he was going to do. He would have to refrain from using his supernatural strength in order to make it look like this was a fight between humans. While he would be sure the men he was about to kill knew he was a viatari before the end, he still had to make sure no one else knew.

The man continued to speak, "The viatari will never know what hit them. I only hope Anders and Lyna hurry up with the preparations to take out that witch they call a Chancellor."

Barty chuckled. "All in good time. I thought the elderly were supposed to have all the patience! I'm sure we'll be discussing this thoroughly in the next—who's there?"

Both men jumped back deeper into the alleyway and pulled daggers out. Zael stood before them, his hands behind his back and his face a mask as he watched the two slowly relax as they recognized him.

"Kurt!" Dave said in surprise. "My, young man, you must be more careful sneaking around in the dark like that, we could have killed you!"

"I could say the same about you," Zael said, his voice steely. "I just noticed your figures in the distance and came to see what was going on."

Barty put away his weapon. "I was just telling Dave the good news. I killed one of the viatari all by myself! And all it took was the venom that Anders provided me. The rest of them will be helpless against our new weapon."

"So I've heard."

The two humans glanced at each other and shifted uneasily.

"I must say, you don't sound too excited, Kurt."

"Aye," Dave agreed. "What's got you so riled up, young'un? You're looking mighty fierce right now."

Zael didn't answer with words, but quickly drew his dirk and thrust it deep into Dave's heart. The old man gasped in shock but then twitched and soon became still, his eyes wide with horror as Zael's hair slowly melted back into its natural silver and his gray eyes turned blood-red.

"No. . . ."

The viatari captain turned to Barty now, his fangs bared menacingly.

"You're one of them. . . ."

Barty swung wildly with his right fist while he reached with his left for his dagger. Zael easily dodged the first attack and flicked his dirk at Barty's other hand, forcing the human to drop the weapon he had just managed to pull out. Barty tackled him and the two rolled on the ground, struggling for dominance.

Zael felt his dirk slide out of his hand and scatter across the stone alley. Barty punched him in the face, the blow stinging him just enough for a fresh wave of rage to fuel him. The viatari captain jammed his fist into the man's side. He felt bones break. Barty screamed and his breathing grew laborious. Now Zael smashed his face into Barty's, causing a stream of blood to gush from his temple area.

Barty rolled away, clutching his side and his head. Zael gave him no respite and tackled him, quickly getting on top of him. He pulled the man's hands away and kneeled on them so he couldn't move. He looked to his right and saw a faint glimmer of metal as the moon's soft light reflected on the dagger Barty had dropped.

Smiling, Zael reached over, grabbed the weapon, and showed his victim what he now had, twirling the blade expertly between his fingers. Barty's eyes widened. He struggled harder. Zael slowly brought the dagger to the man's throat. This human had thought it wise to kill one of Aleganthia's own. Now he would pay: a life for a life.

His hand moved outward in a slow, purposeful manner. Blood spurted, splattering on Zael's face. Barty whimpered and gagged, still struggling, but his movements grew weaker with each passing second until he moved no more. Zael watched the human's face the entire time. He wanted to remember. He wanted the image of this murderer's final moment imprinted in his mind for the rest of his life, so that if he was ever asked by a relative or friend of the slain guard what ever happened to his killer, he would be able to tell them in great detail.

He nodded, satisfied. It was done. He placed the dagger in Barty's limp hand and stood up so he could place another in Dave's when he froze. Looking up, he saw another young man with bushy red hair standing at the end of the alley.

Garrel stood frozen to the spot, his mouth open like he wanted to scream, his eyes wider than those of the two humans Zael had just killed.

"Garrel, what are you doing here?"

"The march was dispersed," Garrel replied numbly. He took a step back. "I was just heading home to my wife. Oh, God, Kurt. You're one of them?"

Zael was silent, thinking hard on what he should do next. His first instinct was to kill Garrel, though he didn't like the idea. This young one wasn't evil like the men he had just killed and he had no personal quarrel with him. But if he spared him, he risked everything. There could be no witnesses.

The viatari captain gritted his teeth as he steeled himself for what he had to do, but before he could move in for the kill, he heard a multitude of voices approaching on both sides of the alley. If the march had truly dispersed like Garrel said, then he was about to be surrounded by a swarm of human witnesses. Zael couldn't be here when they arrived. He looked one more time into Garrel's frightened face, hoping the young human would not be foolish enough to expose his identity to the likes of Anders or Lyna.

Without a word, he quickly retook his human form and rushed past Garrel, who cowered as if he were about to be struck. Zael kept to the shadows as the crowds of humans returned to their homes. When a fair amount of them had passed by, he slipped out of the shadows, merging into the crowd naturally as if he'd always been there. He man-euvered his way skillfully through the masses. With any luck, anyone who saw him would think that his home was closer to the viatari part of Aleganthia and he was just trying to get there.

After a while, Zael found himself alone in the streets. Looking around to make sure no one was watching, he started to run and didn't stop until he was back on his people's side of the city. He reverted to his regular appearance and slowed to a leisurely walk. He glanced over his shoulder and found that he was truly alone. No one had followed him.

A sense of relief rushed through him as he allowed himself to bask in the feeling of accomplishment. He had found the killer and dealt with him. True, Garrel had stumbled upon the scene, creating a potential threat for the future, but he would worry about that when the time came. For now, he couldn't be certain that the human would even expose his cover. If anything, the fact that the man he knew as "Kurt" was really a viatari who didn't fear killing humans who crossed him might scare him into silence.

He hoped that was the case, for Garrel's sake.

Aleganthia's keep loomed in the distance. Zael walked purposefully toward it, thinking of how pleased Salevari would be once he told her what he had done. Perhaps it would even prove to her that this was the proper way to wipe out all human resistance in the city—a task he would be more than happy to carry out.

He smiled at the thought and licked his lips in anticipation, his blood rushing, as he imagined the shock on Anders' and Lyna's face when he brought justice to them—just as he had to Barty.

CHAPTER TWENTY-EIGHT

The consistent beating of hooves against the tunnel floor did little to alleviate the jumbled mess Felix's mind was in. He was constantly trying to stay one step ahead. He was still trying to think of a way to keep the dwarves from fighting each other. His mind also lingered on the task he had given Morteth. The assassin had been only too happy to accept it the next morning, thinking the viatari had won their drinking contest fairly. And now, his thoughts dwelled on the dream he'd had their last night in Kul'Kriegar.

It had been short, disjointed, but there was no mistake he had seen Salevari and Victria in it, and both of them had been in danger. He had difficulty now remembering what the danger was, but the impending sense of doom he had felt when he awoke had been all too apparent. And while his thoughts dwelled on this dream, he knew there was little that would be able to free him from this unwanted distraction.

He had decided not to respond to his sister's letter. Frankly, he was too busy to stop and offer Salevari guidance. She would have to figure out how to lead Aleganthia on her own; and he was confident she could. As for Victria, he hadn't heard a word from her since he sent her to find the acolyte in the Southern Isles. He worried about her every day and when he pictured her bright, cheerful face, he couldn't help but feel his chest constrict into knots. He marveled briefly at the strange sensation but shrugged it off. He missed her—that was all.

Their horses came to an abrupt halt as they reached the end of the tunnel. The viatari carefully guided their mounts down the steep steps toward the cavern floor of Dun'Aldor. Before them, Tinas Gran stood, as impressive as ever with its many towering, column-like edifices, glowing as softly as ever under the light of the giant braziers above.

"Felix," Drathanar called from behind. "What if they don't let us in?"

Felix grimaced. "They will let us in. We will make them hear us."

"Hmph," Aniria scoffed. "They're more likely to attack us now than before because of the stunt Thuradin and Lyrie pulled. And even if they let us through, all we can do is talk. How is that going to keep the dwarves from going to war when all we have working for us on the other side of the aisle is a single assassin's promise to sabotage the viceroy's preparations for war?"

"We must think positively," Drathanar reflected.

Aniria rolled her eyes. "Oh, shut it, Drath. Positivity isn't going to accomplish anything. Thinking realistically might."

Felix glanced behind him curiously. There was just the slightest sign of hurt behind Drathanar's eyes and a new tension seemed to bloom between the pair. He frowned.

This was not the first time he had seen the two bicker. Indeed, it was only Drathanar who could even goad Aniria to have any kind of reaction these days; and any reaction was a good reaction. But lately, he had noticed more venom in Aniria's words and less of a willingness from Drathanar to make his case, as if he was growing tired of the struggle. Felix sighed and shook his head. He really did not need another headache to add to the list. But it would do no good to have the only two companions currently accompanying him becoming liabilities because of personal matters.

Tinas Gran looked even more militarized than it had the last time they were here. Barricades were built along all the city streets they rode through, windows were boarded up, stakes were jammed into the sides of buildings to keep any foe from climbing them. The residents themselves were armed and armored for battle and much too busy preparing for war to notice the three viatari riding past them.

He noticed the air here smelled much cleaner than last time. It appeared they finally fixed the sewage problem Dunkell had left them.

The royal palace loomed over them, but before they could pass into the city's main plaza, a group of royal guards formed up to cut off their approach, shields at the ready and pikes lowered.

Felix recognized the dwarf with the short red beard leading them as the one who had stopped them before.

"What is yer business here, viatari?"

"We have come to speak with the Council once again."

The dwarf guffawed. "The Council will hear no more of yer jabber, viatari. Nae after seeing the state ye left two of its members in with yer last visit."

"Funny you should mention that," Felix replied. He felt his patience draining at a rapid rate. "We are actually looking for those two Council members, specifically. We wish to speak with Myrna Stonebeard and Ayrie Hearthkeeper."

"Hah!" the red-bearded dwarf spat on the floor. "Come ta finish them off? By my father's ale recipes, I'll nae have ye take a step further!"

Felix grinned, revealing sharp fangs. His red eyes flashed dangerously.

"Do you wish to test us, dwarf? Surely you have heard tales of what we can do."

The dwarf's face turned ashen but he held his ground. "I said, by my father's *ale* I'll nae let ye through. Ye cannae fight the entire city."

Felix shrugged. "Perhaps not, but we can at least end your existence quickly enough."

"What's going on here?" a loud, booming voice called out.

The elder viatari looked past the royal guards, noticing a familiar face marching toward them. He wore a regular set of dwarven armor save for the single, multi-layered, plate spaulder that sat heavily on his left shoulder. His shoulder-length black hair flowed behind him as he trudged along.

"Ah, Garadin," Felix said, allowing himself to relax again. "Finally, a dwarf with some reason."

"Felix," Garadin didn't sound too pleased. "Why have ye returned here. I thought we made it quite clear last time that our differences cannae be overcome."

"I wish to try again," Felix replied honestly. "While I hold no ill feelings toward your cousin, Thuradin, it is clear to me that bringing him last time was a mistake, as it caused a stir with two of your Council members in particular."

Garadin dismissed the royal guards and snorted. "That's an understatement if I've ever heard one. Ye should have heard the two of them after ye left."

"Which is why I have returned. I wish to speak with Ayrie and Myrna specifically—both to apologize for springing Thuradin on them, and to discuss seriously about the days ahead."

Garadin sighed and looked back toward the palace. "Felix, ye must know after having fought with ye I hold ye in high regard, and it is because of that that I will lead ye ta the two lasses. However, this cannae become a common occurrence. This will be yer last chance ta convince us—them, especially—of yer cause."

"I understand."

"Very well," Garadin put his fingers to his mouth and whistled sharply. A few buildings down, a guard emerged leading a ram already dressed for travel. The animal bobbed its horned head up and down in greeting to its master as Garadin hoisted himself up onto the saddle. "Let us ride. The lasses are in Fungar Hrathor at the moment, which is less than a day's journey."

With that, he spurred his mount and the beast sped off at a gallop down the streets. The viatari followed and soon found themselves in another tunnel, the flames from the torches installed into the walls flashing by.

As the hours passed, Felix pushed his horse forward until he was riding next to Garadin. Of all the dwarves he knew, he had never suspected this one to be the leader of the Council. Garadin had mentioned having a great deal of respect for him, a feeling he shared for the dwarven warrior.

"Why is it you?" he shouted so that the dwarf could hear him over the rushing wind.

The dwarf sighed; his eyes tired. "Why am I their leader, do ye mean?"

Felix didn't respond, waiting.

"I did nae desire this. I've always disagreed with Dunkell about the burrowers and the fact that he was doing nothing ta prepare us for what is undoubtedly an imminent burrower invasion . . . I'm no leader, Felix—aside from leading dwarves inta battle—but I knew something had ta be done."

"And what if you are wrong about what is coming," Felix asked. Garadin looked at him questioningly. "The digging your people have been hearing. Even when a breach is made into one of the dwarven caverns, if a stream of burrowers were to come through, those would be The Turned One's burrowers, not the ones your people have fought for centuries. You know there is a difference between them."

"There is no difference," Garadin waved his hand dismissively. "A burrower is a burrower. If The Turned One has any sort of influence over them, it is ta tap inta their natural bloodlust and barbaric natures ta make them an even more formidable threat."

"If my people thought like you, we would make war on the Men of the plainlands just for being humans. But that would make no sense, because we can see the difference between those The Turned One corrupted and those that remain undefiled."

"Humans are a different case. Anyway, as a dwarf, I've nae dealt with them long enough ta form any sort of solid opinion on the matter. I can only take yer people's word on their nature."

"I do not know what prejudice has taken hold of the dwarves over the centuries, but you must see the difference between the two types of burrowers. They do not look the same, nor act the same. They do not even fight the same. The difference comes from the involvement of The Turned One. It twists them into something they are not. If the dwarves continue as they have been with regards to the burrowers, Thuradin's sacrifice will have been—"

"Bah!" Garadin spat, his lips twisting as if he'd just eaten some moldy cheese. "Do nae speak ta me of him. He chose his path."

A light appeared ahead, suggesting the end of the tunnel.

"Do you know his story?"

"There's nothing ta know," Garadin said gruffly. There was a pause, then his eyes seemed to stare a thousand miles ahead of him as he continued, "I used ta look up ta him. He was everything I aspired ta be: commander of the royal guard, one of the fiercest warriors in our Kingdom, beloved by the people and feared by our enemies," his face hardened, "and the fool threw it all away. I don't know his reasons and, frankly, I do nae care. He betrayed our Kingdom when he murdered Ronorim and that's all there is."

Felix was disappointed to hear Garadin say this. He hadn't been present at the final battle between the dwarves and the burrowers, but he'd heard accounts of what had happened from Victria. He wondered if Garadin would have a change of heart if he were to hear the same accounts.

They exited the tunnel and stopped at the edge of a drop off, a green cavern spreading out before them. Unlike the other dwarven caverns, this one was full of life and not just bare stone. Mushroom fields spread out as far as the eye could see as well as fields of moss. Some of these fields cultivated the smaller variations of mushrooms, but there were also many plots where mammoth-mushrooms shot skyward, growing nearly as tall as some of the towers the dwarves had built.

From the cavern ceiling hung giant orbs of light, which he couldn't even guess as to how they functioned. However, they lit up the entire cavern much better than the braziers of Tinas Gran. He saw an irrigation system of ditches filled with clear water running through each field and connecting to a central well somewhere deeper in the cavern. Farmers with ropes tied around their midriff hung from the top of the mammoth-mushrooms, tending to them while a line of rams, burdened with produce, trudged underneath.

In the distance, Felix could make out a cluster of buildings standing around, and built into, the thick stalagmites. It seemed the dwarves of Fungar Hrathor, rather than building their own towers as the other clans did, preferred to make the natural features of their cavern work for them.

"Don't get me wrong," Garadin spoke up as he observed the dwarven farmers watering mushrooms or picking at the moss. "I still respect his fighting prowess. He remains a fierce warrior—that much was proven ta me at the battles of Zane and Garon. But I cannae forgive him for what he's done ta us."

He was silent then, and he wasn't the only one. Felix turned his attention to his two companions, who hadn't said a word since Tinas Gran. They both glanced testily at him before looking away. Aniria's brows were furrowed much like they always were when she was thinking of unpleasant things and Drathanar . . . well, Felix had to admit, it still looked like Aniria's words had gotten the better of him.

He shook his head—he couldn't have these two distracted during their task. There was a reason he had only brought Aniria and Drathanar rather than bringing all of the viatari under his command. The others were to remain in Kul'Kriegar to keep the viceroy protected, under close watch, and help Morteth with his task as best they could. He wished they were all here with him now to offer their support. He feared, as things stood right now, he wouldn't be able to rely on Aniria or Drathanar.

But before he could take the two viatari to the side to talk to them privately, Garadin spoke again, "Come, let us go down ta the farming community. I'm sure Ayrie and Myrna will be there waiting for us."

"Do they know we're coming?" Felix asked as they started down a steep slope to the cavern floor.

"No, but I'd be surprised if they haven't seen us already. This is a smaller cavern than most, as ye can tell, and the tunnel entrances are always watched. They'll know a dwarf and three strangers have just arrived."

Sure enough, no sooner had they started down a dirt path than two figures riding hard toward them appeared ahead.

"Ah, there they are. Told ye, lad. Let's wait here for them. Give our mounts a rest."

They stopped, and minutes later were joined by Ayrie and Myrna, who both looked outraged.

Ayrie brandished her spear. "Garadin, what in Nythirim's name are ye doing bringing them here?"

"Calm yerself, lass," Garadin raised his hands in a peaceful gesture. "They're just here ta talk."

"That's what they said last time," Myrna seethed.

Garadin nodded, conceding the point. "Without *him*, this time."

Felix noticed the two female dwarves had been trying to peer behind him as if searching for another member in their party. At Garadin's words, though, they relaxed—though Ayrie kept her spear out, resting it against her shoulder.

"Ta what do we owe this displeasure, then?"

"First, I have come to deliver some news," Felix said, cutting straight to the point. "And I will not mince words. Your assassins failed to kill Dunkell—" the Council members shared dark glances, "—but they did kill the viceroy of Kul'Kriegar. Dunkell has appointed a new one, Edana

Hartshield."

"Ugh, madwoman!" Ayrie scowled. "Of all the dwarves ta pick as viceroy."

"Is she really that bad?" Myrna asked.

"Oh, ye don't know the half of it. The fact that he's appointed her means he's starting ta mean business."

"You are correct in a way, though I do not believe Dunkell intended for Edana to go this far," Felix said.

Garadin's eyes narrowed. "What do ye mean by that?"

The elder viatari sighed as he considered the best way to phrase his next few words. "Edana is on the warpath. She is preparing for battle at a much swifter pace than I am comfortable with and my attempts to convince her to seek peace through diplomacy have failed."

The dwarves were silent as they absorbed the news. Felix took their silence to mean he had their attention so he continued, "I have left most of my viatari there to try to stop her progress and I have hired help for sabotage and delaying purposes, but I have come here first and foremost to ask you not to give them any reason—*any* reason—to justify an attack. It is vital, now more than ever, that we try to come to an agreement through negotiation."

"This news disturbs me," Garadin muttered, looking at his fellow Council members. "If Edana truly is on the warpath, then we must speed up our own preparations. Knowing her mind, she'll come for Fungar Hrathor first and seize our food supply."

"Agreed," Ayrie said, her lips set in a grim line. "I'll start commissioning more troops ta be trained in Tinas Gran and Dun'Burell while we still have the time."

Myrna chipped in, "I'll help with establishing defensive measures here and training the Farmers' Militia so that we can hold off an early attack in case our troops don't arrive in time."

Felix felt a growing sense of dread. The dwarves had accepted his news, yes, but not how he wanted them to. He had hoped they would have been shocked into an earnest desire for a peaceful solution, but it appeared he had seriously misjudged them. If anything, now they were absolutely determined to go to war.

Garadin turned his attention to Felix. There was something in the warrior's face that the viatari wasn't sure he liked.

"We thank ye for the warning, Felix. Ye have given us time ta prepare, and we won't forget that. However, and I know ye may nae like it, but ye must understand that we cannae allow ye ta return ta Kul'Kriegar."

"Excuse me?"

The dwarf glanced at his companions, both of whom nodded encouragingly. "Ye know our plans now. Nae all of them—but enough ta do us harm if ye were ta tell the new viceroy. I must ask that ye remain here with Myrna in Fungar Hrathor, or even return ta Tinas Gran with me, where ye will stay safe from all the fighting."

Aniria laughed, drawing everyone's attention. She eyed the dwarves, her voice dripping with contempt as she spoke. "You cannot seriously believe that you can hold us here against our will, or that we would willingly become your prisoners."

"Aniria—"

"It is just a precaution for our sake, I intend ta let ye go as soon as I can—and, of course, we would never do anything ta mistreat ye. Ye would be more guests at our palace than prisoners."

A farmer passed them on the road, watching their little exchange curiously. Myrna had mentioned a Farmers' Militia. Felix wondered how many of the farmers around them were a part of that and how well they could fight. Thinking of Myrna, he looked at her, astounded by how much she reminded him of Thuradin, were he younger. He sympathized with the anguish his dwarven friend must feel, knowing his daughter was a Council member, a traitor to the Kingdom. If the Kingdom prevailed, it didn't take much imagination to know what fate would befall her.

I promise you, Thuradin, Felix thought. *I will save your daughter from this. I just need to discover a means.*

Myrna caught him looking and raised an eyebrow, but nothing was said between them as Aniria replied to Garadin's offer.

"When will you dwarves stop being so stupid and realize there is a greater enemy than yourselves?" Aniria growled, her red eyes narrowing. "The Turned One is the *real* enemy. She would kill everyone you love and the ones she spared she would corrupt to do her bidding. They would be mindless slaves!"

Ayrie spit on the ground. "If an outside force dares attack us, then we will fight them ta the death. But that's nae what's happening right now. Right now, we need ta focus on winning a better future for our people."

Aniria laughed harshly. "Having a disjointed government that will spend more time bickering instead of working together would be better for your people than a single, strong leader bred for the task?"

"Ye need nae tell me the dangers of the acolyte," Garadin said before Ayrie could bite back with her own words. "I know of the threat she poses."

"If you do, then you're all the more a fool for involving yourself with this petty squabble for power instead of focusing on the greater battle."

"Aniria—"

"No, I will *not* be silent! I will not hold my tongue!" she shouted, glaring at Felix. "If these three were half the dwarf that Thuradin is, they wouldn't hesitate to devote themselves to the greater cause rather than to their own selfish desires." Now she looked directly at Myrna, whose eyes had gone wide, both with shock and anger.

Garadin roared with fury. "I will nae be so insulted by the likes of ye!"

"Garadin," Felix pleaded, in as calm a voice as he could muster. "She—"

"No," the dwarf said sharply, anger burning deep in his eyes. "No, Felix, I will nae calm myself and I will nae forget what she has said. She has insulted our honor and she will pay for it."

Aniria scoffed. "I spoke only the truth. If you'd rather I insult you, then so be it: *Gürl gath hæt-u.*"

There was a moment of shocked silence during which Garadin's face grew as red as a river of blood. He let loose another roar, and, drawing his sword, moved to attack Aniria but his lunge was easily blocked by Drathanar, who maneuvered his horse between them.

His eyes were as wild as his hair as he stared down the Council members.

"You don't touch her."

Felix looked around. Many of the farmers who had been tending their crop were now moving in toward them with axes, hoes, scythes, hammers, and whatever else they'd managed to grab hold of. He recognized the set look on their faces. These farmers were ready for a fight.

He turned back to the Council members hoping he could salvage the situation, but such a hope died immediately. Garadin was yelling obscenities as he swung his sword again and again, trying to attack Aniria—but each time his attacks were intercepted by the Dalyran general. Ayrie let loose her own war cry and kicked her ram to charge them. The suddenness of her actions caused her mount to rise onto its hind legs in surprise, catching her off-guard as she tumbled to the ground.

And Myrna. Myrna simply sat there, her eyes still full of shock, but now mixed with something else. It was a look Felix couldn't quite identify, but whatever it was grounded her where she sat, separated her from the events happening around her. Felix couldn't help but think, as he tore his gaze away to better figure out how to escape their predicament, that he had only ever seen the same expression on Thuradin when he thought of his daughter.

CHAPTER TWENTY-NINE

Yelling drew Felix's attention back to the situation at hand. Garadin continued to shout his rage at Aniria as he tried to get past Drathanar while Ayrie was creeping her way around for a flank attack. Several farmers now surrounded them and were closing in. Felix knew there was little else he could do to keep this situation from escalating even further—but he had to try.

He dismounted and moved between Garadin's mount and his viatari companions, keeping an eye on Ayrie in case she moved in for an attack. Garadin glared, but took a deep breath and allowed his ram to be pushed back. Felix looked him in the eye, wishing he could convey everything he felt so an understanding could be reached, but he knew it was impossible.

"We will be leaving now."

"Oh, no, ye won't," Garadin seethed. "Ye will leave when we say so. Ye'll be coming with us no longer as our guests, but as our prisoners."

"You do not want to make us your enemies, Garadin," Felix said, a hardness entering his voice.

"It is ye who will regret making enemies of the Council, viatari."

Felix sighed, brows furrowing, all pretenses of civility gone as he stared down the dwarves surrounding them.

"Do not force our hand," he called out loudly so all the surrounding farmers could hear. "If you attack, we will defend ourselves—and we cannot guarantee that we will always be able to pull back our blows."

There was scattered murmuring among the farmers but they held their ground. No one threatened them in their own cavern. Garadin waved his sword in the air and pointed it at the three viatari. "Capture them, show them the might of axe and hammer!"

Felix quickly turned to his companions, resigning to the fact that a battle was upon them, and said, "Incapacitate. Try not to kill them."

Drathanar and Aniria nodded, keeping their weapons sheathed.

They jumped into action just as Garadin kicked his ram forward. Felix landed nimbly on the back of the beast and swung at the dwarf's head. Garadin managed to avoid the first few swings, leaning back and forth in his saddle as if he were drunk, before the elder viatari finally landed a hit. The dwarf groaned and slid out of his saddle, landing hard on the dirt path.

Ayrie's war cry pierced the air around them as she charged, her spear aimed directly at Aniria's heart. She never got close. Drathanar tackled her from the side, sending her flying several feet. She landed with a grunt and tried to get up quickly, but Aniria was already on top of her. With a triumphant grin, the female viatari brought down her fists on the dwarf's armored head, crumpling the helmet around her face and knocking her out.

Myrna watched this transpire, outraged. She pulled out a

horn from one of her saddle bags and blew into it three times, a deep, loud note bursting from the other end and reverberating through every hanging stalactite, every pebble on the path they were on. The call sent the farmers into action and they yelled in unison as they charged the three viatari.

Drathanar and Aniria made quick work of them. Within minutes, every farmer was on the ground, bruises already forming on the spots where they'd been struck. Some with greater injuries cried out in pain.

Myrna moved to blow on her horn again but Felix snatched it out of her hands before she could. She shouted a curse, pulling her sword out and swinging it in a wide arc, trying to catch Felix's side. The elder viatari dodged her attack easily and struck at Myrna's wrist, forcing her to drop the blade.

Her ram snorted angrily and lowered its head, but a few soothing words in Viatar and the beast was again complacent. Frustrated by her mount's passiveness, Myrna tried to dismount, but Felix was already by her side, grabbing hold of her to ensure she stayed in her saddle.

"Stay where you are," he ordered as she tried to shake him off. "Out of respect for your father, we will not harm you."

"Ye need nae spare me just because I am his spawn!"

Felix tightened his grip. "Stay. We will be gone soon."

She gasped for breath, "Ye will nae escape us. We will find ye and arrest ye for this betrayal."

"I cannot betray what I did not feel loyalty toward in the first place."

Felix smiled sadly at the young dwarf and then, with a nod of his head, stepped away. Aniria and Drathanar were right behind him as they remounted and sped away from the scene.

"For wanting to keep the peace," Drathanar called out. "You were quick to fight."

"There was no other option at that point," Felix said somberly. "Just as there are very few options for us right now."

Ahead of them stood the entrance to the tunnel that would lead them back to Tinas Gran, but its doors, which the elder viatari hadn't noticed before, were now closed.

"We're trapped."

"What do we do, then?" Aniria asked, her horse pawing at the ground nervously as her grip on the reins tightened.

"We go into the mushroom fields," Felix said. He glanced behind them. In the distance, he could see a sizeable host of dwarves forming up and preparing to hunt them down.

"Head for the fields with the giant mushrooms. It will be easier to hide in them."

"And what about our horses?" Drathanar asked, "I will not give them up to the mercy of the dwarves. For all we know they might eat them."

"We will not give up our mounts," Felix reassured him, dismounting and cupping his mouth over his own horse's ears. "Just as there is a tunnel here that leads to Tinas Gran, I am certain there is one that leads straight to Kul'Kriegar as well."

"Great. We should head for it, then." Aniria said as Felix approached her horse and did the same thing.

Finally, he went over to Drathanar's mount and repeated the process. When he finished, he patted the steed affectionately and then looked at his companions with determination.

"Dismount. We will remain in this cavern and continue on foot. We have unfinished business. I have just told our horses to ride around the cavern's edge until they find another tunnel and to take it back to Kul'Kriegar."

Drathanar and Aniria appeared taken aback by this, but they followed his direction and dismounted, taking their weapons, some food, and other supplies with them. The horses snorted in farewell as, together, they trotted off, following the cavern's wall away from the road they were on.

"What business could we possibly still have here?" Aniria asked, her surprise ebbing away and turning into frustration. "Talking with the Council has led to failure *again*."

"Not entirely."

"Hmph. Enlighten me."

The sound of gruff voices that had only been a buzz in the distance moments ago now grew more distinct as the dwarves they belonged to drew near.

"There is no time to explain presently," Felix gripped Aniria's shoulders and hoped that she could recognize his sincerity. "I will explain when we do not have a mob of angry dwarves on our tail. Right now, however, we must head for those mushroom fields before it is too late."

Aniria reluctantly nodded and they took off at a fast pace, pushing through the first rows of smaller mushrooms which grew as high as their upper thighs. The dwarves spotted them from the road and gave chase but as soon as they entered the fields Felix lost sight of them.

Once they were moving between the stalks of giant mushrooms, the environment around them changed. The air within these fields was musty and old. There was the heavy odor of fungi all around and Felix had a feeling the stench would be with him for weeks. But they pushed on.

Felix pointed up at the dark brown gills that made up the underside of every mushroom. "Climb up and hide within the underside of the heads, we should be able to fit inside. Try not to breathe in too much, I have a feeling the air up there could have adverse effects on our ability to stay awake."

They each split off to a different mushroom and deftly climbed the tall, thick stalk. Felix forced himself in between the rubbery gills, clawing his hands deep into the meat of the fungi in order to fight gravity's pull.

The stench was overwhelming. Felix did his best to breathe in as little as possible, but even the smallest breaths brought with them a fresh wave of nausea and disorientation. He shook his head and tried to think of a pleasant smell—wine, a flowery meadow, anything. If his brain could just picture it, maybe he could trick his nose into smelling it.

And as he searched for something that might save him, the earthy scent of the forest around Aleganthia filled his nostrils, making his heart yearn for home. A picture of Victria, her long, flowing hair flying back with the breeze as she leaned against the railings of one of the numerous balconies in the keep came to mind. His breath caught as he imagined her turning around, grinning at him with the same look she'd had ever since he found her in the woods all those centuries ago—like she knew something he didn't.

Below him the dwarves forged through the mushroom stalks.

"They're nae here!" One called.

"They must have kept running," another grumbled. "Keep moving!"

The dwarves moved on, not once looking up. Shaking his head to clear it of the distracting images running through his mind, Felix waited a few more minutes after they were gone before dropping to the ground. Aniria and Drathanar dropped down next to him, both gasping for air.

They sat there on the spongy ground for some time as the dwarven voices grew fainter and fainter.

"So, what now?" Drathanar asked.

"First," Felix groaned as he pushed himself back onto his feet. "We must find a good place to hide. We cannot stay in these fields."

"I'm not moving until you tell us concretely what we're going to do." Aniria declared, crossing both her arms and legs. "I got us into this mess, I know. But I need to know that we're not just wasting our time by being here—that we can do something to fix it." Felix could tell she was serious about not moving, but even now he couldn't bring himself to snap at her. Her words and actions had escalated their talks with the dwarves, true, but he knew where they had come from.

"Do not worry, young one," he reached his hand out to pull her up and she took it. "I do not blame you for what you said. I know in your heart you were speaking for Balinarus and Kalenar."

Her face froze in shock for a moment, her eyes wide and fearful like a child's.

"Don't say their names," she breathed.

Felix could only grip her shoulder and squeeze, hoping it could convey some small sense of comfort. *How much longer must it take for her to heal?* He wondered.

"As to your question, Drathanar," he said, also pulling the Dalyran general up to his feet. "We do what we hired Morteth to do. We sabotage the Council's preparations for war."

A light rekindled in Aniria's eyes. "Finally. Action."

Drathanar, too, looked like he approved, but there remained some hesitation. "What would that entail?"

"Walk with me and I will explain," Felix said.

They meandered under the giant mushrooms, no longer worried about being seen. The dwarves would comb through every field in the cavern searching for them, but it was unlikely they would return to this area for a second look so soon. For now, they were safe to move at their own pace. As they walked, Felix explained his plan.

"Since a diplomatic approach has been unsuccessful in achieving our goals, we must look to other methods to keep them from civil war. Right now, the only thing I can think of would be to sabotage the Council's preparations."

Felix spread his hands out, his eyes studying every mushroom they passed under as small, yellow spores drifted down around them, like snow.

"This cavern is the Council's food supply. They will need to send food shipments and other materials to their armies marching from Tinas Gran. If we can stop those shipments, destroy, or take those supplies, disassemble any defenses they build within this cavern, we might be able to prolong the ignition of this war long enough for a long-term solution to present itself."

Aniria smirked. "So, essentially, you don't have a plan yet. That's a first."

"I am still thinking of one," Felix corrected her, ignoring the jab. "But I need more time and this will give us that time."

"Sabotage won't work if they capture us," Drathanar noted.

Felix nodded. "Indeed, which is why we must first look for a place where we can stay hidden. Once we are out of these fields, we will look for a cave."

"These are *dwarves* we're dealing with," Aniria almost laughed as she pushed a smaller mushroom out of her way. "Don't you think they'll check their own caves?"

"Not these dwarves. They are farmers. They will be more concerned with tending to their crop, especially now that they are gearing up for war."

"Fine," Aniria conceded. "Let's say we do this and we're good at it and manage to keep the Council's army from leaving this cavern to attack Kul'Kriegar. What about the dwarves in Kul'Kriegar? How are we supposed to make sure Morteth is keeping the viceroy in check while we're here."

"Morteth will send me reports every now and then to keep me updated on his progress with the viceroy. We've developed a system."

"What, he's going to write you letters?"

The elder viatari shrugged. "Something like that."

They exited the mushroom fields and were back on the uncultivated, rocky floor. Ahead of them was the cavern wall. Felix glanced around, hoping to find an obvious cave for them to hide in but no such luck.

"Come, let us search along the wall for any caves we can use to remain hidden."

They followed the wall for almost an hour before finding what they were looking for. It was a small cave, big enough for them all to fit in comfortably, but not for much else. The entrance was also small—and well hidden—in fact, they might have missed it entirely had they not been so close to the cavern wall in the first place.

"This is a well-concealed cave," Drathanar observed, standing at the entrance and looking out toward the several towns of Fungar Hrathor which were directly in their line of sight. "And it gives us the perfect vantage point to see their movements. Do you think the dwarves know about this cave?"

"Oh, yes," Felix said, walking inside and settling down. "Well, at one point they did, anyway. If I am not mistaken, they were the ones who dug this one out."

"They created this? Then shouldn't we move on? Surely they will find us if we stay here."

"Do not worry," Felix yawned. Much had happened today and the strains of it all were catching up to him. "As I said before, they knew about it at one point, but no longer. This cave looks to have been made during the period of dwarven expansion, when they were scouting out the neighboring caverns for good locations to build more cities. It looks to me like this was a scout's cave from that time."

"How can you tell?" Aniria asked skeptically, though she, too, entered the cave without much hesitancy and leaned back against the wall to rest.

"Because of the size of it, its entrance, and where we found it," Felix said with a shrug, closing his eyes now and hoping sleep would take him soon. "The entrance is unnoticeable unless you are right on top of it, the size is large enough for a dwarf or a group of dwarves to dwell in during long scouting missions, and it gives a perfect view of the surrounding area. Dwarven scouts during the expansion must have used this place to look for any signs of danger within the cavern—to see if it was inhabitable."

"And you inferred all of this just by the size of the cavern and where it's located." Aniria scoffed.

Felix shrugged. "Believe me or doubt, but I have studied dwarven history deeply. I know this cave would have been used regularly by scouts of that time, but knowledge of this place will have been lost by the general public over the centuries."

"Lucky us."

"So, we're safe here," Drathanar said, finally coming into the cave himself. "And what do we do now?"

"We wait and see what the dwarves will do first."

Aniria sighed heavily. "I'm sick of waiting. I want to *do* something."

Felix raised an eyebrow but kept his eyes closed. "Patience, young one, there will be plenty of action in the days ahead."

With that, he said no more and let his mind wander as he drifted off into a fitful sleep, the sound of dwarven voices in the distance no longer a worry for him. There would be plenty of time to deal with them tomorrow.

CHAPTER THIRTY

Two weeks passed and the viatari still found themselves hiding in a cave. There was little difference from when they had originally stumbled upon it, save for several loose sheets of parchment marked with lines of chaotic writing spread out across the floor. Aniria and Drathanar were leaned up against the wall asleep, Aniria's head leaning just slightly toward the Dalyran general. Felix, meanwhile, kept watch.

Just outside of the cave was a small outcrop of boulders near the edge of a ridge that provided a commanding view of the whole cavern. He had discovered this spot the day after they had settled into their temporary living quarters and he had come back many times since to keep track of the dwarves' movements.

The past weeks hadn't only consisted of observing and resting though. No, just as Garadin, Ayrie, and Myrna had promised, the dwarves were beginning to mobilize for war—and the most obvious sign of this was through their food shipments. It was normal for food to be shipped from Fungar Hrathor to other parts of the Kingdom; but lately the carts carrying them had grown larger, been more densely packed, and passed through much more frequently.

"They are rushing the food out of here," Felix had said

the day he noticed the increased shipments. "Which makes sense. If they are mobilizing an army, they will need to send food out quickly enough to keep all those dwarves fed while they march and train."

"So what?" Aniria scraped another line down the cave's wall with her fingernail and looked at Felix with extreme boredom.

"So, an army cannot move on an empty stomach."

Aniria smirked. "Yes, they can. They may not like it, but they can."

Felix glanced at Drathanar, who shrugged and nodded in agreement, though with whom he couldn't tell.

"Well, even if they can still march here without food, they will not be in good shape for battle."

"I think you forget it's dwarves we're talking about."

"Even dwarves need to eat," Felix insisted, an edge to his voice. "My point is, it may not seem like much, but we need to intercept those food shipments and destroy them."

"That food may not be going to feed an army," Drathanar pointed out. "What if they're meant for civilians in the other dwarven cities. We'd be starving them too by destroying these supplies."

Felix nodded. "You are correct. This is not ideal, but we must act. In this case, the most important thing is keeping the relative peace at any cost, and for us right now, that means we destroy those food shipments."

After a few more words his companions finally came to agree with him. And so, every day, they had gone out to lie in hiding within the mushroom fields by the road. They intercepted every food shipment that tried to pass them.

At first, the shipments had been unguarded and the cart drivers were unable to do anything but watch and cower as

the viatari ransacked their goods, occasionally using torches
they had obtained from past raids on the farming community
to burn the produce. Every now and then, they would consume the life essence of the dwarves' rams. This continued
for several days. Eventually, though, word of their raids
reached the dwarves in charge and soon the viatari found
themselves facing off against shipments with details of up to
twenty guards.

This made the task more difficult, but not impossible.

They continued raiding, doing all they could to avoid
killing the dwarves—rendering them unconscious or disarming
them instead. Sometimes the guards were too much, though,
and managed to drive them back.

It was around this time that Felix began receiving reports
from Morteth in the form of letters.

As they had planned, once Felix had found a base from
which they could maintain their operation, he had sent a
messenger mole Morteth had given him with a description
of their location written on a small sheet of parchment that
he had then tied around the mole's neck. The mole already
knew where it was meant to dig to, having been tamed and
trained by Morteth himself, and so it had burrowed away as
soon as the message had been secured. After that, it was up
to Morteth to recruit his own assassins or other shady
characters to deliver updates to Felix.

One of them had found the viatari during the night,
asleep in their caves, and had nearly lost his life by waking
Felix up. After a quick scuffle that resulted in little more
than a broken nose for the dwarf, Felix had finally taken the
short letter and read it.

Felix, hope ye're well. Took some—er, all—of the dynath

stores in K'K for meself. Saw Viceroy E today. Safe ta say she's nae pleased.

I'll keep ye updated. Do nae respond.

--M

By the time he looked up from the letter the assassin was gone. But the reports continued coming in, each time in the hands of a different character. Based on what he was reading, Morteth was pulling all of his resources to do the job the viatari had assigned him, which Felix was grateful for.

So far, he had done everything from contaminating the soldiers' ale supply so that they all had terrible bouts of alcohol poisoning to disassembling the dwarves' mobile cannons so that they fell apart at the slightest touch and had to be reassembled. It made what they were doing in Fungar Hrathor seem insignificant in comparison. Still, everything seemed to be going well enough to delay the coming civil war, and for that, Felix was pleased. But this glow of success couldn't last, and Moreth's latest report, which had arrived earlier that morning, proved it.

Felix, E has found me out. Abandoned HQ. Kept meself safe, but cannae continue operations. 'Twas all in vain though, anyway. She's already managed ta restock her supplies and rebuild everything I destroyed. Bloody efficient, that woman. She's due ta march out in a few days. I'll do what I can but I doubt it'll be ta much effect. I've done all I can, viatari, but she is coming.

--M

The news was disheartening, and to make matters worse he had noticed something else as well. Fungar Hrathor had stopped sending out shipments of food for the past few days. Felix had a feeling this meant the army Garadin had called for was close, but he had no evidence to prove it. Still, his gut feeling was strong. They were running out of time.

Leaving his position by the outcrop of boulders, he walked back to the scout's cave, a new idea forming in his head. It wasn't a good idea, and it was risky, but it was all he could think to do—though how he was going to convince his companions to join him, he didn't know.

The sound of his footsteps in the shallow cave woke the two viatari. They yawned, stretched, and greeted Felix with grimaces as they rubbed the sleep from their eyes. Aniria stood up and began pacing in their small space as she always did.

"Any new shipments?" Drathanar asked.

"No," Felix said. Something in his voice must have been different because they both looked at him, suddenly tense.

"Felix," Aniria said with some concern. "What's wrong?"

He held up the latest report from Morteth. "Edana is coming. And I believe Garadin's army is almost here as well."

Aniria cursed. "So, it's all been for nothing!" She resumed pacing with renewed vigor.

Drathanar studied Felix for a long time before speaking. "What makes you think that?"

"What other reason would the dwarves here have for withholding the shipments they had been sending out except that the army they were feeding with those shipments is almost here? I think they have been storing their food these past few days so they can host the army when it arrives."

"So, that's it, then?"

Felix shook his head. "Our objective remains the same."

"But what can we do now?"

Felix was silent. He had a plan, but didn't know how to pitch it in a way that didn't sound absurd. Aniria's pacing stopped and she looked at him, a spark of realization in her eyes.

"You mean to burn their food stores."

Felix nodded.

Drathanar's eyes widened. "All of them?"

Again, Felix nodded.

"Felix, that's too far!" Drathanar ran his fingers through his wild hair as he looked at Aniria for support. When no help came, he continued on his own. "If you do this, you'll starve the entire cavern—no, the entire Kingdom! The dwarves—all of them—will suffer through a terrible famine until the farmers here can produce a new crop; and who knows how long that might take. This will do nothing but invite more violence—except now it will be over food."

"What choice do we have? I cannot think of anything else we might do to discourage these dwarves from going to war with each other, can you? If you know a better way, please, tell me."

Drathanar said nothing and instead stared blankly ahead in shock.

"I still need time," Felix murmured. He was tired, had been since they arrived in the Kingdom, and he was frustrated with himself because of his inability to think of a long-term solution for the dwarves. "I still need time to think of a way to reconcile the two dwarven factions. Nothing has come to mind yet."

"It's been two weeks, Felix," Drathanar said, not unkindly. "If there was a way, you would have thought of it by now. We cannot prevent a war from happening indefinitely through sabotage."

"No," Felix agreed. "But we can buy more time."

Drathanar growled in frustration. "Felix, there is no solution here! In a case like this, neither side is willing to compromise. What we need to do is pick a side and help end this war as quickly—"

"I'm in."

Drathanar gawked incredulously at Aniria, who stood with her arms crossed, an impish smile playing on her lips.

"What?"

"I'm. *In.*" She said again to Drathanar. "This is just the sort of drastic action I thought we needed to take in the first place. It's not a permanent solution but it's *something*," she turned her fiery gaze to Felix, "and I will help you carry it out."

Felix inclined his head in appreciation. Drathanar bared his fangs in displeasure but finally leaned back against the cave wall, drawing his sword to inspect it, a dark mood taking over.

"If she goes, I go," he muttered.

"I don't need you to protect me."

"And yet, I will continue to do so anyway."

Aniria rolled her eyes in exasperation. "When do we go?"

"Tonight," Felix said resolutely, grateful for his companions and their willingness, despite their personal misgivings, to follow him. "We go tonight."

There was no natural indication of when night fell within the mountains. For dwarves, having lived within them for so long, they were simply attuned to the passage of time in the outside world and so always seemed to know when night fell and morning came. Luckily for the viatari, they did not have to rely on such instinctual feelings to know when they had to move out for their task.

The giant orbs hanging from the cavern ceiling were a great help in this respect. Wanting the farming cycle to be as regular as it was in the outside world, the dwarves of Fungar Hrathor always turned the orbs off during the night, leaving nothing to light the cavern save for a few braziers and torches scattered throughout the area.

It was dark as the viatari made their way through the mushroom fields toward the farming community but it was still possible to see. They were careful to steer clear of the scattered campsites with raging bonfires, and moved stealthily through the rows of giant stalks. Felix doubted there were any farmers out tending to their fields this late, but he didn't want to risk discovery at all—so they had taken the longer route toward the storage silos, circling around the entire town so as to enter from the back.

They'd known about the silos ever since they arrived in this cavern. They were hard to miss. Two massive, cylindrical towers were all there was when it came to the dwarves storing their food. The towers were made of stone, so burning it from the outside would be pointless; however, if they could reach the top where the hatch into the silo should be, they could drop a torch inside the structure and the rest would fall into place.

But things wouldn't be so easy, Felix realized as he saw the structures looming before him. Now that they were closer, he could make out a series of walls surrounding the two towers. These walls weren't tall, but they would require some skill to climb over. There were also a series of stakes surrounding and even implanted into the silos themselves. It was as if the dwarves had expected an attack and went out of their way to give these two buildings as much protection as they could.

Felix couldn't help but grin. The dwarves may have gone through a lot of effort to protect what was theirs, but this was nothing to a viatari.

Moving with graceful fluidity, the three viatari scaled the walls with ease, reaching the top and jumping over to the other side within a matter of seconds. They did the same with the second wall, except this time they ran into a guard as they reached the ramparts.

The dwarf's eyes widened as the red-eyed beings suddenly appeared before him. He reached for a horn tied to his belt but before he could touch it Felix was on top of him and rendered him unconscious with a swift blow to the head. The dwarf groaned and fell limp.

"Great," Drathanar hissed. "Now what do we do with him? If another guard comes this way and discovers his body we'll be discovered."

Felix searched up and down the ramparts. He couldn't see anywhere they could stow the dwarf's body out of sight so he propped the guard up against the battlements, crossing his arms snugly.

"There. Now he could be sleeping."

Drathanar eyed him skeptically. Felix shrugged. "It is the best we can do. It will buy us some time at least, so let us waste no more of it and move on."

They jumped over the next few walls, running into a few more guards along the way and dealing with them in the same manner. Within a matter of minutes, they stood below the silos, which towered over them.

"There doesn't seem to be a ladder," Aniria noted.

"The dwarves probably have some mechanism that stows the ladder away when not in use," Felix thought out loud.

"Well, if that's true, then we've wasted our time," Drathanar glanced over his shoulder. "We don't have time to find a ladder."

"No," Felix agreed. "But you give up too soon, general." He pointed up at the stakes implanted into the stone towers.

"That is our ticket to the top. We will climb up the silo using those stakes. They look strong enough for one of us to stand on at any time so we will jump from one to the next."

"Good idea," Aniria didn't waste any time and launched herself onto the lowest level of stakes, then on to the next, and the next. Felix followed suite. Drathanar stood where he was for a few seconds, a scowl on his face, but he, too, eventually began to climb.

The going was easy enough. Stakes were spaced close enough that no viatari had to jump a great distance to reach the next, but the task still required a great deal of balance and precision. One false move and they would fall to the ground. They could certainly survive such a fall, Felix thought, but being so high up, it would likely break some bones.

As they neared the top, Aniria pulled out an oil-drenched torch she'd had strapped to her back—as they all did—and lit it with a few strikes of flint and steel. Flames flared, lighting their immediate surroundings. Felix couldn't help but think how easily that single light would give away their position if any dwarven guards looked their way. They had to move quickly.

There were only a few more stakes to jump to before they reached the top. Aniria deftly hopped from one to the next until she was close enough to pull herself onto the silo's roof. Felix focused so he could follow the same path when he heard a whirling sound slice through the air.

There was a sickening thud, a short, startled cry and then Felix saw Aniria fall to the ground, an axe embedded deep into her shoulder. The torch she carried fell with her but before its light was lost, Felix looked up and immediately realized what had happened.

Several jeering dwarven heads poked out over the side of the silo, waving their arms in triumph and shouting into the darkness. They had been waiting for them.

Aniria crashed to the ground and lay there motionless. Before Felix could decide what to do next, the dwarves began hurling spears and firing arrows on their position. A few missiles dug into his chest, but Felix easily pulled them out, thankful the dwarves didn't use poison like humans did. He searched for Drathanar to tell him to fall back but the Dalyran general was already on his way down, and Felix saw why.

He had thought it strange why there had seen so few guards in such a heavily protected area. But now it was clear to him that they had been in hiding, waiting for the viatari to make their move. Now, several dwarves came out into the open to finish off Aniria, who still lay on the ground unmoving.

Drathanar fell upon them, his curved sabers out and swinging wildly. He cut into the first few dwarves with ease, all pretense of mercy gone. The dwarves fell where they stood, blood gushing from their various wounds. The remaining warriors fell back into a more defensible formation.

Not wanting to leave Drathanar on his own, Felix jumped down the stakes as well, dodging the arrows and spears that were still being sent his way. He hit the ground and ran over to Drathanar, who stood over Aniria, guarding her against the dwarves, his face pale with concern.

Felix bent down to inspect Aniria's wound and was relieved to see she was still breathing. The fall hadn't been enough to kill her, as he had suspected, but he could tell it had caused much damage. The axe in her shoulder had missed anything vital so he pulled it out swiftly, forcing Aniria to cry out in pain.

Her eyes fluttered open weakly. "Wha—what's happened?"

Felix put a finger to her lips. "Quiet. You need to rest and let yourself heal. We will get you back to safety." Doing his best to keep any more bones from breaking, he picked her up.

"Drathanar, let's go."

The Dalyran general turned, saw that Felix had Aniria in his arms, and nodded. Together they rushed through the remaining dwarves and made their escape. Felix couldn't scale the walls very well with Aniria in his arms, so the two viatari made their way to the gates—which were simple wooden doors—and kicked them open.

Dwarves streamed in from everywhere, trying to stop their progress but they were no match for Drathanar's skill and cold rage. He cut down all who crossed them, but still the guards kept coming. Eventually, they managed to break through the last wall and were back in the open, enraged dwarves right behind them.

"Quickly," Felix said, panting. Aniria was growing heavy in his arms. "Run through the mushrooms back to the cave."

They took off at full speed, giving the dwarves no chance to give chase. Mushroom stalks rushed by them as they ran back the way they had come. All pretense of stealth gone, they made it back to their cave within a short amount of time.

Once inside, Felix gently laid Aniria down so that her regenerative abilities could take full effect. She lay there, gasping in pain, her eyes clenched shut. Drathanar sat by her side, his blades already cleaned and put away. He grabbed her hand fiercely and held it, his eyes never leaving her face.

Felix slumped against the cave wall, his mind running through what had just happened, trying to make sense of it all. The dwarves had known they would come for the silos. And the fact that they had been thwarted meant that the stores of food would survive to be used to feed the coming army. They had failed, and Felix feared now that nothing could stop the dwarves from going to war.

"I told you it was a bad idea," Drathanar said bitterly.

Felix nodded.

"So, what do we do now?"

The elder viatari sighed and brought the edge of his tunic up to wipe the sweat off his face. He glanced once more at the two younger viatari and then looked away, his mind on Morteth's final message.

"When Kul'Kriegar comes, I fear there will be very little we can do."

CHAPTER THIRTY-ONE

The atmosphere in Maleres was starkly different to what Victria had grown accustomed to in her short time with the vashi. It had a similar feel to Zessarix in that it was a large city, but that was all. Many of the buildings were built around large marble statues of vashi. She noticed that each one of these figures of the past were clothed in flowing robes and held their arms outstretched as if in prayer. Looming over them in the distance was the temple. It was impressively large, held up by a series of colossal columns. It was every shade of blue and green that Victria could imagine. The individual shingles on the slanted roof glimmered like scales.

The vashi here were different as well. Rarely did they see any guards on patrol or anyone carrying weapons. Most of the denizens they passed, as they left their mounts in the stables and began walking through the streets, were like the statues that flanked every street corner. They all wore the same flowing, pearl robes with golden sashes tied around their waists. None of them stared at the newcomers as they passed—in fact, they didn't seem to notice them at all. Victria wasn't alone in noticing the differences.

"This is no place to start a resistance," Tera murmured.

Avmoshir let out a soft hiss, "I would advise you not to judge the fighting spirit of my people so rashly, human, even those of this sacred city."

"So, where are we going?" Victria asked. "How do you plan on getting help?"

"We're going to see my aunt," the young vashi responded. "She is one of the most influential vashi of Maleres. If anyone can help us, it will be her."

Walking to Avmoshir's aunt's home meant passing near the city's large temple. As they walked under it, and Victria was able to get a closer look at the massive structure, she couldn't help but feel that something within the temple was calling to her. It was as if she were being encouraged to enter the building, that she had to see what was inside. The feeling was not of her own desire, nor something she imagined. It felt alien, and yet familiar.

She turned to her companions, "Do you feel that?"

Tessa and Natiari raised their eyebrows together. "Feel what?"

Tera shook her head, distracted. Serania looked around as if there might be something in the water around them, but found nothing. Madira just shrugged and walked on.

So, she was alone with this feeling. She shook her head, but couldn't shake the urge to go inside. She stared at the giant edifice once more, the feeling growing stronger with each passing second, but finally she turned away and continued following Avmoshir.

A short time later, they stopped in front of a compact, two-story house. It was several shades of pink and red, and made up entirely of coral. Avmoshir hesitated, but forced himself up the few steps leading to the door. He knocked.

Nothing.

He knocked again, louder this time. And before he had even finished, the door flew open, revealing a tall vashi woman with flowing green hair and sparkling eyes. Her face broke out in a large smile and she lunged forward, taking Avmoshir into her arms.

"Oh, little Av, oh, you've gotten so big! It's been so long since I've seen you!"

Victria thought she looked kind, but something about her struck the viatari as odd, as if she'd seen her somewhere before. She tried to think of when, but nothing came to mind.

"Tell me," the vashi said. "How is your father, your mother? I'm surprised they let you come here alone with such strange company."

For a moment, words failed Avmoshir and Victria thought he might let his emotions overtake him. The young vashi swallowed hard, forming his next words with every ounce of strength he could muster.

"They're dead. Koranam had them assassinated."

The vashi's face paled.

"Dead? Koranam? It cannot be."

"I'm surprised the news hasn't reached this city yet," Serania whispered to Victria. "I would think Koranam would want to broadcast his ascendance to power by now."

As quietly as she tried to be, Avmoshir's aunt must have had excellent hearing because she snapped out of her shock and addressed the viatari directly. "News does not travel as quickly as you might think, especially between Zessarix and Maleres. Now if I may ask, who are you—what are you—and why are you in the company of my nephew?"

"They are a race called the viatari," Avmoshir said. "Though that one—" he pointed to Tera, "—is human. They protected me from Koranam's assassins and got me out of the city."

Avmoshir's aunt's features softened when she heard this, a trickle of warmth returning. "I see. In that case, you are welcome here. Please, come in. Call me Meri."

They entered the coral house, drying instantly, and quickly filled up the hallway. Meri closed the door behind them and led them to the kitchen, where she lit an everlasting fire and put a metal kettle over it.

"Allow me to make you all some tea. I'm sure it's been a long journey. And while we wait for the water to boil, you must tell me the details. I cannot believe my Koranam would have fallen so far."

"*Your* Koranam?" Serania repeated, confused.

Meri looked at them steadily, and suddenly Victria realized why Avmoshir's aunt looked so familiar. Her eyes weren't as vivid as the orange one she had grown accustomed to seeing in Zessarix and they certainly didn't hold the same hostility, but they were the same in all else. Her hair was similar, her face, Victria was sure even the lower half of Meri's body would be black as well, if she could see it under her robes.

"Yes, *my* Koranam. He is my son."

There was a shocked silence as everyone made the connection. For a moment, Natiari and Tessa looked like they might pull out their weapons but a quick shake of the head from Victria discouraged them.

Meri grinned, looking even more like the tyrant they had come to detest. "You look quite surprised."

"Yes, well. . . ." Victria didn't know what else to say.

"It's just, after dealing with Koranam for the past few days," Tera stepped in, glancing at the others for some help. "You're just so . . . nice."

Meri laughed but her smile faded quickly and her eyes

softened as if remembering something fondly. "You would not be the first to think so." She moved toward the kettle, which had begun to whistle, and extinguished the everlasting flame. She took out several small glasses and poured an orange, frothy liquid into it.

"This is my special blend," she said, handing each of them a glass. "Made from sea-crab grass I grow myself in the garden."

Victria blew on the hot beverage and took a sip. She was not accustomed to trying new drinks. The last time she had done so was when she was negotiating a treaty with the then-King of the dwarves, Ronorim Ironaxe—which had involved lots of ale. It had not been a good night for her.

She found she enjoyed the tea, though. As the liquid touched her tongue, it brought with it a fruity taste with a sharp tang that lasted long after she finished her cup. It also caused a fizzy sensation within her nose which tickled more than anything.

Meri indicated they should all sit down at her table as she poured herself a cup.

"You must understand, Koranam grew up like any normal vashi. He was even great friends with Avmoshir—"

"A friendship that seems to have meant nothing," Avmoshir muttered.

Meri nodded, her voice laced with sadness as she continued. "So it would seem. I do not defend what my child has done—to kill his own uncle . . . still, he was not always like this. He grew up a happy boy. He had a father who loved him. A mother who doted on him. But tragedy has a way of changing us. With the death of his father and his sister—my daughter—" here her voice broke, and she had to take a moment to compose herself. Closing her eyes and shuddering, she continued, "—my daughter, Adry, he changed. They were killed by human fishermen, you see. Fishermen who had entered our waters, far beyond the reef. I never saw those two again. Koranam was there. It was he who told me that the fishermen had pulled our family out of the water, returning only their heads. My boy, despite the shock and terror he must have felt, had to bury them quickly, so as to keep them from becoming food for scavengers. It scarred him. Ever since that day he's been different, angry. Dark. He hates humans with a passion; hates his own people, I think, for not doing anything about it."

There was a moment of silence as they all digested the sad account.

"I do not pretend that all humans are good," Tera said softly. "But many are, especially the fishermen—some of whom have been the best of my friends. If I ever discovered which boat and which captain was responsible for such a reprehensible act, I would kill them myself, and I'm sure I wouldn't be the only human in the southern ports to do so."

Meri inclined her head, "Your words comfort me. I never grew to hate the humans as my son did, despite what they've done to my family. I found it easier to forgive."

"I remember that day," Avmoshir spoke up, his gaze distant. "I remember noticing the darkness enter Koranam, changing him little by little. I am only sorry I could do nothing to help him grieve. But this is no excuse for what he has done to me. He has taken away my family just as the humans took away his. He has become the very monster he hates."

"Yes," Meri said. "As much as it pains me to hear of his fall, I will do what I can to make amends for him and help you. That is why you have come to me, I presume?"

"It is," Avmoshir finished the last of his tea. Victria could tell from his face he was wishing it had been something stronger. "I intend to retake Zessarix."

"No easy task. Knowing Kor, he probably has an army of supporters behind him."

"Which is why we must build our own."

Meri grimaced, but nodded. She turned to the viatari, "Make yourselves at home. I have many rooms in this house where you may rest. Avmoshir and I will be here for some time discussing plans. You do not have to stay for it if you do not wish to."

The viatari stood up and, after thanking their host, left to get some much-needed rest. Only Tera and Tessa stayed at the table to join in the discussions.

Victria, while she understood Avmoshir's intense desire to retake his seat of power as soon as possible, could not help but feel frustrated by his obsession. Sitting at the table, hearing about Koranam's past and knowing that any future plans would only involve fighting, if not all-out war, brought her to the conclusion that this struggle for power would require a great deal of time.

She wanted to help Avmoshir, after all, she had promised Araxie that she would protect him, but at the same time, this was not her reason for being in the Sea of Scales. Days had passed and still they were no closer to finding The First One's brother than they were when they first entered these waters.

How long would they have to stay in the vashi world, helping Avmoshir retake his home? Weeks? Months? All the while the world outside, *her* world, would fall deeper into peril as The Turned One and the Creature remained unchallenged within their stronghold of the Three Spires.

She shook her head, returning to the present. She realized she had been wandering through the hallways of the second floor. Looking to her left, she noticed a magnificent land-scape painting—or, at least, the vashi version of art.

The frame contained a thin sheet of water behind the glass. Small pieces of kelp and seaweed decorated the interior, swaying back and forth as something within the frame caused the water to continuously move so as to portray a current. It was as if the image was alive, a living rendition of the artist's mind. At the center was a large tower of coral, several colors in different sections, the arms of much of it reaching out well past the lengths of the frame. And at the very base of the cluster of coral, Victria noticed a small smudge.

She leaned in, trying to figure out what it might be. The image clarified, revealing a small, cylindrical chest. She couldn't be entirely sure of any features, as they were so miniscule compared to the rest of the painting. But her heart began to race as an idea entered her mind.

Racing back downstairs, she barged into the kitchen, where Meri and Avmoshir had been discussing in low tones with Tera and Tessa listening in. They all looked up at her in surprise.

"Meri," she gasped. "I'm sorry to interrupt—"

"What's the matter, dear?" Meri asked, slightly concerned. "You look like you've seen a saran."

"I need you to come with me," she turned to Tessa and Tera, "I've discovered something that might give us answers, or a hint at least, but I need you to verify it for me."

Victria just about pulled Meri off her chair in her excitement.

"Wait!" Avmoshir called out, rising from his own seat.

"We're still discussing—" But they were already out of the kitchen before he could finish. Victria led Meri up the stairs and quickly retraced her steps to the painting. She sighed with some relief when she saw the small chest at the base of the coral tower was still there and hadn't been something from her imagination. She pointed it out just as Avmoshir, Tessa, and Tera joined them.

"Can you tell me what that chest is?"

Meri peered at it for a moment, but shook her head. "I can't, actually. I've always wondered about it myself. Why would the artist add such a small, strange chest in the center of an otherwise gorgeous depiction of the Throne of the Deep?"

"This is the Throne of the Deep?" Tessa asked, her eyes widening as she realized why Victria had demanded their attention.

"Yes," Meri said, still studying the chest. "A beautiful depiction of it. When I saw it in the markets I knew I had to buy it. It is a wonder of the world, incomparable to anything else in these waters, yet few people ever go there."

"It's just a painting," Avmoshir said impatiently. "If you're done with your art lesson, Victria, we have important matters we still need to discuss." He tried to lead Meri off with him, as Victria had done earlier, but Meri didn't budge this time.

"Now that you bring attention to it, though," she said, lost in thought. "There is something familiar about that chest." She thought for a moment and then clapped her hands. "The temple! That's where I've seen it before! This chest looks exactly like the statue that stands in the middle of the temple. Though, why the artist added it in . . . I'm still not sure I understand the connection."

Now Victria's heart threatened to jump right out of her

chest as the excitement of her discovery filled her with a sense of triumph. This chest, if she was correct, was depicting the acolyte they had been looking for. If there was a statue of the acolyte in the temple of Maleres, maybe there would be more information on it as well, such as a specific location within the Throne of the Deep.

She turned to Tera and Tessa, who both looked ready to rush out with her. "We need to visit this temple, now."

Meri eyed them questionably. "The temple is beautiful and holds many artifacts from our people's past, and I would recommend anyone go if they haven't gone before, but where is this excitement coming from?"

"They think they'll find something to help them acc-omplish their own task," Avmoshir sounded bitter. "That's why they're in our waters. The only reason."

"Well, you should guide them through the temple then," Meri suggested. "Help them find what they seek."

"What?" The young vashi turned to his aunt, bewildered. "I don't—why should I?"

"Because you've been there many times before and know the temple inside and out. I remember how often you used to go as a child."

"But our discussions—"

"We've discussed enough to begin preparations," Meri said. "While you are away, I will reach out to those who I know will be able to help us and some who might need a little convincing. With any luck, by the time you return for dinner we should already have the start of a small army on our side."

Avmoshir frowned, his eyes shifting between his aunt and the viatari. "Very well," he finally said, though he didn't look too happy about it. He turned to Victria, his distaste clear.

"Gather your other companions and meet me by the front of the house. I will guide you through the temple."

Victria thanked him and rushed off to fetch Serania and the others. She was excited, despite the tension she realized she had unintentionally created between her and Avmoshir. She understood the frustration he must feel, but wondered if there was something deeper that was growing this animosity he seemed to feel for her. She shook her head, saving those thoughts for later. Now was not the time to dwell on them. Now was the time for answers. For the first time since they had entered these waters, she was glad they had come. They were finally making some progress.

CHAPTER THIRTY-TWO

The temple loomed over them once more. It hadn't taken much time for them to return here, since Meri lived only a few blocks away. The walk had been pleasant. Victria enjoyed observing the vashi as they went about their daily lives, even if the only thing she saw were couples strolling in what could only be described as the vashi version of a park or out in one of the cafés drinking hot beverages. It was relaxing and distracted her from the dire reality of their present situation.

As they began ascending the thousand steps—Avmoshir had mentioned beforehand that there were literally one thousand steps they had to take before reaching the main entrance of the temple—Victria kept her eyes glued to the columns holding up the giant, slanted roof. She didn't feel her legs burning and only once looked away to see how far they had come. She was surprised to find they had already made it halfway up, and though she barely felt the strain of taking these steps, it was clear she was nearly alone in that.

"Why can't we just swim to the entrance?" Natiari asked breathlessly, leaning on her thighs with every step she took. "Surely that would have been easier?"

Avmoshir, who had been climbing each step with perfect

posture, all the while maintaining his brooding mood, turned and answered with his usual bored tone. "It would be rude. It is expressly forbidden to swim up to the entrance of the temple of Maleres. Anyone who seeks to enter this sacred place must prove their earnestness by making it up the stairs without resting or giving up. If the stairs are too much for you, you must not have really wanted to enter the temple in the first place."

He turned back around and resumed climbing the stairs, though Victria thought she detected the smallest hint of satisfaction on his face.

"These stairs would not be such a problem if we had our regular strength," Madira groaned as they continued the climb.

"It's like we're human," Tessa added, wiping her brow as if she were sweating, then remembering they were underwater.

Natiari grunted in agreement, "I'm looking forward to returning to the surface world, if only to not be this weak anymore."

Tera appraised the three viatari with humorous eyes. She looked like she might take a jab at them but instead chuckled, shaking her head, and continued up the stairs with renewed vigor.

They trudged the rest of the way up in silence and spent only a little time to rest once they climbed the last step. The large, marble gates of the temple were already open, flanked by several strands of seaweed, swaying as if beckoning for them to pass through.

Victria didn't know what to expect when she stepped inside, but it wasn't this. The interior was just as spacious as the temple's size suggested, but it was dark. Small torches hung off of coral sconces on the wall, their tips lit with small tongues of everlasting flame. This provided only a dim light for the entire space and gave everything a green tint.

Looking around, she saw statues lined up ahead of them of many powerful vashi, each one wielding what appeared to be the same harpoon. They walked toward this line of statues, who all looked unfamiliar save for one.

They stopped before the figure at the end of the line, the well-chiseled features of Araxie glaring down at them. He held his golden harpoon high over his head, as if he were about to strike someone below him. She knew immediately why they had stopped here first and spared a glance at Avmoshir.

The young vashi looked up at the likeness of his father, his own eyes sad but determined. He pulled out the golden harpoon he had strapped to his back and held it before him as if in offering.

"I promise, father, I will take back our seat of power and avenge your death."

"Avmoshir," Tera said gently after a while. "Are all these statues—"

"Yes," he said. "From my father down to the first Supreme Overseer, almost all of these statues represent an ancestor of mine."

"Almost all?"

Avmoshir shrugged. "The Supreme Overseership is not a monarchy, where power is assured to pass on to the son of a king, though that is how it has been done lately. There have been times in the past where the Supreme Overseer saw fit to pass his title and power over to someone else not of his family. My family, however, has had the privilege of serving in the position more than most."

He shook his head, his sullen mood returning. "Anyway, we should keep moving."

There were few other vashi within the temple. As they walked deeper inside, Victria saw a group of three robed figures which she recognized as waterseers. They watched them pass by with suspicion but did nothing to stop them. She felt many sets of eyes suddenly on them. She hadn't seen them before, but there were several guards hidden in the shadows, their armor glinting faintly from the dim lights surrounding them. They wielded tridents double their height and looked like they knew how to use them. Avmoshir noticed them, too.

"The temple guards will not attack you unless you try to take or break something. Don't worry about them. But also be mindful of where you're going, you wouldn't want to break something by accident. You wouldn't last two seconds against one of the temple guards."

Victria nodded, she didn't need to be told that to know the truth behind it. She had a feeling that even with her regular strength and speed, the temple guards would still be a challenging opponent.

They came to the center of the temple, where a few more waterseers meandered about, speaking in hushed tones. There was a hole here in the center of the ceiling, which let in much more light than the dim torches did. The hole focused what light it let in so that it landed squarely on the giant statue before them, illuminating it.

"For being called a temple," Madira noted, "there really hasn't been much that hints at any religious worship."

"That is because this temple was not made for that," Avmoshir responded in the same hushed tones that the waterseers used. "It was made to house the history of our people. From this place we learn where we came from and what we've done up to the present day. There are other wings of the temple we haven't walked through yet that contain countless murals and paintings to tell these stories."

"Are you planning on taking us to them?" Serania asked. Victria noted a tremor of excitement in her voice. She bit her lip to suppress a smile. Even if Serania wasn't a wanderer anymore, wanderers were renowned for their love of knowledge. That love, apparently, had not faded.

"If you wish," Avmoshir sighed, not sounding too thrilled at the prospect. "We can begin with this statue then, carved millennia ago by one whose name has been lost to time. It depicts the birth of our race and is perhaps the most important piece of history we have. Without it, we would know very little of our origin."

Victria paced slowly around the sprawling statue, taking in every detail. In the center stood a giant figure with a humanoid torso, but a serpent's tail. Staring at the face, she thought it looked more serpentine than human. Muscles rippled throughout the being's body, rigid in his eternal position. Her eyes traveled down to the hands, which were outstretched toward the ground in a gentle pushing motion.

From one hand she saw several smaller figures pouring forth. She recognized the vashi, much of the ocean life, even the saran, but there was one race she did not recognize. They looked much like the vashi, but whereas the vashi inherited more of the humanoid features of this being, this unknown race seemed to have inherited the more serpentine one.

Victria reflected on the scene before her. Avmoshir had not yet finished explaining the origin of the statue, and so hadn't mentioned what it actually depicted, but something about what she was seeing seemed familiar. Like she had heard this story before. Serania stepped next to her, her eye devouring the many sculpted figures coming out of the giant being's hand.

"This feels familiar, but I don't know why. It's as if I've seen this scene before."

"I feel the same," Victria said. "Though I don't believe it's from something I've seen."

Her eyes moved to the being's left hand, the only part of the statue she hadn't inspected and gasped. In contrast to the right hand, the left had produced only one thing—a small thing, at that. Sitting there alone, seemingly unimportant in appearance, was a chest. It was different from the others she had seen before—with a cylindrical base and a dome for a lid—but she knew this was the acolyte they had been searching for.

She turned to Avmoshir, "What does this scene depict?"

The young vashi frowned, "I was just getting to that. The main figure in the center is said to depict our creator, Ocaeus, god of the seas. This scene is of our creation where we poured forth from his hand like waves on the beach. Not long after this event, it is said that Ocaeus disappeared from our world, never to be seen again."

"And what about that chest?" Victria pointed at the left hand. She already knew what it was but she wanted confirmation. She now realized why this story was so familiar. Serania and Thuradin had told her about the images The First One had shown them of the creation of their races. It appeared that the vashi had a similar history. But she still wanted to hear it from the vashi themselves, to confirm what she now knew had to be true. Avmoshir glanced at it and shrugged.

"It's just a vase or something, no one has ever under-stood why the sculptor included it or what it means."

"You mean your kind has had it right in front of you this whole time and you never knew? Never even—"

"And what, if I may ask, isss it that we never knew?" A commanding yet silky voice came from behind the statue. From a back room emerged a tall female vashi, her long golden hair flowing like a cape behind her as she slowly approached them. She was flanked by two temple guards who, now out of the shadows, looked even more menacing.

Victria was unsure how to respond or to whom she was speaking, but she figured she had to be important to have her own guard. Even Avmoshir showed respect by greeting her with a deep, graceful bow. She radiated power and it was more than just a feeling. Victria could see the water around her churn as if it were ready to boil in an instant.

"High priestess, it is an honor to see you again," the young vashi approached, gently pressing his lips against one of the high priestess' moon-stone rings. Allow me to introduce my guests in these seas, the viatari and the human, Tera. My father allowed them entry. I'm sure he had his reasons, though I struggle to understand them myself."

The high priestess looked down and gently caressed Avmoshir's cheek. "I sssee your father isss not here now and that you carry hisss golden harpoon. I am sssorry to sssee that he hasss passed from thisss world. How, if I may ask, did it happen?"

"Through treachery," Avmoshir's visage darkened and he said no more.

The high priestess nodded. "It painsss me to hear it. I pray the oceansss will punish those responsible for sssuch evil."

Avmoshir bowed again and then addressed the viatari. "This is Una, our high priestess. She leads the waterseers and is in charge of all of Maleres."

"Enough with the pleasantriesss," Una waved her hand dismissively, sending a pulse of water that pushed them all back slightly. "I desire to know what thisss viatari claimsss to know about the chest made by Ocaeusss."

Victria presented her own little bow. Unsure of how she should address Una, she gave her answer as simply as she could.

"What you see there depicts more than a chest. It is an acolyte, a being made by the first gods to maintain the peace and order of this world when the gods went away. . . ." She went on to explain everything The First One had told her. This was, she realized, the first time Avmoshir had heard the whole explanation as well. He had not been in the room when she explained it to Araxie and hadn't been in the Assembly Hall when the Supreme Overseer explained it to the Assembly. Perhaps now he would understand why they were here and the urgency behind their task.

When she had finished explaining everything, including the reason for their presence, Una did not waste any time with questions.

"I sssee now why the watersss brought your wordsss ssstraight to my earsss for my attention," the high priestess said. Victria thought she looked thoughtful, but couldn't tell if that was a good sign or not.

"For millennia, the high priest—or, in my cassse, priestess—hasss tried and failed again and again to decipher the purpossse behind the chest. We have ssstudied the ssstatue, even entered the Throne of the Deep on numerousss occasionsss to try and understand the mystery, but to no avail. If thisss chest isss what you sssay, then it isss more precious than we could have possibly imagined. I assume, sssince your purpossse isss to retrieve the acolyte, you have come here to ask my permission to enter the Throne, yesss?"

Victria nodded. She had to admit, she was taken aback by how bluntly the high priestess had identified their purpose.

"I give it freely," Una said. "The watersss would have warned me had you been deceptive, but they remain calm. And sssince that provesss your ssstory to be true, it isss clear we vashi must do what we can to aid thossse who ssseek to put an end to thossse who only wish to bring destruction— even if it meansss parting with a treasured creation of Ocaeus."

"But the Assembly," Avmoshir stammered. "They have yet to decide if these strangers should be allowed to even see you to ask for permission."

Una laughed, a soft sound that the water around her seemed to echo. "And yet, ssseen me they have. Besidesss, the watersss give me troubling tidingsss from the Assembly in Zessarix. I would not trust their word at thisss time."

The high priestess turned to leave but a sudden thought brought her attention back to the viatari. "While I have given you the permission you ssseek, you cannot enter the Throne alone. You must be escorted by a vashi, and there isss none I would trust more to escort you than the bearer of the golden harpoon."

For a split second, Avmoshir looked furious, but his face quickly relaxed and he bowed low. "As you wish, high priestess."

With that, he turned and stormed out of the temple, the

viatari and Tera following close behind.

Victria was pleased with how things had turned out, and as they walked out into the bright waters of Maleres, she could not help but feel a sudden urge to depart immediately. The sooner they retrieved the acolyte, the sooner they could return to the surface and their home.

"When will we leave?" she asked Avmoshir.

"I'm not taking you."

Victria stopped in her tracks in shock, but realizing the young vashi had no intention of stopping with her, she hurried to catch up with him. "But you told the high priestess—"

"I cannot deny her to her face, but I have no intention of taking you to the Throne of the Deep."

Victria frowned. "Why not?"

Avmoshir whirled on her, the rage so clear in his eyes they appeared to be burning with it. His anger was so overwhelming, he could not even control his speech, which he and his father typically excelled at.

"Becaussse I have a cccity to retake. I have a family I mussst avenge! And even if you will not help me like you sssaid you would, that will not ssstop me from doing it myself!"

"What makes you think we won't help you?" Victria asked, bewildered.

Avmoshir hissed. "Becaussse there'sss nothing in it for you. I heard you back in the cave on our way to Maleresss. You want to trade your aid for my loyalty to your causssse? Well, I refusssse. Once I retake Zessarix and take my father'sss placcce, I will be sssure to banish you and your kind from our watersss. You have brought nothing but misery to me."

"Avmoshir," Victria said gently. She understood now what the young vashi was referring to but it was clear he had not listened to the whole conversation she'd had with Natiari. "I admit it would be helpful to have the aid of the vashi when facing the evil that threatens our world, but that is not the main reason I want to help you. I promised your father—"

"What is a promissse to you? I don't know you."

"No, but—"

"Enough of thisss! I will not take you and that isss final."

Now it was Victria who was angry. She reached out and grabbed Avmoshir by the back of his neck just as he began to walk away, yanking him back. The young vashi hissed and drew his father's golden harpoon, swinging it at Victria's head. There was a loud clang as Serania stepped in, blocking it with her sword. The entire time Victria stared deep into Avmoshir's golden eyes.

"You *will* take us," she stated, baring her fangs. She did not want to do this, but if the game that had to be played was one of intimidation, she had no choice but to play it—and win. She would not let the whims of this boy be the cause for their failure.

The young vashi struggled to break free but her hold on him was vice-like.

"You cannot forcccce me."

"No, but I can make sure the high priestess knows what you just said. Did you not hear her say how the vashi must play their part in this fight for our world? How pleased do you think she will be when she discovers you not only refused to help us retrieve what we need to ensure victory, but also intended on banishing us and isolating yourselves from the rest of the world? Then again, that's *if* you manage to take back Zessarix. Do you think the high priestess will be willing to lend the aid of Maleres to one who disobeys so readily behind her back?"

Avmoshir hissed again but said nothing. Victria was certain the message had been well-received. She let go of the young vashi and was pleased to see he didn't swim away. He glared at her with hatred. But finally, he nodded.

"I will tell my aunt where we are going first. Meet me at the stables and have the mantas ready." He moved to walk away but stopped after a few steps. "I will take you to the Throne of the Deep, but then I never want to see you or your companions again."

CHAPTER THIRTY-THREE

The tension in the water was palpable as they rode out of Maleres. Avmoshir hadn't said a word since their departure and Victria, feeling it would be inappropriate to make idle conversation in such a situation, kept silent as well.

They headed south, urging their mounts upward to stay close to the water's surface. It was rough riding. The waves pulled them in all directions as they traveled. But this way, they had a clear view of their surroundings—there would be no attacks from above. Eventually they dove back down close to the reef to find a cave or gorge where they could make camp for the night. They found a nice clearing surrounded by a cluster of sizeable anemones where they guided their mantas to a stop and hopped off.

"I don't think we'll be in too much danger here," Victria said. "Madira, if you can get some everlasting fire going, we can have a hot meal—well, Tera can, anyway."

Tera winked as she gathered all their belongings together. "I appreciate it."

"Serania can do the cooking. Tessa, Natiari, swim around our location to make sure we're safe from anyone who might have picked up our trail. Avmoshir—" she turned to address the young vashi but found that he had slunk off far away from them to the very edge of the clearing, close to the anemone. Victria frowned. She had hoped that including him in their camp preparations might help chip away some of the tension that existed between them. She walked to where he had set his things.

"Avmoshir,"

The young vashi stiffened but did not turn to face her.

"Why are you setting your things here? It's safer if we stay together. Besides, you'll be cold without the fire."

"I'll be fine."

Victria paused, hearing the anger in his voice. She understood why it was there, knew it was partially her fault and partially Koranam's, but she still didn't appreciate his attitude. This was not a time for games or politics. She felt her patience ebb away with each passing second.

"Well . . . we can still use your help. Serania is sorting through the food for tonight's meal and she could use help from someone who knows what they're doing when it comes to cooking underwater."

Avmoshir laughed bitterly. "I have no interest in cooking for your human pet. The less I have to do with you people, the better. Now, leave me."

Victria bit her tongue to keep herself from saying something she might regret. There was no use in escalating this feud. She didn't want to risk alienating the young vashi even more than she already had and then have him running away in the middle of the night. He might try to do it, anyway, she thought.

She walked back to her companions. Tera glanced her way, saw the expression on her face and nodded knowingly.

"You shouldn't be surprised."

"I know that!"

Tera raised an eyebrow. After a deep breath, Victria tried again. "I'm sorry. I know that, but that doesn't keep it from affecting me. His attitude is contagious."

"Maybe you should apologize," Serania suggested as she continued rummaging through their bags of fish, seaweed, sea legumes and other foods. "I'm sure you realize it, but it will do no good if we make enemies of the vashi, and that boy is going to be their Supreme Overseer—if he manages to retake Zessarix."

"But he won't listen to me. I doubt he'd accept my apology."

"You should do it anyway," Madira chimed in. "Sorry if I'm butting in, but just making an apology is the first step to healing. It doesn't often work right away, but once you make it, the healing process can begin. And like anything, for the wound to disappear it will take time. Even if he rejects your apology, it will still stick with him in some way that might make him change his mind in the future."

Victria glanced between her companions and frowned. What Madira said made sense. What they all were saying made sense. Things could not continue this way. Her eyes drifted back to Avmoshir's separated camp. Now was not the time, though. The wounds were still too fresh, the anger too hot. She would try tonight, give him some time to cool off. And give herself some time to think about how she could approach him.

There were no bioluminescent jellyfish to light the waters that night. Only their small flame of everlasting fire allowed them to maintain visibility, even if it was very little. The tongues of green flame danced in its miniature brazier, keeping them warm and providing brief flashes of color as the orange, pink, and blue tentacles of the surrounding anemone caught the light.

The viatari and Tera sat around the fire. Not a word had been said since nightfall. Avmoshir remained separated from them, slumped over by the edge of the clearing. Victria had kept an eye on him, but he gave no indication that he planned to escape.

"I wonder how Thomas is doing," Tera spoke suddenly, her voice penetrating the night like a needle. "We've been gone almost a week now."

"Not that I know him," Serania chuckled lightly. "But from the little I saw of him I have no doubt he's still out on some island, fishing peacefully."

Tera grinned and nodded. "Yes, you're probably right."

Serania turned to Victria, all pretense of nonchalance gone. "So, are you going to apologize? It's decision time."

Victria blinked. "What, right now? In the middle of the night?"

"Well, you've spent so much time already doing nothing about it."

She frowned. All eyes were on her, waiting to see what she would do. She stood up, opened her mouth as if to rebel against their ridiculous idea, but nothing came out and instead she turned and marched off to where Avmoshir sat.

The coldness of the waters hit her without warning as she walked away from the flames. With each step she took, she hoped for some sudden inspiration that might help her figure out how exactly she should apologize. What should she say? What should she apologize *for?* She had no idea, and she feared she might lose her temper with the young vashi because of it and only make things worse.

Only a few feet away from Avmoshir, she could see now

that he was shaking. She wondered if the cold really was affecting him despite his claims that it wouldn't but a series of clogged sniffling told her it wasn't just the frigid waters causing him to tremble.

She looked away, berating herself as she remembered how viciously she had spoken to him, how she had threatened him. With all the dangers they had been facing and the immensity of their task, there was one simple fact that she had completely overlooked. Avmoshir was only a child, one who had just lost both of his parents, no less. And though she still didn't have a clue what she might say, she could hear words passing through her lips on their own.

"It's warmer by the fire."

Avmoshir sat upright and stiffened, all signs of trembling coming to a swift halt. He cleared his throat several times before speaking.

"The vashi are not affected by the cold waters as your kind might be. I have no need for a fire."

"Still," Victria had made him talk, that was a good sign, surely. "I think it would be good for you to be around the fire with us."

And now the familiar sneer in his voice returned. "Why? Afraid I'll run away?"

"Yes," Victria said truthfully.

The vashi turned his head slightly but didn't respond, waiting for something more.

"Yes, we're afraid—I'm afraid—that you might run away, might abandon us when we need your help the most. Just as you're afraid we might abandon you."

"You already have abandoned me," Avmoshir hissed. "You put a desire for a bejeweled chest above my need to retake my city, my home, to avenge my father who died in my arms. You never intended to help me in the first place."

"But we did—we do," Victria had taken a few steps closer and knelt down so that she was level with him, though he still had his back turned to her. "I promised your father I would protect you, and if you intend on doing something as dangerous as going against Koranam and all his cohorts, I will be by your side. You said you heard our conversation at the cave but you didn't hear it all or you would know that I keep my promises."

The young vashi's hissing softened. "How can I believe that? I don't know you. You don't know me."

She put a hand on his shoulder, but he violently shrugged it off and stood. Victria stood as well, wondering briefly if perhaps she had pushed too hard. But he just stood where he was, still like a statue.

"You have to trust me."

Avmoshir did not respond.

"Anyway," Victria said once she realized the conversation between them was over. "I just wanted to apologize for how I treated you earlier. I was wrong to threaten you and attack you like I did. You are not our hostage and I don't want you to feel that way. I hope you will forgive me, Avmoshir."

The young vashi kept silent, even as Victria turned and made her way back to the fire. Nothing was said by her companions as she reclaimed her seat. They could tell by her face how well the encounter had gone. Serania nodded her approval.

The night wore on and most of their party laid back to go to sleep. Tessa and Madira volunteered to take the first watch. As Victria rested her head against the soft ocean sand, she glanced in Avmoshir's direction and saw him still standing there as he had been when she left him. She closed

her eyes and prayed that things would change with time, as
Madira had said.

By noon the next day they were able to see the outline of
the Throne of the Deep in the distance. By evening, they
were at its base, straining their necks back as they gawked at
its size.

"It must breach the surface," Tera said, her mouth open.

Avmoshir shrugged, temporarily forgetting his mood. "It
is my first time here as well. I honestly have no idea."

Victria thought Tera might be right. The Throne of the
Deep was like a giant, continuous pillar of coral, rock, and
barnacle shells all stacked on top of each other in inter-
secting layers. Farther up, the coral branched out with their
arms, providing a type of canopy, like a tree. It was all sorts
of colors from blue to yellow to black and as she beheld this
wonder of the world she noticed movement out of the
corner of her eye.

Shifting her gaze, she saw a small gam of sharks pushing
lazily through the water, circling around the left side of the
Throne. There were other oceanic wildlife as well, small
schools of colorful fish and even an octopus or two jetting
between the arms of the coral, but after their last encounter
with sharks she was wary of them.

They hadn't seen any of Koranam's servants since they
left Maleres but that didn't mean they were safe. Any
creature could be under the control of his waterseers and
they would never know until it was too late.

"Come on, let's go," Serania pointed toward the lower end
of the Throne's base. "I think I see a passage that leads
inside."

They left their giant manta rays free to roam and hunt for

plankton and continued on foot. Upon entering, the world outside seemed closed off, as if there was nothing that existed, save the coral that made up the Throne. Victria would have thought from the arrangement of different sea creatures and rocks that made up this place and how chaotic it all seemed from the outside that there would be the same sense of chaos inside. She was surprised to see that there was a clear sense of order with the placement of every piece of coral and stone that made up this passageway as well as the hallway they entered after.

A whirlwind of color passed them by as they continued looking around. Nothing was bland to the eye, but it was almost too much to behold.

"This is why, I think, only the high priests and priestesses are allowed to come here," Avmoshir winced, rubbing his eyes. "This place is too much, as expected from something made by a god."

"It's gorgeous!" Madira exclaimed, her eyes bright as she took in all the different shapes and sizes and colors of the coral around her. "It's like a never-ending underwater forest."

Natiari scoffed. "You and your plants."

"While they might look like plants," Tera pointed out. "Coral are actually living creatures. They eat a type of plankton, very much like our mounts."

Victria gawked at her, impressed. "How do you know all of that?"

Tera shrugged. "Thomas. He knows everything about the ocean."

They moved from one hall to the next, each one as spacious, if not more so, than the last.

"We could walk or swim through here for days and I

don't think we would ever fully explore this place," Serania said.

Avmoshir seemed to agree. "It would be easy to get lost in here."

"Watch out!" Tessa drew her dirk and moved to the front, ready for battle.

Above them, two lines of sharks swam back and forth through the hall. Victria couldn't prove it, but she felt certain that they were watching them with their unblinking black eyes.

"They won't attack us," Avmoshir said after a while. "Unless we give them a reason. I think they're the guardians of this sacred place."

Tessa lowered her blade and put it away, keeping her eyes on the sharks. "What could they be guarding?"

"I think I know," Serania mused. "They must be like what the crystal sprites were for The First One. The sharks serve the acolyte we're looking for."

"Hm," Victria kept a hand on the hilt of her dirk. "Still, keep your guard up."

"So, which way should we go?" Tera's voice rang out from afar. She stood a fair distance ahead of them facing the end of the hallway, which branched off in two separate directions. They rushed to catch up.

"How should we choose?' Madira asked. "What if we make the wrong choice and we get lost here like Avmoshir said? What if it's for days?"

"We don't have time for that." Victria agreed.

"Well," Serania thought for a moment, running her fingers through the strands of hair covering her right eye absently. "When I found The First One, I only found him because he was shooting out a pillar of light in the sky—like a power source. Maybe the other acolytes are similar."

"Avmoshir," Victria turned to the young vashi, the only one who still had his eyes on the sharks. "Do you feel any difference in the waters coming from either hallway?"

Avmoshir finally looked away from the predators circling above and swam before the two openings, closing his eyes. He pointed to the left.

"There is a slight current coming from this hallway. I don't know what it is, but I also don't see how there can be a current in an enclosed place like this."

"Left we go, then," Victria said. Everyone followed her into the next hallway, which, after a few minutes, led to an open, spacious room. During their walk, Victria wondered why everything in this place was so gargantuan. There had to be a reason, but none came to mind. Now, however, as she stared in shock at the saran in front of her, she understood why.

The creature's serpentine head faced them, its sharp fangs jutting out of its mouth. Its beady black eyes were trained on them and Victria was certain they were about to die. There was no use fighting this thing, if what the vashi said about it was true. There was nothing left to do but accept their fate. All because they had made a wrong turn.

They stood there, knowing any second might be their last, but the saran stayed in place, hovering in the water.

"Why aren't we dead?" Victria whispered.

Avmoshir hesitantly moved closer to the saran until he was mere inches away and inspected it. "I-I think it's asleep."

"With its eyes open?"

The young vashi shrugged. "They must be like sharks. I know many creatures of the sea that sleep with their eyes open. Not much is known about the saran, as I've told you before, but I will say, we are incredibly lucky right now."

"Was the current you felt earlier the saran's breathing, then?" Serania asked, moving around to the side of the creature with everyone else.

Avmoshir shook his head. "No, because I still feel the current. It's stronger now." He swam upwards, and after looking around, he pointed toward a narrow hole in the ceiling. "There, that's where it's coming from. It looks like we can fit if we go one at a time."

Victria swam up to join Avmoshir, keeping her eyes on the saran in case it woke up—not that there was anything she could do if it did, she realized. Now that she was closer to the hole, she could feel the current as well. It was strong. Too strong to swim through. She said as much to Avmoshir.

The young vashi agreed. "Even I would struggle against that current. You would have no chance. It would just spit you back out."

"What could cause such a strong force, though?"

"Who knows? It makes no sense to me."

Victria studied the hole again, and felt a shiver run down her spine. There was an urge within her to go through it, as if she had to, as if her life depended on it.

"I think we have to try to go through it anyway."

"How are we going to do that?" Serania asked, joining them along with the rest of their companions.

Victria grinned. "Through sheer willpower."

Natiari snorted. "You sound like a dwarf."

"I guess they've rubbed off on me, then. I'll go first."

Victria dashed into the narrow orifice, using all the strength she could muster to try and make some distance before the current wore her out. But it was no use. She only made it a few feet before the current pushed her out of the hole completely.

"Do you want to look for another way?" Avmoshir asked.

"No, we have to go through this way."

"Why?"

Victria looked at Serania, who had asked the question. There must have been something on her face that conveyed how she felt because an understanding seemed to come between them.

"You feel something, don't you?"

"He has to be on the other side of wherever this hole leads to."

Without waiting for anyone to try and talk her out of it, Victria dashed once more into the hole, this time grabbing onto the coral that made up the sides of the tunnel. She expected the coral to break, fragile as they usually were, but these seemed to be sturdier than others she had encountered during her time in the seas. They made excellent handholds and even though the current was strong and bore down on her like a hurricane, she slowly continued climbing up.

After a few minutes of this, she glanced behind her to see how much progress she had made. She saw Serania and the others climbing behind her. They had followed her lead. Avmoshir was swimming, using all his vashi strength to fight the current. Victria wondered if he would be able to maintain that pace the whole way.

She returned to the task at hand and focused on climbing, gritting her teeth as the current only grew stronger the farther she went. She noticed the water was also growing colder and soon felt her hands grow numb. Still, she climbed. Even when the coral turned into sharp stone, cutting into her flesh, she climbed. She would not stop, refused to give in.

Her entire purpose was to retrieve the acolyte and if she couldn't bear this small suffering to do it, then she would be a failure. And she could not, would not, return to Aleganthia as a failure. Not when the future of the world depended on her.

After what seemed like an eternity, Victria saw a light shining ahead of them.

"It's the end of the tunnel. It has to be!" She yelled, but her words were swept away by the current. She shook her head; she would just have to hope that her friends would continue struggling just as she was. She pulled herself up, one stone at a time, almost mechanically at this point. Not a moment too soon, just as her strength was at the point of giving out, she managed to pull herself out onto the other side.

She collapsed. Noticing belatedly that whatever current had been pushing on her had disappeared. She heard her companions climb out, groaning as they fell next to her. Even Avmoshir looked exhausted as he finally emerged from the tunnel, his chest heaving as he slowly sank to the floor.

Victria sat up, still breathing hard, and observed their new surroundings. The room they were in now was as spacious as the last and just as colorful. But they were not alone. She froze, her heart hammering in her chest as she caught sight of the cylindrical chest standing in the middle of the marble floor.

It was the same one she had seen in the painting, the same one she had seen being held by the statue at the temple of Maleres. It was the acolyte they had been searching for for weeks, a brother of The First One. And as she thought this, as if on cue, transparent, green tendrils slowly began to slide out of the chest.

CHAPTER THIRTY-FOUR

Salevari was furious. She wanted to vent, to yell, to destroy every piece of furniture unfortunate enough to be in the room with her. She wanted to rip the maps and tapestries off the walls and throw them out of a window. She wanted to take out her sword and swing it wildly at Zael, at Simon and Kent, at everyone in this city who brought her nothing but problems and never solutions. Aleganthia was a never-ending battle and as soon as she fixed one problem, another would take its place.

Before her stood Simon and Kent, their own faces livid. The bodies of Dave and Barty had been discovered the day after the riot, though the fact that Zael had been the one who carried out the killing remained unknown. Despite this, Simon and Kent were quick to realize that a viatari had performed this act of retaliation.

"We want answers," Kent demanded forcefully. "What happened last night cannot be allowed to happen again. If humans and the viatari are to work together and trust each other, as you've said numerous times, you must discover who did this and bring them to justice. An investigation must be opened."

Salevari glared at him, wanting to laugh. With each passing

day she came to understand more and more of the human language, which meant she could now speak with Kent more directly rather than through Zael or Simon like before. She preferred the times when she hadn't understood what Kent was saying, though. It was annoying enough dealing with Simon.

"An investigation?" she seethed. "Like the one you said you would perform when my viatari guards were murdered?"

"Yes," Kent hesitated. "It is only fair—"

"Your investigation did NOTHING!" Salevari could no longer hold back her temper. "It was not because of you that we discovered Anders and Lyna's plot, it was because of me."

Kent's face turned red, but he kept his composure and tried again. "Still, this cannot be allowed to continue."

Salevari closed her eyes and took a deep breath to try and calm herself before responding. "No," she finally said, crossing her arms. "It cannot. However, you cannot expect me to keep my people from defending themselves now that they've discovered that they're being targeted by the same humans they've risked their lives to save."

"So you will do nothing?" Kent asked in disbelief.

Salevari glanced at Simon, wondering if he had anything to add to the conversation, but he only studied her curiously. She frowned. There was something unnerving about his adeptness at hiding his thoughts.

"No, Kent, I'm asking you to trust me," Salevari said. "Do you really think I would invest so much time and energy into building a working relationship with you humans only to throw it away by letting my people rampage against yours? Believe me, I will speak with the one responsible for this act. I hope you realize, though, that at least one of the men killed was the one responsible for the most recent murder of *my* people."

"How do you know this?"

"Because the one responsible listened in on their conversation before confronting them. The one named Barty confessed to the killing."

"Then," Kent spoke slowly, his face slack. "You already know who is responsible."

Salevari sighed. They were talking in circles now and she didn't have all day to waste on Kent's desire for answers.

"Yes, I know who did it. No, I will not hand them over to you—yes, I will speak with them—severely—to ensure this never happens again. No, I will not tell you who it is."

Even Simon looked incensed by the time the Chancellor had finished speaking. "You'll *speak* to him? This is no childish misstep, Salevari. He or she murdered two of our own!"

"Yes, as retribution for one of those men murdering ours," Salevari shot back. "You see, there *is* a difference in this. These murders were not done out of hatred for humans. Your people, however, kill us out of prejudice and a reckless desire to eradicate us from the face of the earth. So believe me when I tell you I can assure you that this won't happen again—especially if you give me those antidotes I've been asking for."

Simon scoffed and shook his head. "And how will that ensure this doesn't happen again? If anything, it will give your people more reason to attack ours, seeing as we will truly be helpless without our poisons."

Salevari rolled her eyes. Such idiocy would never have been tolerated in Dalyr. She envied the viatari she had left in charge of her city. She had received nothing but stellar reports of peace and calm ever since she'd left. She'd like nothing more than to return home and sit on the banks of the river that ran through the center of their canyon city and leave this all behind.

"We move back to the issue of trust. I tell you now, Simon, if you and your people cannot learn to trust mine, then we will never be united even against a common enemy like the Creature. I ask you again, will you give my people what we need to protect ourselves?"

Simon frowned. He was not pleased and Salevari knew it, but she didn't care so long as he continued working with her. As long as that happened, she would make sure they all got what they wanted.

"I've created a few batches of an antidote for this new strain of poison, but it's difficult to make. I will need more time to make enough for your purposes. In the meantime, that will give us a chance to learn how to better trust each other."

Salevari thought she detected a hint of sarcasm but she let it slide. She had doubts about Simon's claim that he was having difficulty with the antidote. Humans never had trouble when it came to their poisons and antidotes and Simon was clever. But if time was what he was asking for, again, then she would grant it—for now. There were other more pressing matters she had to attend to.

"Fine. But just know, Simon, our time is not infinite. We cannot wait forever. Will that be all?"

Simon and Kent nodded and inclined their heads, displeasure written all over their faces. The door was opened for them by one of the guards and they walked out. Salevari sighed. She was relieved that this ordeal was over with, she just wished it was all she had to deal with today. Alas, such a thought was fanciful.

"Bring me Zael."

The guard by the door nodded and left, returning several minutes later with the captain in tow. Zael kneeled before Salevari and bowed his head, avoiding her gaze.

"Stand up and look at me."

He did so. Salevari saw that there was no remorse in his eyes, nor fear that he would be punished. She would have found his confidence rather amusing were the situation not so serious.

"Do you have anything to say for yourself?"

"I did what I felt was right."

Salevari frowned. "You disappoint me, Zael. I would have thought you possessed more restraint and patience. Do you realize you nearly destroyed everything we've been working towards for the past several weeks?"

A moment of uncertainty flashed through the captain's eyes. He frowned, unsure of how to respond. "If it is my resignation you seek, I will gladly give it."

The Chancellor shook her head. "Oh no, you will not escape so easily. I still have uses for you. You may not be Drathanar, but I still see your potential. However, I need to know that I can count on you always. I've kept you from the humans' grasp this time. Do not make me regret it."

Zael bowed his head again, this time respectfully. "You will not regret this, Chancellor. I thank you for granting me another chance and I regret the trouble I have caused you."

Salevari bit back a grin. As she had said, he was no Drathanar, and she knew he did not want to be. But the two had such an uncanny sense of duty she could not help but compare them. Still, she had to at least pretend that she remained irritated with him.

"You can thank me by continuing to serve our cause. If there is one thing I am pleased about with your recent vigilante action it's that it will undoubtedly force Anders and Lyna to accelerate their plans. They will come for me sooner than we originally anticipated."

Zael frowned, confused. "Why would that please you, if I may ask?"

"Because," the Chancellor licked her lips hungrily. "We will be rid of them all the more quickly, and I can finally put all my attention on the Creature and his darimun. You may not have realized it at the time, but your act of vengeance will make those dissident humans believe they are being targeted by us. They will want to get rid of me now more than ever, thinking it will throw us into disarray."

"How do you know all this?"

"I have a feeling," Salevari smiled knowingly. Anders and Lyna were clever and dangerous, but they were still driven primarily by fear of the viatari. That fear, now amplified, would make them stupid and their recent successes would make them overconfident. A perfect combination.

"But I need you to make sure that my feeling is correct. I need you to get into another one of their meetings and verify what I just told you. I need to know what time and day this will happen and how. You must not fail me in this. I don't mean to sound dramatic, but the fate of this city and our relationship with the humans may very well depend on it."

Zael saluted, his thin lips pressed into a determined line. "It will be done."

Without another word the captain exited the room, the door slamming shut behind him. Salevari sighed again. Playing these games of subterfuge with the humans was so tiring. She would have much rather preferred to charge in, blade in hand. It would have saved them so much time, but she understood the need for discretion with this delicate operation she was planning.

Time. She thought of the reports she had been told by her scouts earlier that morning. Her jaw clenched as pressure built up in her chest. They were running out of time. The darimun attacks were growing larger and fiercer. It was rare now that the viatari could successfully defend a town without suffering a few casualties.

Soon, she knew, the Creature would grow tired of playing with them and would send a sizeable force to wipe out the remaining human towns, and perhaps, Aleganthia as well. She had to make sure the humans and viatari had put away their prejudices by then. She would not be able to focus on battling the Creature if she also had to watch her back for human assassins.

She stood and walked over to a map of their region. Three more towns were circled in the southern plains—the Creature's next targets. Viatari defenders had already been sent out as well as the first human parties. She prayed that they could work successfully together. If they could, they were one step closer to their ultimate goal. If not . . . well, she didn't want to think of what that might mean.

She left the room, moving to one of the keep's many windows and opening it. A gust of fresh air rushed in, filling her lungs, and she felt the pressure in her chest dissipate a little. She stayed there for some time, watching the crowded streets below her as the city's inhabitants went about their business. She looked up and caught sight of the Silent Mountains in the distance, the clouds parting enough for her to catch a glimpse of their snowy peaks. She leaned against the windowsill and closed her eyes, feeling the breeze and thinking of quieter times, of simpler times.

CHAPTER THIRTY-FIVE

The sun was at its zenith as Zael meandered through Aleganthia's marketplace, taking his time as he made his way to the human quarter of the city. It was a hot day, made all the more so by the cloudless sky. The viatari captain felt droplets of sweat forming on his brow but he ignored the small discomfort. He was lost in thought, absent from everything else happening around him.

He felt conflicted. His meeting with Salevari had not gone as he had envisioned. He had expected her to be pleased with his report that he had carried out justice. Instead, he had been rebuked, chastised. The human leadership was obviously displeased, and he was grateful that Salevari still found enough value in him to protect him from their clutches. As he remembered this, he felt a twinge of shame from his actions.

And yet, he also felt angry. He shouldn't have been reprimanded. Had he done nothing, the murderer would still be on the loose, able to kill more viatari at his pleasure. Salevari was playing a long game, Zael knew, but he could not help but feel that she was doing nothing to counter the human threat they faced. And that was something he could not do, not at the risk of viatari lives. Still, he was duty-bound to his role.

Though, now his role carried some risk of Garrel outing him. Had he told the others what he had seen or kept his silence? Zael had no way of knowing. Garrel had a family to worry about, so he wanted to believe the young man would distance himself from this conflict so as to protect them, but there was always the chance that Zael had misjudged Garrel's character. For all he knew, he could be walking into a trap today.

He was so lost in thought that he didn't notice their presence until they were right in front of him. Almost a century had passed since last he saw them, but he recognized them instantly. He knew their sharp, hawkish features, their elegant clothes, well-groomed hair. He had already been in a foul mood, but now he was seething as he leered at the Rauans. He glanced around for their children, the ones who used to be his playmates, but they were nowhere to be seen.

The Rauans looked shocked, as if they hadn't expected to run into him. That much was probably true, Zael thought, as he noticed their baskets full of fresh vegetables along with caged birds, rabbits, and squirrels in their hands. They were on their way home from the market.

"Zael. . . ." Kur Rauan started to say, but nothing more came out of his mouth.

"My, how you've grown since last we saw you, Zael." Yalar Rauan said nervously, her eyes like saucers but filled with what emotion, the viatari captain couldn't say.

"How—how have you been?" Kur asked.

"Don't," Zael seethed, barely able to rein in the resentment building up inside him. "Don't act like you care."

Yalar's eyes softened. "But we do, Zael. Not a day goes by where we don't think—don't regret—"

"Enough. The blood of my parents is on your hands and you did nothing, never even bothered to ask for forgiveness."

Kur stepped forward as if he wanted to reach out and offer some comfort but Zael recoiled.

"Is it too late to ask that of you?"

"Excuse me?"

"Will you forgive us now for what we did—for our cowardice that day? Not a second goes by where we do not regret it and all the pain it caused you."

Zael felt his eyes burn as a memory of his parents smiling down at him flashed through his mind. He shook his head angrily and pushed past the Rauans, cursing them and making Kur drop his basket of vegetables.

"Zael!"

He kept walking, refusing to turn back, not even to see the pained looks he imagined—he hoped—were on their faces. Such a sight might have given him some small pleasure, but he'd much rather not see their pathetic faces ever again.

He entered one of the city's public lavatories and transformed into his human form, still trembling from the encounter. Of all the viatari who still lived in Aleganthia, he had not expected to run into the Rauans. He had taken great pains in the past century to avoid them—purchasing a home on the opposite end of the city, becoming familiar with their daily schedules so he wouldn't accidentally run into them as he just had. Something must have gone wrong in their day for them to be out in the market at noon rather than the morning.

He slapped himself and glared into the mirror hanging

on the far wall. He had to focus. As terrible as it was to run into remnants of his detestable past, that didn't change his present situation and he couldn't let it affect his performance. He had a job to do.

Shaking his long blond hair, he checked his teeth to make sure they were flat and that the rest of his human illusion was intact. Satisfied, he stepped out again and headed toward the *Nomad's Hut*, where he knew he could find some information on the next meeting.

He pushed through the simple wooden door into the dimly lit inn and stopped. The mood inside was unusual. There was no festive music being played, hardly any raucous laughter or yelling across tables. It was so quiet that Zael could hear the clang of metal in the kitchen, the sizzling of oils, and the clattering of plates as patrons received their meals from the barmaid.

Looking around, the viatari captain noticed something interesting as well. It appeared the humans and viatari were avoiding each other. The viatari sat on the far end of the building, clustered together, and the humans sat on the other side. Hardly anyone was in the middle. Zael met the innkeeper's gaze. Valar shrugged and shook his head warningly. Despite his human appearance, the innkeeper recognized the viatari captain. The fact that he was in his human form could only mean trouble was brewing.

In fact, Valar wasn't the only one who recognized Zael for who he was. Several viatari glanced his way, muttering to each other as he sat down at one of the more crowded human tables. The humans noticed the attention Zael had received and looked at each other with raised eyebrows. A few who Zael had never met before leered at him suspiciously.

"How 'ya, Kurt?" one of the older men at the table asked.

"I'm alive," Zael replied. "And you?"

"Still kickin'," the old man chuckled. "Gentlemen, for those who ain't in the know, this here is Kurt. He's one of us."

"Is he, now?" said one of the strangers, a beefy man who looked like he hadn't missed a meal in his life and that he lifted heavy rocks for a living. "Never seen him around before."

"I've been busy," Zael shrugged, sounding bored as if this wasn't his first time being questioned. "Haven't been able to attend the meetings recently. And you are?"

The beefy man frowned, "Name's Ted. Rhymes with 'dead' if you catch my drift. I've only recently joined," he turned to the old man, "are you sure this one's alright? It just seems strange for him to pop in right as we're about to go over . . . well, you know."

The old man chuckled again; his voice raspy. "Yes, I'm sure. He's been with us before. I and many among us can vouch for him."

The beefy man leaned back in his chair, a frown still on his face as he continued to study Zael. "Fine, then."

The old man nodded, pleased, and brought his attention back to Zael, "What brings you to us today, Kurt?"

"After yesterday's march I couldn't stay away," Zael said, letting a small dose of excitement enter his voice. "I wanted to hear what happens next."

"There's no decision on that yet," one of the other men around the table said. "But that should be decided by Anders tonight."

"So we're meeting?"

"Yes, at dusk. Same building. Do you know the new phrase? It was changed when we lost Dave and Barty. Lyna says it's just an extra precaution so only the ones she knows they can trust attend."

"Well, they know they can trust me," Zael said, flashing an encouraging smile, though it killed him inside. "What's the new phrase?"

The man was about to tell him, when Ted interrupted again. "Just a moment, I'm sorry to be bringing this up again, but how do *we* know they can trust you? What exactly have you done?"

Zael rolled his eyes. He was growing tired of this Ted. He asked too many questions. And despite his looks, his mind seemed to be fairly sharp.

"I may not have killed any viatari myself like Barty managed to do, but I am still part of this campaign. I hate those leeches just as much as you and want them all dead. I want their blood to run through the streets of their own city."

"Don't mind him, Kurt," another man said with a chuckle. "You know how the new refugees are; all paranoid at first. He'll come around."

"Only if there's reason to," Ted growled.

Zael ignored him. "So, what's the new phrase?"

The man at the end of the table cleared his throat. "It's really quite simple. When you knock on the door, the guard will say, 'night falls on this white city,' and you reply with, 'and a blood moon rises.'"

Zael nodded, repeating the words so he wouldn't forget. "Catchy. Thanks. I'll be sure to attend. Do you know what will be discussed?"

The old man at the other end of the table grinned,

revealing deep gaps in his teeth. "What we've all been waiting for," there was a sudden weight of tension around the table as every last man and woman there hung onto the old man's words. "Salevari."

Zael stayed with the humans for a while longer before excusing himself, saying he had a few errands to run before the meeting. Ted glared at him the whole time, still suspicious—but he was the only one. The rest of the humans grasped his arm, telling him not to get into too much trouble before the meeting. Zael laughed as he said his farewells and then exited the inn.

As soon as he was outside, the smile melted from his face. So, this was it. Tonight was the night they would lay out their plan to bring down the viatari. This was what Salevari had been waiting for. But the meeting was not until dusk, and it was still early afternoon. There was plenty of time before he had to go to Anders's house.

Yawning, he turned right and began making his way back to the viatari part of the city. It was most likely going to be a late night. Since he had the spare time, he might as well use it to get some rest. As he walked, though, he could not help but think of the new refugees that had joined Anders and Lyna's campaign, especially Ted. He, more than any of them, didn't seem to buy into his Kurt persona. He would have to tread carefully around that one. He started to go through a number of backstories, reasons for joining this little movement, reasons why he hated the viatari, things he hadn't had to think too much about when he was fooling the others.

Again, he so lost himself in his own thoughts that he didn't see the elderly lady in front of him until he ran into her. The old lady grunted as she hit the cobblestone street.

Zael, suddenly pulled back to the present, looked down at her with a scowl. But as he watched her struggle to get back up and noted her frailty, his irritation faded away, replaced by a strange sense of pity. This old woman was human but he found her to be no threat at all. If anything, he felt a strange obligation to help her.

He bent down and grabbed her by the arms, lifting her gently back onto her feet.

"Oh!" she said, wiping the dust off her knees and sides with her gnarled, wrinkled hands. "Why thank you, young man. I'm sorry for running into you. I must pay better attention to where I'm going!"

"Not at all," Zael inclined his head respectfully. "The fault was mine. I hope you are unhurt?"

"I think so," the old lady said happily, bending down to retrieve the basket she had dropped. "I may look frail but, by the plains, I never seem to even get a scratch on me—oh! Better not jinx it, hmm?"

She cackled and Zael couldn't help but grin along with her good humor.

"Is there anything I can help you with, perhaps?" He asked, though he wasn't sure why he still felt compelled to do so. "I think it's the least I can do for knocking you over."

"Well, I'm just heading over to the market to buy some ingredients. Do you speak any Viatar?"

"A little. Enough to get by," Zael said before he could stop himself. He didn't know who this woman was, but even if she was non-threatening, he couldn't risk her discovering his true identity, either. And yet, he found himself unable to back out of his offer to help. He shrugged. It would be easy enough to fool her so long as he kept his interactions with the other viatari at a minimum. Besides, this would help kill some time before the humans had their meeting.

"Thank you so much, eh, what's your name?"

"Kurt."

"Well, thank you, Kurt. I appreciate the help, young man." She looped her arm around his, taking him by surprise, and together they made their way down the street toward Aleganthia's market. They passed a few viatari along the way who, recognizing Zael, shot him strange looks. He ignored them, but couldn't help but feel a slight burning trickle through his cheeks.

"What town are you from, Kurt?"

"Halshire," Zael said without hesitation. He had decided early on that this would be a good origin for his human self since it would allow Simon to back him up if it ever became necessary. Already, he had fooled the refugees from that very town into thinking that he had always been a part of their community. There would be no one who could refute his claim. "I came with the others when the viatari defended us from the darim—from the demons."

"Nice town," the old lady said. "I'm from Westir. Unfortunately, while the viatari got us out, they couldn't save the town. It now lies completely in ruins."

"I'm sorry to hear that."

"Ah, don't be," she patted his shoulder as if she were the one consoling him. "I've found a new home here and a new family."

This surprised the viatari captain. "You consider Aleganthia your home?"

"Of course! Why wouldn't I?"

"Well," Zael wondered how far he should go with this. He had just met this woman but already he felt at ease around her, which was dangerous. "With the viatari—"

The old lady scoffed, waving her hand dismissively. "The viatari? The viatari saved us! We humans were all set to be wiped out by those demons, but here we are with a second chance—and it's thanks to them. By allowing us into their city they've also allowed for us to make this place our new home, which I do gladly."

"So you don't distrust them at all?"

"On the contrary," she beamed. "I find them quite enjoyable. I think any one of us who desires to continue the old feuding and hatreds we used to have for each other is being foolish—like those two young men who recently wound up dead. I remember hearing one of them talk a big storm about how they were going to kill some viatari. No surprise to me that he wound up dead for causing trouble."

Zael could not help but be impressed. This was the first human he had encountered who didn't have even an ounce of suspicion or ill-will toward the viatari. If only more were like her, he thought, then the humans and viatari could really work together to defeat the Creature once and for all.

They walked in relative silence the rest of the way. The market was not too crowded this late in the afternoon, but it was enough to force Zael to guide the shuffling old woman in his company through so she wasn't knocked over. As they moved past the various stands and stalls, the elderly woman would point at the things she needed and Zael would communicate with the stall keepers to ask for a price. Many of the viatari running the stalls recognized Zael in his human form but, thankfully, kept their mouths shut. Still, they offered him an odd look every now and then when they saw who he was with and realized what he was doing with her.

They spent a few hours browsing. The old woman was meticulous when picking out her ingredients, grabbing individual vegetables again and again to feel their textures and mumbling to herself about salt and other spices. Nor was she afraid to haggle. Through Zael, she would negotiate prices down to as low as the stall keepers would allow before making any purchase. It was a long, arduous process. But finally, basket full, they left the market with Zael carrying the spoils of the day.

He glanced at the position of the sun and figured he had maybe an hour before the meeting started. He would arrive on time, though with the slow pace they were currently walking, he would make it with only minutes to spare.

He shifted his grip on the basket, looking through the goods that had been bought.

"This is quite a few ingredients for one person."

The old woman cackled. "For one person, yes, but it's just enough for dozens of little persons."

"Little persons?"

"I run an orphanage."

"I didn't know we had one."

"You didn't," the old lady said sadly. "I started one for the human children who lost their families in the demon attacks. Many are maimed and disabled. All of them are good kids. They're the new family I mentioned before, ever since I lost mine in Westir. They've been particularly good this week, so as a reward, I went to the market to buy the ingredients I needed to make my famous Gra'mama stew."

"Gra'mama?"

"It's what they call me," she shrugged, looking up at Zael, staring deep into his eyes. "You're welcome to come and join us. There will be enough for you to have a bowl as well."

Zael smiled. "I appreciate the offer, but, unfortunately, I have an errand to run myself after this. Another time."

"Another time."

They reached the intersection where they had first run into each other. Zael handed the heavy basket over to its owner.

"Well," the old lady said. "Thank you, young man, for your help today. I would not have been able to buy any of these ingredients at such a bargain without your help."

Zael chuckled. "It was my pleasure. I will have to take a page out of your haggling book the next time I go to the market myself."

The old lady laughed. "It takes a lifetime of practice."

She turned to leave but then paused and faced him again, her face serious as she stared into his eyes. The viatari captain couldn't help but think of his mother when she used to scold him for keeping secrets from her.

"You're a viatari, aren't you."

It was more a statement than a question. Zael felt a shiver run down his spine. How did she know? How had she figured it out? He replayed the events of the day in his head, trying to pinpoint where he might have given himself away. If she had been able to figure it out so easily, could there be others among the humans who also knew?

She smiled and raised a hand placatingly. "You don't have to answer. If you are in your human form, there must be a reason. I hope you succeed in whatever it is you and your Chancellor are trying to accomplish—for all our sakes. Just tell me one thing before we part ways."

Zael found his voice, though it sounded weak and unlike anything he had ever heard. "And what would that be?"

"What's your real name? I know it can't be Kurt, that's so un-viatari."

Zael was tempted to give her a fake name, but even though

she had discovered his identity, he still did not feel that she was a threat. If anything, he felt she had a certain charm about her that compelled those around her to speak the truth.

"Zael Windkeeper is my name."

The old lady nodded with satisfaction and curtsied. "It was nice meeting you, Zael."

And with that, she turned and hobbled away. Zael watched her go and was about to walk away himself when a sudden thought occurred to him.

"Wait!"

The old lady stopped and turned with a raised eyebrow.

"Will you tell me your name as well?"

There was a pause. Then the old lady cackled. Her voice sounded old, older than it had before.

"Oh, I'm just an old woman and very soon my name won't matter anymore. Farewell, Zael Windkeeper." She turned a corner and walked out of sight.

Zael was rooted to the spot, wondering what it was he had just experienced. He felt warm when he thought of the old lady, like a thin layer of peace had come over him that even the sorrows and rage of his past couldn't penetrate. He shook his head, snapping out of his daze. The sun was lower on the horizon now. The meeting would begin soon.

He rushed off toward Anders' house, his mind occupied with the day's events. If there was one thing he needed right now, it was focus, but it seemed to elude him with every step he took. At least there was one thought in his mind that was crystal clear. It was new, one that the old lady had planted and one that changed how he viewed his mission.

She had given him hope for the humans. They could be good. They could adapt, change, and make the right choices.

Perhaps not all of them, but some. And while he had no love for those who would be attending this meeting, perhaps not all of them deserved the fate that they were leading themselves to. Perhaps some could be persuaded to leave. Determined, he quickened his pace. He would not be late. He wanted to give them that chance.

CHAPTER THIRTY-SIX

Zael paused outside of Anders' house to catch his breath. He could hear the low buzz of conversation coming from inside. The meeting had already begun, but they couldn't have discussed too much.

He knocked.

The buzz inside died instantly and a lone voice spoke from behind the door, "Night falls on this white city."

"And a blood moon rises."

There was a series of clicks as the door was unbolted and locks were undone and then it swung open and Zael was admitted inside. It was as dim here as it had been at the inn, with only a few candles, most of them on the stage where Anders and Lyna stood, to light the place.

"Welcome Kurt," Anders said. "We're glad you could make it."

"Sorry I'm late."

"Not at all. Take a seat wherever you wish."

Zael made his way around the dozens of occupied tables toward an empty one in the far corner. He noticed many of those in attendance steal glances at him, most of them new faces he didn't recognize. Clearly, Ted had spread word of his suspicions to the others. Zael would have to tread lightly with so many eyes on him, especially if he intended to convince as many people out of this uprising as possible.

"As we were discussing," Anders continued, his voice reaching everyone easily. "We must take a moment to acknowledge the death of our friends, Dave and Barty. We know they were killed by a viatari, though the perpetrator did a fair job in making it look like they had done each other in. But we knew them. They were the best of friends. They would never have killed each other."

There was a moment of silence as everyone who had a drink lifted it in commemoration.

The silence was broken by Lyna, her soft, sweet voice like poison to Zael's ears. "While we honor their sacrifice, we must also understand what this means. Barty was killed because he killed a viatari guard. He begged us to let him do it and we provided him with the poison. The fact that he was targeted and killed soon after his accomplishment, and the fact that the viatari who killed him clearly knew what he had done, means that those leeches are on to us. We must accelerate our plans."

There was excited murmuring in the crowd, though some sounded uneasy.

"Now, dear," Anders cleared his throat, his own uncertainty unmistakable. "We've discussed this. We must not be hasty."

"But we must," she shot back. "We have enough poison to do what we need to do. The longer we wait, the greater the risk of being discovered and stopped by the viatari. We need to take out Salevari while we still have the initiative."

"Lyna—"

But Lyna was now addressing the crowd and didn't care to let her husband finish. "What say you? We may have started this uprising, nurtured it as we would a rare orchid, but without you this orchid will never bloom. Shall we kill their leader?"

There were several cheers, though Zael was pleased to note that not everyone joined in. Clearly, there were still some misgivings. He scanned the room to see if he could identify from their expression who might be uncommitted to the plot. He noticed Ted staring back at him from across the room. The beefy man looked ready to kill, though he couldn't tell if that was just because of the poor lighting.

"We've had a plan formulated for some time now and I think it's time you all heard it," Lyna continued.

"Lyna, I really don't think—"

"Hush now, my husband, the people have spoken. Let me explain to them what we must do."

The couple shared a look and an understanding seemed to pass between them. Anders took a step back, giving Lyna the full spotlight. And she took it with glee, a smile playing on her lips as she spoke of murder and destruction.

"Exactly three nights from now we will carry out our mission to assassinate Salevari. My husband and I have thought long and hard on the best way to accomplish this and what we've come up with is a three-part plan. The first, most important part will be the ones who go to take out the viatari Chancellor. There will be only a certain number of us who set out to do this. Late at night, when most of the city is asleep, we will make our way through the empty streets to the viatari's keep. There will undoubtedly be guards patrolling along the way. If we run into any, we kill them quickly so no alarm can be raised. Once we reach the keep, we will scale its walls, climbing up to one of the highest levels of the building."

Lyna began to pace around the stage as she continued, a fire in her eyes, passion in her voice. The crowd listened in utter silence, hanging off her every word.

"Once we make it inside, one of us will drop a torch from the window and that will signal a separate group to execute their part of the plan. We will kill every viatari in sight as we make our way to the bottom floor. Salevari will be the target, but there's no guarantee where she will be. She's been known to have an irregular sleep schedule so there's a chance she's in her room sleeping and there's a chance she's wandering the hallways. Either way, as long as we kill everyone we see we should manage to kill her in the process. Everyone's weapons will be imbued with our new poison, so killing the viatari shouldn't be difficult."

Lyna took a breath. Just like everyone else, Zael was enthralled by her—and with each word he heard, his disgust grew. He could taste bile on his tongue and struggled to keep his face passive. Luckily, no one, not even Ted, was paying him any attention.

"Now, for the second part of the plan," she continued. "Those who are left behind will gather together and hide in this house. One of you will need to be on the roof as a lookout so you can see the signal when we drop the torch. Once you see it, you need to head to Aleganthia's southern gate and open it—kill anyone you meet along the way as well as those manning the gates and surrounding ramparts. Anders and I have managed to secure the aid of the people of Ulad, a small village only a day's ride from here. They've pledged to send a force of well-armed, well-trained warriors to help us destroy the viatari—but only if we can get those gates open, so this part is vital."

This information shocked Zael. They had saved Ulad

from a darimun attack only a week ago. And this was their reward. . . .

"Once you've opened the gates," Lyna said, her eyes bright and manic as she shouted the last part of her plan in triumph, "They will rush in and together you will tear through this city, street by street, house by house, burning and killing everything as you go until there is not one viatari left alive!"

Cheers and applause broke out among large portions of the crowd and even those who had once seemed uncertain clapped in appreciation of the brilliant plan. And brilliant it was, Zael had to admit. If Salevari had not sent him to spy on these humans, they would have been taken completely unaware by such a bold move; and with the new poison the humans had created, he doubted they would have been able to recover from the shock in time to defend themselves properly.

This was priceless information. In a way, the survival of Aleganthia rested on his ability to make it out of this meeting alive and it was for this reason that he joined in with enthusiastic applause, even though it disgusted him. He had to get out of this meeting and soon, and he knew the perfect way to do it without raising suspicion; and at the same time, it would allow for those who might not want to partake in this brutal plot to walk out.

The cheering died down so Lyna could speak again.

"Three days from now we will be liberated from the leeches who have tormented us for centuries. We will no longer have to live in fear of them, having our boys and men and women waste away in endless battles against them. This will be our greatest moment as a race and, with luck and determination, we will prevail!"

Another round of cheers surged through the room. Zael

stood up, catching Lyna's attention.

"Yes, Kurt, is there something you wish to add?"

"Yes, if I may."

Lyna inclined her head.

"As brilliant as this plan is, make no mistake that it will be a dangerous night for us—and I do not believe I need to remind anyone what will happen to us should we fail," Zael saw a few heads nodding and several worried looks cast between tables, "that is why I move that we make participation in this completely voluntary. Due to the magnitude of the danger, I do not believe it would be right to force those who might be uneasy with the plan to join in."

"I second that," a young voice said from the middle. Zael saw Garrel rise from his seat, looking at him with thankful eyes before turning to Anders and Lyna. "Kurt is right, we should have the option to walk away."

Lyna leaned in close to Anders and they spoke with each other briefly before she addressed the crowd again.

"It is a fair point," she finally conceded. "Those who do not wish to participate are free to go. We will not keep you or force you to risk your lives—especially if you do not believe in the cause as we do."

There was a moment where nothing happened, and then the sound of scraping chairs filled the room as several people left all at once. Those that stayed glared angrily at them leaving. They jeered and called them cowards, but still people continued to leave until the room had been emptied to almost half its original attendance.

Garrel, too, got up to leave. Zael watched him walk to the door and nodded gratefully. He was one of the good ones and he was glad he had the mind to save himself from the gruesome fate Salevari would undoubtably plan up for those who remained. And now, he knew, it was time for him to go as well. He stood up and made his way for the door.

"You too, Kurt?" Lyna asked. There was a note of genuine hurt in her voice, as if she hadn't really believed so many would leave their cause. "I had thought better of you."

Zael turned to reply, but the room suddenly filled with a deep, throaty laughter.

Ted slapped his large belly, glaring at Zael once he finally managed to regain his composure. "Of course this one wants to leave," he said. "He's a *viatari*, after all."

There was stunned silence. Ted's accusation rang in Zael's ears and he felt his heart skip a beat, but he kept his face passive, knowing that even the slightest hint of fear or uncertainty would give him away.

"Here we go again," he rolled his eyes. "Ted has been suspicious of me ever since he met me in the *Nomad's Hut* earlier today. However, as many of you should know, I have been here since the beginning. The reason I'm leaving, though, is because I cannot, in good conscience, partake in a plot that would endanger the rest of our people in this city should it fail. If even a small group of viatari manages to escape, they will fetch help from their dwarven allies. You can be sure that there will be retaliation and I do not wish to be the reason for that."

"Say what you want, viatari," Ted growled, crossing his arms. "I know the truth of what you are."

"Don't be ridiculous," Zael's eyes narrowed. Of all the risks to his discovery, he would never have imagined this beefy, ingrate buffoon would be the one to pose the most danger.

"Ted, on what do you base your accusations?" Anders asked.

"Yes, I'd like to hear this too," Lyna said, uncertainty in her voice.

A triumphant smile stretched Ted's face. "I saw him today interacting with the viatari vendors in their market like it was nothing. The viatari all seemed to recognize him as well."

Zael could feel all eyes turn to him. "That's hardly evidence. If you did see me there, you would have also known that I was only there because I was helping an old woman buy ingredients, since she couldn't speak any Viatar. I think the question is, though, if me being in the market is such a scandal, why were you there watching me?"

Ted brushed aside the question. "So, you admit you speak the viatari's language."

Zael scoffed. "Yes, after all the time I've lived here I've managed to pick up enough Viatar to get by. I have to buy food from them every now and then, too, you know. I don't know anyone here who hasn't had to."

He looked around as if looking for support and thankfully many of those around him were nodding in agreement.

"Yes," Lyna said, though she still sounded wary. "Ted, that's hardly any reason to make such an accusation against Kurt. We've known him ever since we moved here, so unless you have some damning evidence. . . ."

Ted was visibly frustrated, his face reddened and his bushy eyebrows drew together as he stood up and pointed at Zael, his voice harsh and loud. "Of course he's a viatari! Even the old woman he says he was with realized he was one of them and called him out on it. And he *admitted* it to her! I heard it with my own ears."

"Kurt?"

"Yes, she made the claim I was a viatari, but she was also

old and senile and I'm fairly certain she was a little crazy. She had also taken a long time at the market and I was ready to be rid of her but she wouldn't leave until I answered her questions so I said whatever she wanted to hear to make her go. She was the reason I was late to this meeting."

"Do you know who this old woman is so we might bring her in to see for ourselves what she has to say?" Anders asked.

"If I knew I would tell you," Zael said. "But she wouldn't give me her name. She just told me that since she was old giving me her name wouldn't matter. Ted can attest to that as well if he was truly close enough to hear everything."

"Ted, did the old woman say that?"

Ted hesitated for a moment but eventually grunted in assent. "Yes, but she also asked him for his name—his true name—and he admitted to being a viatari by the name of Zael Windkeeper."

This brought about a series of nervous murmurs as most in the room recognized Zael's name.

"That is the name of the viatari closest to Salevari," Lyna breathed. "How is it that you know that name, Kurt?"

Zael's heart was pumping hard, but he still managed to control his features and his voice as he answered. "Believe it or not, I've actually run into him many times as I'm going about my day. He seems to be everywhere in this city. When the old lady asked me for my name, believing I was a viatari, I just told her the first name that popped into my head."

"Oh please," Ted guffawed, his toad-like features all the more prominent as his smile returned. "How is it you're the only one who's run into this Zael Windkeeper several times? Has anyone else seen him during their time living in this city?"

Most in the room shook their heads and looked at Zael with newly suspicious eyes. Lyna, too, was glowering at him, as if considering the best way to kill him. This was bad, Zael knew. He could not fight all of these people nor did he want to. Even if he managed to escape with his life, if his identity was exposed, then all his work spying on these people would be for nothing. The humans would just change their plan since the one given today would be compromised and the viatari would be caught off-guard in the end.

"This man is crazy."

Zael turned to see Garrel was still in the room, shaking his head in disgust at Ted. Garrel understood who he was, understood what it would mean to allow him to escape this house with his life—and yet, here he was defending the viatari captain. He could not help but feel an enormous sense of gratitude for the human.

"I saw Kurt when we marched toward the keep the other day. Why would he be there if he was a viatari? Of course he's human! Didn't you see him there?" Garrel asked those around him. They nodded hastily as everyone's attention turned to them. Zael knew for a fact that these men hadn't seen him at the march, but the sudden pressure from the question allowed themselves to think that they had.

"If you really are human, then," Ted marched over to where Zael stood and towered over him, his eyes filled with venom. He looked ready to throttle the viatari captain where he stood. "You should know the answer to this simple question: what is the name of the poison we use to nullify the viatari's strength?"

Zael relaxed and worked hard to conceal his sense of triumph. He remembered a conversation he had overheard between Simon and Salevari as the human wanderer had identified and explained a few of the humans' poisons. "Obviously, that would be Sun's Fury, which we apply mostly to arrows so we can weaken them from afar."

Ted stepped back in shock, his face paling. "You shouldn't know that. How do you know that?"

The room burst into laughter and their attention turned back to Lyna and Anders who shared a look of relief.

"I think it's clear to us all that Ted's accusations are baseless. Please take a seat, Ted."

"I'm telling you, he's viatari!" Ted yelled, his face still red. He raised his fist as if to punch Zael, but the men around them stood up and tackled him to the ground, restraining him until he was calm.

"There will be no fighting amongst ourselves," Lyna said calmly. "Kurt, you're free to go. I'm sorry about Ted and his accusations. I hope you know, though, that if you walk out that door you will miss out on all the glory and honor we will gain and the praise we will receive from our people when we successfully destroy the viatari."

Zael patted Garrel on the shoulder and turned him toward the door, leading him out as well as himself.

"That is, *if* you are successful," he called back as he pushed through the door. "And I wish you luck in that endeavor."

And with that the door slammed shut and the dim light of the meeting disappeared behind them. Garrel and Zael stared at each other for several minutes, then they both nodded and walked away back to their respective homes. There were no words between them, none were needed. Each one recognized what the other had done for them. And that was enough.

CHAPTER THIRTY-SEVEN

Heat was all that there was in the magma caverns. Trickles of sweat beaded Thuradin's forehead as he exited an outlying tunnel the burrowers had led him and his companions through. He looked behind him at Lyrie and Borim and saw that they were just as uncomfortable.

"It has ta be hotter than a furnace in here," Borim grumbled, his voice echoing. "How is it that we aren't suffocating?"

Thrak'mig and Hrack snickered but said nothing as their heads swiveled back and forth, as if on the lookout for something.

"Enchantments to armor," Brap explained, scratching the nape of his neck with the sharp end of a dagger. "Lurt use heart of fire, make metal strong so you no burn." A mischievous smile spread on the burrower's face. "No jump in magma, though. You still melt."

"It's amazing how yer people can control fire like that," Lyrie whistled softly as she reached for a pool of magma near them and held her hand there for several seconds without flinching. "How do ye do it?"

Brap grinned appreciatively and placed a finger to his lips. "No tell."

A loud crash ahead brought them all to a halt and the burrowers began grunting to each other with some urgency. Krunt said something in their own tongue and the others agreed. It seemed as if they were in some sort of danger so Thuradin kept his voice low as he asked, "What is it?"

Brap faced the dwarves with a finger to his lips, his chiseled face deadly serious. "Must be silent. Giants hear."

Thuradin remembered hearing about the fire giants and fire spiders from Gruk-Gruk's telling of the story of Gul, but he wasn't too sure what these creatures might look like if they truly existed. Their surroundings stretched on for miles in this immense cavern. If there were giants, surely they would be noticeable, but he could see no sign of them—until the floor erupted right in front of him.

A foot the size of a house smashed the ground only a few feet from where they all stood. Thuradin's mouth popped open as he craned his neck all the way back to see the enormity of the creature before them. It stood as tall as the trees surrounding Aleganthia. Had they been standing only a few steps to their right they would have been crushed.

The giant's skin was made of rock, but it did not appear completely solid. In fact, it looked more like plates of rock floating along a body of magma. Red seams sprawled along the giant's body like veins and its eyes burned crimson.

So far, it had not noticed them. The burrowers were as still as statues, and the dwarves followed suit. Brap had mentioned in Trek-ti how they would need to enchant their armor and weapons in case they had to fight a fire giant, and Gruk-Gruk had told them how Gul had fought and conquered these creatures. But seeing them in person, Thuradin could not believe such a feat could be accomplished. How could they, beings so small, take down something so massive?

The giant moved unbearably slowly, groaning softly with each step, which is why Thuradin hadn't noticed it before. Now, though, he recognized how many there were inside this cavern. A few he had mistaken as rock formations with streams of magma flowing down their height sat around a pool of molten rock, others leaned against the cavern wall, blending in. And some, like this one, patrolled around the middle, wandering without purpose.

They remained where they were for at least half an hour before the giant was finally far enough away for them to begin moving again. They crept along the edge of the cavern, hugging the wall until they stumbled upon another tunnel. Only once they had gone inside did Thuradin feel safe enough to talk again.

"Those fire giants are aptly named."

"Aye," Borim agreed, letting out the huge breath he had been holding. "I'm glad we weren't noticed because I cannae imagine how we would fight that thing."

"With weapons," Brap said, now picking his teeth with his dagger. "Giants big, but slow. Easy to move around. Weapons, armor, and shield made strong my Lurt, can cut into anything and block almost anything."

"My question is how did that giant nae see us?" Lyrie asked.

Thrak'mig pointed to his eyes and shook his head.

"They couldn't see us?"

Thrak'mig grunted in affirmation.

"Creatures here are blind," Brap explained. "Magma make bad eyes, but good ears. That why we be silent."

Almost an hour passed before they exited the tunnel into what looked like the same cavern but a different section.

Here waterfalls of magma slowly cascaded over cliffs of burning rock into larger and deeper pools of the orange, bubbling liquid. There were more giants here as well, a pair of them floating in the burning pool as if it were a lake.

Brap led them across the spacious cavern without so much as a second thought, only watching his footing so as not to kick any loose rocks. Luckily, no fire giants were near them this time and they made easy progress. They reached the edge of a cliff that overlooked more of the area. Krunt grunted and pointed to a small hole sitting along one of the walls further out. Brap clapped him on the shoulder and grinned.

"Almost there."

There was another grunt, soft and tense. Thrak'mig was gazing up and then over the cliff to the bottom. He grunted again and jerked his head to the side, encouraging Brap to look for himself. If a burrower could grow paler than they already were, Thuradin thought, Brap had just done it.

"Very careful down cliff," he whispered. Thuradin leaned over the edge to see what could have spooked their guides so much. He saw clusters of large oval rocks that glowed a slight reddish color.

"Eggs."

Brap pointed toward the ceiling, and, lifting his gaze, Thuradin felt his skin crawl as he saw the fire spiders Gruk-Gruk had mentioned in his tale of Gul. They were giant spiders, at least double his size. They were as red as a flame, with black markings on their abdomen that, like the giants, made it look like they wore plates of armor made from the surrounding rock. He couldn't make out many more details as they blended so well to their surroundings. There were at least twenty of them and they all hung suspended in the air within their intricate and expansive system of webs composed of orange spider silk.

Borim gasped and Lyrie whimpered as they too noticed the giant spiders. Thuradin felt a soft hand slip into his. He glanced at Lyrie whose face was ashen. He could tell it was taking everything in her to keep from trembling. He squeezed her hand in what he hoped was a comforting gesture.

"If we fight them, we fight them together," he said softly to her. "I've got yer back."

She nodded and then abruptly let go of his hand, her face suddenly a similar color to the magma around them.

"We go down," Brap whispered. "Careful. Move around eggs, no break them."

The dwarves climbed down the cliff edge easily enough with the burrowers leading the way. Thuradin had never seen anyone maneuver around rocks as well as the dwarves. He had always thought his race superior when it came to the basics of rocks and metal. But now, he had to admit, he was impressed.

They began carefully maneuvering their way around the eggs. The spiders' spawn would wobble every now and then but otherwise did nothing as they passed. Thuradin half-expected one of them to suddenly burst and for a million baby fire spiders to crawl out and swarm them, but thankfully that did not happen.

"Ooooo,"

Thuradin glanced behind him and saw Borim lift his foot and place it delicately in front of the other, almost as slowly as the fire giants did. His face was scrunched up, his eyes only slits as he moaned with each step, "Ooooo."

"Borim!" Thuradin hissed. "Get a hold of yerself."

"Ooooo,"

Finally, they made it past the last cluster of eggs, to which

Borim and Lyrie both sighed heavily in relief. Thuradin, too, was just as glad to be past their latest obstacle.

"We move on," Brap grunted. They began walking again at a steady pace toward the next tunnel.

"Just a moment," Borim said weakly. "I just—" he leaned against the rock wall next to him and became sick. And just as he finished emptying his stomach, the wall he had been leaning on shuddered.

Instantly alert, the burrowers spread out as a fire giant's leg came crashing down where they had been standing. What had been mistaken as part of the cavern wall had in fact been a sleeping giant, and Borim had just vomited all over it.

The fire giant roared with displeasure and lifted another foot to try and stomp on them again. The burrowers had been right, though. The giant was terribly slow and by the time its foot came crashing down, the burrowers and dwarves were well clear of the impact area, though they were still peppered by flying debris and embers.

"Time ta test these enchantments," Thuradin grimaced as he charged at the nearest leg. He swung both of his axes inward, expecting them to bounce off the giant's stone plates, but he was surprised to see the plates give way as easily as butter. Magma gushed from the giant's wound and Thuradin just managed to avoid it spilling onto him before going in for another attack.

The giant roared now in pain as the burrowers, as well as Lyrie and Borim, joined the attack. They hacked at the giant's leg like it was a tree, inflicting minor cuts each time. The fire giant tried to crush them again with its other leg but each time it tried the burrowers and dwarves managed to step out of the way and would then swarm that leg and cut into it as well.

Despite its thickness, they eventually managed to cut through the leg completely and the fire giant toppled over like an oak onto its side where it lay there, groaning and roaring its frustration. Thuradin wiped the sweat from his brow, readying his axes to move in for the kill, but Hrack stopped him. The burrower shook his head.

"Why?" Thuradin asked, confused. "We should finish it off."

"No time," Brap pointed behind them. "Other giants come by later and kill him. Right now, we run. Spiders come."

Thuradin whirled around as did Lyrie and Borim. The sounds and tremors from their battle with the fire giant had indeed caught the attention of the fire spiders which were now lowering themselves from their webs.

"We cannae fight them all," Lyrie said, her voice weak.

Borim was sick again.

"No," Brap agreed. "Too many. We run to tunnel. Can't follow us in."

Without another word they all turned and ran at full speed toward the small hole in the wall that was their next destination. The spiders gave chase. Their long, spindly legs granted them greater speed and, before long, the giant arachnids were right behind them.

The burrowers leapt into the tunnel, passing through its narrow entrance with ease. Lyrie and Borim struggled to do the same, wasting precious seconds.

A high-pitched shriek, almost as if in glee, came from behind. With little choice, Thuradin spun around, his axes flying, and embedded them into the nearest spider's head. The creature shuddered, its eight black eyes blinking rapidly as its legs curled up beneath it. Thuradin ripped out his axes and swung again, batting away the mandibles from another spider.

"Thuradin, get in here!" Lyrie shouted from within the tunnel.

Thuradin leapt back as one of the spiders tried to impale him with its legs and he shoved himself through the entrance and onto the other side. The spiders tried to follow but could only fit their legs through, which Thuradin promptly lopped off. Shrieking with rage, but realizing their prey had escaped, the spiders retreated to their webs and all was silent once again.

"That was reckless of ye," Lyrie scowled.

"There was nothing else ta do, I had ta buy time for ye two!"

Before more could be said, Brap intervened. "No more talk. We almost arrive."

They walked in darkness, feeling for the tunnel walls to guide them through. Though he usually could sense the passage of time within the mountains, being so deep within them now, Thuradin couldn't tell how long they spent walking like that. He knew his legs were growing tired. The air around them was getting hotter and more stifling. And there was the unmistakable sound of splashing liquid up ahead.

The cavern they walked into was not bright with light by any means, but it was lit up substantially by the constant glow of the ocean of magma before them. Thuradin had thought the previous cavern had been the largest he had ever seen, but no. This one was endless. He could not see the other side, couldn't tell how wide the walls stretched out for. All he could see was the molten rock.

"Welcome," Brap said, a toothy grin on his face as he

watched the dwarves' stare in awe, "to Magmasea."

Giant waterfalls of magma poured out from holes in the ceiling, hundreds of feet in the air, which was what had been producing the splashing sounds Thuradin had heard. Magmasea was still, save for the churning areas hit by the waterfalls, glowing with an orange aura. The heat radiating from the sheer number of molten substances should have been unbearable to any living being, but because of the enchanted armor they now wore, Thuradin only noticed a little more sweat running down his face.

"How do we get across that?" Borim asked incredulously

Brap said something in his own tongue to his burrower companions and they ran off to one side of the rocky shore toward a pile of stone slabs.

"We paddle across on boats."

"Excuse me?"

"On these," Brap pointed at the slabs of stone canoes that his companions were dragging toward the shore.

"Ye must be joking."

Brap shrugged. "No. Boats safe. Made of enchanted rock so they no get hot or melt. Only way across."

The dwarves looked at each other, unsure of how they should proceed. Hrack, Krunt, and Thrak'mig came up behind them and began pushing them toward the stone canoes with grunts of encouragement. Realizing there was no other way across Magmasea and knowing they had to reach the acolyte no matter what, the dwarves finally relented and allowed themselves to be led to the boats.

Borim and Thuradin entered one canoe, having paddled one before with Serania. Lyrie sat in the front of the canoe next to them, with Brap in the back. The third was taken by Hrack and Krunt. Thrak'mig sat alone in a smaller vessel.

They grabbed their paddles, which were made of stone as well, and pushed out from shore. Thuradin felt his stomach lurch as the stone they sat in wobbled with the sea's current. Their armor might be enchanted, but as Brap had told them before, if they were to capsize and fall into the magma, they would perish. Terribly. With this in mind, and realizing he was sitting at the front of their canoe, he was extremely careful to not splash Borim with an overcompensated stroke.

He gripped his paddle with white knuckles as he dipped it into the red, hot liquid and pulled. Their canoe pushed forward smoothly, and they began their journey across the endless sea, each member of their party acutely aware of how many inches of enchanted rock separated them from certain death.

CHAPTER THIRTY-EIGHT

Nothing but the orange glow of magma surrounded them. The shore had long since disappeared and what made their situation even more unnerving was the fact that Thuradin had no idea how much time might pass before they saw anything resembling a shoreline again.

He stretched his arms for what felt like the hundredth time since they'd set out. They had been paddling for the better part of two hours with no sign that they might stop and rest soon. No one spoke; everyone was too focused on keeping the canoes from tipping over. At one point, Lyrie nearly caused her canoe to capsize when she had twisted around suddenly, as if to strike up a conversation. Her stone boat had rocked treacherously but Brap, being the skilled rower that he was, managed to compensate the shift in balance and regained control of the canoe.

"No speaking," he had said afterward rather harshly. "Sit still."

Lyrie hadn't tried to move since, not even to paddle. In fact, she was so still Thuradin had begun to think that she was a beautifully carved statue rather than the dwarf lass he knew.

Another few minutes passed with nothing but silence before Borim broke it.

"Bah! I cannae hold my tongue any longer. Thuradin, do ye really think that we're going ta find an acolyte in the middle of all this?" He waved his stone paddle around at their surroundings.

"I don't know," Thuradin said truthfully. "It seems ta me that something has ta be here. After all, this is probably the most impossible place we could find within these mountains. I'd categorize it as a wonder of the world just for that."

"Just for a big pool of magma?"

"Come now, this is no mere pool. This is an *ocean*. How many oceans have ye seen made of this stuff?"

"Hmph, few enough."

"More like none, ye stubborn, old—"

"If speak of black chest," Brap called out from their left. "It is there. I see it before."

"Are we close, then?" Borim asked, grimacing as a small fleck of magma splashed up from one of his strokes and singed the tips of his fingers.

"Hmm," the burrower thought for a moment. "Hard to say. We know we close when we see Ta'Ka."

"Ta'Ka?"

"Don't ye remember?" Lyrie's mouth barely moved but she projected her voice well enough to be heard as she kept still in her canoe. "In the tale of Gul, Gul had ta face off against this Ta'Ka before encountering the black chest. We've faced the fire giants and fire spiders from the tale, it's obvious that we'll have ta face that fire bird next."

"How do ye know it's real? It could just be a legend." Borim shrugged.

"So could the acolytes and darimun and the first gods, yet they're real enough," Thuradin countered.

"When we meet Ta'Ka," Brap continued. "We fight her and win—only way to see black chest."

"And how do we fight a bird presumably made of fire?"

Hrack grunted on Thuradin's right and lifted a heavy, metal contraption. A large, thick spear was loaded inside, its jagged head poking out. Harpoons, Thuradin realized. They would shoot down the bird with harpoons.

"We shoot it down?" he asked. "Just like that?"

"Ta'Ka not easy fight," Brap said solemnly. "Very dangerous. These help bring Ta'Ka down so we fight her."

Thuradin and the dwarves took this in silence as they continued paddling forward. He had no idea what he should expect from the upcoming battle. It certainly did not sound like an easy fight, but he shook out any doubts before they could form. They would serve only as distractions.

Krunt was the first to notice something was wrong. The burrower stuck out his finger, grunting loudly, his eyes wide with anticipation. Thuradin's gaze followed his finger and he saw what had caused the burrower to stir.

Ahead of them, the magma started to change into a lighter shade of orange. And it was boiling. The liquefied earth around them frothed and small waves rocked their canoes as a massive form breached the surface.

Streams of magma poured off the creature and back into the sea and Thuradin could do nothing but sit back and gawk and wonder how they could ever possibly emerge victorious. If it were up to him, he would turn the canoes back around and come back with an army—then, at least, they'd have a chance. Instead, they floated ever closer to the legendary avian with a measly seven warriors.

Ta'Ka was a giant bird completely made of fire. Its wings, instead of consisting of feathers, were made up of many individual flames. The same could be said for the bird's body, its feet and talons, even each individual tail feather. And each flame glowed a different shade of orange or red so that it looked like the bird shimmered in midair. In fact, the only thing about this legendary monster that didn't look to be made of fire were its black eyes—like coals—and its long, sharp beak.

Ta'Ka flapped its fiery wings, shaking off the last bits of magma onto the approaching party and lifted itself into the air, where it stayed, hovering—watching them.

"What now?" Lyrie asked shakily.

The burrowers did not respond. Instead, they began mounting their harpoon launchers, securing them onto the head of each canoe. Ta'Ka screeched a warning, forcing Thuradin to cover his ears. The single call, like many swords scraping against rock at once, was loud enough to burst eardrums.

"It's nae attacking us," he noticed as the avian continued to hover.

"Not yet," Brap agreed. "But *she* will soon, closer we come."

There were three loud clicks as the burrowers finished setting up their weapons. Krunt, Thrak'mig, and Hrack looked at Brap for the signal to attack. They continued floating forward, drawing closer to Ta'Ka, who released another, shriller cry—this time a challenge.

The bird dove for them. Brap shouted in his own language and the burrowers launched their harpoons. The jagged, metal missiles soared through the air with a *fwoosh*, a thick chain of steel attached to the end. Ta'Ka never had a chance to react as all three harpoons embedded deep into her body.

The fire bird screeched furiously and flapped her large wings, sending waves of heat at the dwarves and burrowers as she tried to escape them. The canoes rocked violently as the bird struggled but somehow they all managed to keep from capsizing. The burrowers pulled on a small lever at the side of their harpoon launchers and the chain linking to each shaft began to pull back in. Ta'Ka flapped her wings harder, but the pull from the three harpoons, each at a different angle, was too great and the bird was slowly forced to descend.

As Ta'Ka was pulled in closer, Brap and the others grabbed long spears, which Thuradin realized—looking down—had been stowed at their feet. He went ahead and grabbed his own metal shaft and lifted the heavy weapon, admiring for a moment its elegantly-cut crystal tip. No doubt these weapons were specially made to fight this creature.

Thuradin rose carefully to his feet and settled into a fighting stance, being sure to maintain his balance so as not to tip the boat over. He glanced over his shoulder and saw Borim's face scrunched with concentration as he worked to keep their vessel steady.

Brap stood at the back of his canoe with remarkable grace, the spear in his hands leveled. Lyrie was crouched low, sword in hand. As Ta'Ka came closer, Thuradin felt the temperature rise tremendously, though the burrowers seemed unbothered by it.

Once the avian was nearly on top of them, Brap lunged. Ta'Ka had been too busy trying to dig out the harpoons impaling her body to take notice of the four stone canoes beneath her. That changed as Brap's crystal-tipped spear entered her body.

Streams of hot magma flowed from the wound as the

legendary creature screeched in pain. The magma would have drenched Thuradin had Borim not moved with lightning speed and covered him just in time with his shield, deflecting the stream as the force of it pushed them farther away from the bird.

"Thanks," Thuradin gasped. Borim nodded, his face taut with focus as the canoe rocked underneath.

Thrak'mig struck next from the side. The burrower laughed in triumph as his spear penetrated, but too soon. Ta'Ka turned suddenly, ripping the spear out of his hands, and swiped at him with molten talons.

The talons passed straight through the burrower, cutting him into several pieces. Laughter was still in his eyes as his head rolled into the sea below. The rest of him fell back into the canoe.

Hrack and Krunt both roared angrily and tried to lunge with their own spears, but the avian avoided this by diving into the sea, creating large waves—one of which capsized the canoe the two burrowers were on.

Thuradin watched with growing despair as Hrack fell into the orange sea below. His gurgling cries echoed in the giant cavern as his body was enveloped by the magma, but they soon died out as he sunk below the surface. Krunt managed to jump before the canoe tipped over completely and landed in Brap's vessel, which was still nearby.

Lyrie tended to him as Brap moved in for another attack. Thuradin, too, not really knowing what else to do, tried to inch closer to the bird's side so he could strike. Ta'Ka floated on the molten surface ahead, eyeing them angrily. Knowing no other possible weak points, Thuradin had his sights on the bird's depthless eyes, hoping that, if he lunged with enough force, he could drive the spear all the way through the avian's brain.

But before another attack could be made, an unfamiliar voice echoed through the cavern.

"Unhand my guardian, trespassers. I shall deal with you myself."

Thuradin didn't know what to make of this. Brap, however, complied immediately, lowering his spear and severing the line connecting his canoe with Ta'Ka. The bird, too, seemed to understand what had been said. She shook her head wearily and took flight once more, soaring away a distance before plunging back into the sea.

Now that there was no immediate threat, Thuradin sighed heavily and sank back onto his bench, dropping the spear back where he had found it. He glanced at Lyrie, who was visibly shaken even as she took care of Krunt's toes, which had been singed by the magma.

"That was something," Borim said, his voice hollow.

"Aye," Thuradin said. "Give me a horde of darimun any day."

After resting briefly, the two remaining canoes continued their journey through Magmasea. This time, however, only minutes passed before they saw the beginnings of an island take shape before them.

This island was unlike anything Thuradin had ever known. It was made entirely of black stone. Obsidian was his initial thought, but it seemed to be glassier—and when they landed and set foot upon this lonely island, he realized the material was harder even than crystal. He couldn't identify the material no matter how hard he racked his brain. He would have liked nothing more than to take a few samples to study its properties, but he restrained himself.

They had little time for sightseeing, however. Immediately,

a flurry of transparent, vibrantly yellow tendrils surrounded them, their source a long, rectangular chest lying in the island's center. Thuradin, despite the apparent danger they were in, felt his heart swell with a sense of accomplishment as he realized they had found the acolyte within the Silent Mountains.

This acolyte's artifact was made of obsidian. It was black, but unlike The Turned One, the black color was simple and sleek and gave off no aura of evil. There was gold plating along the corners and a line of jagged crystal ran all the way around the lid's edge. Three large rubies were embedded in a triangle on each of the artifact's sides

The voice coming from the artifact was deep and fierce, "Never before has a dwarf come so deep in the mountains to seek me out. Tell me why I should not simply end your existence."

"Yer brother sent us."

The yellow tendrils hovered in place for a moment and then gradually receded until they were nearly back in the artifact.

"My brother?"

"Aye, The First One. He sent me ta tell ye that ye are needed ta help quell yer other siblings."

"I take it the Creature and my daring sister, The Turned One, have awoken, then?"

"Aye."

"This is disturbing news," the acolyte said, his voice no longer fierce, but calm and thoughtful. "I had felt their presence, of course, but I had hoped I was mistaken. If my brother needs me, I will of course go to him and help put a stop to our monstrous siblings. Allow me to see where he is. . . ."

One of the yellow tendrils floated lazily to Thuradin's forehead where it made contact. Instantly, an image of The First One in the Watcher's Quarter in Aleganthia came to mind, and, just as quickly, it disappeared as the tendril retreated.

"Ah, the children of Arokun, I will travel to him immediately. Together we will be a force to contend with. Has he sent others to seek out our other siblings as well?"

"Aye."

"Good," the acolyte hummed. "I assume you dwarves will be aiding in the fight against our wayward siblings. This is good. I remember how much turmoil the world was in when the Creature and The Turned One nearly conquered it last time. It is about time the dwarves did their part to protect our natural way of life."

"Thuradin," Lyrie whispered as the acolyte went on about his years of sleep. "What is this . . . thing?"

The acolyte chuckled, his voice like gravel. "You need not whisper. I can hear you just as well."

"Forgive her," Thuradin said hurriedly, fearing Lyrie's words might have provided some insult. "She hasn't seen one of yer kind before."

"I understand," the acolyte said. "You need not fear me, dwarf. My name is Faenerus. I was created and placed here by Nythirim himself to watch over his other creations—primarily, the burrowers and dwarves."

"Ye were made ta watch over us?" Borim asked incredulously. "The dwarves have never even heard of yer existence."

"Yes, well," the acolyte seemed to shrug with his tendrils. "I suppose that has much to do with your kind being too busy killing off the burrowers. I must say, you kept me quite occupied doing what I could to keep them from extinction as your kings took army after army against them."

Thuradin felt a stab of shame, and worse, he couldn't deny the accusation. Still, he felt obligated to defend his people.

"We have changed since then. Much has been sacrificed ta separate our two races ta ensure peace between us."

"But have your people really changed?"

Thuradin didn't know what to say to this, and apparently neither did his companions. The burrowers, so far, had done nothing but gaze reverently at the artifact in front of them, but now they looked at their dwarven companions and snickered.

"I know all that goes on within these mountains. Even now, your kind are preparing to war with each other because you cannot agree on whether you should be getting ready to kill more burrowers. Tell me, if you hadn't collapsed the tunnel between your two races, would the dwarves still be fighting the burrowers?"

Thuradin didn't have to think too much on that question. He knew the acolyte was right, though he was loathe to admit it. He hung his head as he said, "Yes."

There was silence for a moment, then the acolyte spoke again, now in a more determined tone.

"Do not let your shame consume you. You cannot change the past, but you can affect the future. I go now to join my brother in this coming war against my other siblings. We will need all races of Azar to do their part if we wish for a decisive victory."

Thuradin looked up, wondering where the acolyte was going with this.

"This includes the humans, the viatari, the dwarves, the vashi, *and* the burrowers. While I am charged to watch over your two races, I cannot force either one of you to bend to my will. And so, it is up to you."

"What are ye saying?" Borim asked. "That we need ta convince the burrowers ta fight with us against the Creature and The Turned One?"

"Not just that. You must also convince the dwarves that the burrowers are not the enemy, a task you may find more challenging than it was to find me."

Faenerus started to shimmer, and Thuradin knew that he was preparing to teleport to The First One's location. They had perhaps only minutes before he was gone.

"What ye ask is impossible," Thuradin protested. "We cannae simply heal the divide between our two races in just a few days. War is already upon us!"

The acolyte considered the dwarf for a few moments. "If it is truly impossible, as you say, then there is no hope for victory against The Turned One and the Creature. We have already lost."

Thuradin felt his feet leave the ground and looking around he saw everyone else was floating as well and had begun to glow. He remembered when The First One had done this to him and Serania in the Crystaline Forest. He knew what was coming.

"Where are you sending us?"

"Back to the city of Trek-ti. You can begin your next task by convincing the burrowers to join the fight. Then, it will be up to you to convince the dwarves."

The glowing around their bodies grew intense and Thuradin knew they had only seconds before they were transported through the white nether.

"Do not let your doubts control you," the acolyte cont- inued to say. "Luck be with you. I will see you again when you return to Aleganthia."

With that the acolyte vanished and the light around their bodies continued to grow brighter until they felt a strong tug and were pulled into the void.

CHAPTER THIRTY-NINE

They were deposited on a small cliff, the city of Trek-ti sprawling out before them. Tiny lights flickered in the distance from the numerous candles and torches lighting up the burrowers' homes. Thuradin had no idea how long they had spent searching for the acolyte named Faenerus, but, clearly, night had fallen.

Brap and Krunt began making their way down to the city, prompting the dwarves to follow. The silence between them all was heavy. With all the danger they had encountered, the loss of Thrak'mig and Hrack had been forcefully pushed to the back of everyone's mind as adrenaline had taken over, helping them to survive. Now, however, in the silence and emptiness and calm of the dark cavern they were in, their deaths came to the forefront.

Thuradin had not known the two burrowers well, but he admired their courage. They had faced Ta'Ka without fear—and he decided that this was the way he would remember them.

"I am sorry about yer friends," he said, and he realized he meant it. They were not just words to him. Finding Faenerus would have been impossible without their sacrifice.

Brap inclined his head in thanks but said nothing in

reply. They walked on, but it could not continue in somber silence. There was too much to discuss.

"So, what do we do now?" Lyrie asked.

"We do what the acolyte told us ta do."

Borim scoffed. "Ah, aye, a simple task. Do ye truly believe the burrowers would join forces with us? Helping Dunkell with favors is one thing, but an alliance? I don't know, Thuradin, the acolyte made many good points about our people—though I hate ta admit it."

Thuradin shrugged. "It isn't about convincing them ta join us—the dwarves—but us—the world. They don't have ta be our friends, but we all are a part of this world. If it is destroyed, we both lose."

"But we've already tried that argument," Borim pointed out. "Gruk-Gruk isn't convinced he'll be touched by the evil we fight; he'd rather fight it alone if it comes at him."

"Aye, but what if this time it wasn't us who was telling him he must fight, but someone he respects?"

"Faenerus," Lyrie's eyes lit up. "The burrowers basically see his word as coming from Nythirim himself."

Borim grunted. "He'd still be hearing it from us."

"Brap and Krunt could testify on our behalf in this matter and that should help Gruk-Gruk believe what we say."

The two burrowers in question did not seem to be listening to the conversation happening behind them—or, they didn't care. Borim raised an eyebrow.

"As helpful as our friends here have been so far, it doesn't seem ta me that they're too enthused ta continue aiding us."

Thuradin thought for a moment. He didn't believe Brap and Krunt would be unreasonable in this matter, having been present for Faenerus' instruction. He was sure, at this point, if he asked for their help in this, they would give it. Still, this was no time to leave things unsaid or questions unasked. Too much was at stake, and there was not enough time.

"Brap."

The burrowers kept walking. Thuradin pulled ahead a little closer and called out in a louder voice.

"Brap!"

The burrower sighed, but turned to face him.

"Know what you will ask."

"Then, what's yer answer?"

The burrower shrugged. "I no decide. Faenerus say we fight, we should fight. But, Gruk-Gruk make final choice."

Thuradin nodded his understanding and they continued walking, only now reaching the first few blocks of the city. He and Borim shared a glance. Brap's words seemed to strengthen both of their points so that neither one was more correct than the other. The burrowers respected and adored the acolyte hidden within Magmasea because they knew he was a powerful creation of the earth god, Nythirim. If he wanted something from them, they would strive to fulfill his wish. However, they were not blind slaves and still had free will, as Faenerus had pointed out. The ultimate decision on whether to obey would rest on the shoulders of their leader.

It seemed the fate of the world would be decided on how well they could convince an old, mad—at least, Thuradin thought so—burrower High Chieftain to join their cause. He only hoped the weight of an acolyte's word would be enough to ensure their success.

They were now only a few hundred yards from the entrance to the High Chieftain's hall. The streets were, for the most part, empty—save for a few guards on patrol. Brap turned, his face passive as he addressed his dwarven companions.

"This far as you go."

The dwarves gave each other the same confused look.

"Shouldn't we report our success ta our King and yer High Chieftain?" Lyrie asked.

Krunt grunted, as did Brap. "We make report. You wait. See Gruk-Gruk later."

Thuradin's eyes narrowed. "How much later? Tomorrow? Time is nae a luxury we have ta waste. Besides, we wish ta see our King."

"King safe," Brap said in an almost bored manner. "King go to house here in Trek-ti. He stay there. You too. Go. Eat. Sleep."

"Ye heard what Faenerus told us. I'm telling ye we do nae have time—" Thuradin felt a hand on his shoulder. Turning, he saw Borim shake his head.

"Eat," Brap said again, turning away and making his way with Krunt into Gruk-Gruk's hall as he called back to the dwarves. "Sleep! We talk later."

Thuradin watched the two burrowers hobble away. He was fuming. He would have liked nothing more than to rush up to them and force them by the blade of his axes to take him to Gruk-Gruk. Now that they had obtained the aid of the acolyte within the Silent Mountains, there was a new objective in his mind that took complete precedence. To stop the Dwarven people from falling into civil war.

He hadn't heard any news on the matter since he had left to come here with Dunkell; and, he had to admit, he was a little worried. He was confident in Felix's abilities to play the diplomat, but he didn't think that would be enough to stop the coming conflict—it would, at best, only delay it. Felix sometimes thought too highly of the dwarves for his own good.

No, if the dwarves were to be restrained, they would have to stop themselves by their own efforts. Or they would need a miracle. Either way, it couldn't be done from these burrower caverns.

"Bah!"

Thuradin turned away and stormed off, followed closely by Lyrie and Borim. Neither said anything at first, but after a few minutes of walking around without clear purpose, Lyrie spoke up.

"Maybe it's nae as bad as ye think. Maybe they'll reach out ta us by tomorrow and we'll be on our way home."

Thuradin scoffed but looked at Lyrie with some concern. He thought he detected something off about her statement; as if she hoped it wouldn't happen.

"Tomorrow? Ye give them too much credit."

"Ye see, those kinds of statements and sentiments are what we as a people are going ta have ta change if we want ta work together with them."

Thuradin grimaced. "Ye're right. I apologize for my ill-chosen words. But that still doesn't change the fact that time is nae something we can waste. We cannae afford ta risk being here for weeks."

"And if we have ta wait that long anyway?" Borim asked.

Thuradin didn't want to think about that, but he had a feeling that was how events were going to play out.

"If it happens then we'd better pray ta Nythirim every day that our kin don't go crazy with all the time they're going ta have ta hate each other. I would hope, though, that Dunkell has something up his sleeve ta keep us from wasting away here."

"I don't know," Lyrie said, sighing softly as they neared the house where Dunkell stayed. It was a simple abode made with a combination of rocks and mud. Nothing fancy. One would never guess that a king was inside.

"Worrying about it isn't going ta change the fact that we cannae do anything ta help right now. Besides . . . maybe staying away from home for a couple of weeks is a blessing in disguise."

Thuradin's eyebrows raised to their fullest extent, Borim stopped with a similarly surprised expression.

"Why would ye think that?"

Lyrie looked shocked as if she just realized what she had said. She opened her mouth to explain but nothing came out. It looked like she wanted to say more. But at the last second, she cast her gaze down and her mouth clamped shut with a grimace. She swayed where she was for a moment, lost in whatever memories or thoughts that had suddenly entered her mind. Thuradin didn't think they were pleasant ones.

Finally, she shook her head, coming out of her stupor. She mumbled a "good night" and before either Thuradin or Borim could question her further, she opened the door into their temporary home and walked in.

Thuradin thought he saw the glistening birth of tears in her eyes before the door closed and blocked her from view. And for the next few minutes, as Borim and he remained outside to discuss future plans, he felt a sharp pang of concern strike his heart.

As worried as he was for her, Lyrie's outburst fell to the back of Thuradin's mind as days turned into weeks, just as he had feared. With each passing hour, he grew more furious at the burrower High Chieftain for wasting their time. And worse, there was little to do in this city.

They could explore it, yes, so long as they were under guard. But after the first few days of doing this, they had exhausted everything the city of Trek-ti had to offer, from their mud-wrestling rings to their meager markets. They had seen all sorts of burrowers and all of them looked on the brink of starvation.

Indeed, there was little food in the city. That, along with the stuffy atmosphere within the cavern from the lack of a ventilation system brought a lot of suffering to the burrowers and so the sense of vibrancy that often came from city life was not there. Thuradin couldn't help but feel responsible for the decrepit state of life here, since he had been the one to collapse the tunnel, which in turn had brought about the food shortages and lack of air supply. He hated being reminded of the unintended consequences of what he'd wrought, and so for the past week and a half he had stayed indoors. Waiting. Thinking

Dunkell had urged patience. He was confident in Felix, not only to delay the coming civil war long enough for them to return, but also in his people, that they were good enough to not let themselves fall into a destruction that Thuradin was sure had already started.

As night began to fall on another day, Dunkell burst into the small house they were in, a triumphant grin on his face.

"He wants ta see us."

Thuradin jumped up, the axe he had been sharpening falling to the floor with a heavy clank.

"Finally. What are we waiting for? Let's go!"

The dwarves rushed out and hurried to Gruk-Gruk's hall. Thuradin was eager to leave this place. He thought better of the burrowers than he had before—at least, he tried to—but he missed being around dwarves. Besides, seeing the burrowers so close without being forced to fight them still disconcerted him.

Before too long, they were once again in the spacious hall with a red-moss mat dominating the floor. The orbs that surrounded the burrower High Chieftain glowed brighter than before and seemed to radiate power.

As for Gruk-Gruk, he stood facing them, his scepter in hand as if he were going to use it as a weapon. Thuradin tried to read his face but, it being so weathered and eternally grumpy, he couldn't take too much from it. Looking around, he saw Brap and Krunt standing to the side with several of the High Chieftain's aides, their faces blank like statues.

"King Dunkell," Gruk-Gruk said in a raspy voice as he bowed his head slightly. "I welcome you back to my hall."

Dunkell returned the bow. "High Chieftain, I am happy ta return so we may speak on matters of great import."

"Yes," the burrower High Chieftain's gaze fell on Thuradin for several moments before reverting to the King. "I have heard the report given to me by those I sent with your dwarves to see the acolyte. I was sorry to hear about the loss of two of my servants."

"As was I," Dunkell said somberly. "Though I understand they died bravely in battle against a fierce monster."

"Yes, Ta'Ka is very fierce . . . My son, Brap, has also told me what was said when they encountered the acolyte. I assume you have been told the same?"

"I have."

Gruk-Gruk grunted and sat down within the square of crystal orbs. "I cannot say I do not adhere to the words of

Faenerus without an enormous amount of thought. His words weigh on me more than many know. However, the final decision, as I'm sure you've already been told, on whether to obey lies with me."

"I understand," Dunkell said. Thuradin glanced at him and noticed a determined fire in his eyes he had not seen before when he had simply been a prince. Perhaps he had the means to bring the burrowers to their side on his own. But looking at the High Chieftain again, he couldn't be sure that anything might change his mind.

"Ye have heard what your acolyte has ta say, now hear me. As King of the Dwarven Kingdom, I ask ye ta aid nae just the dwarves, but the viatari, humans, and the rest of the world with the burden of stamping out this evil we face today. Only together can we defeat the Creature and The Turned One. I vow ta ye as King, that yer people will nae encounter hostility from mine any longer. After we're done here, I intend ta do what I must ta quell the current rebellion occurring in my kingdom and eradicate the last vestiges of prejudice and hatred that my people have held for too long. When we're on the battlefield together, my people and yours will see each other as brothers in arms. That is my vision."

Gruk-Gruk closed his eyes. He chuckled softly. "It is a good vision, though I am unsure it can ever become anything more. You must know my answer already."

"But—"

Thuradin couldn't take it anymore. The High Chieftain's complete disregard for his King's earnest request was the last straw. He would not leave without making the old burrower see reason.

"Forgive my intrusion," he began, catching everyone's

attention. Dunkell shot him a look that all but said to be quiet, but he ignored it. Gruk-Gruk opened his eyes and glared at him with severe distaste. "I know ye must hate me, and ye have reason ta."

"It is rude to interrupt—"

"I apologize for all the suffering I caused yer people by collapsing the tunnel connecting ye ta the outside world. I'm sorry for the deaths ye had ta suffer at the hands of my kin. But that is in the past and cannae be changed. I know that, as do ye. What we are speaking of right now is the future."

"Thuradin, I really think—"

"Yer people cannae live like this for the rest of time. They will eventually run out of oxygen, or food, or simply the will ta keep living. Ye need access ta the outside world, and in the same breath, ye need ta make friends with my kind and those who live outside the mountains. Ta start, the best way ta prove ta my kin that the burrowers are actually good and civilized is by showing up ta fight off those burrowers who've been corrupted by The Turned One. The dwarves will recognize the difference between ye two and will come ta their senses. They would see ye as comrades.

"If ye fight with us, this world has a chance at being saved. If we win this war, everyone will know it was because the burrowers chose ta fight with us. Yer kind will gain the respect and friendship of nae just my race but every race in this world. Yer people will have free access ta the outside world again. Yer people can live, nae only survive, but only if ye choose ta fight with us. Because if ye don't, nothing will change. If we lose, ye will have no one ta help ye when the corrupted acolytes come for yer home—and if they don't, ye will slowly die off on yer own anyway."

Thuradin took a deep breath. He had said much, ignoring

his companions attempts to stop him. Now that he had said his piece, though, he felt satisfied. Gruk-Gruk continued glaring at him, his one working eye cold and steely. However, the other burrowers—the High Chieftain's aides, the guards, even Brap and Krunt—looked at each other and at him with a new sense of hope and respect. There were low grunts of approval as they discussed what had just been said with each other.

"Silence." Gruk-Gruk growled. The command was low, so low Thuradin could barely hear it. But it was obeyed, and every burrower in the hall fell silent and stood as still as statues.

Dunkell stepped forward, putting his arm out for Thuradin to step back, which he did.

"I apologize for that outburst," the King said. "But what Thuradin says is true, and I hope ye will truly consider fighting with us. For now, though, we will leave ye and return ta our homes—give ye some time ta think it over. Ye know how ta reach me if ye've made a final decision."

With that, Dunkell turned and, forcing his fellow dwarves to do the same, moved to walk out of the hall. But Thuradin wasn't quite done yet.

"I think ye will make the right decision in the end," he said loudly so that his voice carried through the entire hall. "I just hope ye don't make it too late."

"Let's go," Dunkell commanded, pushing Thuradin to turn around and walk out.

The dwarves were silent as they walked out of the city and back toward the narrow passageway that would take them home. For a moment, Thuradin thought Dunkell and the others might be angry at him for what he had done, but he didn't believe there was anything to be angry about. What he had said was true. And perhaps the only way to make Gruk-Gruk join them was to tell him the truth. Still, he did recognize he had overstepped.

"I apologize, Dunkell, if I overstepped where I shouldn't have."

The dwarven King kept silent for a moment more, but eventually replied. "I accept yer apology. That was a meeting between leaders and ye had no right ta interject yer talking points inta it. However," he looked down at Thuradin with an approving grin, "that doesn't mean that what ye said wasn't true, and I'm glad ye said it."

They climbed the stone steps with little discussion on what they should do next. No one knew what could be coming. For all they knew they might walk out into the middle of a battle raging in Kul'Kriegar. Thuradin hoped that they exited the tunnel only to find that nothing had changed, that Felix had been able to keep the peace while they were gone.

When they first entered Kul'Kriegar, that's exactly what Thuradin thought had happened, but this hope was quickly extinguished. The city was eerily quiet. There was hardly a soul walking through the streets, except for one particularly shady one who was even now running toward them.

Morteth Shadowmeld was breathing hard as he skid to a stop in front of them. His dark leather armor looked worn and there were some areas where it was clear a quick repair had been made.

"Morteth," the King began, "what—"

The assassin shook his head. "No time," he huffed, "Edana Hartshield emptied the ci'y of all its warriors and marched down ta Fungar Hrathor."

"She's done *what?*"

"They left yesterday," Morteth continued. "I 'magine

she'll be arrivin' any minute now."

"What about Felix?" Thuradin asked.

"After ye left, he . . . convinced me ta stay 'ere and delay Edana's plans for war. I did me best, bu' she's a mad woman. I've ne'er seen such efficiency—there was only so much I could do."

"Ye did fine," Dunkell said firmly, gripping the assassin's shoulders. "But what about Felix, where has the viatari gone?"

"He and some viatari wen' down ta Tinas Gran ta try and talk some sense inta the Council 'gain. They wound up in Fungar Hrathor and he's been tryin' ta delay their own preparations for war. When Edana left with her army, the viatari who had stayed back 'ere went ahead of her ta join Felix."

Dunkell nodded, absorbing all this information in an instant and quickly coming to a decision. He looked at his fellow companions. "We ride."

They all nodded and rushed to the stables, quickly readying the rams they would need to take them to what Thuradin feared would be a full-fledged battle. Morteth was preparing his own ram with them.

"I'm joinin' ye," he said with some excitement when Thuradin noticed him. "I want ta see this through."

Once their mounts were ready, they burst out onto the streets and veered toward the tunnel to Fungar Hrathor. No words were shared as they rode, the sound of hoofbeats being the only one that echoed within the stone walls.

CHAPTER FORTY

They were rooted to the spot. Victria didn't think there was any external force keeping them from moving, more likely, everyone was frozen because they had no idea what might happen next. What if they were too late? What if the enemy had reached this acolyte first?

But nothing happened.

The green tendrils that slid out of the chest merely swayed back and forth soothingly, like a field of seaweed. The acolyte didn't even greet them or wonder what they were doing here, as Victria half-expected him to. Seeing that no action was being taken, she inched closer to inspect the artifact.

Different in shape than the artifacts she was accustomed to, at one point it might have been called beautiful. Its domed top appeared to have been made of white opal, and the base had mostly been golden. Now, though, after millennia of sitting in the ocean, the precious metals and stones that made up this artifact were almost completely encrusted by barnacles and other sedentary sea life. A few pearls lay embedded across the artifact's main body and, in some places, there were small species of coral and anemone growing from it.

She had to admit, she felt underwhelmed by the state of this acolyte. Could he really make a difference in this coming war?

Tera approached from the other side and stretched her hand out to touch the artifact. As soon as her skin made contact, the green tendrils recoiled, as did she. A moment later, they returned to their previous, peaceful state, as if nothing had happened.

The human scoffed. "I know this is the first acolyte I've ever met, but I must say, in terms of appearance, I'm not too impressed."

"Well, I'm *so* sorry I fail to live up to your mortal standards."

Tera froze and looked around as if expecting someone else to have suddenly joined them in this room. Victria took a few steps back out of respect and readied herself mentally for the task ahead: convincing an acolyte to go to war.

The jovial voice spoke again, his voice like a cascade of beads falling on a tile floor continuously. Or, Victria corrected herself, like waves.

"May I ask what the creations of Ocaeus and Arokun are doing here in my throne? And the identity of the one who has touched me? I seem to be unable to identify her creator."

"My name is Victria Bloodletter and these are my viatari companions. Avmoshir here has been our guide and led us to you. And this—" she motioned toward Tera. "—is Tera, a human."

"Human?" The acolyte's tendrils trembled. "I have never heard of humans and I cannot seem to place their creation. ...This troubles me."

"And why we have come," Victria continued, determined. It had become clear to her within the first few seconds of their interaction that this acolyte was a little odd and easily distracted. "Is because of your brother, The First One."

"Ahhh, my brother. Yes. Always busy. Always working. What is he up to now that he desires my help?"

Victria frowned. The First One had said his brother wouldn't need too much convincing since they would all have already sensed their sister's awakening as he had. Either he had overestimated his siblings or the acolyte of the Throne of the Deep was toying with her. She decided to play along for the time being. Acolytes were ancient beings, even more so than the viatari. There had to be a reason behind this.

"I'm sure you've already felt it yourself, but your sister and brother The Turned One and the Creature, have awakened and—"

"Ah, those two," the acolyte seemed to make *tsk* sounds as if addressing a naughty child. "Always inseparable, they were—still are, I suppose."

"Yes," Victria said slowly, taking a breath to keep her composure. This acolyte was certainly testing her patience with his incessant, pointless remarks. "And The First One is currently doing what he can to defeat them once and for all. He sent us to call you for aid."

The acolyte sighed. "My brother is *so* needy. He never seems to take a break, always working for this world. All the time! And every time he needs something, he comes to me for help. He interrupts my rest, my slumber, to help him be busy. Will there ever be an end to it?"

Victria didn't quite know how to respond to this, but she was beginning to worry this acolyte might actually reject her request—something she had not planned for.

Luckily, Serania stepped in. "It is not just your brother who asks for you, but we do as well. Without you, and the aid of the other non-corrupted acolytes, we will surely lose this coming conflict."

Laughter filled the room. "If there's one thing that I noticed, even in my slumber, it is that war is already here. Still—" the green tendrils edged closer to them and seemed to inspect the viatari as well as Avmoshir who only stood there, his mouth hanging open and his eyes bulging in wonder. "—it does interest me that my brother's pursuits have brought together two creations of the First Gods—"

"—the dwarves are also part of our cause." Victria interjected.

"Are they now? The creations of Nythirim, hmm? And I'm sure, knowing my brother, he will have sent for Faenerus and Veliris as well."

"He has," Serania confirmed. "We have envoys en route to their locations even as we speak."

"Hah. I would hardly call you envoys. Still, this situation interests me enough to give you a chance. I will offer my aid, but it does not come free. If you wish for me to join my brother—wherever he currently is—you must do a few things for me first."

"We'll do anything you ask."

Victria glanced at Serania, wishing she hadn't been so quick to agree. This acolyte was a tricky one and she didn't have the faintest idea what the tasks might be. What if they couldn't be accomplished?

The acolyte seemed to think the same thing and laughed. "Young one, do not be so quick to make promises if you don't know whether you can keep them. But, if you are willing to try, the tasks are as such—" the green tendrils drew back from them and formed together to create an image of a spiked plant. "—this is cuttleweed, a weed of little use for those who don't understand its properties as I do. It is found in abundance within a gorge to the west of here. I want you to gather fifty separate cuttleweed stalks and bring them to me. Be sure to cut the stem near the base of the root instead of pulling it out. If you try to pull, the weed will attack you with its many thorns."

Victria glanced at her companions, who wore the same incredulous expressions, which were only amplified by the next task the acolyte shared with them. The tendrils shifted again, creating another shape—this time showing a fish with a single, straight blue line down the middle.

"This is known as the bluegill fish. They are extremely fast and only travel in small schools, making them difficult to find. A gentle approach will be needed in order to not scare them off. Once you've captured one, I want you to extract three of their shiniest scales and bring them to me. Lastly," the tendrils writhed and then formed into a craggy rock poking out of the ocean as waves rolled all around it. Upon closer inspection, though, Victria saw that this was no rock.

"This is the peak of my Throne. It pokes just above the water as you can see, and as you may have noticed, it is also *covered* in barnacles and mussels. Pry them off and throw them back into the sea. Do all of this and I will lend you my aid."

There was silence for a minute as the viatari stared blankly at the acolyte. The acolyte, however, seemed to take this silence as acceptance. "Excellent! There is a tunnel behind me that serves as a direct exit from my Throne, you can use it to return here once you complete your tasks. It will be much easier than the route you took before."

"Are you serious?" Victria couldn't help but ask, thinking of all the time they would waste performing these tasks.

"Victria—" Serania began, but Victria would not back down. Not after all they had risked to get here.

"Is this a joke to you? The fate of the world is literally at stake because of *your* siblings. And you want to waste our time with these—these pointless chores?"

The acolyte's tendrils stretched out and thickened as they surrounded Victria. Tessa and Natiari looked ready to step in, their hands on their weapons, but a quick shake of the head from Serania held them back.

"It heartens me that you see these tasks as pointless," the acolyte's voice remained jovial, but that didn't mask the hint of malice now mixed in. "Because that is how I view what you are asking me to do. My time and labor are not free; They are more valuable to me than anything. If you want my aid, you will pay for it—and I have given you the cost. Now go," the tendrils withdrew and reverted to their regular size. "And be silent as you leave. I would not want the saran below us to wake and eat you before you finish your tasks."

Knowing there was nothing they could do or say to change the acolyte's mind, the viatari, Avmoshir, and Tera swam around him and entered the tunnel he had pointed out earlier. Within minutes, they had exited the Throne of the Deep. And Victria was still fuming.

"How dare he? I think I would rather have the Creature on our side than that imbecile."

"What do we do now?" Tera asked.

"Well," Serania gripped Victria's shoulder and squeezed it gently. "First thing we must do is keep our wits. We still need this acolyte's help; and as much as I don't like him either, it looks like the only way to do that is to complete these tasks."

"You're not ssserious."

They all turned to Avmoshir, who looked even more furious than Victria. "What he asksss isss for you to waste your time! Ssso a little magic voice comesss out of a box. It doesn't ssseem to me that he will be much use with your sssurface conflict."

"He has a point," Tessa muttered. "This acolyte looks useless compared to The First One. Is it really worth our time to try and gain his aid?"

"What else can we do?" Victria shot back. "Return to Aleganthia empty-handed? No. As much as I hate this and agree with Avmoshir, we must do what he asks. I trust The First One, and if he says we need his brother's help for this war, we will not return until we get it."

"Thisss isss a waste of time!" Avmoshir hissed, outraged. "You would rather pick plantsss and pry off barnaclesss from a rock than help me take back my city?"

"It's not what we want to do," Victria grumbled. "It's what we must do. Now the question is which one should we do first?"

"Maybe we should split up," Madira suggested.

All eyes turned to her.

"Well," she looked around like what she was thinking should be obvious. "If we have three tasks to do, we can do them faster by splitting into three groups and doing them at the same time."

"That could be dangerous," Serania said uncertainly.

"But it would be faster," Victria thought for a moment. She liked the idea but also understood Serania's desire for caution. "As for Koranam, we haven't seen any sign of him or his henchmen in days. These tasks should take no more than a couple of hours at most if we split them. We'll be fine. Just be sure to remain alert for anything suspicious."

"In case you're wrong?"

Victria ignored Serania's quip and assigned groups. Avmoshir knew about the bluegill fish and where to find them so he and Tera were assigned that task. Madira, Tessa, and Natiari were sent to the surface to remove barnacles. Serania was paired with Victria. After agreeing to regroup at their current location within the next two hours they all went their separate ways.

Together, Serania and Victria retrieved their mounts and urged them westward. They quickly found the gorge the acolyte had mentioned and dove into it, all the while keeping their eyes peeled for roaming sharks or patrolling vashi.

The acolyte had not been lying when he said the gorge had cuttleweed in abundance. As they dismounted, leaving their mantas hidden beneath a ridge that jutted out over them, Victria thought it looked like a green field of wheat.

Serania cracked her fingers, her eyes scanning the water above them. "Let's get this over with so we can get out of here. This is a perfect spot for an ambush."

They left the cover provided by the ridge and went out into the open. Serania pulled out a short knife and began cutting the cuttleweed from the base, tossing them into a bag that Victria held behind her.

As time passed, Victria's sense of danger left her. She had scanned the waters around them a dozen times now with no hint of anything lurking around them. She could tell, though, by Serania's tense movements, that the wanderer did not feel the same. "It's not like Koranam or his vashi would have any reason to suspect we would be out in the middle of a gorge harvesting cuttleweed, right? *I* would never have imagined us doing this either."

"Hmph, that's true I suppose."

Serania yelped and pulled back her hand, tiny ribbons of blood following her movement and mixing into the water. "Agh! Blasted plant. Its thorns are like claws."

"Don't pull them."

"Thank you for that timely reminder."

Thorns were hardly the only issue they ran into while gathering the cuttleweed. Sea fleas seemed to have made their homes within the beds of weeds and would swarm the two viatari as their home was harvested. Victria tried swatting them away but the pests were far too nimble and by the time they had gathered fifty individual stalks of the detested plant, the two were covered in unbearably itchy bites.

"I wonder what the acolyte could possibly have in mind as a use for these weeds," Victria said as they remounted their mantas, which flapped their fins happily as they sucked up the sea fleas into their mouths.

"These things would hardly be any good for a fire," Serania muttered, tying off the bag that held the cuttleweed to her mount's harness. "Ugh, I'm just glad that's over with. Let's go back and see if the others had a better time than we did."

They returned to the Throne, managing to find the tunnel leading directly to the acolyte's lair easily. They stayed there, keeping watch as their mounts circled each other playfully.

"There!"

Above them, three silhouettes emerged, their movements clearly those of a manta ray. Tessa, Natiari, and Madira were soon floating beside them, though they looked none too happy about it.

"I hate barnacles!" Natiari seethed furiously.

"What happened?" Victria asked rather alarmed. She had rarely seen her so riled up.

"The things were nearly impossible to remove," Madira explained. "We had to take our weapons out and scrape them off—"

"If *only* it had been that simple, Madira!" Now Tessa joined in, just as upset as Natiari. "We had to scrape them off but they wouldn't come off completely. There was always some little remnant of shell that would stay behind, not to mention the residue they leave behind. . . . I feel like we've been scraping for hours. I wish we had picked the stupid weeds instead."

Serania's eye flashed. "Let me tell you—"

"Wait! Look!" Victria pointed to their right, where Tera and Avmoshir had gone off. There was a single figure moving toward them, and it was definitely not traveling with the graceful movements of a manta.

"Do you think it's an enemy?" Tessa asked.

"It could be. Hard to tell from this distance."

"They're moving pretty slowly." Natiari noted.

Madira nodded. "It is about time for Tera and Avmoshir to come back. Maybe it's them?"

"But there's only one figure," Victria murmured with a growing sense of worry. "Do you think—"

Serania nodded. "It is. It's Tera. Alone."

Tera was swimming toward them as fast as humanly possible. She looked angry, but her features softened when she caught sight of the viatari, who had ridden out to meet her half way.

"Tera, what happened?" Victria asked, not seeing any wounds on her or any sign that she had been in a fight. "Did Koranam find you?"

"Hah!" Tera laughed. "I wish that was what had happened. No, this is worse—because if anything happens to that boy now it'll be on his own damn head!"

"What do you mean?"

"He left me! Stranded me. We had found one of the bluegill fish and he told me to approach it from behind, said I had a better chance of not spooking it since humans swim slower than vashi." She gritted her teeth and punched her right hand into her left. "Then, while I was approaching the fish he took my mount and sped off!"

Victria understood Tera's fury, she would feel the same had Avmoshir tried that with her, but all she felt now was fear for what might happen to the young vashi she had promised to protect. Did the fool not realize the danger he had put himself in?

"Did he say where he was going?"

"Did he need to?" Tera scoffed. "It's obvious he's going back to Maleres to continue his little plot to retake Zessarix."

"Should we go after him?" Madira asked.

"More importantly," Natiari interjected. "Did you manage to get the scales from the bluegill?"

Tera blinked for a moment, stunned, then shook her head. "No, I'm afraid I scared it off when I started yelling curses at Avmoshir *for stranding me in the middle of the ocean.*"

Natiari clicked her tongue in disappointment. "What a pity. I suppose this means we have no choice but to go after him now—since he's the only one who knows how to find those fish."

"We would have done so, anyway," Victria said, slightly peeved. "Come on, let's go. We ride until we find him. We will not rest until we do."

Tessa and Natiari groaned but followed along as they all sped off back to Maleres—Tera, sharing a manta with Serania.

Please, be safe, Victria hoped as the ocean floor passed by in a blur below her. All alone, Avmoshir would present the perfect target for Koranam and his cohorts to attack. The young vashi might be a talented warrior, but even he couldn't fight off all his enemies at once.

Please.

CHAPTER FORTY-ONE

"I think we need to split up again."

The words were out of Victria's mouth without much thought but as they left her lips she knew it was the right decision to make.

"Are you crazy?" Serania pushed her manta forward next to Victria's. "If Koranam's vashi can find Avmoshir, they can find us too—and we're not able to fight them as effectively as he is. We need numbers."

Victria knew she was right, but she also knew they still needed to take the risk.

"We also need to cover more ground," she countered. "Night will fall soon. What if we miss him entirely because he took a different path back?"

"I agree with Victria," Tessa chimed in. "Besides, the faster we find Avmoshir, the faster we can go back to the Throne of the Deep—the faster we get out of these waters."

Serania grimaced but even she had to concede the point. "And if we still don't find him?"

"Then we rendezvous at Maleres and hopefully find him there."

"Fine. How are we splitting up?"

Victria thought for a moment. They were all in a weakened

state here so none of them—except Tera—were at full strength when it came to fighting. She shook her head. There was little point in strategizing. They needed speed more than power, anyway.

"Natiari, you're with Madira. Keep going straight. Serania, you're with Tera. Go east for a few miles, then head to Maleres from there. Tessa and I will go west."

The three groups went their own way with few words said between them other than a quick "be careful."

Victria and Tessa sped off a fair distance westward before veering back north and resuming their journey to Maleres. Tessa kept her eyes on the ocean floor while Victria observed the waters above and around them, searching for any sign of the runaway vashi.

"There!—Oh, wait, never mind," Tessa shook her head. "Everything moves in this place because of the current. I don't know how one would even begin to track someone else. Do you really think we'll be able to find him?"

"We have to," Victria said resolutely, though in her heart she felt the same doubts as Tessa. The ocean was simply too big and there were no clear trails to follow. They didn't have a heightened sense of smell like the vashi that could detect specific scents from miles away. Even so, she would not give up on searching for Avmoshir until he was found.

"We have to. It's my fault he ran away."

"Victria, no it—"

"It is! If I had not been so cruel to him back in Maleres— there had to be another way to convince him to help us—but I just—"

"Stop it," Tessa said sternly, "You shouldn't blame yourself if he gets hurt as a consequence for the stupid action *he* took."

Victria felt like pins had been pushed into and through her heart at the thought. "But I promised his father I would protect him. And now . . . now he's gone. If he winds up dead because of this, I just don't know."

Tessa grunted disapprovingly but said nothing. The two had known each other for a long time, knew each other's moods and thoughts. Knew what was important to them.

"We'll find him. I'm sure we'll find him."

But night fell and they had yet to find any trace of Avmoshir. The ocean grew dark. Every now and then they would come across a stray cluster of bioluminescent jellyfish and they would be able to see the path ahead for a brief instant, but it was always just a glimpse.

"Come on," Victria said. "We need to descend and keep the ocean floor in sight."

"Victria, we're already almost touching the sand. We need to stop for the night and set up camp."

She shook her head. "No, if we stop and Avmoshir doesn't then we lose ground that we won't be able to make up. The only way to catch up to him is to keep riding."

"And if we keep riding but pass him because we can't see him in the dark, what then?"

Victria didn't have an answer to this, and Tessa knew it.

"We need to set up camp." She said again.

Victria didn't like it, but it didn't look like they had much choice. She had hoped to find Avmoshir before night fell. Now she could only hope that the distance between them would not continue to grow, that they would find him to-morrow.

"Fine. But you're taking first watch."

They patted their manta rays, bringing them to a stop, and dismounted.

"I don't know what good a watch will do, since I can barely see five feet in front of me."

"Better than no watch," Victria yawned. She laid down on the sandy floor without unpacking any supplies and, within minutes, fell asleep. But even in her dreams she could not escape the darkness and found herself running, tired, scared, looking for a source of light.

She gasped and opened her eyes. For a moment she thought she was still asleep, but then realized the ocean was just as dark as her dream.

"Nightmare?" Tessa asked from nearby.

"Just a dream," Victria murmured. "Is it my turn?"

"Not yet, you've only been asleep for about half an hour. Lie back down. I'll wake you when I get tired."

Victria grimaced. She wasn't sure she wanted to go back to sleep in case she had the same dream. But she had to be rested during their search for Avmoshir or she risked overlooking a sign of his presence, so she forced herself back down and closed her eyes. But now sleep wouldn't come. Instead, her thoughts wandered until they focused on Felix and what he might do in her position.

Would he continue into the night like she wanted? No, she decided. He never let emotions rule his thinking when it came to making decisions. That was one thing she had always admired about him.

She wondered, not for the first time, why thoughts of Felix so often barged into her head these days. She worried for him, which, she decided, was normal. They were long-time friends, after all. But she also wished he was here with her now, and it wasn't solely so that he could take the reins of leadership from her. Her heart quickened, and she felt a soreness within that she had not felt before.

Finally, she had to physically shake her head to clear her mind. As much as she might like for such thoughts to lull her to sleep, she could not afford to remain distracted, even now. As a final image of Felix slipped away a new idea bloomed in her mind.

She often tried to think like Felix when a situation became difficult and that often led to her discovering the solution to any given problem. What if she applied the same idea for finding Avmoshir?

By all appearances, Victria appeared to be asleep, but her mind was working overtime now. If she were a young vashi who had just lost his father and was driven by rage or grief and not necessarily by logic, where would she go? She remembered Avmoshir's initial desire to challenge Koranam in the Assembly Hall to enforce his right to rule and it was like a sudden shock ran through her spine. Could it be that Avmoshir wasn't heading for Maleres at all, but was returning to Zessarix to challenge Koranam by himself? Surely, he couldn't be that foolish.

But, as she began to think more like the young vashi, she knew with a growing sense of dread that he could indeed be that foolish.

"I think I know where he's gone!" Victria bolted upright, her eyes wide with panic.

"Did you take something before going to sleep to give you weird dreams?" Tessa smirked, clearly amused.

"I'm serious. He's not heading back to Maleres!"

Tessa hesitated. "You mean, Avmoshir?"

"Yes!"

"And how do you know this?"

"I *thought* like him."

"Uh-huh," Tessa yawned. "Go back to sleep, I'll be

waking you up in a little bit for your turn at the watch."

"But—"

"Victria, it's still pitch black around us and we can't see a thing. We'll continue this in the morning, when there's light. Go. Back. To. Sleep!"

Victria grumbled but laid back down and closed her eyes once more. She was sure she was right, and also sure she wouldn't be able to sleep now with all these thoughts going through her head. It would be a long night, but she was okay with it as long as she was right in the end.

Avmoshir was beyond angry.

He was angry at Koranam for usurping his family's power and killing his parents. He was angry at his aunt who had promised to help him but was taking too much time talking for his liking. And most especially, he was angry with the viatari for first forcing him to lead them to the Throne of the Deep like he was their tour guide and second for thinking, even for a moment, that he would be fine with doing any of those pathetic, menial, servant tasks the acolyte had ordered them to do.

He'd had enough. If no one in all the Sea of Scales would help him take down Koranam, he would do it himself. If the viatari wanted to stay behind and pick weeds and do some housecleaning for the acolyte, they could waste their own time. Why they would even want that thing's help he would never understand. He wasn't impressed by the acolyte and wondered how in the name of the ocean Ocaeus could ever create such a useless thing.

Avmoshir took a deep breath, trying to clear his mind. He had to focus, to prepare mentally for what was to come. If he was to take on Koranam alone, there was only one way. A ruler's duel, a challenge that could only be issued and carried out in the Assembly Hall. A ruler's duel was a unique right that only those with claims to the Supreme Overseership had. It was a brutal fight to the death with whatever weapons could be found and it only ended when the blood of one of the contestants filled the room.

For this to happen, though, Avmoshir would have to make his way back to Zessarix. It would be a long journey—even longer now that he had sent the two manta rays he'd had north toward Maleres as a false trail in case the viatari decided to follow him. His legs burned, but he had to make as much distance as he could before letting himself rest.

By the next day, he would be near the edge of the Trench of Fear. It would take another day to cross it without a mount. After that, since he still had to avoid the surrounding towns to keep a low profile, it could take up to a week before he would arrive to Zessarix to challenge Koranam. In a week, this nightmare he had been living in for the past several days would be over and the first action he would take as Supreme Overseer would be to banish the viatari from vashi waters indefinitely.

He had suffered enough at their hands. This nightmare began when they showed up and, while they may not have assassinated his father themselves, he had a feeling they had in some way been the reason Koranam had gone to such extreme measures.

The scales on his right shoulder prickled, as if something were crawling on them. As a vashi, he was able to feel the vibrations in the water to detect movement. Something had caused a disturbance just ahead of him and to his right. Looking up, he could see figures approaching from the distance. It was a small gam of sharks, led by three vashi, each with their weapons out.

Avmoshir hissed in frustration. "Not now!"

He drew his father's golden harpoon, its enchantments humming with power and coursing through his hands as he prepared for battle. He was outnumbered, but that didn't mean he wouldn't fight. He could not claim to be the son of Araxie if he simply allowed himself to be captured.

These were Koranam's agents, he was certain of it. He doubted they would try to kill him—wanting to capture him instead—which worked in his favor because he would certainly try to kill them.

The sharks came first. They rushed in with a burst of speed, their numerous, sharp teeth ready to tear into his flesh. He dodged The First One, spinning and sinking. As he did so he lunged upward with his harpoon, knowing that another shark would pass above him. His golden blade pierced straight through the shark's midsection, stopping it in its tracks. Blood burst from the twitching creature and filled the water, driving the other sharks into a frenzy.

With the sharks distracted by the blood, Avmoshir tried to lunge at another hunter but found his attack was blocked by the trident of one of the vashi. The other two descended upon his flanks. They all wore black outfits with black masks so he couldn't identify them, but he could see their eyes, eyes of a predator who had just caught their prey.

Avmoshir tried to escape by swimming up, but the vashi to his right had expected this and threw a net just as the young vashi made his move. Avmoshir's webbed feet were caught in the netting and he felt himself get entangled. He hissed and tried biting his way out, but the seaweed the net was made of was well-woven. It proved too resilient to break under a vashi's bite.

He glared at his three captors defiantly. "I challenge Koranam to a ruler's duel. Take me to Zessarix so we may end this."

His captors glanced at each other, then burst out laughing.

"There'll be no duelsss for you, boy," one of them said.

"Yesss," another nodded enthusiastically. "You're our prisoner now. Koranam will reward usss handsomely for your capture."

Avmoshir felt iron chains being tied around his feet and chest by the third vashi. He tried to struggle, but it was no use. The chains were connected to each other with a click and the young vashi was constricted to the point where he could barely move.

"Come, brothersss," one of his captors said, hissing triumphantly "Let usss return to Zessarix ssso we may claim our reward."

"Wait." One of the vashi eyed Avmoshir. Avmoshir, seeing this as a challenge, leered back, doing his best to portray a fierceness he did not feel. Deep down, he was terrified. He didn't know how he was going to escape this.

The black-clad vashi laughed. "Thisss one ssstill hasss sssome ssspirit in him. It will be a jellyfish on our legsss if we must remain vigilant for our journey back to the capital just to keep him from escaping."

"Ssso, you sssay we must break hisss ssspirit first?"

"Yesss."

Avmoshir didn't like where this was going. A sinking feeling formed in his stomach. "Koranam will not reward you if you kill me. I know for a fact that he wants me alive so he can end my life himself."

The captors laughed once again, their voices dry and harsh.

"Obviously," one of them replied. "Do you take usss for

foolsss?"

"We will not kill you," the one Avmoshir took to be the leader of the trio grinned. "But you will wish we had. We will take you to the Trench of Fear first, then we will travel to Zessarix."

And now Avmoshir was truly afraid. "You're not going to drop me in there. You wouldn't."

"We won't drop you, we'll be sssure to have your netting sssecure ssso we can reel you up and down like the humansss do with their bait. There'sss no reward if we lossse your body."

The vashi cackled and began swimming in the same direction Avmoshir had originally been heading—toward the Trench of Fear—only, Avmoshir no longer wished to go this way.

He felt himself trembling, but couldn't bring himself to stop. There were rumors of what lived—or rather, unlived, in the Trench. Spirits of all sorts were said to reside in the dark. Anyone unfortunate enough to be sent down there, wound up having their life essence sucked out of them. The spirits never sucked out too much to kill their prey, just enough to leave even the strongest vashi a broken, rambling husk. A continuous food source for them.

The young vashi looked back the way he had come. He wondered if he should hope for the viatari to come after him, but realized it would be pointless. He had purposefully led them off his trail. They would be in Maleres by tomorrow, too late to save him.

He had failed. He had failed his father, his people, everyone. He bowed his head, still thinking desperately for some way he could escape, some miracle he could pull off. But nothing came to him. As far as he was concerned, he was already dead.

CHAPTER FORTY-TWO

"Are you sure about this, Victria?" Tessa asked.

Victria finished sucking out the life-energies of the fish they had caught soon after setting out that morning. It was a paltry meal compared to what they had been given in the cities, but it was enough to give her a fresh boost of energy, which she sorely needed after a restless night.

"I'm sure. Don't you think it would be just like Avmoshir to try something like this? Besides, the others are still headed for Maleres. If I'm wrong, they will find him there."

Victria's eyes were glued to the ocean floor as their manta rays coasted toward the Trench of Fear. So far, there had been only a few traces of life—a small school of fish here, a pair of giant clams there. As they drew nearer to the Trench, though, life became even more sparse.

"Do you see that?" Tessa pointed ahead.

Just a short distance before them rose a small cloud of dust. Something was disturbing the ocean floor. It could be something as simple as a predator sniffing out their prey hiding in the sand; she had seen such a thing during their time here. But it could also be Avmoshir making a run for it, having sensed their presence—or even worse, he could be in the middle of a struggle, fighting for his life.

"Come on," Victria said, a new urgency entering her voice as the last thought stuck. "We need to hurry."

They pushed their mounts to new speeds and descended upon the scene within a matter of minutes. It was hard to tell what was happening within the cloud of dust. Tessa brought her manta around and had it swoop just over the area, flapping its fins hard so that the dust cleared for just a few seconds.

Victria felt both disappointment and relief. What had caused the dust cloud was a small battle between a pack of large crabs and a few strange fish she thought looked to be made of sand. Avmoshir was not here, but that also meant he wasn't in immediate danger—at least, not in this particular area.

"Hmph," Tessa grunted when she realized what they had stumbled upon. "Just some crabs."

Victria was already turning her mount away. "Let's keep moving. I think we'll reach the Trench soon."

She proved to be correct in her assumption. Shortly after they had resumed their search, the first signs of the Trench appeared in the distance. Victria felt shivers run down her body as some instinctual fear of falling into the black abyss returned to the forefront of her mind.

She scanned the ocean floor around them and then looked ahead toward the edge of the Trench. Her eyes narrowed as she noticed several figures swimming casually toward it. She couldn't tell if they were vashi or not; but if they were not, what could possibly desire to be so close to this terrible place? This warranted a closer look.

After pointing them out to Tessa, they veered toward their new targets, leaning back so their mounts rose to a higher depth to minimize their chances of being detected.

"Those are vashi," Tessa confirmed. They circled over the party in question, trying to make out more details. "And I think I see two, maybe three sharks as well."

"How many vashi?"

Tessa clicked her tongue as she considered. "I think four. It looks like two of them are carrying another, and the one being carried looks like they're struggling—you don't think. . . ?"

"I do. Let's dive on them. They'll know we're coming before we're close enough to strike, so keep your weapon drawn in case they really are enemies." She drew her own blade, taking a deep breath as she prepared herself mentally for a fight.

"Victria, there's only two of us," Tessa warned her. "There's no way we can take them all, especially with those sharks."

"We focus on the sharks first, then. We dive as steeply as we can for speed so we can determine quickly if Avmoshir is with them or not. If we see that he's not, we make a run for it. I'm sure our mantas can outswim those vashi and sharks."

"I wouldn't be too sure of that . . . but if you already have your mind set, I know better than anyone that there's no changing it," Tessa drew her dirk. "Let's do this."

They dove, keeping their bodies close to their mounts. Water surged past their faces, making it difficult for Victria to keep her eyes open. Even so, she saw the vashi below her stiffen and look up almost simultaneously. For a moment, they just stood there, confused, seeing the giant manta rays but not the riders pressed against their backs. Not all of them remained so oblivious, though. Now that they were close enough, Victria recognized Avmoshir trapped in a net and tied together with iron chains being carried by two of the vashi. Her heart leapt with relief that they had finally found him—and just in time, it would seem.

"Victria!" he cried out, startling his captors into action.

"Foolish boy!" Tessa hissed. "Could he not have kept his mouth shut for a second longer?"

Had Avmoshir not said anything, Victria and Tessa might have managed to swoop in unopposed, killing at least a few of his captors before they realized they were under attack. Now, Koranam's henchmen moved to defend themselves.

Victria swung her dirk, trying to catch one of the vashi in the throat, but he pulled back just out of range. Before she could swing around for another attack, he thrust his trident at her mount, which she only just managed to parry. Tessa's dive had no better luck.

Now the sharks were upon them. Victria ducked low as one charged at her head, narrowly avoiding its dangerous maw. She swung behind her blindly, catching the shark on the back but not doing too much damage. She leaned right and her manta responded immediately arcing around for another attack—but the shark had the same idea.

Victria looked up at a gaping jaw of daggers nearly upon her. Reflexively, she thrust her sword arm forward putting it inside the predator's mouth, her blade penetrating through its roof, stabbing where she hoped the brain was. The shark thrashed. Victria, still holding onto her weapon, was torn from her mount, her arm ripped into by razor sharp teeth.

She let go of her weapon and pulled out her arm, nursing it and hoping the shark would die soon so she could retrieve her blade. For the time being, though, she was defenseless. She didn't even have her natural strength to assist her with hand-to-hand combat. She searched for Tessa, hoping she was still alive. She was only a few feet away, her situation no better. Behind her, one of the sharks floated dead while another feasted on her manta mount.

But the sharks weren't the only enemy. The three vashi who had captured Avmoshir surrounded them, their tridents pointed at the viatari's throats.

"Well, look who we have here," one of them said.

"The ssstrangersss from the Assembly. Koranam will be even more pleased when he learnsss that we've killed you."

Stunned, Victria realized there was no way out of their predicament. Tessa was still armed, but she wasn't, and they were fighting in the vashi's element. Their regenerative abilities could help keep them alive long enough to prolong the fight, but without any further aid, they were defeated. She sighed. It was all she could do. After two long millennia she had not expected it to end like this, in this place. So far from home.

A shadow loomed over them, blocking out all light from the outside world for what seemed like miles. Everyone looked up, their eyes bulging as they took in the giant form of a saran approaching them. The creature was so close, Victria could see its reptilian eyes shifting between them, analyzing the food sources before it.

The vashi were the first to react. They all hissed in fear and swam for their lives, dropping their tridents in their haste to escape.

But it was no use.

Victria had been told several times how dangerous the saran was, how it was impossible to fight, how it was the true master of the seas. And now she understood why the beast was spoken of with such reverence and awe as the giant serpent, with one flick of its body, covered the gap between it and the escaping vashi.

The saran opened its maw and, instantly, Koranam's agents were gone. There hadn't even been time for them to scream as the creature's long, sharp fangs tore into them. The saran swallowed and slowly turned to face the viatari.

This was it. There was no escaping this.

"Victria," Tessa whispered.

"I know."

The saran glided toward them leisurely until one of its eyes was before them. Victria could see her own terrified reflection in it. They hovered there like that for a few seconds and then the saran turned away, curving its body through the water slowly and gracefully as it returned to roaming the seas.

Victria let out the breath she had been holding, a stream of bubbles erupting from her mouth. She gasped for air. Had she been on solid ground, she knew her legs would not have been able to hold her and she would have collapsed from the sheer terror she felt. Tessa was in no better condition.

"How are we—still alive?" She gasped.

"We should not be."

They sank to the ocean floor where Avmoshir lay, his face as pale as a vashi could get with their colorful scales.

"We have the luck of the universe," he said. "I feel like I could take Zessarix back single-handedly now."

"You had that feeling before already. That's why you left, isn't it?" Victria said. She wasn't trying to accuse him, but Avmoshir's face fell as he nodded mutely.

After a while, they recovered from the shock of their ordeal and got back to work. Tessa cut through the netting while Victria undid Avmoshir's iron chains.

"Why did you come for me? I thought you would have

been happy to be rid of me."

Victria shook her head. "I promised your father I would protect you. I told you that as well, and I meant it. I'm sorry if I've made you feel otherwise, if I've made you feel like we didn't care for you. We do, and we will help you retake Zessarix—but you must understand these things take time."

"I don't like waiting."

"No one really does," Victria chuckled. "But the things we desire the most, the goals we wish to accomplish—they gain their greatest value when we're patient. Your people will be more impressed with you as their leader if you bide your time and strike when the moment is right than if you run into Zessarix alone with no plan and make a fool of yourself. One of the greatest qualities of leadership is patience."

"Then I shall fail as Supreme Overseer."

Victria grinned. She couldn't help but see herself reflected in this young vashi now.

"Patience is learned. You will make mistakes to begin with, I'm sure. But given time, you will learn what it means to lead—just as, I'm sure, your father did when he first became Supreme Overseer. What has happened here will just be the first of many lessons in that subject."

The iron chains came loose and the last of the netting was finally cut away. Avmoshir swam out and stretched, his face lighting up as he felt the water move freely around him once more.

"Thank you, Victria, Tessa, for freeing me. Even I can admit I would have been doomed without your timely rescue. And thank you, Victria, for your words."

"Will you continue on to Zessarix by yourself?" Victria asked, moving to retrieve her dirk from the shark she had killed.

"Do I have a choice?"

"There is always a choice," Tessa said. "But we would be lying if we said we didn't want you to come back to Maleres with us."

Avmoshir's face scrunched in confusion. "Why Maleres? Have you already finished the acolyte's tasks?"

Victria shook her head. "No, we still have to retrieve three scales from a bluegill. But Serania and the others should nearly be at Maleres by now. They're still looking for you. We will have to return there to meet up with them before we go back to the Throne of the Deep."

"That would be a huge waste of time," Avmoshir said. "I will return with you, but we will not waste any more time with this pointless back and forth."

He whistled sharply, a small stream of bubbles escaping his lips. Almost immediately, a pair of swordfish appeared in the distance, approaching at impressive speeds. They were circling the viatari within seconds. Avmoshir spoke to them softly, in a language that was not of the vashi, but one Victria and Tessa could just as well not understand.

Once he was done, the swordfish shot off and were gone the next instant.

"What was that?" Tessa asked.

"Those swordfish will find your companions and tell them to head back to the Throne."

"But none of us speak . . . fish."

Avmoshir laughed. "The language is called Ichthys, and in that case the swordfish will tell the manta rays. Either way, we shall meet your companions at the Throne. Now come—" he urged the two viatari to mount the one remaining manta ray, indicating he would swim beside it. "—let us finish this task of yours quickly so we can return to Maleres and focus on the more important task of retaking my city."

They were back in the acolyte's lair. His green tendrils swayed as calmly as they had the last time. Nothing had changed as far as they were concerned, except that the viatari were more determined than ever to obtain this acolyte's help.

They had finished the menial tasks they had been given—Avmoshir harvesting the three bluegill scales they needed himself—and once they had all reunited outside the Throne of the Deep, they had made their way inside.

Victria stepped forward, presenting the items that had been requested. She placed the three sacks of cuttleweed they had gathered, the three shining scales from the bluegill, and a single barnacle as proof they had removed them from the top of the Throne before the artifact.

"We have done what you asked."

Green tendrils swooped down and enveloped the items, taking them into the artifact where they disappeared from sight.

"So you have, so you have," the acolyte's jovial voice filled the room. "I thank you, little ones, for being so cooperative."

"Will you join us, then, in fighting The Turned One and the Creature?"

There was a pause.

"Not quite yet. There remains one more thing I must ask of you."

"You said you would help," Serania stepped forward, her fangs bared. "We don't have time to waste on any more silly tasks, even if they come from you, acolyte!"

"I assure you, this one is quite simple. And you may call me by my name, Scorpus. I think you've now earned that right."

From one of the many large tunnels leading into the room a large beast snaked its way through, swimming to the ceiling and hovering there, eyeing them all with its reptilian eyes.

"Another saran," Avmoshir breathed.

"We're dead," Serania whispered, all her anger immediately dissipating.

"Not yet, you're not," Scorpus hummed. "The saran serve me as my protectors and agents. They are my ears, eyes, and hands in this watery world. You need not fear them just as you need not fear me, so long as you do not make yourselves my enemies."

Victria grimaced. It looked like they had no choice but to accept the acolyte's demand.

"What else do you want us to do?"

"I want you to tell the truth."

A tendril reached out and stuck itself onto everyone's forehead.

"I will ask each one of you a very personal question. You must answer truthfully. If all of you do so, you will have earned my aid—for I value honesty above all. But if one of you lies, you will see your end within the maw of my protector. And don't think you can get away with half-truths. I will be able to discern truth from fiction with the aid of my tendrils."

They all nodded. It seemed like an easy enough task. Victria wondered what questions Scorpus could possibly ask, since he should have no way of knowing about their personal lives—except, maybe, for Avmoshir.

"Excellent! We shall begin with the daughter of the

Chancellor of Dalyr."

Serania's eye widened. "How did you—"

"Ah, ah, ah. I will be asking the questions."

Victria paled. Somehow Scorpus knew who Serania was, where she had come from, and who her mother was. If he knew so much already it could very well be he *did* know everything about them. She began to suspect this task would not be as easy as she initially thought. If someone was asked something too personal, or something they didn't wish to share with everyone else in the room. . . would they lie to save face, even if it meant certain death?

"Serania, for your specially enchanted Eye of the Gods, which you so cleverly hide behind your hair, you offered two sacrifices—one being your own eye, and the second being the body of your father, which you had to dig up out of its grave to present to the Guardians at the Temple. My question to you: was it all worth it?"

Victria looked at Serania in shock, expecting her to deny such a terrible allegation, to look disgusted that Scorpus would even suggest she had done such a thing. But instead Serania simply turned pale, her mouth agape but no words coming out. Finally, though her voice was weak, she did speak.

"I have half a mind to use my eye on you right now."

Scorpus chuckled. "It would have little effect, I assure you. Your answer?"

Serania stood there for a minute longer, but finally, she closed her eye and gritted her teeth. "Yes, it was worth it."

"Excellent! I see your thoughts. Now that others know your secret, I only hope none of them choose to inform your mother. I can only imagine how devastating such a discovery would be."

The tendril attached to Serania's forehead retreated into

the artifact.

"Now we move on to Tessa."

All eyes shifted to her, wondering what secrets she could be hiding. Her normally serious face cracked with doubt as she wondered herself what revelation might be coming.

"Are you still considering switching sides in this coming war between acolytes?"

A deadly silence followed. Tessa? A traitor? Victria couldn't believe it, wouldn't believe it. She had known her since they were young. She would never . . . would she?

Annoyance marked Tessa's face as she responded. "I *never* considered it. What you're referring to was a temptation the Creature put inside my head when we confronted him in Inadarim over a year ago. It was a temptation influenced by his corruption, nothing more. I would never betray my friends, my people."

"Hmm," Scorpus withdrew his tendril from her forehead. "Very good. Now, to Natiari. Why did you let your little sister be devoured by that bear while you hid behind a bush?"

Natiari's eyes glistened with tears and she fell to her knees. She choked as she spat out the words. "It was the only way I thought that I could survive. But I found the bear and killed it once I realized the horrible thing I had done and how wrong I was."

"Indeed," Scorpus murmured, another tendril retreating into his artifact. "Much too late, if I may say so. Now, Tera— hah! You already know what I am about to ask, do you not?"

Tera had a dangerous gleam in her eye as she glared at the acolyte, but she spoke back defiantly. "Just say it. Since you already know the answer, I'm not afraid to share it."

"Very well, do you still intend on betraying the viatari?"

The viatari eyed her with suspicion. Serania's words in Halding Port came back to Victria, and she wondered now if she should have listened to her instead of choosing to believe in the potential good of their human guide.

"I admit I had planned on doing so when I first realized they were viatari, but I didn't. And now I would never consider doing so. These ladies have become friends of mine, closer friends than some of the humans I know. I would give my life for them."

Victria sighed inwardly, ashamed that she had second guessed Tera at all. She didn't understand what the point of these questions was, all they seemed to do was create tension, instill brief moments of doubt. Still, she couldn't help but feel some comfort in finally knowing the full truth about Tera. Now she knew with absolute certainty that they could trust her.

"Madira," Satisfied with Tera's answer, Scorpus had moved on. "If you are so close to Natiari, your cousin, why did you not seek her out sooner?"

Madira hesitated, suddenly taking an interest in the floor. "Because for the longest time I wished she was dead. Our families grew to hate each other after what happened at the Lone Tree and my parents died with that hatred so I saw it as my duty to keep it alive. When I saw her, though, during that time that she came to Dalyr to drive out Anzo, those feelings melted away and I could feel nothing but love for her."

Natiari nodded encouragingly and pulled her into an embrace, "It's okay, I understand."

Madira smiled, clearly relieved.

"Avmoshir, your aunt has asked you not to kill your

cousin, Koranam, should you defeat him in the coming battle. Will you obey her wishes or do you intend to avenge your father's death by killing his killer?"

Avmoshir hesitated but finally hung his head. "I will only kill him if he tries to kill me. I will only disobey my aunt if it is to save my own life—though, I wish to kill him with every scale on my body."

"Hah! Very good everyone, so far you have all been truthful. But now we go to the last of your members, and we shall see if she can be truthful with herself. Victria,"

Victria racked her brain for what the acolyte might ask her. Her original hatred for the dwarves? Her sadness for Dragos' death? Her doubts as a leader?

"Victria, whom do you love?"

Victria's mind blanked. She felt everyone's eyes on her but dared not acknowledge them. She could only stare at Scorpus, wondering if he was serious.

"I will let you know silence is not an answer."

Victria thought of what she should say. Well, she had to tell the truth, obviously, or they would all die. Did she love anyone?

Felix's face popped to mind, making her heart skip a beat. She frowned, puzzled. Surely, not Felix. She admired him, certainly. Looked up to him, yes. She had thought about him many times during their times apart. But that was because he had always been the first; the first viatari to save her, the first to show her her own worth, the first to help her improve. He was the first. No one could be like Felix. And she knew she didn't want anyone who wasn't like Felix.

Her mind fuzzy, her heart hammering, cheeks burning, she replied with the words she had been hiding from herself since the very beginning, though it felt like someone else was speaking them.

"Felix. I love Felix. I've loved him ever since I first met him."

A wave of heat poured down her body and then the acolyte's tendril separated from her forehead and went away.

"Very good. You have all been truthful and, as I've said, I so love honesty. I will help you in your war against my siblings."

Scorpus continued talking, but Victria hardly heard him. Her mind was still reeling from her personal revelation. How had she not recognized these feelings for so long? She felt a hand on her shoulder and saw Tessa and Natiari at her side, smiling warmly and looking at each other knowingly.

"You knew?"

"Please," Natiari scoffed. "It was obvious to anyone with two eyes."

"Well that probably explains why I never saw it—since I only have one," Serania mused, a silly grin on her face. "But everything makes sense now."

"If you ladies are finished congratulating each other," Scorpus brought their attention back to him. "I will teleport myself to Aleganthia to join my brother, but I understand you still have some things to take care of in this realm, so I will send you back to Maleres through liquefaction. It has been lovely meeting you all, and I look forward to working with you in the future."

With that, Victria felt the liquid moving around them, a squeezing of the body, shortness of breath, and then they were back in Meri's house. Meri blinked rapidly, startled by their sudden appearance. The tea she had been pouring into a cup overflowed and spilled all over her table.

Victria turned to her companions. Any tension that was created by the questions they had faced was now gone. It felt like they were all a little closer now. Victria wondered if that had been the acolyte's intention all along—to tighten their bonds through honesty.

"Scorpus is right," she said, taking a seat next to Meri, who had finally stopped pouring her tea and looked ready to ask a million questions. "We have a lot of work to do if we hope to take back Zessarix."

CHAPTER FORTY-THREE

Salevari studied the two human leaders before her, their faces ragged with exhaustion as she told them what Zael had discovered three days ago. She'd had much time to think in those three days and she knew what she had to do even before Simon and Kent could fall to their knees and beg for mercy for their people.

"Stand up, both of you," something in the calmness of her voice must have caught their attention, because they did not hesitate to obey, though they looked unsure of what was coming.

"I did not summon you two here to kill you and your kind despite the treachery some of your people have planned against me. I have called you here to give you warning. As you may have already guessed, tonight will be one filled with blood. I want you to make sure you and your people stay indoors. That way, there is less of a chance of innocent life being lost. No doubt, those involved with this treachery will ignore your pleas to stay indoors—which works fine for our intentions."

"And what might those be?" Simon asked, surprised that he and Kent had not been blamed for this threat.

"Isn't it obvious?" She glanced at Zael, who nodded encouragingly. They had discussed this earlier. There was only one way to rip out the dissent among the humans by the roots so that it never reared its head to threaten them again. "Those who rise against us must die—all of them."

"Is there no other way?" Kent asked, his voice pleading. "Perhaps if Simon and I talked to them—"

Salevari held up a hand to silence him. "There is no other way. Those involved have made their choice. They've made it clear that they hold no respect for your leadership. Your words would be wasted. I cannot run a city if my people and I must constantly watch our backs. No, they must all die, and hopefully with them will die the hatred our races have held against each other for so long. The only difficulty will be to make tonight look like self-defense."

Kent sighed heavily and wept, unable to meet the Chancellor's eyes. It was an expected reaction. As a leader, his job was to protect his people. In this case, however, there was nothing he could do to save them. Simon, for his part, maintained his composure.

"You want them to attack you here?" he asked. "You know the names of those who are guilty, why not just slay them where they live."

"I've explained this to you before, Simon," Salevari replied. "It is the same reason we let the darimun attack your towns first before we jumped in to save the day. If I send my guards into the human quarter and kill all who oppose me without anyone else knowing about their murderous treachery, what will it look like to the common civilian?"

Neither Simon nor Kent responded. They knew. But for the sake of them all being on the same page—which she desperately needed—she continued, "It would look like we went on a rampage for no reason, like we massacred you humans for sport. It would create more hatred between us and the cycle would repeat. But if we catch them in the act, allow them to come within a single step of accomplishing their goal, and then kill them in self-defense—"

"Then it will look like those who died brought it upon themselves," Simon finished. "And the viatari will appear blameless to the commonfolk."

The Chancellor smiled. "Exactly. Now, Zael here," she motioned toward the viatari captain, who was as still as a statue, "has managed to uncover the full extent of their plan, so I know where they will attack and which parts of the city will see the brunt of the violence. What I need—"

The doors to her throne room burst open and a single viatari, a young female, dragged herself through, her hair bedraggled and her armor torn in several places. She nursed her twisted right arm with her left as she stumbled forward. Her mouth hung open as if to speak but no words came out as her legs finally gave in and she collapsed.

Salevari rushed forward and caught her just before she hit the floor.

"Guards!" she yelled.

Moments later, two of her own guardsmen from Dalyr rushed in, their weapons out.

"How did this young lady get past an entire keep full of viatari without anyone helping her?" She yelled at them, furious by what she saw as a gross display of carelessness. She could not tolerate any of it—especially not tonight. "You, bring her food and water—and you, bring a healer here immediately. Move it!"

The guards rushed out. The young female moaned and Salevari gave her her full attention.

"What's your name, dear? How is it you've arrived here

in this state?"

"A-Alari," the viatari winced. "I was in charge of the scouting division for the western regions n-near Lake Lunadar."

"Was?"

"They're all g-gone!" Alari gasped, her eyes bulging. One of the guards returned with a jug of water, a glass, and a pair of squirrels. Salevari poured the water and put the glass to Alari's lips. She gulped it down greedily, spilling a fair amount onto the rug floor. When presented with the squirrels she bit into them like a ravenous animal and sucked them dry of life within seconds. She coughed, some color returning to her cheeks.

Seeing Salevari before her again, her eyes refocused and she continued her story, "They caught us by surprise. Slew everyone. We couldn't hold them back. I barely made it out."

"Who could have wiped out an entire scouting division?" Salevari asked, though in her heart she already knew. They were out of time. The moment she had been dreading had come, and at a terrible time.

"The darimun," Alari groaned. "Too many to count. Heading for the mountains."

The other guard returned, a healer in tow. The healer bent down and examined the young viatari's wounds closely. After a quick inspection, he nodded and turned to Salevari.

"She will be fine. Her regenerative abilities look to be healing her as we speak."

"But she came to us from Lake Lunadar like this, how could it be taking so long for her to heal?"

"I was a lot worse than I am now," Alari whispered, and before anything more could be said, the young scout's eyes drooped as she fell unconscious. Salevari grimaced and looked at the guards she had called in. "Take her to one of the vacant rooms where she can rest."

The guards bowed and did as they were told, lifting the scout gently between them and shuffling out of the room, the healer following close behind.

"We are out of time," Salevari took a moment to collect her thoughts, then turned to face Simon and Kent. "The Creature is through playing games. He now moves to destroy us."

"Do you have a plan?" Simon was the one who had asked it but it was clear that the same question was on everyone's mind. This was something she had been preparing for ever since Felix left. Now it was time to see if her preparations had been worth all the trouble.

"Yes," she said steadily, hoping to portray an air of confidence. "Kent, I want you to gather your envoys and send them to the human towns who are friendly to us but decided to remain in their homes. Tell them they must mobilize all of their forces and gather in the foothills south of Aleganthia's forest. I will send my scouts to keep eyes on the darimun's movements. Once they have all gathered in the foothills, I will send a messenger to tell them where to go for battle."

Kent nodded and rushed out of the room, leaving only Simon and Zael.

"Zael," Salevari turned to the one viatari who she had entrusted so much to in these past several weeks. "I need you to gather our own forces. Have them ready to depart as soon as the sun rises tomorrow. We need to move fast. I have no doubt the Creature will direct his darimun to attack the humans' location once he realizes they're out in the open."

"What about the raid tonight?"

"Have everyone in the keep ready for battle. We will cut the humans off as they enter this building and slay them. Have a sizeable force hide around the southern gate and another in the forest. As soon as that torch is dropped, as you told me, the humans will move to open the southern gate. Intercept them and kill them. Those in the forest will surround the humans waiting for the gates to open. Once they drop that torch, it will be our signal to wipe them out in one fell swoop," she looked at Simon, "do you have any objections to this?"

Simon pursed his lips but shook his head.

"Good, because now I need you to deliver. This plan, and the one I have to defeat the darimun, will be no good if we don't have the antidote you created to counter the poison they use to paralyze our regenerative abilities. I need it now. There is no more time for games or hesitation. You either trust us, or you don't. Decide."

Simon looked troubled. No doubt, a part of him wanted to deny her this vital piece of the puzzle, doom the viatari to get back at them for what he saw as their part in his fall from grace as Halshire's chief. But he also knew that without them, he would have remained disgraced—never having a chance to redeem himself by saving Halshire from the darimun. Not only that, but without the viatari, the humans were sure to perish under the Creature's onslaught.

"I will bring them to you," he said resignedly. "Right away."

Salevari nodded, pleased and thankful with how things were turning out. If their luck held like this, everything would go according to plan. The human assassins would be wiped out, Aleganthia would be saved from the darimun, and she would have completed the momentous task Felix had entrusted to her. And then, perhaps, she could have a little peace and quiet—at least, for a little while.

The sun was low on the horizon. Zael watched it sink for a moment longer before continuing down the path he had taken. He had already passed down Salevari's orders to those who needed to know and the time was quickly approaching for Lyna and Anders to begin their attempt to topple the viatari. But before he joined the others in the keep for what would undoubtedly be a bloody battle, there was one thing he had to take care of.

He knocked on a door he thought he would never touch for the rest of his life. Footsteps came from within and he felt his heart beat through his chest. The door swung open, revealing a startled Kur Rauan.

"Zael!"

There was a commotion from further inside the house as Yalar came rushing to the door as well. She saw Zael and froze in place, as if paralyzed.

Zael's first instinct was to run, to abandon this silly idea he had been entertaining ever since his encounter with the old woman three days ago. But he stood his ground. He knew he had to do this, if only for his own benefit. Still, he could not help but feel disgust as he looked at the two viatari responsible for his parents' demise.

"Can—can we invite you in?" Kur asked uncertainly. He moved slightly to the side as if half-expecting Zael to push through him, but the viatari captain shook his head.

"I only came for one thing," he said, staring both of the Rauans straight in the eyes. "Centuries ago, we all went out hunting near Lake Lunadar. We'd done it countless times before for as long as I can remember. It was how we grew in friendship, how we came to consider each other as family."

Yalar sniffed behind her husband, who continued to stand where he was, his eyes downcast.

"You were farther ahead than us the last time we went. You would have seen that huge party of humans coming our way long before we did. But you never came back to warn us. You ran away. You abandoned us like the cowards you are, leaving my parents to their fate. It is ironic, because it is entirely due to their own sacrifice, their own bravery, that I can stand here before you today, ready to forgive."

Kur's eyes widened and Yalar gasped.

"Zael, you don't know how much it means to hear you say that."

"Please," Yalar said. "Won't you join us for our evening meal? There is so much that we can discuss."

Again, Zael shook his head and ground his teeth. It was taking every ounce of discipline to keep from letting loose his rage on these two. But he kept his temper in check. He would remain calm. He would be the better viatari.

"Do not mistake my meaning. I forgive you freely for how you wronged my family, how you wronged me. But I do not forget. I will never forget. Things can never be the same between us. That is all I came to say."

With that, he turned and walked back the way he had come. He half-expected the Rauans to call after him, as they had always done in the past when he was younger. Back then, he would often leave something behind at their house so they would have to bring it to him later. That way they could spend more time together. They had been, for the longest time, like a second family to him.

But no such thing happened. Instead, he heard their door

slam shut. He continued walking, gazing up at the darkening sky as he made his way back to the keep. He thought of the human elder he had helped. He wasn't quite sure what it was, but something had clicked in him after they parted ways that day, and as hard as forgiving the Rauans had been, he was glad he'd done it. His chest felt lighter, his mind felt at ease. There were no more distractions from his past, no more feuds or old hatreds. Now he could focus on the present.

He was ready for tonight.

CHAPTER FORTY-FOUR

This would be a night to remember, Anders thought as he and his wife, Lyna, made their way out of their private room and into the spacious hall they had cleared out for their meetings. Inside the hall stood nearly thirty brave men and women willing to put their lives on the line for a chance to make history. They all stood in light, form-fitting black body suits with a thin layer of supple leather armor adding some extra protection. They all wore masks, or simple black cloths to hide their identities. Many had even gone so far as to smear their faces with charcoal so that any lights outside did not betray their pale skin. A hush fell over the crowd as they turned to face their leaders.

"On behalf of the entire human race, Lyna and I thank you for coming tonight. This night, we will free our kind from the shackles of fear that have bound us for countless generations. Tonight, we destroy the viatari and rid the world of monsters. Tonight, we secure a future for our children, for our families."

There was no cheering. But Anders expected this. This late in the night, it would be foolish to expose their position and intent—no matter how much they may have wanted to express their excitement.

"Everything is in place for this plan to succeed," Lyna said. "You all know what must be done. Anders and I will lead the way. Good luck."

Anders glanced at the beautiful woman next to him, his heart swelling. This would be the culmination of their efforts. They had spent countless sleepless nights planning for this, creating the poison. When they finally did get some sleep, they had dreamt only of this night. They had bled for it. And now it was finally here. Even though Lyna had already covered her face with a black cloth, he could tell she was grinning in anticipation as she waited for him to lead them out into the streets.

He tied his own cloth across his face and pulled a thick pair of black goggles he had invented long ago to help improve his vision during the night. He jumped off the stage he and his wife had used for weeks now to stir up the people and strode toward the door, ripping it open and rushing into the night. There were soft footsteps behind him as the others followed.

They darted through the dark alleyways and into the wider streets, sticking to the shadows to avoid detection. Anders slowed his pace once they passed out of the human quarter of the city. This was where the real danger began. They had to remain undetected to keep the element of surprise at all costs for this plan to succeed. If the viatari ended up discovering them with enough time to prepare a defense—well, they just wouldn't have the numbers to follow through with the plan.

As they rounded a streetcorner, two viatari guards on patrol came into view. Anders smiled. Perfect, their first targets. The two guards were walking away from the party of humans. Anders and Lyna, crept forward slowly, careful not to make any noise with their steps. They drew daggers from their belts, the blades glistening a sickly yellow from the poison they had been imbued with. Indeed, everyone's weapons had been imbued with the poison—from the arrows people carried in their quivers to the spikes some had attached to their gloves.

Close enough to strike, Anders lunged in unison with Lyna. They both drove their daggers deep into the viatari's backs, reaching over to cover their mouths in case they yelped from the shock. The viatari shuddered and slowly sank to the floor, going limp before their heads hit the ground.

They moved the corpses to the sides, into the shadows where no one would stumble upon them until it was too late, and moved on. Having studied their patrol patterns, Anders expected to run into a few more guards on the way to the keep, and he was right. Most of the time they took the viatari out with one of their bowmen, but every now and then someone was brave enough to creep up behind the guard to kill them with their own hands.

So far, things were going swimmingly. Only an hour had passed and they'd already reached the keep. Anders looked up at the tall stone walls they needed to climb in order to reach the higher levels of the building. Behind them, though hidden in shadows, was a trail of the first victims of the night. He breathed in deeply and let all the air out in a satisfied sigh. Knowing Aleganthia's streets ran with the blood of its own people was thrilling, and he was looking forward to going back when this was over to cut off the heads of those he wanted to stick on a pike in front of their own gates.

He especially looked forward to doing that with Salevari's

head. He would make sure hers was at the front. It was only fitting that she led her people even in death.

They began to climb the walls. The stones at the base of the keep all the way up to the midsection were uneven and provided plenty of handholds and footholds for them to use. Still, they had no ropes or protective gear to keep them from falling when they reached the higher altitudes and the wind came into play. And some of them did fall. They moved slowly to conserve energy and were careful to avoid the windows. Even so, the climb proved too much for some. Once they reached the midsection, at least four of their members lost their grip. Each one fell to their deaths with their arms outstretched, as if welcoming it. No one screamed, just as had been discussed earlier. Silence was key, even with death. Anders would be sure to honor their heroic sacrifice once this was all over.

They reached a point during their climb where the stones smoothed out and became more even, making it impossible to continue the way they had been. Still, they needed to climb higher to reach their target room. With one hand, Anders and a few others in the party reached into their back pockets and pulled out a propulsion tool with a trigger mechanism he had invented. Attached to the mouth was a grappling hook and a long line of rope. Once the trigger was pulled, the hook would be ejected with a force much greater than they could create by simply throwing it.

They shot it upward, aiming for the keep's roof. Most of them were successful in planting their hooks. After tugging on the ropes a few times to ensure their hooks were secure, they continued the climb. One by one, they gripped the ropes and used their legs to push themselves higher.

Anders was tempted to look down, to see how far they'd

come, but he kept his eyes on the target. Only a few more feet and they would be able to break into the room they had picked to start their assault. Only a few more feet and they would be able to realize his dream and destroy the viatari. Just a few more feet and they would finally avenge all the family members killed by these monsters. They would finally avenge the deaths of his children and parents.

The viatari had been waiting for over an hour for the humans to attack. Salevari was surprised, and couldn't help but feel a little disappointed, by how long it was taking them to reach her. She had purposefully helped make their path easier by telling the guards on patrol to allow the humans to sneak up on them when the time came and to not fight back.

The humans should have been running through the streets, thrilled by their apparent success, eager to reach her. And yet, according to the continuous reports she was receiving, they had remained cautious, moving at a slow pace and not daring to take any chances. It was probably wise of their leader to do so, but it would do little in the end to help them.

The sound of glass shattering and muffled footsteps came from the other room—the ones the humans had picked to start their attack. Salevari smiled. It was finally time to rid herself of these pests.

She drew her sword, a long, slender saber and wrapped her fingers around the grip of her small buckler, rolling her shoulders as she prepared for the upcoming battle. She looked around. She had at least a dozen guards with her in the room, all standing against the wall and out of immediate sight. Simon and Kent were there too, though they wouldn't come out until the invaders were surrounded.

Once the humans finished gathering in the room next door, Salevari knew, they would start making their way through the keep to slaughter any viatari they found. Little did they know that as soon as they stepped through the doors leading into this room, they would find themselves surrounded by the viatari she had with her as well as another group of twelve she had hidden in the room they currently occupied. This way, they could ensure they ensnared all of the humans, like a pack of wild boars.

Still, she was not foolish enough to think just surrounding them would be sufficient. With their weapons undoubtedly coated in poison, she had given each viatari present a capsule filled with the antidote Simon had finally provided to her. The capsule had been created by Simon to be carried in their mouths, out of sight. If any of them were struck by one of the humans' weapons, all they had to do was bite down on the capsule and swallow and the antidote would do the rest. She had given these capsules to the guards on patrol as well. That way, she could be sure that any guards "slain" by the humans would survive their wounds.

The door burst open and the humans flooded in. A fair amount, Salevari admitted, but not too much for them to handle. Immediately, the viatari guards stepped out of the shadows, shields held out in front and swords and spears pointed directly at the humans. The humans huddled together ready to fight, but looked less sure once the second group of viatari rushed in from behind and blocked any path of retreat.

Salevari stepped forward, clapping.

"Well, well, well. I'm glad you finally made it. I've been hearing of your exploits in my brother's city for far too long. I thought it was time I witnessed it myself. If you'd be so kind as to tell me which one of you is the leader?"

Two humans stepped forward, one male and the other female, both with angry embers burning in their eyes.

"So this must be Anders and Lyna. I must ask, did you manage to drop your torch before you came in here?"

"Yes," Anders growled. "And soon the streets of your city will run with blood as our other members let in an army to wipe you out."

Salevari clicked her tongue as if to a child. "An army? Hardly. The group I sent out into the forest to take care of them reported their numbers could not be more than forty. That's no surprise, really, when the only real help you can get comes from a small village. Needless to say, as small as they were, they won't be bothering us ever again."

Anders paled and seemed lost for words.

"How?" Lyna asked, her eyes crestfallen. "How could you have known?"

Zael stepped forward, immense pleasure written on his face. He waited until all the humans' attention was on him and then transformed into his human form, he remained as Kurt for a few moments, staring triumphantly at Anders and Lyna before reverting. His red eyes were hungry for the kill.

"I knew it!" One of the larger, beefier men yelled in fury. "I told you he was one of them!"

"So what now?" Anders said, his voice bitter. "Will you kill us all? When our leaders hear of this—"

"The leaders you think of as incompetent?" Salevari interrupted. "Simon, Kent, would you like to come out now?"

The two human leaders came out of the shadows, their faces grim as they appraised the thirty humans they knew must die.

"How could you betray us like this?" Anders was now livid, his voice growing hoarse as he shouted every curse he could at Simon and Kent.

"You are the ones who betrayed us," Simon said. "Because of your foolishness, you've cost all of these people their lives and risked endangering all of ours as well."

"As much as I don't like this, I must agree with Simon," Kent said. "You should have trusted my judgement Anders, Lyna. Now you must pay the price."

"How can we trust you when you throw your lot in with these *monsters*?" Lyna seethed. "Are we the only ones who still care about all those who have died by their hands?"

"The old feuds are what need to die," Kent replied softly. "There is a greater evil out there that we must focus on. And without the viatari, there is no hope in facing them."

Salevari cleared her throat, bringing the attention back to her. "Now, I'm sure you understand the situation you're in. And with Simon and Kent as my witnesses, let it not be said that I am not merciful. I am giving you one chance, Anders, to make the right decision. Lay down your arms, surrender, and we will let you live. You may no longer live in Aleganthia, but you will have your lives."

But Anders was already shaking his head. "We've come too far. If we must die, we will at least take you with us!"

He lunged at Salevari, his dagger sinking deep into her chest.

She stumbled back, eyes wide with shock. "Kill them."

The viatari guards yelled and charged in, skewering some with their spears and slashing away with their swords at others.

Salevari felt a burning in her chest and a numbing cold creep in along her arms. Quickly, she bit into the capsule she'd had resting under her tongue and swallowed. At first, nothing happened, and she feared Simon had tricked her and had given her a false antidote. However, the next second, her wound began to heal and she could move her arms again.

Baring her fangs, she gripped her saber and jumped into the battle, tackling Anders just as he was about to stab another one of her guards. His daggers clattered on the floor as he hit the wall, his eyes rolling from the impact. Salevari didn't give him any time to breathe, though. She rushed over as he tried to get up and slammed her knee into his face, sending him reeling. She placed her blade against his neck.

"Anders!"

Salevari glanced over her shoulder and saw Lyna trying to push her way to them. She might have made it, too, but just as she seemed to find a clear path to reach her husband, Zael stepped in front of her, bringing his dirk up and twisting it deep into her belly. Lyna gasped and coughed up blood, her eyes slowly sinking as she continued to stare at Anders, who was still struggling to get up.

The Chancellor turned her attention back to him. He pushed himself back onto his knees and coughed, wheezing as he did so. He stared calmly into her eyes, and then closed his own.

"We have failed."

"Yes," Salevari said, swinging her saber clean across his neck. "You have."

Anders toppled over and soon the room was still as the remaining humans in his group were also killed. The floor was sticky with blood. Salevari took out a rag and wiped her blade clean. She turned to Simon and Kent, who had stayed in the same spot, watching the massacre. Both were beyond pale.

"These are your people," she said, sheathing her saber and clapping Zael on the shoulder as she made her way past them. "You should bury them however you wish. I leave them for you to deal with."

"And where will you go?" Kent asked, his voice hollow.

"We have another battle tomorrow," she replied. "I'm going to bed."

She stomped out of the room, undoing the straps of her armor as she walked and letting the pieces fall where they may. She sighed and took a moment to look outside. The moon sat high over the clouds. People would wake up tomorrow and discover what had happened here. Perhaps there would be an initial uproar from the humans, a final spurt of defiance, but once they learned what had truly transpired, they would calm down. For now, though, the city was peaceful, and she was certain it would remain that way.

CHAPTER FORTY-FIVE

"The humans are in position, Chancellor, but the darimun close in on them as we speak."

"Will we arrive in time to position ourselves adequately?" Salevari asked the scout standing before her. To her side, columns of human and viatari warriors surged past her, their footsteps pounding dully in unison on the soft, damp earth.

"Not at this pace," the scout replied. "We're still several hours away."

"How long do you think the humans can hold by themselves?"

"It's hard to say—they are much weaker than we are—but a significant force has rallied in the foothills. They may hold as long as an hour before their lines crumble."

"Then we need to quicken our pace. Go back to the field and bring me reports as the situation changes. Zael—" Zael rode up behind her, his face eager for the coming battle. "Spread the word, starting at the front of the columns: We're doubling our pace again. We must reach the humans to reinforce them before the darimun get the chance to destroy them."

Zael nodded and urged his horse forward at a quick gallop. He soon disappeared in the trees. Salevari stayed where she was for a moment, thinking.

She knew this day had long been coming. She'd known the Creature would send out an army large enough to wipe them all out once it became apparent that viatari and humans were working together and she was ready. Now that the human defectors within Aleganthia had been dealt with, she felt calmer about the coming battle. This would be their greatest test to see if their two races could truly be allies—and that possibility was made easier without the likes of Anders and Lyna.

She had woken up that morning refreshed, despite getting only a few hours of sleep. Since then, the day had been non-stop. She had quickly strapped on her armor and weapons and made her way out of the keep to inspect the army. Two thousand viatari, some mounted on horses, others on foot, had stood ready to move out. The humans had added another thousand to their numbers.

After sharing the location of their destination with the officers of the host, they had moved out, an air of urgency in their movements. They all knew they were on a time limit to save the humans who had already gathered to face the darimun. The Creature would not wait for them.

At first, Salevari had feared the humans would be unable to keep up with the viatari, who were faster on foot. But they had and continued to do so. The need to save their fellow man was a good motivator and kept their feet moving, and the adrenaline would keep them energized enough to fight when it came time for battle.

You will have to hope their adrenaline will be enough, I will not be able to supplement them with my auras from this distance, The First One said in her mind.

Salevari had not taken The First One out with the army,

preferring that he stay with the garrison she had left to defend the city in case the Creature attempted to sack it again like he had last time. Still, while The First One had acquiesced to her wishes, he had still imprinted himself upon her so that they could continue to communicate, much like how he had done with Thuradin only months ago.

"Well, as long as there are no surprises we should be fine."

At that moment, Simon and Kent rode up to Salevari, both dressed in heavy mail armor and armed to the teeth. The Chancellor counted at least five different daggers strapped to different parts of each one's body—and she was sure there were more hidden in places she couldn't see.

"Today is the day," Simon said. "You do have a strategy for what we're about to face, don't you? Because I remember how ferocious these demons can be."

"I do," Salevari said. "Though, whether or not we can execute that strategy properly will depend on how quickly we can get there."

Simon grunted. "Either way, I suppose we will make our stand against this Creature. It will be interesting, at least, to see whether this new poison Anders discovered will work the same way on the demons," he glanced curiously at her, "Do your people know?"

Salevari frowned. Before they had departed Aleganthia, Simon had come to her with the recipe for the poison Anders and Lyna had created to paralyze the viatari, which they had found after raiding their home. It was a simple recipe and large batches could be made in minutes. As soon as she had seen it, the idea that it could be used against any powerful being, like the darimun, had popped into her head and she had told the human wanderer to make several batches of it to apply to the weapons of his people. She had not told any of the viatari, not even Zael.

"Just as you trusted us enough to give us the antidote for this poison, I trust you and your people to find a better use for it than what Anders wanted. I only hope it is not a mistake."

"It is not," Kent said fiercely. "Your people will have nothing to fear from us."

"Good, then ride on ahead. We must cover as much ground as possible if we are to win the day."

They rode and marched like never before—out of breath, sore, sweating, but still they pushed on. Their armor wore down on them, their weapons felt like deadweights, but that did not stop them as they entered the foothills and crested the last series of hills they needed to reach the battlefield.

Those on horses made it first. Salevari looked out on the scene before her. The humans she had summoned seemed to number around two thousand, but the darimun were much more. She had arrived just in time to watch the corrupted beasts swarm down from the surrounding hills on the opposite end, their intention to crash into the human army obvious. The host of humans shuffled back nervously. Others looked around, no doubt expecting their reinforcements to appear any second. A few pointed at her lone figure.

As those on foot caught up, Salevari took some time to observe the Creature's army more closely. She could see the corrupted forms of every sort of beast, each one grossly enlarged from their regular size and oozing the same purple mist. There were snakes, wolves, deer, bears, even hawks and bats. The Creature had gone out of his way to corrupt as much wildlife as he could to create this army. Thousands stormed down the hills, mere minutes from crashing into the human lines.

The front ranks of humans settled into a battle stance, shields at the ready and interlocked with spears lowered. Salevari's decision was made, as much as she didn't like it— there was not enough time to deploy her army the way she desired. Despite the scout's reports, she doubted the humans below could fend off such a force of darimun for more than ten minutes, especially without the new poison the humans in her own host had at their disposal. If they were to save these humans, they had to act fast.

"Form ranks," she ordered, urging her horse back and forth along the hill. "Quickly! Viatari and humans, together, we go to save our lands from the evils of the Creature. To-gether, we shall emerge victorious. Defend each other as you would your brother or sister—" she raised her saber just as the first few ranks of the army below them absorbed the brunt of the initial impact from the darimun. She looked to her left. "—Zael, take half of our forces and swing around the left flank. I will swing around their right and we will meet in the middle. Kent, lead our cavalry. Take them all the way around the back and defend our flanks from any reserves they may have, then crash into their rear. Go, now!"

Kent and those mounted warriors near him burst into action, the sound of galloping horses fading away quickly as they rushed to maneuver around the large army of darimun.

Satisfied that everyone understood what was at stake here, she lowered her saber.

"Fight now for your families! Fight now for your homes! Fight now for Azar!"

Humans and viatari roared together as they rushed down the hill. They maneuvered around the humans holding the center and crashed into the darimun's flanks. Salevari rode her horse into the thick of the battle, using its weight for a stronger impact as she crashed in, then hopped off onto the nearest darim she could find, swinging her heavy saber down hard and severing its head almost all the way through. The darim fell under her weight and she rolled away just as one of the hawk-like darim lunged for her from the air. She swung blindly behind, felt her sword clip something, and heard a shriek of pain.

She did not have long to revel in her small triumph. A sharp searing agony ripped through her belly, and she felt blood immediately drench her legs. She brought her buckler before her, deflecting a second attack as a bear-darim tried to rake her again with its claws. She brought her sword down in a chopping motion but the darim easily avoided it, this time moving in from the side to pounce on her. Salevari rolled away again, but toward her enemy instead of away. The darim had not expected this, and fell limply as she plunged her blade into it from behind.

She groaned. Her regenerative abilities were already dealing with the wound in her stomach, but it could not numb the pain. She heard a terrified scream and then a human fell to the ground next to her, his neck broken, eyes bulging. She looked up.

Above them, the hawk and sparrow-darimun circled, swooping down to pick up individual humans or viatari, clawing and pecking at them the entire time, only to drop them to their deaths. She looked to the skies in Aleganthia's direction. Any minute now. . . .

And sure enough, she saw specks in the distance steadily grow larger as the Lyruun and their riders arrived. The Lyruun rushed through the flying darimun, sending many plummeting to the ground as they unleashed their blue and green mists. Once the initial surprise had worn off, some of the flying darimun rallied together to take down the Lyruun riders, but the damage to their ranks was already too much. Salevari grinned, satisfied, and returned her attention to the fight before her. Before long, they would have control of the skies, and, with that, she was sure of victory.

She fought tirelessly for what seemed like hours, her saber swinging wildly around her as darim after darim tried to overwhelm her. Occasionally, she would catch glimpses of a human or one of her own falling to a darim. Each time she witnessed it, a sense of rage grew within her which she unleashed upon the enemy, leaving behind a trail of death.

The earth trembled. And though she already knew the reason, she could not help but glance at the darimun's rear, which had so far been left open. Their mounted forces, led by Kent, charged down the hills the darimun themselves had gone down moments before and crashed into them, creating havoc for the Creature's forces.

The sound of horse cries, human cries, and the horrible growls and yips of darimun filled the sky. Salevari felt her ears grow numb as the barrage of sounds pounded them. Her nose was assaulted by the thick smell of blood and guts and she felt, with sudden clarity, how heavy her limbs were.

In a moment of respite, she tried to see how the battle was faring around her but found she could see very little. She was deep in the fight. All she saw was a mass of bodies; many lying on the ground, but many more still standing and fighting. She shook her head. She needed a bird's eye view if she wanted to have any idea of their situation.

She whistled sharply, hoping that Halon, the stable master, had released As'ven just as she'd requested. She worried briefly that, even with the superb hearing that Lyruun had, the sound of battle would drown out her summons. But no sooner had she whistled than she noticed one of the Lyruun break from formation and dive straight for her.

As'ven landed, breathing blue mist at the darimun around her as she quickly mounted him.

"*Oss ferath!*"

As'ven flew up, just as she commanded, at incredible speeds—Salevari clung on to the reigns tightly and closed her eyes as the wind rushed past. Within seconds, the Chancellor was as high as the clouds. She looked down and observed the battle raging below her. Luckily, she could still make out her own ranks, the dwindling light of the sun reflecting off their armor, and those of the Creature's.

As far as she could tell, there did not appear to be any breaking points within her lines. Everyone was holding their ground. Indeed, she noticed that the circle they had created around the Creature's forces was slowly shrinking. They were taking ground. They were winning.

She scanned the land past and around the hills they were fighting in, but didn't see any reserve forces of darimun waiting to outflank them. Kent had done his job. This was it. This was all they would have to face to save their lands from being ravaged by the corrupted beasts.

She felt giddy at the thought that they were going to win the day, but stopped herself. The battle was not won until it was over—and it would be a while before they were done cutting down every last darim they had trapped. Until that time came, anything could go wrong.

And just as she thought that, Salevari saw the darimun organize for a last-ditch effort. A long line of large bear-darimun formed in the middle of their lines and pushed their way through until they reached the front rank of the human's center. The force behind their charge was too much for the humans to handle. Many went flying into the air, many more were trampled.

They are on the verge of breaking. The First One warned.

Salevari thought for a moment, an idea forming.

"Down," she called to her mount. As'ven obeyed instantly, diving toward the lumbering darimun who were trying to create an opening for their fellow beasts to escape through. She tapped on her Lyruun's serpentine back three times, signaling that he should breathe mist, which he did. The darimun below her melted away. A few snake-darimun tried to lunge at her as she flew past but she was just out of their reach.

The humans on the ground cheered as the Chancellor passed by and once again formed into a solid wall of shields, preventing the darimun from escaping. Satisfied that there would be no other major obstacles to break their lines like the bear-darimun had almost done, she directed As'ven to land so she could dismount and then sent him back to rejoin their air forces in wreaking havoc on the enemy in the middle.

The day wore on and the light of the sun began to wane as human and viatari fought together to slay every last darim caught between their lines. The darimun, lost in their bloodlust, never wavered as most armies might have done once it became clear that defeat was inevitable; and so the fighting remained fierce up until the last one was killed by a band of spear-wielding humans.

The last darim, once a wolf, reared back on its hind legs, snarling, and then toppled onto its side, unmoving. Then, there was silence.

Salevari looked around, breathing hard, as did most everyone else, expecting more of the Creature's forces to pour forth from the hills. But none came. The humans fell to the ground, exhausted, and simply sat there, staring blankly ahead with their mouths hanging open in shock.

The Chancellor saw Simon and Kent greeting each other happily on the battlefield. Kent's arm looked mangled but other than that he seemed fine. Simon looked untouched, though the dark red streaks of blood on his blades banished any thoughts Salevari might have had that he had somehow avoided the fighting. His eyes met hers and a new understanding seemed to pass between them. One of mutual respect and real trust.

They had won the day. And as this realization washed over the survivors, humans and viatari began to cheer. Many wept as they embraced each other, uncaring what race the other was, just happy to see that the other had made it.

The sun set, replaced by the moon shortly after, which shone a gentle white light on them all.

Well done.

Salevari grinned at The First One's simple praise. She swept the hair out of her face and wiped the sweat from her brow as she looked toward Aleganthia. There would be celebrations tonight—mourning, too, for those who had died in this battle—but plenty of celebrations.

She was not so deluded as to think this was any sort of final victory against the Creature, however, and especially not against The Turned One, but it was a victory for today. Their evil had been thwarted by the unity humans and viatari had mustered—a unity she had helped foster. Because of that, there would be some peace and time to prepare for the next battle.

When Felix returned from the Dwarven Kingdom and learned all that they had done, he would know it was because of her. She had led the charge, the planning—she had *led* like she had never had to lead before. And she had proven her own capabilities to herself. That, in itself, was something to celebrate.

CHAPTER FORTY-SIX

Thuradin wasn't sure what he would see when they arrived to Fungar Hrathor, but he knew it couldn't be promising. Would they come upon a pitched battle, with scores of dwarves lying on the ground killed by their own kin? Could they arrive in time to stop it? Worse, what would they discover of Felix and his viatari? Thuradin hadn't expected them to stick around and fight if war truly broke out, but if they wound up getting pulled into it. . . .

"Thuradin," Lyrie prodded him as their rams kept stride together, concern in her eyes. "Do nae dwell on it. Ye're going ta make yerself sick. Focus on the task at hand."

"I share yer worries," Dunkell said, and indeed the King's voice was ragged as if it was anticipating how much it would have to be used in the near future. "But Lyrie's right, there's no use in letting yer imagination run amok. We must see what the situation is for ourselves. Fungar Hrathor should be just ahead. Prepare yerselves."

After a few more minutes of riding, the tunnel opened into a spacious cavern and the five riders stopped, rooted to the spot. Borim shook his head slowly.

"I never thought I'd live ta see the day."

"While I don' have allegiance ta either side," Morteth

grimaced. "This cannae be good for business."

Thuradin was speechless. Before them should have been the sprawling mushroom fields of Fungar Hrathor with farmers tending to them. Now, the cavern was completely transformed.

Barricades lined up all along the tunnel they had just exited—though, by the looks of it, they had been broken through recently—and more were scattered throughout the cavern. There were a number of iron guard towers standing as tall as the tallest mushrooms where before there had been none. Fires raged in many locations, creating a smokescreen that covered the ceiling and dimmed the orbs of light that normally lit up the cavern.

A little ways ahead, two armies faced off against each other. The Council's forces stood with their shields locked. Edana's forces were the same. Neither side had engaged yet. It looked like the battle would take place just outside of the farming community that housed the cavern's population. However, as Thuradin studied the formations being utilized and guessed at what tactics might be in the minds of the commanders, he noticed a third party on the battlefield.

Right in the middle, between the two armies, stood Felix and his small retinue of viatari. They stood in a circle, their blades drawn and facing outward as if daring both dwarven armies to attack them at once. Based on the fact that the two hosts were holding their ground rather than charging into each other, Thuradin surmised that even now Felix must be holding off this major conflict with little more than his words.

"Come," he said, pointing at the viatari. "We must move quickly if we are ta reach Felix in time."

Lyrie gasped. "What are they doing? They're right in the

middle of it!"

"Typical," Borim shook his head but grinned with approval.

Dunkell nodded. "Aye, let us ride—and let me do the talking." He looked pointedly at Thuradin, to which the former commander raised his hands as a sign of compliance.

It was a short ride to the battlefield, but Thuradin feared that at any single moment their luck might break and whatever charm Felix currently held over the dwarves would fail. He pushed his ram as hard as he could, his eyes glued to the scene, waiting for the slightest sign of movement in the dwarven ranks. As they drew near, they could hear some of what Felix was saying.

"—listen! You do nothing here, accomplish nothing here, except death and destruction of your own kind and the world at large. This battle only serves the benefit of the Creature and The Turned One who will be thrilled to hear of the weakness of the dwarves."

"Ye dare call us weak?" That was Garadin. Thuradin recognized his booming voice anywhere, especially after the past few months of fighting with him. "Ye know nothing of this matter, viatari. Now, for the last time, leave this battlefield and return home! I do nae wish ta have ta fight ye as well."

"For once the Council and I are in agreement," yelled a voice that, while shrill, clearly demanded great respect. Thuradin guessed this was Edana Hartshield, the new viceroy of Kul'Kriegar. "If ye will nae honor our alliance and help us defeat these rebels, then ye are better off crawling back ta yer home. This is a dwarven matter—"

"This is a *worldly* matter!" Felix raged. It was not often that the elder viatari let anger get the best of him, but Thuradin could feel the heat in his words alone. "What you do here affects us all and may lead to our doom as well!"

"Halt!" Dunkell yelled. "Stop everything!"

They had made it. Dwarves from both armies gawked as they rode past and into the middle ground where the viatari were. Felix saw them and his face instantly broke out in relief.

"I have never been happier to see you than I am today, King Dunkell. And you, Thuradin."

"What am I," Borim muttered. "Rat feces?"

The elder viatari chuckled. "I am always glad to see you, Borim."

Dunkell turned his ram to face the Kul'Kriegarans. "My people! As yer King I command ye ta stand down. Edana Hartshield, if ye would join me here in the middle," he turned again, this time to face the Council's army, "and if members of the Council would oblige me by speaking with me in the middle as well?"

There was silence within the cavern. Then, a path formed within the Kul'Kriegaran ranks and a heavily-armored dwarf on top of an equally-armored ram trotted forward, battle-axe in hand. On the Council's side, five dwarves rode out toward the center, though at a much more leisurely pace.

Dunkell muttered greetings to both sides as they drew near, but their attention was not on him. The Council members glared at Thuradin, most of them with clear hostility, though he noticed Myrna's eyes no longer held the same intensity as the others. She looked sullen, like she would have rather not seen him. But there was no hatred, rather, she appeared conflicted. He wondered what might have changed since last they met in Tinas Gran.

"There's no time for this lunacy," Dunkell said, drawing everyone's attention to him. "I will get straight ta the point.

Edana, I appointed ye viceroy of Kul'Kriegar so ye could look after the people in my absence. Why have ye raised an army against them?"

Edana pulled back the visor of her helm, her face aghast at the accusation. "My King, I raised this army ta crush those who would oppose ye, so that the realm might return ta order and peace."

"A king is nothing without his throne. There is no king, you fool."

The King's gaze fell on the council member who spoke.

"Andarthol, I knew yer father well when I was a prince and was saddened when I heard he died in battle. But he would be ashamed of ye now if he heard ye speak. He valued loyalty ta the crown and the name of Ironaxe above all else."

"Enough of this," Garadin said gruffly. "What have ye called us here ta talk about this time, Dunkell, or are ye just wasting our time?"

"No, I'm hoping this time spent talking will benefit us all. I've called ye here ta convince ye—the both of ye—ta lay down yer arms and return ta yer homes."

Ayrie guffawed. "And why would we do that?"

"Because if we fight each other, we will nae have the strength ta repel the invasion the acolytes will make on our caverns. And then, we all lose."

"As we've told ye and yer viatari friends several times now," Garadin growled, his impatience mirrored by his ram's shuffling back and forth. "Those acolytes are nae a threat ta us presently. Right now, the biggest threat ta us are the burrowers digging just outside our caverns. Can ye nae hear it, Dunkell? It grows louder by the day! And ye've done nothing ta prepare us for this invasion."

"Come now Garadin, ye fought in Aleganthia with the viatari. I've heard yer report and Felix's own account of that time. I admit ta nae taking the imminent invasion seriously enough, but it was because I did nae wish for any misunderstandings between dwarves and burrowers ta grow from our people's unwillingness ta distinguish a difference. Who do ye think is controlling those burrowers—if there are any—ta dig inta our caverns for an attack? I can tell ye right now, it isn't the ones that Thuradin stopped us from massacring a year ago."

Garadin's eyes narrowed. "And how do ye know this?"

"Because I just returned from speaking with them."

"Aha!" One of the other council members who hadn't made too much of an impression on Thuradin the last time they'd met—Lunthir was his name—pointed a fat finger in the King's face. "Even now ye conspire with the enemy ta betray yer own people."

"They are nae the enemy," Dunkell glowered at the accusing dwarf. "And if ye don't mind, I'd appreciate it if ye kept yer fat, sausage of a finger out of my face." He turned his attention back to Garadin. "I speak truthfully, Garadin, the burrowers who live beneath our caverns are nae the enemy, but The Turned One is, and if there are any enemies digging inta our caverns it's going ta be her corrupted burrowers and humans. I promise ye that. I also promise ye that we cannae face them divided as we are."

Even as the King finished his promises, though, Thuradin knew it was to no avail. Garadin was already shaking his head. He turned his mount back to return to his army. The rest of the Council followed suite, though Myrna glanced back with uncertainty.

Thuradin wanted to call out to her, to bring her over to

their side, but considering they had just failed to stop the now-inevitable battle, he realized he didn't want her in the middle of it—literally—she would be safer away from him for now.

"Edana," the King turned to his viceroy, "pull the army back ta Kul'Kriegar. I do nae wish ta witness my own people slaughtering each other."

"My King, if we do that, they may take the fight ta Kul'Kriegar."

"Or they'll abandon the battle just as we are. Edana, as yer King I am commanding this of ye."

Edana thought for a moment; and for that moment Thuradin thought she would obey, but the sound of marching from the other side seemed to make her mind up for her. The Council had ordered its army forward. The viceroy's shoulders slumped.

"Ye are my King and I am loyal ta the crown. Which is why I will nae blame ye if ye strip me of my title, rank, and everything else I hold dear when we return ta Kul'Kriegar."

"Edana, listen ta me—"

"But," Edana continued. "My first duty is ta protect ye, sire, and right now that army poses an immediate threat ta yer safety. I intend ta bring my warriors forward so we may defend ye with our lives."

And with that the viceroy spun her mount around and rode off quickly back to her own troops where she signaled for them to charge.

"Wonderful," Felix sighed heavily. "What do we do now?"

Dunkell thought for a moment. "We go back ta yer original plan."

Felix blinked, confused. "I do not believe I understand

what you mean."

The dwarven King looked down at him with somber eyes. "Ye were standing here in the middle of the field with yer viatari without knowing if we would arrive. What did ye intend ta do had we nae arrived and the two armies had met for battle?"

"I suppose we would have held our ground and fought both sides to keep them from fighting each other."

Dunkell nodded. "I thought as much. That's exactly what we'll be doing, then."

Lyrie turned to Thuradin, her face grave. "This is suicide. We cannae hold back a single army by ourselves, much less two."

"I don't know, lass," Borim said, scratching his chin with the edge of his hammer. "Thuradin's gotten us out of many a bind in our lives, being the brilliant commander that he is. So, what say ye, commander, how shall we get out of this one with our lives?"

"We don't."

"Ah," Borim smiled and smacked his shield. "Brutal honesty for once. Just what I wanted ta hear."

The two dwarven armies did not rush in, but advanced with a slow methodical march. The dwarves on the front line smashed their spear shafts onto their shields repeatedly, creating a resounding and ceaseless din.

The viatari separated into two lines, each one facing a different host. Thuradin drew his twin-axes. They would die here; he was sure of it. Caught between two armies, both of which he'd be fighting against, he doubted he would last long. He glanced at Lyrie, saw the resignation in her face as she pulled her tight blonde bun apart and let her thick locks fall back onto her shoulders. She drew her sword and readied herself for battle and Thuradin couldn't help but think how glad he was that they had been able to spend some time together again before the end.

The dwarven armies now ran at a slow jog. There remained a few hundred yards between them but it would only be a matter of seconds before the two sides met. He noticed with some relief that there was no artillery from either side. For that he was grateful. The situation they were in right now was hard enough without having the earth exploding around them as well.

Dwarves from both sides were now close enough that Thuradin could see their faces. There was fear, anger, uncertainty. He didn't think any of them really wanted to be here right now.

But just as steel was about to clash against steel, the ground itself shook, stopping both armies in their tracks as everyone was forced to focus on keeping their footing. Many failed and were thrown onto their backs.

"What the—"

"Over there, look!"

"The cavern is breached! West side!"

Thuradin looked toward the western end of Fungar Hrathor, but couldn't see anything aside from a thick cloud of dust. He narrowed his eyes, waiting to see what might come out of this newly-made tunnel and prayed that whatever it was, in some way, might help them out of this dire situation.

CHAPTER FORTY-SEVEN

They were a fair distance away, but based on the lumbering gait of the intruders, their hunched over figures and egg-shaped heads, Thuradin knew them for what they were.

Burrowers. But judging from their size, he knew they weren't any regular burrowers.

"Fellow dwarves!" Dunkell bellowed, urging his ram to gallop back and forth between the two armies so all could see and hear him. "The time has come! Our caverns are under attack. I do nae care about the differences we have, royalist or separatist, join me now and fight ta protect our home from these invaders."

And with that the dwarven King rode off, his large two-handed axe raised high in the air as he let loose a war cry.

"Come on," Thuradin said. "We must protect the King." He, Borim, Lyrie, Morteth, and Felix and all the viatari moved at once to catch up to Dunkell. As he ran, Thuradin noticed a few other dwarves running alongside him, then a few more. He glanced over his shoulder and realized the two armies had merged.

For a split second he thought they had joined to fight each other despite the King's call for unity, but he quickly realized they were running alongside each other, both sides shouting their desire to protect the King. Those dwarves with rams shot ahead of everyone else, as did the viatari, to catch up to Dunkell before he reached the enemy by himself. Ahead of them, the farming community of Fungar Hrathor began to burn.

"Is it just me," Lyrie said with measured breaths. "Or are those burrowers attacking us."

"Aye, those are burrowers," Borim huffed. "But nae the ones we were staying with these past few weeks."

"Wha' do ye mean by tha'?" Morteth asked, two lethally curved daggers popping into his hands. "A burrower's a burrower. I cannae believe the Council was right about 'em diggin' through the mountain."

Thuradin frowned. If Morteth was under the impression that these were the same ancient enemy the dwarves had fought for centuries, he could only imagine how many other dwarves thought the same. To do so would be a mistake, and could cost them dearly in the future.

As they reached the outskirts of the farming community, the legion commanders began shouting orders at the top of their lungs for everyone to form ranks just outside of it. Thuradin nodded in approval. The army would be more effective as an organized unit rather than a mob pouring into the fight. Besides, so much smoke was coming from the town that he couldn't even see the enemy who might only be a few hundred yards in front of them—even now he could hear their guttural yells and brief clashes of steel.

From the smoke burst out Dunkell and the ram riders who had followed him as well as the viatari and a handful of dwarven civilians. It appeared the ram riders had already taken quite a few casualties, their grim faces hinting at how difficult this upcoming battle would be.

"Do we have artillery?" The King asked.

"Aye," Garadin said, all business. "I had ordered some from Tinas Gran ta join us. They should be entering Fungar Hrathor by now."

"Good, go tell them ta hold their position by the tunnels. We will need them ta buy us time for a retreat."

"A retreat? But—"

"Ye do nae yet know their numbers. I myself have caught only a glimpse. We cannae fight them here in the open like this. They will surround us and kill us ta the last dwarf."

"It is true," Felix said. "Even with us fighting by your side, our odds of defeat are all but certain if we stay here. We need to move into a more confined space so we can protect the flanks and control where the fighting occurs."

Garadin considered for a moment, then nodded. "Very well, I understand. I will relay yer orders."

As Garadin rode off, Dunkell addressed the army once again. "This is nae the time for arguments or great speeches, so I will only say this: the enemy that has invaded us are indeed burrowers, but nae the ones ye are all familiar with. Ye may nae understand yet, but ye deserve ta know the truth. These come from the outside world and, as I was told by those brave dwarves who fought them before with our viatari allies, have fallen under the corrupting control of one of the fallen acolytes who seeks ta destroy our world and our way of life.

"This battle will be more difficult than any previously fought, but we must fight ta the last! For ta fail will mean the end of our people. This enemy is nae ta be taken lightly. Fight smart, fight hard. Fight with the strength of all dwarvenkind at yer back and we shall emerge victorious."

The dwarves cheered loudly, many banging their axe heads

and spears against their shields in approval. The King leaned down from his ram and spoke with the nearest legion commanders. Thuradin was just close enough to hear him.

"The community here is lost. We've saved as many as we could. For now, we will fall back ta the tunnels and fight the enemy there. Order yer dwarves ta make all haste. I want two lines of fifty as a rear guard in case the enemy try to attack us while our backs are turned. They're ta hold the line at all costs."

"Aye, my liege!"

The commanders relayed the orders and in a single movement, the army smoothly turned and began making their way toward the tunnel to Tinas Gran. Behind them, two lines of dwarves formed just far enough away to act as a buffer in case of a sudden attack by the enemy.

Thuradin stayed with the rear guard. He would ensure that this line held at all cost. His blood boiled at the thought of the upcoming fight. His focus was so complete he didn't even notice who was standing next to him.

"This will be the first battle we fight together."

Thuradin's head snapped to his right at the sound of Myrna's voice. She didn't meet his eyes but she didn't need to. Her presence and words were enough for him to understand.

"Enemies approaching!"

Thuradin looked behind him, his focus returning, and saw a wave of corrupted burrowers rushing out of the smoke toward them, howling in bloodlust.

"Rear guard!" he called, raising his axe and pointing it at the oncoming burrowers. "Turn and lock shields! This line shall nae break no matter how many come at us."

The burrowers crashed into them like a rock slide but

the line of shields held strong. The burrowers' strength was just as Thuradin remembered. Several of them crushed the dwarves opposing them with a single swing of their weapons.

"Hold!" Thuradin yelled as he parried a sword away from his face. "Hold and fight! Do nae let them through!" He dodged another attack from the opponent facing him and lunged, planting his axes into the burrower's knees, severing them. The burrower cried out as he fell allowing Thuradin to finish him off.

Next to him, Myrna fought two burrowers at once with her short sword and iron buckler. Thuradin could only spare a few seconds to watch her. He could tell from her form and movements that she was a skilled fighter and for a moment a warm flow of pride filled his heart. He chuckled as another burrower tried to crush him with a hammer, but instead wound up without a head as Thuradin maneuvered swiftly around him.

His brief moment of pride turned ice cold, however, when he heard a sharp yelp to his right. He looked for Myrna again and saw her on the ground, her sword gone, a single burrower looming over her, weapon raised.

Thuradin's vision turned red. He roared furiously and charged into the burrower with all his strength, sending him flying into a fire raging in one of the nearby mushroom fields. The burrower screamed as the fire consumed him, but the dwarven commander had already moved on. He turned to Myrna and helped her back onto her feet. She retrieved her sword from the burrower she had run it through and then turned her gaze to him with a mixture of shock and a little bit of awe.

"Stay focused," was all he could say before the earth in front of them began to explode. The burrowers cried out in shock and a fair number of them fell, never to move again.

"Cannons," Thuradin grinned. "They've finished setting up. It's our turn now. Rear guard, fall back ta the tunnels!"

The cannons provided the perfect cover for the dwarves to disengage and run as fast as their feet would carry them toward the rest of the army. The burrowers faltered for a moment but the emergence of reinforcements from behind the smoke emboldened them and they resumed their push forward.

Artillery fired continuously, inflicting heavy casualties on the burrowers but more poured out of the smoke until it seemed like the whole cavern might be crawling with them. The explosive projectiles were enough to slow them down, though, and soon Thuradin and the rear guard had rejoined the others at the mouth of the tunnel.

There was no time for rest. Despite the continuous cannon fire, the burrowers had continued pushing forward and even now overran the cannons' positions, slamming into the front lines of the dwarven army. The fighting was fierce and the dwarves hacked away like never before; but even so, many fell to the initial charge and the dwarves were pushed back deeper into the tunnel.

Despite their heavy plate armor and well-crafted weapons, the dwarves had simply never encountered burrowers such as these. Their strength was overwhelming. Their greater size allowed them to reach over the front line and attack those behind. As the dwarves were pushed back even further into the tunnels, the burrowers began to crawl along the walls and ceiling so they could attack from above and to the sides. Dwarven archers and spear-throwers did what they could to pick them off, but they couldn't get them all.

Thuradin's face was splattered with blood as he cut through

one burrower's neck. He took a moment to wipe his eyes so he could see, but that was the only respite he was allowed before another challenger ran up to him.

They were everywhere.

Thuradin feared that the dwarves had lost their formation and that there was a free-for-all in the tunnel, which would spell doom for them. Their greatest advantage in battle had always been their disciplined formations; but under the onslaught of so many enemies, he wasn't sure if that would be enough.

"Pull back!" He heard Dunkell shouting above the cacophony of steel striking steel and the screams of the wounded and slain. "Pull back and reform!"

The dwarves did so, and the burrowers pressed their advantage. The newly formed dwarven line took the impact of a second charge without breaking, but the army as a whole was again pushed back deeper into the tunnel.

Hours passed with no end to the fighting. Thuradin's arms were heavy, his breathing was ragged. His feet could barely hold his weight, but he still managed to somehow find one last scrap of energy every time an enemy approached him. He knew that many others were not so lucky. More fell to the onslaught of The Turned One's forces with each passing minute as the army continued to be pushed back, now at a greater pace than before.

A soft glow appeared from behind the dwarven lines and Thuradin's heart fell as he realized that this glow was from the cavern of Dun Aldor. They had been pushed back all the way to Tinas Gran.

The thought infuriated him. He had seen the city fall under siege once before and it had nearly been sacked that time. He did not want to experience that again. He let out another war cry, mustering all the energy he could as he swung his twin-axes at one burrower after another. Having fought The Turned One's forces before, he was more capable in dealing with their increased strength than he had been during his first encounter. They fell easily to his axes, but there was always another to take their place.

Well, he thought grimly as yet another enemy fell before him, if they were to be pushed back to Tinas Gran, at least there would be reinforcements in the city. No doubt they would notice the horde of burrowers pouring from the tunnel in time to prepare the city's defenses. They needed those reinforcements. Their numbers were dwindling as dwarves left and right succumbed to fatigue and became easy targets for the burrowers.

Dunkell's voice again penetrated the raging chorus of battle. "Back! Back ta Tinas Gran! Inta the city streets!"

Thuradin dodged one burrower's axe swing and punched another in the face in frustration. He then swung around and brought his axes into the other burrower's belly before disengaging and running with the rest of the army out of the tunnel and into the city. Another rear guard tried to form to buy them time, but they were overwhelmed before a shield wall could even be formed. Guttural screams of victory came from behind as the burrowers pursued them into Dun'Aldor.

Bells rang and shouted orders came from all directions as Thuradin exited the tunnel and rushed toward the towering buildings of Tinas Gran. Already, a significant defensive force was forming along the city's streets to create bottle-necks. He estimated the reinforcements to number around one or two thousand. It wouldn't be enough to turn the tide of this battle, but it was better than nothing. And these would be fresh warriors, too.

The defenders opened their lines to allow Dunkell and his warriors to pass through, closing just in time to take the impact from the burrowers who had been close behind. Many who had survived the battle so far fell to their knees, gasping for breath, while the fresh defenders did their part to hold off the enemy. Thuradin looked around in dismay. The outskirts of Tinas Gran had already caught on fire and smoke filled the cavern. At this rate, they would be pushed back to the royal palace, just like last time.

How did this happen? Numbers were always a factor in any battle, but they'd had not only a significant number of Kul'Kriegaran warriors—the best—but also a decent force of viatari on their side, and still they had been pushed all the way back here.

Thuradin's mind briefly returned to the last time the dwarven capital had been under attack. That time, it had been besieged by regular burrowers and Ronorim had been King. The city had almost been lost then, and would have been had the Kul'Kriegarans not arrived at the last moment to attack the enemy's forces from behind.

There would be no rescue from Kul'Kriegar this time.

Dunkell's brows were furrowed as he sat on his bloodied mount, his axe dripping with gore. No doubt the King was trying to think of some way to save this battle, but Thuradin already knew there was no saving it, at least not as they were. In the front lines, some of the viatari did what they could to fight the burrowers, moving from one point to another rapidly to inflict as much damage as possible, but it didn't seem to be making a dent. The bottlenecks were holding, but they would not hold forever against such a large force of The Turned One's burrowers.

Thuradin stood up, his knees shaking slightly from fatigue. Others around him began to stand as well to rejoin the battle. He saw Ayrie pass him by, her iron, crescent-mooned spear caked in dried scarlet. He caught glimpses of Borim, Garadin, and Felix and was glad to know they were still alive and fighting. He hoped they stayed that way.

He looked past the fighting toward the tunnel they had been pushed out of and sighed. Perhaps his hope was in vain. Even now another wave of burrowers poured forth from the tunnel to join the battle.

Thuradin looked again, his breath catching. The burrowers that had just entered Dun'Aldor had also just charged, hacking and slashing, into the backs of their fellows. They were still a distance off and he couldn't be sure with his mediocre eyesight, but he thought these newcomers looked smaller, less equipped with armor and weapons.

And at the head of them was one wielding a brass scepter with a glowing red orb. This burrower was old, missing many of his teeth and at least one of his eyes were milky white with blindness. Gruk-Gruk swung his scepter like a club, smashing in the head of the first burrower he ran into, his army rushing in right behind him.

Thuradin gave a bark of manic laughter, his legs failing him again. All he could do was catch his breath and watch as something he had thought impossible unfolded before his eyes.

CHAPTER FORTY-EIGHT

Most dwarves could not comprehend what had happened. To most, it appeared that more burrowers had joined the fight against them, taking away any slim chance at victory they thought they had. The truth was just the opposite. Dunkell's face lit up with triumph as he drove his ram by each bottleneck proclaiming the news.

"Keep fighting lads! The burrowers have come ta save us!"

Garadin walked up next to Thuradin, watching the spectacle in disbelief. "He's gone mad."

Thuradin grinned at his cousin. "No, he hasn't. Take a closer look at the rear."

Garadin did, studying the enemy's back lines. After a few minutes, his eyebrows rose. "I don't understand."

"Right now, ye don't need ta," Thuradin clapped him on the shoulder and then went off to join one of the bottlenecks that looked like it was beginning to falter. "Just spread word about what's happening so our people don't accidentally start killing their own saviors."

With that he rejoined the battle. Gruk-Gruk's arrival was a miracle as far as he was concerned and he could not help but feel hopeful that they might be able to fight off The

Turned One's forces.

"Push forward, lads!" Dunkell's voice rang out from another street. "Push them out of our city!"

The dwarves yelled and shoved with all their might, forcing the bulk of corrupted burrowers to stumble backwards. The first rank of dwarves took advantage of this and struck down those that were vulnerable, felling many.

Thuradin made his way to the front and swung his axes with all his might, catching two unsuspecting burrowers in the head with the serrated edges. A fresh stream of energy surged through him as he fought, replenishing his mind and limbs. He dodged when he needed to, parried away what strikes he could, and like the veteran warrior he was, waited for the right moments to present themselves so he could deliver a killing blow. The burrowers fell one after the other, and with their access to reinforcements cut off by Gruk-Gruk's warriors, their numbers began to finally dwindle.

But they weren't the only ones to fall. Many dwarves were still fatigued from all the fighting in the tunnel and were too slow or weak in their movements. Far too often, Thuradin saw the head of one of his kin lopped off or smashed in or their body cut to pieces as The Turned One's forces fought with a fierce bloodlust given to them by their master.

A horn sounded from behind. To Thuradin's left a cluster of mounted ram warriors burst forth from one of the inner streets and mowed down the burrower lines, sending several of them flying. The rams screamed as they swung their horned heads back and forth as their riders reached down with sword, axe, and hammer.

The charge caused a ripple of uncertainty to spread along the enemy's ranks. Their attacks came with more hesitancy, more caution. Those in the front tried to move back to create space but they were prevented by their comrades behind them, causing a crush effect that spread through the ranks. More of The Turned One's forces fell and still the dwarves hacked away, now with a vengeance. The taste of victory was in the air, mixed in with blood pouring from the countless fallen bodies littering the streets.

The Turned One's forces continued fighting to the last, leaving nothing but corpses between the dwarven army and Gruk-Gruk's forces in the end. For a moment the two sides stood where they were, breathing hard, regarding each other, an eerie silence having fallen over the battlefield.

Dunkell rode out between them, his hands raised in a placating manner, and Gruk-Gruk strode forward with his scepter raised. The two leaders greeted each other and shared a few words before the dwarven King turned back to his people.

"Fellow dwarves," he said, his voice booming through the cavern. "As I'm sure many of ye witnessed, these burrowers are nae like the ones we have just defended our caverns from. In fact, these have just saved us from certain annihilation. Without their bravery and willingness ta face their own corrupted brethren, this battle would have been lost. Our great city would be a smoking ruin. Can anyone here deny this?"

Silence. A great many of the dwarves lowered their weapons, looking more perplexed than anything.

"This burrower standing next ta me is named Gruk-Gruk, he is their High Chieftain. When we first noticed the sound of digging drawing close ta our caverns, many of ye plotted against me, claiming I was doing nothing ta prepare our people for what was coming. I tell ye now, though, that all that time ye were wasting fighting amongst yerselves I used ta travel ta his realm and ask him for aid. Owing our people nothing, he gave it."

Dunkell scanned the length of his army, all of whom were looking back at him with somber, tired faces.

"If that doesn't speak ta their character, then I don't know what will. These burrowers are nae our enemies. And so, while we gather the bodies of our dead and give them the respectful burial they deserve, I invite Gruk-Gruk as well as the leaders of the Council, and Felix and his viatari ta join me in the royal palace so we may discuss the future our people can have together,"

Thuradin grinned. He had never known Dunkell to be a cunning political player, but with his invitation for talks to begin so soon after giving what once would have been a controversial speech—with no objections from the assembled dwarves—he had managed to regain and assert his authority as King. Anyone who might still oppose him would do so at their own peril since it would now look like they would rather fight just to fight, rather than advancing the cause for peace and dwarven unity.

He couldn't see any of the Council leaders, but he was sure they weren't too pleased with recent developments. They would have to submit if they valued their lives as well as their reputation.

There was a collective sigh of relief as many in the dwarven host collapsed onto the ground, exhausted from the battle. Weapons were put away and the remaining dwarves and burrowers worked together to move the dead and clean up the city streets. The Turned One's forces were gathered together in the rocky fields between Tinas Gran and the tunnel and burned. Entombed dwarves were moved to the numerous Halls of Stone directly beneath the city for their final resting place, and any of the burrowers Gruk-Gruk lost were returned to those who remained to do with as they saw fit.

Walking around and helping where he could, Thuradin saw Borim leaning against one of the far buildings in the city's outskirts. His head was heavily bandaged and his shield arm was in a sling, but he was still alive.

"Ye alright?" he asked as he rushed to greet his long-time friend.

Borim looked up at him with tired eyes. "Aye, but I think we're getting too old for this sort of business."

They both laughed and Thuradin helped him up, leading him deeper into the city so an Enurg'en could heal him properly. They passed a few small groups of burrowers as they made their way.

"Strange seeing them in our city, isn't it?" Thuradin said.

Borim nodded groggily, "Though, it's a nice change of pace nae having ta fight them."

They reached one of the many inner plazas where a group of Enurg'en had set up camp to heal the wounded streaming in from the battle. Thuradin heard a continuous drone of muttered chants as the Enurg'en called on the life forces of the body to heal the various wounds their patients had received.

With a groan, Thuradin set Borim down on a mat and patted him on the shoulder. "I expect ta see ye on yer feet in no time."

Borim grinned weakly. "Aye, see ye soon."

Thuradin turned to walk away and came face to face with Myrna, who stared deeply into his eyes for a long moment before casting her gaze to the floor. He couldn't help but see Agata looking at him through those eyes. His heart hurt briefly, but he pushed the pain aside for the moment. If his daughter had approached him, there must be a reason.

"It's over," she said softly. Her vibrant green eyes found his again and now he could see clearly that there was nothing but confusion. He understood why. He could only imagine what must be going through her mind now, having thought her father was a traitor, having thought the burrowers were the main threat to dwarven existence, only to be proven wrong on both counts.

"Myrna," Thuradin said gently. "Nothing's over." He reached out to brush her cheek, as he thought a father should do, but she instinctively jerked back. She blinked a few times as if just now recognizing what she'd done.

"It's over," she said again. "The Council is finished. The King has the people's loyalty once more. Those of us who led them against him," she grimaced. "We'll be lucky ta keep our heads, I think. So, before I go and meet my fate I just wanted—"

Thuradin pulled her into his arms before she could say more. Her body went rigid but eventually relaxed and he felt her arms wrap around him as well. "Hush now, my daughter. Dunkell will show mercy ta the lot of ye. Ye only did what ye thought was right for our people. He's nae so bad a king as ta overlook that."

They pulled apart and he couldn't help but smile in a way he hadn't in centuries.

Myrna regarded him curiously and, after a brief hesitation, nodded. "I'm yer daughter and yet I feel like I barely know ye. If ye'd like, if yer right about the King and he spares me for my part in this mess, if yer okay with it . . . I'd like ta get ta know ye, ta understand ye. I have questions."

Thuradin felt his heart swell so much from those words

that he thought it might burst and he would die on the spot. He couldn't think of anything to say so he simply nodded, struggling to fight back the happy tears threatening to mark his cheeks. They embraced once more and then Myrna walked off toward the royal palace. Thuradin saw Ayrie join her. The fierce, red-headed lass took him in, her eyes still rather cold. Finally, she inclined her head respectfully, then turned and walked out of sight.

"LYRIE!"

Thuradin and most of the dwarves in the plaza turned to see a fuming dwarf march in from one of the side streets. It was Hork Anvilgar. Thuradin would have recognized his bedraggled, black beard anywhere. It had been a few years since he had last seen him, though. It appeared that the past few years had not been kind to Hork.

Waiting in line under one of the many tents the Enurg'en had set up for healing, Thuradin saw Lyrie's bright, blonde head turn in Hork's direction. Her face paled. Thuradin saw her shrink away ever so slightly.

Thuradin's eyes narrowed. He had known Hork and Lyrie for a long time, but something between them was different. Alarms rang in his head.

"Lyrie, I've been looking all over for ye," Hork said loudly, dramatically. He swept her up in a bone-crushing hug and kissed her as he lifted her off the table she had been leaning on and put her on her feet. She staggered as he let go, clearly in pain. Hork put a hand on her arm to steady her, though he must have gripped a bit too hard as Lyrie winced.

"Come, love, we've much ta discuss back home. I've already got the rams waiting ta take us back ta Kul'Kriegar."

He led her, still gripping her arm, and she did her best to

keep up with his fast pace. They walked toward the stables, which Thuradin realized belatedly he was in front of, and, as they drew near, Hork looked up and locked eyes with him.

They stopped, Hork glaring at Thuradin and Thuradin glaring right back. He felt his blood begin to grow hot. This was not right. This was not the Hork he remembered. His hands balled into fists and he was vividly aware of how quickly he could draw his axes. But one look at Lyrie's fearful face and the violence left him, though he still felt a dull heat in his veins.

"Thuradin," Hork said gruffly. "I must thank ye for taking care of my wife while she left our home ta go on her . . . adventures."

Thuradin took a breath before speaking, just to ensure he could control his tongue. "It was a pleasure ta serve the King together."

Hork moved on, his grip on Lyrie as tight as ever. She glanced his way as she passed and there was something in her eyes he wished he could take away. Suddenly, he remembered all the times they had talked about Hork, how she had always looked like she wanted to say more. He remembered her relief when they had been forced to stay in Trek-ti. All the signs he should have seen became apparent in one instant.

But why do I care? A part of him said. *It isn't my business.*

The answer came quickly: because it wasn't right. He nodded to himself. That was why he was worried about Lyrie right now, why he cared. *But,* that small voice spoke up just loud enough for him to hear it one last time, *is that the only reason?*

"I realize we don' know each other too well."

Thuradin jumped as a voice spoke right into his ear. He whipped around and saw Morteth Shadowmeld, the assassin. Of all the dwarves to have survived the battle, he hadn't really been rooting for this one. Morteth must have seen his thoughts on his face. He chuckled.

"I'm glad ta see ye survived as well, commander, though ta be honest I don' think anyone expected anything less."

"I'm no commander," Thuradin retorted. "What do ye want?"

Morteth slid an arm around Thuradin's neck as if they were the best of friends. "'Tis nae really wha' I want, more wha' ye want. Or wha' I believe ye want. I'm only 'ere ta offer me services, is all."

"And what is it ye think I want?"

Morteth laughed again. "Oh, Thuradin, ye jest. 'Tis nae obvious? Anyone who witnessed yer encounter with Hork just now saw how ye were lookin' at his lass."

"Lyrie?" Thuradin blinked a few times. Had he been looking at her in any way other than with concern? He tried to remember, but the image of Hork dragging Lyrie away from the Enurg'en tents barged into his mind and all he felt was his blood boiling again. "I'm worried about her."

"Mmm," Morteth took out one of his daggers and began scratching his chin with the hilt. "Me thinks ye do more than worry. I mean, as I said before, we don' know each other too well—yet—bu' even I can tell *why* ye worry abou' her."

"Ye think I have feelings for her."

"I know ye do."

Thuradin guffawed and looked up toward the tunnel to Kul'Kriegar. Hork and Lyrie were only specks on the narrow staircase leading up to them now. He wondered what was going through her mind.

"Ye may be right," he admitted. "But even so, she's already a married lass. I've no business with her."

"Indeed," something in the assassin's voice caught Thuradin's attention, as if drops of venom had just dripped from his tongue. "But she doesn' 'ave ta be." He spun his dagger in the air, caught it, and sheathed it all in one fluid movement.

"Are ye saying—"

"Aye, I am, bu' let's nae blurt it out for the whole world ta hear, mind ye."

Thuradin paused to think about it, then shook his head in revulsion at the very idea that he would even consider such a course of action.

"I'll nae stoop ta yer level, assassin. Lyrie's a strong lass. She can handle herself. And if she ever needs help, she needs only ta ask."

"Well, that's nae very nice, bu' I'll forgive ye. In any case, she didn' look very strong ta me jus' now. Those kinds of situations? 'Tis hard for anyone ta break out of—I don' care who ye are. Ye should think it over, commander. Keep in touch. Let me know if ye change yer mind."

Thuradin opened his mouth to respond but before he could, Morteth had disappeared into the crowd, leaving him with nothing but his thoughts. And his thoughts were not good.

CHAPTER FORTY-NINE

They had all barely finished sitting down around the table when Meri got up and began to prepare them a meal.

"It's nothing much," she said, pulling out several vibrantly colored fish and tossing them into a pot with dried seaweed, sliced tubers and a variety of spices. "But it will refresh you and give you some energy. I'm sure you need it. It does not look like you've had a particularly smooth couple of days—especially you, Av."

"A lot happened," Avmoshir waved his hand, brushing away the comment. "We don't have time to go over it right now. Now that we're back, I want to put all our focus into retaking Zessarix. Auntie Meri, were you able to secure any aid from your connections?"

Meri placed a steaming pot in the center of the table, passing out red clay bowls for everyone to eat out of. Victria peered into the pot. It looked like a kind of fish stew, and despite Meri's claims about it replenishing their energy, she doubted it would. Decapitated fish heads bobbed up and down in the broth, staring back at them. None of the viatari looked eager to try it.

Only Tera, famished and without a hot meal for the last few days ladled herself a sizeable helping and began to devour it. Meri took some as well, as did Avmoshir. Finally, not wanting to appear rude, the viatari took some, making sure to keep their portions small.

Meri closed her eyes contently as she sipped from the bowl, licking her lips as the savory broth warmed her body. She then turned to her nephew, a troubled look taking over. "I have, though it's not nearly as much as I had hoped."

She stood suddenly and left the room, returning quickly with a scroll, which she unfurled. Victria saw that it was a map depicting the Sea of Scales as well as some of the human lands north of them.

"I've gained some insight about the situation that you will face in Zessarix, though," Meri continued, her eyes flicking between the various X's she had scribbled over a number of towns. "Koranam has seized control of almost every town in the sea—though Maleres and some of the villages close to us have yet to feel his overreaching arm."

"Is the military with him?" Avmoshir asked, a tremor marking his words.

"For now. The vashi in Zessarix believe you are dead, though rumors have begun to spread that you are not since no body was ever recovered. However, Koranam is still accepted as the Supreme Overseer; and the military serve him because of this. But, if you were to come into the scene, prove that you still live and are ready to lead, it might change things."

"Koranam would never just let him casually swim in, though," Serania said. "And I suppose we don't have the means to attack the city and force him out?"

Meri shook her head. "I spoke with the leaders of the neighboring towns and my friends in the temple as well as the High Priestess herself. We have a few waterseers and some volunteers willing to fight—I think about twenty in total—nowhere near enough for a direct engagement."

"But if I were to charge into Zessarix with them, wouldn't the military switch to our side once they saw me, as you said?" Avmoshir ventured.

"If we send you in with those volunteers as your 'army,' Koranam will easily misrepresent it as an isolated attack of dissenters before word can spread that you're leading them. Even without my son, there would be confusion among the guards and soldiers as they try to figure out what's going on. They would see the attack and feel compelled to repel it. You could be killed in the fighting before anyone understood what was going on."

Tera pursed her lips. "And with only twenty vashi, I don't think you would even be able to take on Koranam's main supporters, let alone the military."

Here Meri smiled, which seemed to lift Avmoshir's spirits—the task before them had begun to look impossible, but if Meri had an idea. . . .

"Not in an open, drawn-out battle, but if we were able to take them by surprise—"

Tera's eyes lit up. "We attack them during the night?"

"Yes. My sources tell me most of Koranam's agents are goons and criminals or spineless politicians. They will melt away once my son loses his power. However, there are some important vashi who are throwing their weight to him. They are the representatives from Kesmur and neighboring towns. I have a list of their names and where they live. They must die. Once they are dead, my son will stand alone with no one to help him—and then, perhaps, he will come to his senses and come home to me."

Meri glanced cautiously at Avmoshir, who nodded. "For

everyone's sake, I hope for that too. While I wish to take revenge on him for slaying my family, I do not want to inflict that same pain onto you, Auntie Mer. I will do all I can to see that no harm comes to him. But tell me, what of the people? Everyone believes me to be dead, but are they also on his side?"

Meri hesitated. "I've received mixed reports on that question. Some support Koranam and others don't, it seems."

"I have a feeling that more will be on Avmoshir's side rather than Koranam's in the end," Tessa grinned.

"What makes you so confident?" Victria asked.

"Do you remember when we were in Pashir and I had a little . . . outing with some of the locals?"

Victria frowned. She *did* remember that. She also remembered thinking what a foolish thing it had been for her to do, how unlike her. She had never known Tessa to open up to others so quickly and the way she had done so had seemed irresponsible. She wondered why she brought it up now.

"Well, while I was getting to know the locals there, I asked about Araxie to see what type of leader he might be. To see who we might be dealing with."

"He was a great—"

Tessa held up a hand, stopping Avmoshir mid-sentence. "Yes, he was a great leader—we know that now, but back then we didn't, and I wanted to find out as much as I could as quickly as I could since we had entered such an alien world. My point is, no matter who I asked, they could not stop talking about him and how great he was. The vashi were extremely loyal to Araxie. I believe that loyalty will easily pass on to his son."

Victria was impressed, and now she couldn't help but feel some guilt that she had thought so poorly of Tessa after learning the reasoning behind her escapade.

"Then we have only one obstacle to overcome?" Avmoshir asked, somewhat in disbelief. "Is there nothing else we must do? No other enemies to look out for? We simply assassinate the representatives who back Koranam and win Zessarix back?"

Meri chuckled. "It will not be as simple as you make it sound, but yes, it is just the one task—though, you must also personally face Koranam yourself while the representatives are being silenced."

Avmoshir nodded, a fire coming into his golden eyes giving him a look eerily like Araxie's.

"How soon can we leave?"

"I will have the volunteers and waterseers gather and supplies made available for your journey. If all the prep-arations go as planned, you will be able to depart by dawn. Oh!—"

Avmoshir wrapped his arms around Meri, nearly knocking her over.

"Thank you, Auntie Mer. Thank you. You can trust me to not harm Kor. I'll make sure he gets back to you in one piece."

A sad smile touched her face as she hugged the young vashi back. "Thank you for that, Av. Anyway," she stepped back, motioning toward the pot of stew still on the table, "I've got a busy day ahead of me if you want to leave by morning. Finish up this stew for me and put the pot away, will you?"

She left the kitchen with a little wave. Avmoshir sat back down, eagerness etched onto his face, hope burning in his eyes as he went back to eating. Victria had actually enjoyed the meal herself and was about to get another helping when

Serania cleared her throat.

"Victria, will you go on a walk with me?"

Victria saw in the wanderer's eye that there was some-thing more than just a walk on her mind. The questions Scorpus had asked them returned to her and she felt as if weights had been tied to her legs as she stood up and followed her out of the kitchen.

They went outside, walking down the streets casually, a small school of black and yellow fish circling them for the first few minutes. Once they were well away from the house, Victria expected Serania to explain what was on her mind but nothing was said. They continued in silence down several more streets. As the silence continued, the acolyte's questions grew louder in Victria's mind as well as the answers that had been given. There was one in particular.

"What the acolyte said about you—about what you did—is it really true?"

Serania nodded, though she did not look pleased. "Yes. When I first started my journey as a wanderer, I met a human on an old road that follows the Silent Mountains. At the time, I was looking for ways to become more powerful, for my own protection as well as to help defend Dalyr from any attack. He shared with me rumors of a Temple in the east, past the mountains, hidden in the center of a gargantuan forest with beasts and creatures unlike anything else in the world protecting it from any who wander in.

"He told me about the winged beings there who could grant me the power I sought. I went. I found the Temple and the winged beings. They had the power I wanted, the power I needed, for my people—and, at the time, that was all I thought about. Power like that, though, demands a unique sacrifice. The Guardians don't give things like this," she pointed to her hidden eye, "for free. And so, I gave them what they wanted. My own eye and—and my father's corpse. It was an awful thing I did. Still, I don't regret it. Rarely have I used the powers contained in this eye, but without it, I know I would not be here with you right now, alive."

"And your mother—Salevari doesn't know? Didn't she ever question what happened to your eye?"

"She knows only that I sacrificed my real eye for it, nothing else. And she must never know. No one must know outside of those who heard it at the Throne." Serania looked almost timidly at Victria, as if she expected her to shout out her sins to the whole world.

"I won't tell if you don't."

Serania chuckled. "Now we come to what I wanted to talk to you about. I always wondered why you seemed to hate me so much every time I visited Aleganthia."

"In my defense," Victria couldn't help but smile at the thought of how she used to behave, unaware of her own feelings, yet jealous of a potential—but impossible—relationship between Felix and Serania. "I didn't know you were his niece because he never told me."

"So, you discovered our relation. That explains why we suddenly became friends. How did you connect the dots?"

"Actually, Thuradin and Borim had to explain it to me."

Serania grinned. "Clever dwarves."

"Yes," Victria thought for a moment. "Come to think of it, they probably told me because *they* knew I had feelings for Felix."

"Well, like Natiari said before, everyone except for you and Felix already knew."

"You didn't."

Serania nodded. "Fair point."

They were silent for a moment, but now something else bothered Victria that she had to know the truth. "Do you really think Felix doesn't know?"

Serania's laugh seemed to bounce off the thick stalks of seaweed flowing around them as they passed through an underwater park.

"While Felix is incredibly clever and perceptive with the logical parts of life, I have learned that he is not the brightest when it comes to the emotional aspects. I don't think he has a clue. Which brings me to my next question: Will you tell him?"

Victria thought about this. She tried to imagine herself taking Felix to the side to speak with him alone, looking into his ancient red eyes, his calm, collected face, and saying the words out loud. She couldn't imagine anything past that, though. Would he be surprised? Embarrassed? Would he say the words back?

"I don't know if I should."

"You should."

"But what if—"

"Don't think about the 'what ifs.' Just do it. Especially now that you realize your own feelings. There is no reason to hide it anymore."

Victria supposed she was right, but that still didn't make it any easier. Every time she thought about how such an interaction might go, she felt her cheeks burn unbearably.

"Well, we have to survive this first."

Serania picked up a piece of broken coral and examined it as they walked. "Yes. Do you think this plan that Meri has thought up will work?"

"I don't know. Anything could go wrong. I hope it does, though. I'm ready to go back home."

"What will we do with Tera when this is over, then?"

Victria hadn't thought of that. She had grown so accustomed to Tera's presence she felt as if they had known each other for many years.

"I sometimes forget that she's human. I suppose we go our separate ways after this."

"I half-expect that she will choose to come to Aleganthia with us if we tell her it's time to part ways."

Victria smiled at the thought but shook her head. "I don't know if that could happen. It would be fairly difficult to explain why we brought a human to our home."

"Perhaps, or perhaps this could be the beginning of something new between humans and viatari."

Serania stopped walking and grew serious. "We may need the humans for this coming war, you know. They're as much a part of this world as we are. We have to start somewhere."

Victria crossed her arms, a new thought coming to mind. "Speaking of the war, I'm surprised by how easily we found the acolyte and brought him over to our side without encountering any opposition from The Turned One or the Creature."

Serania pursed her lips and looked up at the darkening waters. They had returned to Meri's house. The waters had darkened as they walked and now bioluminescent jellyfish were being placed above the streets by city workers to provide light during the night.

"I wouldn't be too sure of that," she finally said.

"What do you mean? There's been no burrowers or darimun or anything."

"We may not have seen their forces directly, but I sensed something was amiss ever since we gathered in the Assembly Hall with Araxie. Their presence is here somewhere, I know it. And I have a feeling we're going to uncover the shadows they've been working from before we return to the surface."

With that, silence fell. They had discussed much today, and yet Victria felt like there was more on her mind than before. The two viatari stepped into the house, and climbed the stairs, heading for their rooms to rest for the journey ahead. Outside, the jellyfish began to glow as the last of the sun's filtered rays were swallowed up.

CHAPTER FIFTY

Victria felt that time had sped up. Perhaps it was because she was anxious to be on the surface again—to be home again—perhaps it was her imagination; but the three days to Zessarix had not felt like three days. Within the next hour, they would be able to see the city sprawling out in the distance.

While the journey had felt short, it certainly had not been devoid of danger. Koranam's agents were still at large throughout the seas. They'd had to keep a constant lookout for them as well as for any sharks that might be under his waterseers' control. With no small amount of luck, they avoided detection from each patrol that came near their path, sometimes having to veer off course for several hours in order to avoid the larger ones.

At the front of the party rode Avmoshir, wearing full scale and hardened-coral armor. He wielded his golden harpoon and pointed it to the right. They leaned together and their mantas obeyed instantly, turning gracefully toward a set of large pillars standing next to a tall, rugged cliff.

Victria had no idea what these pillars might be for, but the cliff looked like it had been cut into. As they drew close, she saw that scattered on the ocean floor were carts upon carts of cut stone and the machinery used to harvest it from the cliff. Avmoshir steered his mount into one of the several caves that pocketed the side.

"This is a quarry," Victria observed the mining equipment below them as she entered the hollow. Even in this cave there were light fixtures of everlasting fire staked into the ceiling as well as smaller carts fixed to tracks.

"It is, indeed," Avmoshir said, helping her dismount. "This place is where we harvest almost all of our marble to build our towns and cities."

"Won't someone discover us, then?"

"No one mines at night. The workers have all gone home. We'll be safe."

The rest of their party joined Avmoshir as he moved deeper into the cave. He paused after a few minutes and scanned their surroundings, his scaled body quivering as he felt the water's vibrations for any possible occupants besides themselves.

"This is deep enough," he finally said. "We shall rest here until the night matures."

They broke off into small circles to eat and drink and rest from the journey while Avmoshir remained where he was, eyes lingering from one vashi to the next.

"How do you feel?" Victria asked, sensing the young vashi's unease.

"Like I don't know what I'm doing. These vashi's lives are in my hands, as are yours. What if this is a mistake and we all die?"

Victria placed a firm hand on his shoulder and forced his eyes to meet hers. "Mistakes happen. Mistakes always happen. Gods know I've made plenty in my life. But you must not let that breed doubt within yourself. Fight through it. They—

we—need you to fight for us, just as all of us will fight for you."

Avmoshir's face hardened a little and he nodded. "You know, my father used to tell me something similar. He would say hope is the light we must always fight for. To not do so means we remain in darkness."

"I wish I had known Araxie longer," Victria said truthfully. "I think he would have been a great friend to the viatari."

The mood in the cave shifted as the hours dwindled away. Tensions were high. The water seemed to boil with it. They all gathered at the mouth of the cave, Avmoshir in front, facing them.

"You all know the plan. Remain vigilant. Watch each other's backs. We will cross into Zessarix together, but once we've reached the city center, we will split into our set groups. Each one of you knows your target. Our enemies cannot live through the night. And we must not be seen. No alarms can be raised."

Everyone nodded their understanding. Avmoshir, satisfied by this, turned and led them out of the cave. They would swim into the city, rather than ride their mounts. Presenting themselves as smaller targets would offer them a better chance at avoiding detection by the city's sentinels.

They swam over Zessarix, just under the surface of the ocean. Victria could feel the waves above pushing and pulling her with them as she swam. Beneath her spread a sprawling network of lights as the bioluminescent jellyfish floated in place.

With a sharp kick, Avmoshir split from the group with nine of his vashi, one a waterseer, heading for the Assembly Hall at the center of the city. They would cut off any fleeing representatives and fight off any counterattacks Koranam's guards might attempt while the assassinations were underway. The others went their separate ways as well—Victria breaking off with Tera toward the back end of the city. Their target was Alezar, a representative from the town of Zol. He was one of the more vocal supporters of Koranam's and had close ties to smuggling guilds which Meri had discovered were supplying her son's goons with quality weapons.

That ended tonight. Alezar lived in the Meadows section of Zessarix, an area populated by the city's elite. Here the coral houses rose several stories above the ocean floor and were built more for aesthetics than practicality. Victria thought all the houses here were gaudy and unnecessary, but nothing compared to the huge waste of resources that was Alezar's home.

Lamps of everlasting fire burned in all the rooms within and hung off several posts outside in a sprawling garden.

"Oh yeah," Tera said, her distaste clear. "I know this type. We have too many of them in the human world as well, unfortunately."

"All the more reason to take him out."

They sank down to the ground level. It would do no good to swim straight into the house. Avmoshir warned them that these homes would have top-tier security measures prepared for any intruder. Each window and door would be equipped with vibration shells, which were tuned to detect vibrations made in the water specifically by swimming within a certain range. No, a direct approach would only get them caught. If they wanted to break in, they would have to walk and use the shadows from the surrounding greenery and the building itself to sneak their way in.

That wouldn't be easy either, they quickly found out.

Guards were everywhere, patrolling the narrow passages, stationed around the entrances, some were even on the roof. Victria and Tera pressed themselves against a thick bunch of kelp as one guard strolled past.

"It's no use," Tera seethed. "If we want a chance at entering that house, we have to take out some of these guards."

"Can't you just knock them out or something?" Victria asked. She didn't want to kill any vashi if she didn't have to. Guards were generally just regular people doing a job.

"Oh, dear, are you feeling sorry for them? Look at their uniforms and the insignia on their chest. It's the same one as those who attacked Araxie's home and killed him."

Victria saw what she meant. They weren't wearing masks this time, but they still wore the same style of black leather armor as the ones they had found dead in Araxie's home. She searched for the insignia and found it embedded into their chestpiece. Three fish pouring out of an endless hole.

"You're right," she said, all sympathy gone. "But which one do we start with? We can't fight them all."

"No, we cannot. Nor would I want to. It would take too much time and our target would surely be alerted to our presence and escape." She pointed at the guard who had just walked past them. "Start with him. Come in from be- hind and don't let him hear you. It must be a silent kill. I will go for the one standing by the corner of the house. Meet me there when you're done."

Tera drew her daggers from her boots and melted away into the shadows. Victria gritted her teeth and pushed her- self out of hiding, also using the shadows as best she could to keep her own from betraying her. Her target was taking his time with his patrol. He yawned, a strange mix of hissing and gurgling. Clearly, he was tired from a long day, his senses would not be at their best. He might not even re-cognize the warning his vibrating scales naturally gave him as Victria approached.

Only a few steps away now, Victria drew her dirk and with one swift lunge brought it to the vashi's neck and drew her arm back. There was a brief gasp and then a soft gurgling as he drowned in his own blood, then silence. Moving quickly now, Victria pushed the body to the ground, where it floated limply, and dragged it inside one of the seaweed clusters. It would do no good if one of the other guards happened upon the body.

She crouched back into the shadows and moved carefully to where Tera said she would be. As the corner of the house came into view, she noticed there was no guard, and no sign of Tera. Victria glanced around and behind her and then slowly inched her head around the corner to check the entrance.

Two guards were stationed there. Both wielded long, silver harpoons and stared blankly ahead. They never noticed the little human inching toward them from the side. Victria wanted to call to Tera and tell her to come back—there had to be a better approach for attack—but she bit her tongue as Tera inched ever closer to her targets.

She moved carefully, using miniscule and slow move-ments so she didn't catch the guards' attention through their peripherals. Finally, close enough that she could stretch her hand out and grab them, she made her move. Faster than a snake, Tera was up and behind the guards, her daggers flashing under the green flames surrounding them. The guards were dead before their next breath.

Victria helped push their bodies into the corners of the portico and together they went inside, careful to make sure the door didn't creak as they opened and closed it. Once inside, Victria felt more in her element. They dried instantly and now were grounded to the floor without any sense of weightlessness. It limited them in terms of how they could approach the room Alezar stayed in, but it would also affect the guards. No longer surrounded by the ocean, they would be much more awkward in their attacks, less agile, which evened the playing field if they came head-to-head.

They made their way up the grand marble steps in the center of the room to the second floor. The small green flames encased in glass lamps lining the corridors did little to light their way but it still was easy work to find their target's room. At the end of the corridor stood what was the largest and most elegant door of the whole house. There was no competition.

"Open it slowly," Tera whispered. "Just a crack, so I can see if there are any guards inside."

The two pressed themselves against the double doors, making themselves as small a target as possible, and slowly pushed against it. A small crack appeared in the middle. Tera leaned in to take a look.

"Anything?"

"Just the representative. He's in bed. I think he's alone."

They shared a look and nodded. It was time. Victria had killed many times before, but only in battle. Never had she performed an assassination, murdered someone in cold blood. For a brief instant, she wondered if she would be able to do it.

"On three," Tera mouthed, daggers at the ready. "One . . . two . . . three—"

They burst through the doors and rushed for the bed where the representative slept. Victria raised her blade into the air, aiming its point for the vashi's heart, but suddenly she felt something heavy tackle into her. She managed to keep hold of her weapon and rolled as she hit the floor. Looking around, she saw that they had been attacked by two guards. Victria wasn't sure where they had come from—perhaps they had been standing just to the side of the doors, out of sight from Tera's initial probe. Whatever the case, now she and Tera had to kill them, and kill them quickly, if they hoped to reach Alezar, who had woken from the noise.

His eyes bulged when he noticed Victria and Tera and realized their intentions. Whimpering, he gathered the sheets of his bed around his body, reaching for the silk robe hanging off the footboard.

"Eyesss on me, ssstranger," the guard who had tackled her hissed. "I am your opponent."

Victria tried to sidestep him, but he lunged at her with his curved sickle. She parried it just in time but was forced to step back as the vashi drew a second sickle from his back and swung it as well. He laughed with a rasp in his voice.

Tera was doing no better. The guard she faced carried a thick heavy net and any time she tried to step in close enough to use her daggers, he would simply spread it in an attempt to capture her.

Meanwhile, Alezar had managed to get dressed, grab a few of his belongings and was now inching his way toward the glass-paned door at the far end of his room, which led to a balcony. Victria bared her fangs. If he reached those doors, he would be able to make his escape and they would never catch him.

She tried again to sidestep her opponent, but this time she ducked simultaneously, knowing he would aim his first swing where he thought her head should be. She felt the air vibrate above her and then lunged with her own weapon, aiming for the vashi's heart. The guard dodged just in time and countered with his second sickle, tearing into the length of Victria's back with its sharp blade.

She cried out, jumping away before another attack could strike her. The pain in her back was fierce. The blade had cut deep, but already she felt her regenerative abilities healing the wound. She looked for the representative again.

Alezar was now within reach of the balcony doors. He scrambled for the latch and undid it, pushing the doors open with a triumphant cry. Knowing she only had seconds, she did the only thing she could think of, and threw her dirk like a spear straight into Alezar's back. The representative jerked with a sharp gasp as the blade ran through him. Blood seeped into his silk robes and he coughed as he sank to his knees and fell against the wall beside him.

The guard she had been fighting hissed furiously.

"Victria!"

Victria expected to feel the guard's sharp blades tearing into her back again, to feel her own blood seep through her leather armor. But the feeling never came, and instead the only thing she felt was cold fear as she heard Tera cry out next to her. She turned to see the human crumple before her as the guard, who had aimed his attack for Victria had instead run his blades through Tera's midsection.

A pool of blood began to form beneath the human wanderer, who was still breathing but with difficulty. The next thing Victria felt was an intense heat as rage burned through her. She was unarmed, so she grabbed the first thing she found—one of the lamps full of everlasting fire—and threw it at the guard without a second thought.

The guard's eyes widened with fear as the lamp raced

toward him but he could not dodge it. It hit him square in the face and the next thing Victria knew, the room had exploded with a bright green light. She watched in shock as the vashi was consumed by the everlasting fire, his screams piercing her ears and forcing her to close her eyes. She only opened them again once the shrill noise had stopped. The vashi lay on the ground, still burning, his crisp body eaten away and unrecognizable. She looked for the second guard but found that he was already dead. Tera had managed to kill her opponent before throwing herself as a shield to save Victria.

She turned her attention to her human companion, kneeling to inspect the wound, and found it had gone deep. She could not tell how extensive the damage was, but knew there was no way Tera could survive this without help. And soon. But she was no Enurg'en or a waterseer, she could not heal like they did.

"Tera, you fool," Victria felt her eyes burning. "Why?"

"He would have had your—head—" she coughed, droplets of blood spraying Victria's face. "You might—be viatari, but even you—even you wouldn't survive that—dear. Now go. There's nothing—nothing you can do for me. Avmoshir still needs you."

"Don't," Victria said firmly. She couldn't heal, had no training with such things, but even she knew if Tera was to have any chance, she had to stop the bleeding. She found another silk robe in Alezar's closet and bunched it up, pressing it against Tera's midsection and placing the human's hands on it. Tera groaned.

"Put pressure and keep it there. I'm getting you out of here." She went over to Alezar, who stared blankly ahead of him, and ripped her dirk out of his back, sheathing it after wiping the blade on a clean part of the vashi's robes.

Carrying Tera was no easy task, especially in the water. The human was still conscious for now, but Victria knew it would not be long before she succumbed to her wounds. The Assembly Hall where Avmoshir and his vashi had gone was mercifully nearby and as they approached it, Victria could hear fighting. They were only short clashes, no prolonged battles were taking place, but they were there.

Once she was past the main entrance she saw more evidence of the fighting. Several vashi bodies floated around her, rivulets of red mist spreading through the water. A few of them looked to be from Avmoshir's group, but the vast majority of the dead were representatives and a few of Koranam's guards.

"We're almost there, Tera, just hang on," Victria groaned. She was exhausted, her strength had run out long ago and her muscles burned as if they had been touched by everlasting flame, but she pushed on, knowing that for her to stop would mean certain death for the first human she had ever come to care for.

Tera didn't respond, but the viatari could hear her labored breathing so she knew she was still alive. She found the large doors leading into the room where the Assembly gathered and stopped. Voices rang from within, and she recognized both. She pushed through the doors, Tera still clinging onto her back, only to see Koranam standing before her, his back turned to her. Ahead of him, sitting on the seat of the Supreme Overseer, golden harpoon in hand, was Avmoshir.

Looking around, she found the waterseer he had brought with him, treating the wounds of the remaining vashi from Maleres. She raced toward him, gently lying Tera onto the floor. She was deathly pale now, her eyes barely open. The robe Victria had found to stop the bleeding was soaked through.

The waterseer noticed her and saw Tera. There was a moment of hesitation from the vashi, as if he were deciding whether he should try to save a human's life.

"Why are you just standing there?" Victria said, steel in her voice. "Can't you heal her?"

"I can," the waterseer replied, though he still looked hesitant. "Ssshe isss human, though."

"Yes, and she just helped Avmoshir reclaim his title as Supreme Overseer, helped save your people from Koranam's bloodlust and warmongering. And if you don't help her simply because she is human, I will suck out every last drop of your life-energies until you crumble into dust. You will wish you had died a normal death like she will."

The vashi paled and finally nodded, kneeling at Tera's side, feeling her wound and inspecting the damage. There was nothing more Victria could do, and so she stepped away to give the vashi room to work. As the waterseer began using the water around them to heal, Victria's attention shifted to Avmoshir and Koranam, as their back and forth finally registered to her.

"Surrender, Koranam. Your guards have fled, your allies lie dead. You have no one left to save you. I am the rightful Supreme Overseer, and you must give me your loyalty."

"The only thing I must give you, little one, is the taste of my blades." Koranam drew his curved swords and settled into a fighting stance. "Fight me," he hissed. "Fight me for the right to rule the vashi. You say I am alone, that my allies are dead. Hah! I have more allies than you realize, allies who you cannot even comprehend—and I am eager to show you their power. Fight me, little one, just like old times."

"Don't be a fool," Avmoshir said, his voice soft but full of anger. "I am not patient like my father was and it is only my promise to your mother that keeps me from spearing you on the spot—but do not think I will keep from striking you down if you continue to resist. For the sake of your mother who loves you dearly, surrender."

More voices sounded from the corridors leading into the Assembly Hall. Victria recognized them as her viatari companions. She was relieved to learn they had survived the night.

"You cannot win against all of us," she said. Koranam's head jerked in her direction, causing her to gasp. His eyes were completely black, and there was a sickeningly familiar aura surrounding him, as if he emitted nothing but darkness.

"Kill him, Avmoshir."

"What?" Avmoshir balked. "Do not interfere—"

"Kill him, *now!* It's too late to save him. He has been corrupted by The Turned One."

Koranam's lips curved into a wicked smile, revealing fangs as black as his eyes. He spoke, but his voice was mixed with feminine tones, tones dangerously light and dripping with venom, "So, girl, you remember me, do you?"

"Koranam?" Avmoshir held his harpoon before him. "What is this? What have you done with my cousin?"

"Sit down, boy," Koranam mused. "You may have taken back control of your vashi, but it shall not be for long."

"Release him!"

Koranam put a scaled finger to his chin as if he were thinking. "Mmm, I don't think I will. I believe I shall have many uses for this puppet in the future," he laughed terribly, manically. "Until then, boy."

A dark sphere began to envelop Koranam. Before it had completely encircled him though, he glared at Victria one last time. "Do not think you have won, girl. I shall return."

The sphere completed its enclosure and Koranam faded away as if he had been just a shadow.

"What happened?" Avmoshir asked, his eyes bewildered as he turned his head this way and that. "Where has he gone? Someone find him!"

"He's gone," Victria muttered. She should have known, should have sensed something just as Serania had. Of course The Turned One had been here with them, working against them, fighting them every step of the way to keep them from achieving their goal. But what could she have done differently? It was possible Koranam's corruption had not been complete when they first arrived. Had they acted— No, she shook her head. There was no point in thinking of what could have been. It would not change what had happened.

Running footsteps approached from outside and a second later, Serania and the rest of the viatari barged into the Assembly Hall, their weapons out, just as the last vestiges of black smoke from Koranam's escape cleared away.

"What happened?"

"It was The Turned One all along. You were right Serania," Victria turned to Avmoshir, who stared blankly at the spot where Koranam had been standing only moments before. His eyes met hers.

"Is there really no saving him? What will I tell Auntie Mer?"

"The Turned One has him now. Avmoshir, I'm so sorry."

CHAPTER FIFTY-ONE

Thuradin felt as if he hadn't smoked in decades as he puffed on his pipe, relighting it for the umpteenth time that day. White smoke drifted into his face and he breathed in the sweet scent, trying to soak it in and enjoy it, but it wasn't the same.

His feet dangled over the southern wall of Aleganthia as he thought back to the last time he was in this position only a couple months ago. Then, the concept of relaxing and taking in the day had come easily enough. But these days he found his mind too cluttered to simply let go.

Though a few weeks had passed since the dwarves had narrowly avoided a civil war, he still felt conflicted by the aftermath. Morteth's offer came to the forefront of his mind, dangling before him like a carrot on a stick. He shook his head violently, wishing he could send the thought flying. He was not that kind of dwarf. He felt ashamed that he was even still considering such a course of action.

And yet, he could not help but dwell on the fearful visage that had crept through Lyrie's face when Hork came into the picture.

"Ye didn't even say goodbye ta her, ye coward. Ye have no say in this matter," he muttered, sucking on his pipe so much that the wooden bowl grew too hot for him to hold and he had to let it rest beside him to cool down.

Thuradin stared glumly ahead with eyes unseeing and sat like that for several minutes. Viatari guards patrolling the ramparts behind him cast curious glances his way as they passed by. He blinked. In the distance appeared a line of six horses, slowly making their way toward Aleganthia. They were approaching from the southern plains and it would only be another hour or so before they reached the borders of the forest.

A lightness entered his heart as he realized who these riders must be. It had been months since he'd seen Victria, one of his first and greatest viatari friends. Her return was good news, though he wondered who the extra rider in her party could be. He knew for a fact that she had left the city with only four others.

"Lad," he called to the nearest sentry and pointed toward the riders. "Ye might want ta fetch Felix. Tell him Victria has returned."

The guard nodded and rushed down the rampart steps into the city below, making his way to the keep. Meanwhile, Thuradin remained where he was, watching Victria's progress as she and her party drew near. Finally, it came to the point where he could make out their faces and he slapped his knees, laughing loudly as Victria waved up at him.

"It's good ta see yer shining face again, lass," he called down to her. "I'll be down in just a second."

Victria flashed him a winning smile and made her way through the gates, which opened before her. Behind her, sitting lazily on their saddles rode Tessa, Natiari, Madira, Serania, and then someone Thuradin had never seen before. He dumped the remaining leaves of his pipe bowl onto the parapet so the wind could take them, and made his way down to the city streets.

They had known for some time that Victria would be returning soon, since the acolyte she had been after, Scorpus, had teleported into the Watcher's Quarter right next to his brothers a week and a half ago. It was obvious she had been successful, but that didn't keep them from wanting to hear what happened.

By the time Thuradin reached them, Victria and her companions had already dismounted, their horses taken away to the stables by viatari workers. The dwarf and viatari embraced. Thuradin couldn't help but give her a great clap on the back as he took in her earthy smell—though he noticed it was now mixed in thoroughly with a fresh layer of saltiness.

"Tessa, Natiari, good ta see ye as well."

The two viatari grinned down at him and inclined their heads in greeting before saying their goodbyes to Victria and making their own way through the city, Madira in tow.

"They've been anxious to be back here," Victria explained. "We all have. I'm sure they're heading home to take a long, hot bath."

"I don't know about you, but I'm going to keep my distance from water for a while," Serania grimaced, coming up to them. "Hello, Thuradin. It's been some time."

"Aye it has, what—"

The two viatari suddenly tensed, their eyes wide and alert as they finally took in their surroundings.

"Humans," Serania gasped.

"In the city?" Victria added, confused.

Thuradin glanced over his shoulder and saw several men and women gathering by a corner to peer curiously at the new arrivals. He laughed.

"Aye, I was as shocked as ye when I came back. There's much we must catch up on."

"Came back?" Victria repeated. "Where did you go?"

"Home," Thuradin said, and with that word the confusion he had felt before returned and he felt a sudden weight press down on his shoulders.

"You went back to the Dwarven Kingdom?" Victria's eyebrows shot up. "And they didn't kill you?"

Thuradin stroked his beard as he pondered how he should go about telling his story but, in the end, he decided he did not wish to discuss the events that so troubled him—not even to Victria—not yet. Instead, he changed the subject.

"Who's that lurking behind ye?"

"Oh, that's just Tera," Serania said, waving her hand absently.

"Tera?"

The stranger stepped forward, lowering the hood she had been wearing and revealing shoulder-length, curly blonde hair and gray eyes. Thuradin was surprised to see she was human, but only for a moment.

"A human, eh?"

"Yes," Victria grinned. "A remarkable one at that. She helped guide us to our goal and then some."

"I'm more than capable of introducing myself, dear," Tera said, though there was humor in her voice. "You don't have to keep talking about me like I'm some exotic pet you've captured." She bent down to examine Thuradin, "I've met very few of your kind, but judging from your short stature, you must be a dwarf, am I right?"

Any other dwarf might have taken offense at the mentioning of their height, but Tera made her statement with such boldness Thuradin couldn't help but let out a bark of laughter.

"Aye, lass, that I am. Let me be the first ta welcome ye ta the city of Aleganthia," he bowed respectfully and then turned to the viatari. "Come, I sent a guard ta fetch Felix, but let's head ta the keep and meet him there. I'm sure he'll be eager ta see ye—yer mother as well," he added, nodding to Serania.

They made their way through the cobblestone streets, listening to each other's accounts of their recent adventures— though Thuradin made it a point to avoid sharing his own, choosing instead to share the heroics of others. Tera was silent the whole way, content with looking around the city and observing her new surroundings. Before too long, they made it to the main plaza and were only a few feet from the steps leading into the keep when its doors burst open.

Felix and Salevari stood at the entrance, their faces beaming as they saw Victria and Serania making their way up. They rushed down the steps, Salevari leading the way as she pulled Serania into a tight embrace. Felix was close behind and as he reached the bottom of the steps where Victria waited, he stopped and stood there, unsure of what to do. The two locked eyes, and Thuradin put his hand to his lips to smother a grin as he recognized a new, fiery look in Victria's gaze.

"Victria—"

"Felix, you don't know how good it is to see you again."

Felix stood there, his mouth agape like he wanted to say the same thing but nothing came out. Salevari pulled away from Serania and looked back at her brother, bemused.

"If it's okay," Victria continued, determined. "I want to discuss something with you in private."

"O-of course," Felix stammered and cleared his throat. "You can speak with me whenever you wish, Victria. You know I can hardly ever deny you."

Victria grinned sheepishly. "Then how about right now?"

Everyone watched the exchange with knowing looks as once more words seemed to fail Felix. Thuradin could hear the gears turning in his mind as he tried to think of what to say.

"Now? Now . . . yes, of course. Let's just—"

But just then a guard ran into the plaza, eyes scanning the area in a frenzy until finally they landed on Felix.

"Felix," the guard said, the urgency plain in his voice. "Sire, a rider from the east."

Felix's face fell back into its typical solemnity. "That must be from the party we sent to the Eastern Wald. Pulaneus has sent word," he spared a glance at Victria, unsure, "I am sorry, truly, but we must talk another time. Is that alright?"

Victria nodded, though she couldn't hide her disappointment.

"Take us to this rider," Felix commanded, his attention back on the guard.

"Sire, he should be here any moment. I ran ahead, but he was already making his way when I left my post."

Just as the guard finished saying this, out of the corner of his eye Thuradin could see another figure entering the plaza on horseback. He was caked in dried blood and looked tired, but didn't appear injured—at least, not recently.

"Fetch him food and water," Felix ordered as he walked forward, snagging the reigns of the messenger's horse and using his other hand to help steady the rider. "Rilaf, is that you?"

The messenger nodded, swaying in his saddle.

"Come, help me get him down."

Salevari and Serania rushed forward and, together, helped pull Rilaf off his saddle and onto the ground, where he collapsed into a sitting position.

"Been riding for days," he croaked, his voice hoarse and scratchy. The guard who had announced his arrival rushed back with a jug of water and Rilaf took it, draining it in seconds. If this viatari had come to deliver news about the expedition sent to retrieve the acolyte in the Eastern Wald, Thuradin didn't think the news was going to be good. Felix was of the same mind.

"What has happened?"

"They were all over us," Rilaf shuddered, his eyes closing as he took a deep breath. "I shouldn't even be here."

Victria knelt in front of the worn viatari, her calm, red eyes level with his. "But you *are* here, and for that we're grateful. Now it is important that you tell us what happened. It doesn't look like you met the east with success."

Rilaf let out a hollow laugh and shook his head. "We weren't even close. The forest over there is alive with murderous beasts. To make matters worse, it seemed to us that The Turned One and the Creature had unleashed every servant available to them to thwart us during our journey.

"They attacked us in the middle of the night. We were overwhelmed before we could even wake up. Felix," Rilaf stared deep into Felix's eyes, his own dangerously close to madness, "they've taken the acolyte. We failed."

"And Pulaneus? The others? What happened to them?"

Rilaf only shook his head but that was answer enough. Felix grimaced, nodded, and patted the viatari on the back numbly. He turned to a nearby guard.

"Take Rilaf to the healer's hall. Have them treat him for

the trauma he has undoubtedly suffered."

The guard saluted and scooped Rilaf's arm over his neck, carrying him away.

Felix closed his eyes, thinking for a moment, then made a beeline for the keep. Everyone followed, silent, waiting to see what he would do. He led them up the stairs. They climbed flight after flight and it did not take long for Thuradin to realize where they were going.

After several minutes of this, the stairs ended, leaving them standing before a simple wooden door, which Felix opened forcefully. They entered the Watcher's Quarter, the city sprawling underneath them. Three magnificent chests stood before them, transparent tendrils of white, green, and yellow swaying calmly. It was a serene scene that Thuradin could have appreciated much more had there also been a fourth chest present. But it didn't look like that would be a possibility anymore and he feared what that might mean for the future.

"So," The First One said, his ancient voice tinged with sadness. "They have captured my brother."

"They've taken him to the Three Spires, haven't they?" Felix said.

"That is correct," Faenerus answered. "All three of us have detected his presence in those wretched mountains."

"It is very much an inconvenience," Scorpus sighed.

"Then the path forward is clear." Felix's voice hardened. "We must attack the Three Spires and win him back."

Thuradin thought he misheard for a moment. "Attack the Three Spires?" he repeated in disbelief, "That's suicide. Those mountains are impregnable. Ask any dwarf and he'll tell ye the same."

"I do not care what the dwarves have to say on this. It

must be done. If we do not have all The First One's uncorrupted brothers on our side, we will lose this war against The Turned One—and no doubt, your brother and sister intend on corrupting the acolyte we failed to retrieve."

"Yes," The First One agreed. "It would seem that is their plan. Still, the dwarf's words cannot be taken lightly. The Three Spires are wrought with danger, especially now that it has been made the place of operations for my sister. If you are to proceed with this course of action, you must proceed with caution and much planning."

"And with the help of Scorpus and myself, and your new allies, we just might be able to put enough pressure on our sister to distract her long enough for a small party to infiltrate those mountains and save our brother," Faenerus added.

"That is true," Scorpus seemed to hum, but to Thuradin it sounded like bubbles were being blown underwater. "The vashi and burrowers could make this much less inconvenient than I originally thought."

Felix shook his head, "Whatever the case, it is decided. Can I count on you three to aid us in our attack? No doubt we will need you to counter any attacks by your corrupted siblings."

There was a moment of silence as the acolytes consulted silently amongst themselves, their tendrils intertwining with each other and mixing colors. Finally, The First One spoke, his words heavy with a sense of finality.

"We will do what must be done."

"Good."

But Thuradin did not like it, and he would make sure Felix knew that. This was folly. And he had to make sure the elder viatari knew this as well, or they might all very well be marching to their deaths.

"Felix, there must be another way. We cannae—"

He felt a hand on his shoulder and turned to see Victria behind him. She shook her head gently. And though he wanted to disobey, to have his voice heard, there was something about her that always seemed to compel him to obey.

Felix stormed out of the room, making his way down the keep. No doubt, he was on his way to begin planning for the preparations that had to be made for the coming battle. Thuradin regarded Victria once he was gone.

"I'm nae the only one who had something ta say ta him."

Victria nodded sadly. "You were not, but now is not the time. He has his mind set, and we must trust him. He has never led us astray yet. He will not do so now."

She patted his shoulders encouragingly, then left with the other viatari, leaving him alone with the three acolytes.

Thuradin stared out the wide, arching windows toward the north. He couldn't see the Three Spires from Aleganthia, despite how large those mountains were. But as he continued looking, he couldn't help but imagine flashes, like lightning, coming from that direction. Repeatedly, consistently, ominously.

He shook his head and ground his teeth. Whatever happened in the coming days, he would have to have faith that their will, strength, and unity would be enough to overcome the evil they were about to face. He turned to leave the room; his mind even more crowded now with uncertainty than it had been before. And in the dark recesses of his memories, he thought he could hear a soft, rumbling chuckle—like thunder.

Thank you for reading this book, dear reader! As an indie author, I appreciate each and every one of you for supporting me. The best way to support an indie author, aside from buying and reading their book, is by leaving a review on Amazon and/or Goodreads! If you liked this book, I would appreciate it so much if you took the time to do so. Thanks!

DARKNESS SPREADS. . .

With Daniel Fansler's fourth book in the
Chronicles of the First Gods, *Breaking of Wills*. . .

BREAKING OF WILLS

A lone, hooded figure peered over the edge of a rocky outcrop jutting from the side of the mountain. Below, far below, lines upon lines of tents spread out along the foothills of the Northern Mountains. From their vantage point, the figure could even make out the movement of individuals within the camp. And there was a lot of movement. Lines of men, dwarves, viatari, and burrowers gathered together as the army prepared to leave camp.

A battle was imminent, and the crows already knew it. Layers of the black birds circled overhead lazily, patiently.

The figure grunted and shuffled back from the edge, making their way back up the mountain path where a staggered line of similarly-hooded figures waited.

"What did you see, Victria?"

Victria pulled back her hood, if only to let the cold mountain air cool her face for a moment from the thick, stuffy cowl she had been wearing. She regarded the one who had called out to her with cool, blood-red eyes and a smirk, revealing sharp fangs as a breeze played with her long, silver hair.

"I thought we weren't using names here, Tera."

Tera pulled back her own hood, revealing a voluminous

mess of curly, blonde hair and a teasing smile. "We aren't supposed to show our faces here either, dear, now are we?"

"The army is preparing to move out. We'll have our distraction."

"Hopefully it will be enough."

"Enough of thisss banter," one of the figures hissed. By his emphasis on a certain set of syllables, it was obvious this was one of the vashi, a race whose origin was far from the mountains. "Our ssscaled bodiesss are not accustomed to being outside of water for sssuch long periodsss of time. We must find thisss rumored lake asss sssoon asss possible. I don't know how much more of thisss we can endure."

A chorus of approving hisses came from the other vashi in the party.

Tera conceded the point. "Right you are. Let's move on."

The line of hooded figures continued making their way up the mountain path, Lightning flashed overhead ominously.

Adjacent to the path they were on loomed the Three Spires. These three peaks were well-known among the dwarves as the tallest and most dangerous mountains in existence. On a cloudless day, the peaks reached impossibly high, nearly scraping into the blue sky. Now, however, their immense size was well-covered by a thick blanket of rolling black clouds. Even just observing such a sight, though, was enough to make the dwarves in the party shiver. They had heard of the horrors of this place since they were mewling for the mother's breast.

"Why are we here again?" One of the dwarves, an Enurg'en, muttered. "It's mad enough that Felix wishes ta assault this place, but ta send this small force ta try and infiltrate these peaks because of a burrower rumor—"

"No rumor," another member grunted, his hunched back prominent even with a cloak on. "Burrowers once lived here. We know of waters within Three Spires from stories, told from father to son for long time. Same way we know of hot springs on this mountain. We will find."

"Says ye."

"Quiet," another dwarf spoke up with a note of finality. Despite his cowled head, a thick, gray beard, separated into three, thick braids which were, in turn, divided into three segments each by golden bands, spilled out, letting everyone know who he was: Thuradin Stonebeard.

"The burrowers clearly know more about these mountains than we do. King Dunkell and Felix were convinced enough ta send us on this expedition. That should be enough for ye."

"I dunno, Thuradin," another dwarf spoke out, one Thuradin certainly did not care for. "Who cares if there's wa'er in the Three Spires and an 'ot spring on this'n. How is this helpin' our cause? Personally, I'd rather get me blades wet."

"I have no doubt of that, assassin," Thuradin sighed. "Were ye nae listening at the debriefing?"

Morteth Shadowmeld shrugged—Thuradin could almost see the smug look on his face from under his hood. "I may 'ave 'ad other thoughts on me mind."

Thuradin rolled his eyes. "Ta make it simple for ye, then. "The vashi have an ability that allows them ta move from one body of water ta another instantly. We find the hot springs, we teleport inta the Three Spires, we find The First One's lost brother, we teleport out, mission complete."

"Incredible! It's so simple, even a burrower could do it.

I'm sure we'll run inta no enemy forces while we're prancin' 'round in their headquarters." Morteth clapped his hands, "No offense ta ye, friend," he added as one of the burrowers glared back at them.

"Enough chatter," Tera called out from the front. "We need to focus on the task at hand."

Felix had given them three days to find the hot springs and already two had been spent with no result. On this third day, Felix would sally forth and engage The Turned One's and Creature's forces on the presumption that their task to infiltrate the Three Spires was underway. Already, as Victria had reported, the army was on the move.

Time was not their friend.

They trudged on.

The path they were on was not overly difficult to traverse. The mountain was barren of any vegetation. The only obstacle in their path proved to be loose rocks and boulders, the ever-present fear of a rockslide. Thuradin had expected to run into some grattles, giant lizards who typically lived on the mountains, but the size of their party appeared to have dissuaded any potential attack from the predators.

Ahead of them, layers of mist slowly rose. A burrower in their group named Brap sniffed the air. He threw back his hood and turned to face them, his cracked lips curved into a gloating smile.

"We here."

About the Author

Daniel has known he's wanted to be a writer since he was thirteen. His debut novel, *The Lost King*, was written and the world and peoples of Azar born during his senior year in high school. He graduated from Stephen F. Austin State University with a BFA in Creative Writing, which helped him hone his writing into what it is today. He lives in Fort Worth with his wife and children.